James White, Ellen Gould Harmon White

## Life Sketches

Ancestry, early life, Christian experience, and extensive labors of Elder James
White, and his wife Mrs. Ellen G. White

James White, Ellen Gould Harmon White

**Life Sketches**

*Ancestry, early life, Christian experience, and extensive labors of Elder James White, and his wife Mrs. Ellen G. White*

ISBN/EAN: 9783337260811

Printed in Europe, USA, Canada, Australia, Japan

Cover: Foto ©Raphael Reischuk / pixelio.de

More available books at **www.hansebooks.com**

# LIFE SKETCHES.

# LIFE SKETCHES.

ANCESTRY, EARLY LIFE.

# CHRISTIAN EXPERIENCE,

AND

## EXTENSIVE LABORS,

OF

## ELDER JAMES WHITE,

AND HIS WIFE,

### MRS. ELLEN G. WHITE.

STEAM PRESS
OF THE SEVENTH-DAY ADVENTIST PUBLISHING ASSOCIATION.
BATTLE CREEK, MICH.
1880.

# PREFACE.

In the preparation of these pages for the reading public, the honor and glory of God have been in view. The facts presented in this work are evidence that the hand of God has been in the rise and progress of the cause espoused by S. D. Adventists, an outline of which is here given. It has been embarrassing to make prominent on almost every page the lives and labors of those whose names appear on the title-page. But their connection with the work has been so close from its very commencement, that the history of the cause is, in a great degree, their history.

The first design was to make this book much larger, to include particulars relative to Mrs. W.'s visions, her condition while in vision, and many circumstances connected with this whole matter. These, however, with statements relative to many remarkable fulfillments of her visions, and answers to common objections, will be given in another volume, which will contain her likeness in steel engraving. That volume will be the first of a series which will contain her testimonies and general writings not found in the "Spirit of Prophecy."

# CONTENTS.

---

## CHAPTER I.

# LIFE SKETCHES.

## CHAPTER I.

ANCESTRY, EARLY LIFE, AND CHRISTIAN EXPERIENCE.

I WAS born in Palmyra, Somerset county, Maine, August 4, 1821. Bloomfield, Maine, which now forms a part of Skowhegan, was the birthplace of my father, Deacon John White. At the age of twenty-one he commenced life in the new township of Palmyra. At that time there were but twenty acres of trees felled on his land. The old farm is situated on the west side of a body of water which is called, as seen upon the large map of Somerset county, "White's Pond." On this farm my father lived and labored fifty-one years. He spent one year and a half in Ohio, and twelve years at Battle Creek, Michigan, where he died July 5, 1871.

My father descended from one of the Pilgrims who came to America in the ship May Flower, and landed upon Plymouth Rock, December, 1620. On board that ship was the father of Perigrine White, who wore a pair of silver knee-buckles, such as may be seen in the picture of the venerable signers of the Declaration of Independence.

The knee-buckles worn by this man were afterward given to his son, Perigrine White, who was born on the passage to this country, with the request that they should be handed down in this line of the White family to the eldest son of each successive generation, whose name should be called John. My father had those buckles thirty years. They were as familiar to me in my boyhood days as the buttons upon my coat. He gave them to my brother John, a Methodist minister in Ohio, who has passed them down to his son, Prof. John White of Harvard College. When visiting the Centennial Exhibition I had the pleasure of seeing in the New England Log Cabin what was said to be the veritable cradle in which the infant Perigrine was rocked. Also in the Gallery of Art there was a painting representing the landing of the Pilgrims, and the infant Perigrine is sleeping in his mother's arms.

My father possessed from his youth great physical strength, and activity of body and mind. With his own hands he cleared the heavy timber from his land. This revealed stones in the soil, which his own hands removed, and placed into stone fence, to prepare the way for the plow. He toiled on for more than half a century, till the rock-bound soil was literally worn out, and much of the old farm had lost its power to produce crops. At the age of seventy-four he left it and sought rest in the more congenial climate of the West.

His religious experience, of more than sixty years, was marked with firmness and zeal, and yet with freedom from that bigotry which prevents investigation and advancement, and shuts out love for all who seek to worship God in spirit and in truth.

At the age of twenty-one he was sprinkled, and joined the Congregational church, but never felt satisfied that in being sprinkled he had received Christian baptism. Several years later, a Baptist minister came into that new part of the State and taught immersion. My father was immersed, and was a Baptist deacon ten years. Still later he embraced the views held by the Christian denomination of New England, which were more liberal and scriptural than those of the Calvinistic Baptists of those days, and communed with that people. The Baptists called a special meeting. The minister and many of the church members were present. The minister invited several to open the meeting with prayer, but each in his turn wished to be excused. He waited. Finally, my father opened the meeting. They then excluded him for communing with the Christians. The minister made an effort to have some one close the meeting. No one moved. My father closed their meeting with prayer, and left them with feelings of love and tenderness. He soon joined the Christian church, and served them as deacon nearly forty years. During this entire period he was present at every conference meeting held by the church, excepting one, which, according to their custom, was held on Saturday afternoon of every fourth week.

As early as 1842 my father read with deep interest the lectures of William Miller upon the second coming of Christ. He cherished faith in the doctrine of the soon personal appearing of Christ to the time of his decease. He embraced the Sabbath of the Bible in 1860, and observed it while he lived.

My mother was a granddaughter of Dr. Samuel Shepard, one of the first and most eminent Baptist ministers of New England. She possessed great firmness of constitution, a good mind, and a most amiable disposition. Her entire religious experience, for more than sixty years, was marked with a meek and quiet spirit, devotion to the cause of Christ, and a consistent walk and godly conversation.

My venerable parents reached the good old age of more than fourscore years, and kept house alone when father was eighty-five years of age and mother was eighty-two. At Oak Hill Cemetery, Battle Creek, Michigan, are two graves at which are erected two marble slabs. On one is chiseled " Dea. John White, was born April 12, 1785, Died July 5, 1871, aged 86 years." On the other, "Mrs. Dea. John White, was born February 14, 1788, Died January 31, 1871, aged 82 years." Also that remarkable passage of Paul to his son in the gospel, is divided. the first part is engraved at my venerable father's head, " I have fought a good fight, I have finished my course, I have kept the faith." At my beloved mother's head the concluding portion is given, " Henceforth there is laid up for me a crown of right-eousness." 2 Tim. 4 : 7, 8.

In my father's family I stood in the center of nine children, four above me and four below me. But this family chain is now much worn, and nearly half its links are broken. The four above me in years, all live. All below me sleep. Time, toil, and care have made their unmistakable impress on the remaining five.

My remaining brothers are both ministers, one of the M. E. Church, of Ohio, the other of the regular Baptist, of New Hampshire. Two sisters are living. One brother is supposed to have lost his life by the Indians, in returning from California. Another sleeps beside a sister in Mount Hope Cemetery, Rochester, N. Y., while another brother, who died at the age of three years, rests in the old burying-ground in Palmyra, Maine.

My parents say I was an extremely feeble child. And, what added greatly to my difficulties, and cut off their hopes of my life, when less than three years old, I had what the doctors call worm fever, result-ing in fits, which turned my eyes and nearly destroyed my sight. I am reported to have been extremely cross-eyed—not naturally, but from affec-tion of the nerves—a feeble, nervous, partially-blind boy. These are sufficient reasons why I could not enjoy the common advantages of school. And not until I was sixteen years old, when my health and strength greatly improved, and my eyes became quite natural, could I read a single verse in the Tes-tament without resting my eyes. I felt keenly the fact that I was behind my school-mates in education. And with the poor advantages of those times I could do but little toward making up the almost total loss of ten years. I grew rapidly, and at eighteen was ahead of my years in size and strength. This added to my embarrassment as I entered the Academy at St. Albans, Me., at the age of nineteen. I could not then work a simple problem in single rule of three, and I could not tell a verb from an adverb or an adjective, and was deficient in the other common branches. My friends advised me to turn my attention to farming, and not think of seeking an education. But I could not take their advice.

At the close of the term of twelve weeks, I received from the preceptor, C. F. Allen, a certificate of my qualifications to teach the common branches, and the winter following I taught school. This required close study eighteen hours of each twenty-four. A victory was gained. Much of my time previous to this I had viewed myself as nearly worthless in the world, and regretted my existence. But now I was beginning to hope that I had powers to become a man. No privation nor hardship formed an obstacle in my way. My father gave me my time at nineteen, and a suit of clothes. All I asked of my parents in addition to this was three dollars to pay my tuition, and six days' rations of bread to take with me each Monday morning for three months as I should walk five miles to the school.

At the close of my first term of school-teaching I again attended school at St. Albans five weeks, then shouldered my pack and walked to the Penobscot river, forty miles, to offer myself as a raw hand in a saw-mill. In the mill I cut my ankle, which resulted in permanent weakness and occasional painful lameness in my left foot. For twenty-six years I was unable to bear my weight upon my left heel.

At the end of four months I returned home. I had lost much time in consequence of the severe wound in my ankle joint, and after paying my

board during the time lost, I had but thirty dollars
and a scanty amount of worn clothing. In order
to be qualified to teach a school where I could obtain first-class wages it was necessary for me to attend school. I therefore immediately packed up
my books and humble apparel for the school at
Reedfield, Me., then favorably known as being under the control and support of the Episcopal Methodists. During that term my object was to thoroughly qualify myself to teach the common
branches. Besides these, I took up Natural Philosophy, Algebra, and Latin. At the close of that
term I had conquered all the Arithmetics within
my reach, was regarded as a good grammarian, was
prepared to teach penmanship, and was told by my
preceptor that I could fit for college in one year.

My thirst for education increased, and my plans
were laid to take a college course and pay my way,
if labor, economy, and study would accomplish it.
I had but little else to thank but God and my own
energies for what advancement I had made. At
Reedfield I wore old clothes, while my class-mates
wore new, and lived three months on corn-meal
pudding prepared by myself, and a few raw apples.
while they enjoyed the conveniences and luxuries
of the boarding-house.

With the close of this term, also closed my school
studies. I had attended high school, in all, twenty-
nine weeks, and the entire cost of tuition, books, and
board, did not exceed fifty dollars. My apology
for being so definite in this part of my narrative, is
a desire to help those young men who wish to obtain an education while suffering under the unfriendly influences of poverty and pride. A poor
boy may obtain an education by calling to his aid
industry, economy, and application to his books.
Such an one will prize his education, and be likely
to make a good use of it; while the young man

who looks to his father's purse, puts on fine clothes, spends much of his time in fashionable calls, and acts the part of the spendthrift, will not get a thorough education, and will probably make a poor use of what he does obtain.

The following winter, covering a part of 1840 and 1841, I taught a large school, and also gave lessons in penmanship in two districts. And with my winter's earnings in my pocket, I returned home with a firm purpose to pursue my studies.

At the age of fifteen I was baptized, and united with the Christian church. But at the age of twenty I had buried myself in the spirit of study and school-teaching, and had lain down the cross. I had never descended to the common sin of profanity, and had not used tobacco, tea and coffee, nor had I ever raised a glass of spirituous liquor to my lips. Yet I loved this world more than I loved Christ and the next, and was worshiping education instead of the God of Heaven. In this state of mind I returned home from my second and last school, when my mother said to me, "James, Brother Oakes of Boston has been lecturing at our meeting-house on the second coming of Christ about the year 1843, and many believe the doctrine, and there has followed these lectures a good reformation in which most of your mates have experienced religion."

I had regarded what was commonly called Millerism as wild fanaticism, and this impression was confirmed by hearing one James Hall of Maine speak upon the subject at the house of worship at Palmyra. But now that my mother, in whose judgment and piety I had reason to confide, spoke to me upon the subject in words of earnestness, candor, and solemnity, I was shocked and distressed. In spite of me, conviction would fasten upon my mind that these things might be so. But, then, how could I have it so? I was unprepared, and my plans for this life were made. The conversation continued :—

"But. mother, this preacher Oakes, of whom you speak, professes to know more than the Lord and his angels, in teaching the time of the second advent. Christ himself has said, 'But of that day and that hour knoweth no man, no, not the angels which are in Heaven; neither the Son, but the Father.' He is certainly wise above that which is written."

My good mother replied, "'As the days of Noah were, so shall also the coming of the Son of man be.' God gave the time to Noah. The Bible says, 'My Spirit shall not always strive with man, for that he also is flesh; yet his days shall be an hundred and twenty years.' Gen. 6:3. Noah had this time given him in which to build the ark and warn the world. And his message, based upon the word of the Lord that a flood of water would destroy man and beast from off the face of the earth at the close of the one hundred and twenty years, condemned the world. Jesus also says in this connection, that there shall be signs in the sun, moon, and stars, and adds, 'When ye shall see all these things, *know* that it is near, even at the doors.'"

I then appealed to Paul. "The apostle has said, 'For yourselves know perfectly that the day of the Lord so cometh as a thief in the night.' 1 Thess. 5:2. This language is very plain, and shows that as a thief in the stillness of the night quietly seeks his plunder, without giving notice, so Christ will come when least expected, hence this idea of warning the world of his soon coming is a mistake."

"But, James, of whom is the apostle in this verse speaking? Not of Christians, but of the ungodly. They will not receive the warning. They will not be looking for Christ. They will be buried up in the spirit of this world. They will be saying, Peace and safety, and they will be suddenly and unexpectedly destroyed. Not so with those who love Jesus and his appearing. They will receive the warning. They will be looking for, waiting for, and loving the appearance of the dear Saviour, and that day will not come upon them as a thief. Notice with care the two classes mentioned. One is the ungodly. The other is the brethren. The day of the Lord will come on one class as a thief; but not so with the other. 'For when they shall say, Peace and safety, then sudden destruction cometh upon them, as travail upon a woman with child, and they shall not escape. But ye, brethren, are not in darkness, that that day should overtake you as a thief.'"

My good mother was ready to calmly and pleasantly meet all my objections, and I was now disposed to view the subject as worthy of my attention. And when in the house of God I heard my school-mates speak of the love of Christ, and the glory of his appearing, I was deeply impressed that the hand of God was in the Advent doctrine.

As I returned to the Lord, it was with strong convictions that I should renounce my worldly plans and give myself to the work of warning the people to prepare for the day of God. I had loved books generally; but in my backslidden state had neither time nor taste for the study of the sacred Scriptures, hence was ignorant of the prophecies. I had, however, some knowledge of the Bible history of man, and had the idea that the race in six thousand years had depreciated physically, and, consequently, mentally. The subject came before my mind in this form: Man once lived nearly one thousand years. In length of days he has dwindled to seventy. In a few centuries, should time continue, with the same results upon the lifetime of man, the race would cease to exist. I had renounced the doctrine of the conversion of the world, and the temporal millennium, in which the soil and man were to be gradually restored to their Eden state, as taught me by my father. I therefore saw the necessity, in the very nature of things, for some great change, and the second coming of Christ seemed to be the event which would most probably bring about the change in man, and in the earth, to remove the curse and its results, and restore all to its Eden perfection and glory.

My mind turned to the young people of the school I had just left. In that school of fifty scholars, twenty were near my own age, several were older. My school was a happy one. I loved my scholars, and this love was mutual. As we parted, at the close of the last day of school, I said to them, " I am engaged to teach this school next winter, and should I fulfill this engagement, I will not ask one of you to obey my orders better than you have this term." As I found comfort in prayer, I began to pray for my scholars, and would sometimes wake myself in the night praying vocally for them. A strong impression came upon me, as if a voice said, Visit your scholars from house to house and pray with them. I could not conceive of a heavier cross than this. I prayed to be excused, that I might pursue my studies ; but no relief came. I prayed for clearer evidence, and the same impression seemed to say, Visit your scholars.

In this state of mind I went into my father's field, hoping that I could work off the feelings under which I suffered. But they followed me, and increased. I went to the grove to pray for relief. None came. But the impression, Visit your scholars, was still more distinct. My spirit rose in rebellion against God, and I recklessly said, I will not go. These words were accompanied with a firm stamp of the foot upon the ground, and in five minutes I was at the house, packing my books and clothes for Newport Academy. That afternoon I rode to the place with Elder Bridges, who talked to me all the way upon the subject of preaching, greatly to my discomfort.

The next morning I secured a boarding place, and took my position in several classes in the school, and commenced study with a *will* to drive off my convictions. But in this I did not succeed. I became distressed and agitated. After spending several hours over my books, I tried to call to mind what I had been studying. This I could not do. My mental confusion was complete. The Spirit of God had followed me into the school-room in mercy, notwithstanding my rebellion, and I could find no rest there. Finally I resolved that I would do my duty, and immediately went directly from the door of that school-room, on foot, to the town of Troy, the place of my last school. I had gone but a few rods on my way, when sweet peace from God flowed into my mind, and Heaven seemed to shine around me. I raised my hands and praised God with the voice of triumph.

With a light heart and cheerful step I walked on till sundown, when I came to a humble cottage which attracted my especial attention. I was strongly impressed to call, but had no reason for so doing, as it was but a few miles to the school district where I should find a hearty welcome. I decided to go past this house, as I did not wish to find myself in the awkward position of calling upon strangers without some good reason. But the impression to call increased, and the excuse to ask for a drink of water occurred to me, and I stepped to the door and called for water. A man in the noon of life waited upon me, then kindly said, " Walk in." I saw that he had been weeping. In one hand he held the Bible. When I had taken the chair he offered me, this sad stranger addressed me in a most mournful manner, as follows: " I am in trouble. I am in deep affliction. To-day I have buried my dear son, and I have not the grace of God to sustain me. I am not a Christian, and my burden seems greater than I can bear. Will you please stop all night with me?"

He wept bitterly. Why he should so directly open his afflicted mind to a young stranger, has ever been to me a mystery. I could not refuse his invitation, and concluded to stop for the night. I told him my brief experience, and pointed him to Christ, who says, "Come unto me all ye that labor and are heavy laden, and I will give you rest. Take my yoke upon you, and learn of me: for I am meek and lowly in heart, and ye shall find rest unto your souls. For my yoke is easy, and my burden is light." We bowed in prayer, and my new friend seemed relieved. Then we sought rest in sleep. In the morning I assisted him in erecting the family altar, and went on my way. I have neither seen nor heard from him since.

But I had walked only two miles on that delightful spring morning, when all nature, animate and inanimate, seemed to join my glad heart in the praise of God, before the same impression came upon me, as I was passing a neat log cottage. Something said to me, Go into the house. I stepped to the door, and called for a drink of water. And who should bring it to me but a young lady who had attended my school the past winter. As she recognized me, she exclaimed, "Why, school-master, walk in." This family had just moved from the district, three miles, to a new settlement surrounded by forests. The father was absent. The mother and children greeted me with more than usual cordiality, each calling me Master. There was the place for my work to commence. I told my errand, and asked the privilege to pray.

"Oh, yes!" said the already weeping woman. "But let me send out the children and call in my neighbors." Some half-dozen little boys and girls received dispatches from their mother, and cheerfully ran to as many log cottages with the word, "Our school-master is at our house, and wishes to pray, and mother wants you to come as soon as you can." In less than half an hour I had before me a congregation of about twenty-five. In conversing with them, I learned that not one of that company professed Christianity. Lectures on the Second Advent had been given near them, and a general conviction that the doctrine might be true rested upon the people. And as I related my experience of the few weeks in the past, stating my convictions relative to the soon coming of Christ, all were interested. I then bowed to pray, and was astonished to find that these twenty-five sinners all bowed with me. I could but weep. They all wept with me. And after pointing them to Christ, as best I could with my limited experience and knowledge of the Scriptures, I shook their hands, said farewell, and joyfully pursued my journey.

As I entered the district I had so recently left, all seemed changed, yet no changes worthy of note had taken place but in me. The school-house where I had spent happy hours in teaching willing minds, was closed, and my scholars were pursuing their daily tasks in the field and kitchen. I had left them, a proud, prayerless backslider, but now had come to pray with them. It seemed to me that the Lord could not have selected a duty more humbling to my pride. The district was made up of Universalists, formal professors, respectable sinners, and infidels. My employer, who had also engaged me to teach their school the next winter, was an infidel. I lost no time in making known the object of my visit, and in visiting and praying from house to house. No one opposed me. Some were deeply affected and bowed with me. My infidel friend said to me as I asked permission to pray in his house :—

" I am very sorry, Mr. White, to find you in this state of mind. You are a good teacher, and a gentleman. I shall not forbid you."

This reception was decidedly cold when compared with what I had met from others. This infidel was evidently much disgusted and disappointed, but tried to conceal his feelings out of respect to mine. I tried to pray, and passed to the next house. In a few days my work in this direction was finished for that time, and I returned home with the sweet assurance that I had done my duty. A few weeks afterward, however, I visited the place again. A general reformation was in progress, under the labors of a Christian minister. On Sunday, the meeting was held in a barn. The interest was general, and the congregation large. After the minister closed his remarks, I improved a few moments. I felt deeply, and my testimony reached the people, especially my scholars and their parents.

The following summer, lectures were given in the town-house at Troy, and the next winter most of the people of that town embraced religion.

Much of the summer I was unsettled as to duty. I had visited my scholars, and sometimes hoped to be excused from anything further of the kind, and feel free to pursue my studies. But the definite idea of proclaiming the soon coming of Christ, and warning the people to prepare for the day of the Lord, was impressed upon my mind. I did not dare attend school. The Spirit of the Lord had driven me from the school-room once, and in following a sense of duty I had been greatly blessed. How could I resist present convictions, and again try to shut myself away from the Lord, over my books? But how could I renounce all my fondly-cherished hopes of the future ? My brother in Ohio said to me by letter : " Come out into the sunny West, James, and I will help you." "Well," said I, "when I become a scholar." How could I give up my school books, and with my small stock of education think of becoming a preacher ?

A school-mate, Elbridge Smith, who had also been a room-mate at St. Albans and at Reedfield, was a special friend of mine. He was a fine young man, of good habits, yet not a Christian. I loved him for what he was, and we mutually in confidence freely stated to each other all our plans, hopes and difficulties. To this young man I first opened my mind freely upon the subject of the Second Advent, and my convictions of duty to preach the doctrine. He treated the matter with candor, and seemed troubled as he learned from my own lips that I was inclined to believe that Christ would come about the year 1843. He had given the subject no study, but evidently feared it might be so. He replied as follows :

"You know I am not a Christian, and therefore am poorly prepared to give you advice in relation to religious duty. I think of these things more than many suppose, though I publicly take no personal interest in them. I, however, think it well for me, and safe for you, to say at this time, Follow the convictions of your own mind."

I highly esteem this friend of my youth for his candor and good counsel. Who could have done better ? We have met but a few times since, as I soon left that part of the State to proclaim the coming of the Lord, and he for Bowdoin College. He graduated in two years from that time, studied law, and now Elbridge Smith is a judge somewhere in the West.

The struggle with duty was a severe one. But I finally gave out an appointment, and had some freedom. I soon sent an appointment to speak at the Troy town-house. The congregation was large. Had rather a lean time, and felt embarrassed. And what seemed to well-nigh finish me, a good, honest, simple-hearted woman came up to me at the close of the meeting and said: "Elder White, please come to our house and take dinner." The word Elder cut me to the heart. I was confused and almost paralyzed. I will not attempt to narrate anything further that occurred on that day. The remaining portion of the day has ever seemed like a blank. I can only remember my confusion and anguish of spirit as I heard the unexpected word, Elder. I was unreconciled at the prospect before me, yet dared not refuse what seemed to be duty, and turn to my books. I was urged to speak in the presence of two young preachers, and attempted to preach. In twenty minutes became confused and embarrassed, and sat down. I lacked resignation and humility, therefore was not sustained. I finally gave up all for Christ and his gospel, and found peace and freedom.

Soon my mind was especially called to the second advent by hearing Elders J. V. Himes and A. Hale speak several times upon the subject, in the city of Bangor, Me. I then saw that it was a subject that required study, and felt the importance of commencing in earnest to prepare myself to teach others. I purchased Advent publications, read them closely, studied my Bible, and spoke a few times during the summer on the second coming of Christ with freedom, and felt encouraged.

## CHAPTER II.

### THE SECOND ADVENT.

In September, 1842, Elders Himes, Miller, and others, held a meeting in the mammoth tent in eastern Maine. In company with Elder Moses Polly, a Christian minister of my acquaintance, I attended that meeting. I there for the first time saw that great and good man, William Miller. His form and features showed great physical and mental strength. The benevolent, affable, and kind spirit manifested by him in conversation with numerous strangers who called on him to ask questions, proved him a humble, Christian gentleman. Infidels, Universalists, and some others came to him with opposing questions. He was quick to perceive their designs, and with becoming firmness and dignity promptly met their objections and sent them away in silence. So long had he, even then, been in the field, meeting opposition from every quarter, that he was prepared for any emergency.

In his public labors his arguments were clear, and his appeals and exhortations most powerful. The tent in which he spoke was a circle whose diameter was one hundred and twenty feet. On one occasion, when this tent was full, and thousands stood around, he was unfortunate in the use of language, which the baser sort in the crowd turned against him by a general burst of laughter. He left his subject with ease, and in a moment his spirit rose above the mob-like spirit that prevailed, and in language the most scorching he spoke of the corruption of the hearts of those who chose to understand him to be as vile as they were. In a moment all was quiet, and the speaker continued to describe the terrible end of the ungodly in a solemn and impressive manner. He then affectionately exhorted them to repent of their sins, come to Christ, and be ready for his appearing. Many in that vast crowd wept. He then resumed his subject, and spoke with clearness and spirit, as though nothing had happened. In fact, it seemed that nothing could have occurred to fully give him the ears of the thousands before him, and to make his subject so impressive as this circumstance.

God raised up Paul to do a great work in his time.

In order that the Gentiles might be clearly taught the great plan of redemption through Jesus, and that the infidelity of the Jews might be met, a great man was selected.

Martin Luther was the man for his time. He was daring and sometimes rash, yet was a great and good man. The little horn had prevailed, and millions of the saints of the Most High had been put to death. To fearlessly expose the vileness of the papal monks, and to meet their learning and their rage, and also to win the hearts of the common people with all the tenderness and affection of the gospel, called for just such a man as Martin Luther. He could battle with the lion, or feed and tenderly nurse the lambs of Christ's fold.

So William Miller, in the hands of God, was the man for his time. True, he had been a farmer, and had been in the service of his country, and had not the benefits of an early classical education. And it was not until he had passed the noon of life that God called him to search his word and open the prophecies to the people. He was, however, a historian from his love of history, and had a good practical knowledge of men and things. He had been an infidel. But on receiving the Bible as a revelation from God, he did not also receive the popular, contradictory ideas that many of its prophecies were clad in impenetrable mystery. Said William Miller: "The Bible, if it is what it purports to be, will explain itself."

He sought for the harmony of Scripture and found it. And in the benevolence of his great and good heart and head, he spent the balance of his life in teaching it to the people in his written and oral lectures, and in warning and exhorting them to prepare for the second coming of Christ.

Much of the fruits of his labors are now seen. Much more will be seen hereafter. Heaven will be hung with the fruits of the labors of this truly great and good man. He sleeps. But if it can be said of any who have toiled and worn and suffered amid vile persecutions, " Blessed are the dead which die in the Lord from henceforth, that they may rest from their labors, and their works do follow them," it can be said of William Miller. He nobly and faithfully did his duty, and the popular church, united with the world, paid him in persecutions and reproaches. The very name of William Miller was despised everywhere, and Millerism was the jeer of the people, from the pulpit to the brothel.

But, dear reader, if your deed of real estate be registered at the office of the county clerk, rough hands may tear the paper you hold in your hand which you call a deed, and your title is no less secure. And however roughly and wickedly men may have handled the name of William Miller here, when the final triumphant deliverance of all who are written in the Book of Life comes, his will be found among the worthies, safe from the wrath of men and the rage of demons, securing to him the reward of immortality according to his works.

As I have introduced to the reader the man whom God raised up to lead off in the great advent movement, it may be expected that something of his life, experience and labors should here be given. I have room for only a very few sketches from his memoir. He was born in Pittsfield, Mass., February, 1782. His biographer says :—

" In his early childhood, marks of more than ordinary intellectual strength and activity were manifested. A few years made these marks more and more noticeable to all who fell into his society. His mother had taught him to read, so that he soon mastered the few books belonging to the family ; and this prepared him to enter the senior class when the district school opened. But if the terms were short, the winter nights were long. Pine knots could be made to supply the want of candles, lamps, or gas. And the spacious fire-place in the log house was ample enough as a substitute for the school-house and lecture-room.

" He possessed a strong physical constitution, an active and naturally well-developed intellect, and an irreproachable moral character. He had appropriated to his use and amusement the small stock of literature afforded by the family while a child. He had enjoyed the limited advantages of the district school but a few years before it was generally admitted that his attainments exceeded those of the teachers usually employed. He had drank in the inspiration of the natural world around him, and of the most exciting events of his country's history. His imagination had been quickened, and his heart warmed, by the adventures and gallantries of fiction, and his intellect enriched by history. And some of his earliest efforts with the pen, as well as the testimony of his associates, show that his mind and heart were ennobled by the lessons, if not by the spirit and power of religion. What, now, would have been the effect of what is called a regular course of education ? Would it have perverted him, as it has thousands ? or would it have made him instrumental of greater good in the cause of God ?

" Whatever might have been the result of any established course of education in the case of William Miller, such a course was beyond his reach : he was deprived of the benefit, he has escaped the perversion. Let us be satisfied."

William Miller was married in 1802, and settled in Poultney, Vt. His biographer continues :—

" But the men with whom he associated from the time of his removal to Poultney, and to whom he was considerably indebted for his worldly favors, were deeply affected with skeptical principles and deistic theories. They were not immoral men; but, as a class, were good citizens, and generally of serious deportment, humane, and benevolent. However, they rejected the Bible as the standard of religious truth, and endeavored to make its rejection plausible with such aid as could be obtained from the writings of Voltaire, Hume, Volney, Paine, Ethan Allen, and others. Mr. Miller studied these works closely, and at length avowed himself a deist. As he has stated the period of his deistical life to have been twelve years, that period must have begun in 1804; for he embraced or returned to the Christian faith in 1816. It may fairly be doubted, however, notwithstanding his known thoroughness and consistency, whether Mr. Miller ever was fully settled in that form of deism which reduces man to a level with the brutes, as to the supposed duration of their existence. And the question is worthy of a little inquiry, to what extent was he a deist?"

He received a captain's commission, and entered the army in 1810. He returned from the army, and moved his family to Low Hampton, N. Y., to begin there the occupation of farming in 1812.

"As a farmer, he had more leisure for reading; and he was at an age when the future of man's existence *will* demand a portion of his thoughts. He found that his former views gave him no assurance of happiness beyond the present life. Beyond the grave all was dark and gloomy. To use his own words: 'Annihilation was a cold and chilling thought, and accountability was sure destruction to all. The heavens were as brass over my head, and the earth as iron under my feet. *Eternity!—what was it? And death!—why was it?* The more I reasoned, the further I was from demonstration. The more I thought, the more scattered were my conclusions. I tried to stop thinking, but my thoughts would not be controlled. I was truly wretched, but

did not understand *the cause.*  I murmured and complained, but knew not of whom.  I knew that there
was a wrong, but knew not how or where to find the
right.  I mourned, but without hope.'  He continued in this state of mind for some months, feeling
that eternal consequences *might* hang on the nature
and object of his belief.

"It devolved on Captain Miller, as usual in the
minister's absence, to read a discourse of the deacons'
selection.  They had chosen one on the Importance of
Parental Duties.  Soon after commencing, he was
overpowered by the inward struggle of emotion, with
which the entire congregation sympathized, and took
his seat.  His deistical principles seemed an almost
insurmountable difficulty with him.  'Soon after,
suddenly,' he says, 'the character of the Saviour was
vividly impressed upon my mind.  It seemed that
there might be a being so good and compassionate
as to himself atone for our transgressions, and thereby save us from suffering the penalty of sin.  I immediately felt how lovely such a being must be; and
imagined that I could cast myself into the arms of,
and trust in the mercy of, such an one.  But the
question arose, How can it be proved that such a
being does exist?  Aside from the Bible, I found
that I could get no evidence of the existence of such
a Saviour, or even of a future state.  I felt that to
believe in such a Saviour, without evidence, would
be visionary in the extreme.

"'I saw that the Bible did bring to view just such
a Saviour as I needed; and I was perplexed to find
how an uninspired book should develop principles
so perfectly adapted to the wants of a fallen world.
I was constrained to admit that the Scriptures must
be a revelation from God.  They became my delight;
and in Jesus I found a friend.  The Saviour became
to me the chiefest among ten thousand; and the
Scriptures, which before were dark and contradic-

tory, now became the lamp to my feet and light to my path. My mind became settled and satisfied. I found the Lord God to be a rock in the midst of the ocean of life. The Bible now became my chief study, and I can truly say, I searched it with great delight. I found the half was never told me. I wondered why I had not seen its beauty and glory before, and marveled that I could have ever rejected it. I found everything revealed that my heart could desire, and a remedy for every disease of the soul. I lost all taste for other reading, and applied my heart to get wisdom from God.'

" Mr. Miller immediately erected the family altar; publicly professed his faith in that religion which had been food for his mirth, by connecting himself with the little church that he had despised ; opened his house for meetings of prayer; and became an ornament and a pillar in the church, and an aid to both pastor and people. The die was cast, and he had taken his stand for life as a soldier of the cross, as all who knew him felt assured ; and henceforth the badge of discipleship, in the church or world, in his family or closet, indicated whose he was, and whom he served.

" His pious relations had witnessed with pain his former irreligious opinions ; how great were their rejoicings now ! The church, favored with his liberality, and edified by his reading, but pained by his attacks on their faith, could now rejoice with the rejoicing. His infidel friends regarded his departure from them as the loss of a standard-bearer. And the new convert felt that henceforth, wherever he was, he must deport himself as a Christian, and perform his whole duty. His subsequent history must show how well this was done.

" Soon after his renunciation of deism, in conversing with a friend respecting the hope of a glorious eternity through the merits and intercessions of

Christ, he was asked how he knew there was such a Saviour. He replied, "It is revealed in the Bible." "How do you know the Bible is true?" was the response, with a reiteration of his former arguments on the contradictions and mysticisms in which he had claimed it was shrouded.

"Mr. Miller felt such taunts in their full force. He was at first perplexed; but, on reflection, he considered that if the Bible is a revelation of God, it must be consistent with itself; all its parts must harmonize, must have been given for man's instruction, and, consequently, must be adapted to his understanding. He therefore said, 'Give me time, and I will harmonize all those apparent contradictions to my own satisfaction, or I will be a deist still.'

"He then devoted himself to a prayerful reading of the word. He laid aside all commentaries, and used the marginal references and his Concordance as his only helps. He saw that he must distinguish between the Bible and all the peculiar partisan interpretations of it. The Bible was older than them all, must be above them all; and he placed it there. He saw that it must correct all interpretations; and in correcting them, its own pure light would shine without the mists which traditionary belief had involved it in. He resolved to lay aside all preconceived opinions, and to receive with child-like simplicity, the natural and obvious meaning of the Scripture. He pursued the study of the Bible with the most intense interest—whole nights as well as days being devoted to that object. At times delighted with truth, which shone forth from the sacred volume, making clear to his understanding the great plan of God for the redemption of fallen man; and at times puzzled and almost distracted by seemingly inexplicable or contradictory passages, he persevered until the application of his great principle of interpretation was triumphant. He became puzzled only to be delighted, and delighted only to persevere the more in penetrating its beauties and mysteries.

"His manner of studying the Bible is thus described by himself: 'I determined to lay aside all my prepossessions, to thoroughly compare scripture with scripture, and to pursue its study in a regular, methodical manner. I commenced with Genesis, and read verse by verse, proceeding no faster than the meaning of the several passages should be so unfolded as to leave me free from embarrassment respecting any mysticisms or contradictions. Whenever I found anything obscure, my practice was to compare it with all collateral passages; and, by the help of Cruden, I examined all the texts of Scripture in which were found any of the prominent words contained in any obscure portion. Then, by letting every word have its proper bearing on the subject of the text, if my view of it harmonized with every collateral passage in the Bible, it ceased to be a difficulty. In this way I pursued the study of the Bible, in my first perusal of it, for about two years, and was fully satisfied that it is its own interpreter. I found that by a comparison of Scripture with history, all the prophecies, as far as they have been fulfilled, had been fulfilled literally; that all the various figures, metaphors, parables, similitudes, etc., of the Bible, were either explained in their immediate connection, or the terms in which they were expressed were defined in other portions of the word; and when thus explained, are to be literally understood in accordance with such explanation. I was thus satisfied that the Bible is a system of revealed truths, so clearly and simply given, that the wayfaring man, though a fool, need not err therein.'

"'While thus studying the Scriptures,' continuing the words of his own narrative, 'I became satisfied if the prophecies which have been fulfilled in the past are any criterion by which to judge of the manner of the fulfillment of those which are future, that the popular views of the spiritual reign of Christ—a temporal millennium before the end of the world, and the Jews' return—are not sustained by the word of God; for I found that all the scriptures on which those favorite theories are based, are as clearly expressed as are those that were *literally* fulfilled at the first advent, or at any other period in the past. I found it plainly taught in the Scriptures that Jesus Christ will again descend to this earth, coming in the clouds of heaven, in all the glory of his Father.

" 'I need not speak of the joy that filled my heart in view of the delightful prospect, nor of the ardent longings of my soul for a participation in the joys of the redeemed. The Bible was now to me a new book. It was indeed a feast of reason; all that was dark, mystical or obscure, to me, in its teachings, had been dissipated from my mind before the clear light that now dawned from its sacred pages; and oh, how bright and glorious the truth appeared! All the contradictions and inconsistencies I had before found in the word were gone; and, although there were many portions of which I was not satisfied I had a full understanding, yet so much light had emanated from it to the illumination of my before darkened mind, that I felt a delight in studying the Scriptures which I had not before supposed could be derived from its teachings. I commenced their study with no expectation of finding the time of the Saviour's coming, and I could at first hardly believe the result to which I had arrived; but the evidence struck me with such force that I could not resist my convictions. I became nearly settled in my conclusions, and began to wait, and watch, and pray for my Saviour's coming.' "

" From the time that Mr. Miller became established in his religious faith, till he commenced his public labors—a period of twelve or fourteen years—there were few prominent incidents in his life to distinguish him from other men. He was a good citizen, a kind neighbor, an affectionate husband and parent, and a devoted Christian; good to the poor, and benevolent, as objects of charity were presented; in the Sunday-school was teacher and superintendent; in the church he performed important services as reader and exhorter, and, in the support of religious worship, no other member, perhaps, did as much as he. He was very exemplary in his life and conversation, endeavored at all times to perform the duties, whether public or private, which devolved on him, and whatever he did was done cheerfully, as for the glory of God. His leisure hours were devoted to reading and meditation; he kept himself well informed respecting the current events of the time; occasionally communicating his thoughts through the press, and often for his own private amusement, or for the entertainment of friends, indulged in various poetical effusions, which, for unstudied productions, are possessed of some merit; but his principal enjoyment was derived from the study of the Bible."

What can be more natural than for man, as he looks forth upon a world where evil is everywhere present, and the marks of disorder and decay everywhere visible, to inquire whether or not this state of things shall always continue? And what inquiry can be of more interest and importance to the race than that which has respect to the age of the world in which we live? It would therefore be reasonable to conclude that God would give to man a revelation informing him in respect to subjects of such absorbing interest. And the declaration of the Scripture is in strict accordance with enlightened reason, when it says, " Surely the Lord God will do nothing, but he revealeth his secret unto his servants, the prophets." Amos 3 : 7.

The object of prophecy is to forewarn the world of things to come, in time for the requisite preparation, and to inspire the people of God with fresh courage as they see the time for the full fruition of their hopes drawing nigh. No judgment has ever come upon the world unheralded; and none have ever fallen therein unwarned. And if, from the uniform dealings of God with our world in the past, we may judge of the future, then may we conclude that of the events yet to transpire, and above all, the great event in which earth's drama shall close—the ushering in of the great day of the Lord, and the coming of the Son of man—something will be known, and the world be faithfully warned thereof, ere they shall take place.

In calling attention to these things, William Miller and his associates were accused of prying into the secrets of the Almighty. From this charge, however, they needed no better vindication than the language of Moses, in Deut. 29 : 29 : " The secret things belong unto the Lord our God, but those things *which are revealed* belong unto us and to our children forever." Prophecy belongs to that portion of the Bible which may properly be denominated a revelation. It is designed to reveal to us things of which we could not in any other way gain information.

Again, they were met with the plea that the prophecies could not be understood. But says the Saviour, referring directly to the prophecy of Daniel, "Whoso readeth *let him understand.*" Matt. 24 : 15. That many of the prophecies, such as those portions of Daniel which reach to the close of earthly governments, have not been understood, is very true. But to assert that they cannot at any time be understood, is a virtual denial that they are a portion of God's revelation to man.

The prophecy of Daniel, reaching far into the future, could not be understood by the prophet him-

self. Neither could it be understood by any until
the time of the end, when much of it should be fulfilled. Hence the answer of the angel to the anxious
inquiry of the prophet. " And I heard, but I understood not : then said I, O my Lord, what shall be the
end of these things ? And he said, Go thy way,
Daniel, for the words are closed up and sealed till
the time of the end. Many shall be purified and
made white, and tried ; but the wicked shall do
wickedly, and none of the wicked shall understand ;
but the wise shall understand." Chap. 12 : 8–10.
Again says the angel to the prophet : " But thou, O
Daniel, shut up the words and seal the book, even
to the time of the end. Many shall run to and fro,
and knowledge shall be increased." Verse 4.

From the very nature of the prophecy of Daniel,
it was closed up and sealed till the time of the end,
when, most of its prophetic history being past, it was
to be unsealed, understood, and many were to run
to and fro with the knowledge of the great subject
upon which it treats. The result of the increase and
spread of knowledge in relation to the approaching
judgment, which is the great theme of the prophecy,
is also given. The wicked shall do wickedly, and
none of the wicked shall understand. But the wise
shall understand.

As I heard able and godly men present the subject of Christ's soon appearing my mind was deeply
affected with the evidences found in the book of Daniel and the Revelation. The second chapter of
Daniel opens with the kingdom of Babylon, or Chal-
dea, at the summit of its greatness and glory, B. C.
603. Nebuchadnezzar, the Chaldean monarch, as it
is natural for man to do, had been anxiously looking
into the future, and pondering what should come to
pass thereafter. Verse 29. Instead of rebuking or
discouraging this spirit of inquiry in man, God takes
occasion to grant to the king, and through him to

the world, the information which he sought. Under the symbol of a great image he presents before him the most impressive history of the world, from that time on, that can anywhere be found. This image's head was of fine gold, symbolizing the kingdom of Babylon, then existing. In his interpretation, the prophet addressed himself to the king in the following words : " Thou art this head of gold." Verse 38 . The breast and arms of silver represented Media and Persia, which shortly supplanted Babylon in the empire of the world. The belly and sides of brass prefigured Grecia, which, conquering its predecessors, enjoyed its period of universal dominion. And finally Rome, the legs of the image, bore its iron sway over all the earth. In development of the ten toes, said the prophet : " The kingdom shall be divided " [Verse 41] : and so was Rome divided into ten kingdoms between the years A. D. 356 and 483. What next ? The monarch beheld till a stone cut out of the mountain without hands smote the image upon its feet, ground its metallic parts to powder, became a great mountain, and filled the whole earth. The inspired interpretation of this impressive scene is given thus : " In the days of these kings shall the God of Heaven set up a kingdom which shall never be destroyed, . . . but it shall break in pieces and consume all these kingdoms, and it shall stand forever." Verse 44.

The prophetic history of Babylon, Media and Persia, and Grecia, has long since been completed, and that of Rome also has been fulfilled, excepting the dashing in pieces to give place to the immortal kingdom of God. And mark : The stone smote the image upon the feet. And it was in the days of the kings, or kingdoms, represented by the ten toes of the image, that the God of Heaven was to set up an eternal kingdom purely his. This kingdom is not yet established. It is evident that it was not set up at the time of Christ's first advent, from the fact that Rome was not then divided into the ten kingdoms, represented by the ten toes of the image.

Paul looked forward to this kingdom in his solemn charge to Timothy in view of the judgment at the appearing and kingdom of Christ. 2 Tim. 4:1. For this kingdom all Christians were to pray: "Thy kingdom come." Matt. 6:10. James speaks of this kingdom as a matter of promise to the poor of this world, rich in faith. Chap. 2:5.

Adventists never believed, however, that all that is said in the New Testament relative to the kingdom of Heaven relates to the future kingdom of glory. Especially in some of the parables of our Lord does the term refer to the work of grace with the people of God in this mortal state. But if we may be allowed to express the relation between believers and their Lord in this mortal state by the term kingdom of grace, and the future relation of immortal beings with the King of kings by the kingdom of glory, the position that the kingdom was set up at the first advent is not relieved of any of its difficulties. For certainly the kingdom of grace was established immediately after the fall. Adam, Abel, Enoch, Noah, Abraham, and Moses, were as truly the subjects of the kingdom of grace as the apostles of Jesus. With this view of the subject every text relative to the kingdom can be harmonized.

It is true that both John and Jesus proclaimed the kingdom of Heaven at hand. The immortal kingdom of glory was then at hand in the sense that it was the next universal kingdom to come. In the time of the Babylonian kingdom, the kingdom of Persia was at hand. The kingdom of Greece was at hand in the period occupied by Media and Persia. And in the days of that kingdom, Rome was at hand, for it was the next kingdom to succeed. In this sense was the kingdom of Heaven at hand in the days of the ministry of John and of Christ.

In the seventh chapter of this prophecy we have the same great outline of this world's history as symbolized by the image of chapter 2, again brought to view, but in a different form. The prophet here saw four great beasts, explained in verse 17 to be four great kingdoms, corresponding respectively to the gold, silver, brass, and iron, of the great image.

The first was like a lion, and had eagles' wings. Verse 4. The Chaldean empire, as advanced to its summit of prosperity under Nebuchadnezzar, was intended by this beast.—*Scott.*

The second like to a bear, and it raised itself up on one side, and had three ribs in its mouth. Verse 5. A fit emblem of the character and conquest of the Persian nation which succeeded Babylon B. C. 538.—*Prideaux*, Vol. I, p. 139.

And lo, another like a leopard, which had four wings and four heads. Verse 6. This was the emblem of the Grecian or Macedonian empire, which for the time was the most renowned in the world. It was erected by Alexander the Great on the ruins of the Persian monarchy, and it continued in four divisions under his successors. The leopard being exceedingly fierce and swift, represented the kingdom, and especially under Alexander, its founder, but the swiftness of the quadruped was not an adequate emblem of the rapidity with which he made his conquests; the leopard had therefore four wings of a fowl upon his back.—*Scott. Prideaux*, Vol. I, p. 380. *Rollin's Hist. of Alexander.*

And behold a fourth beast, dreadful and terrible, and strong exceedingly. Verse 7. The kingdom that succeeded Greece was Rome, the invincible fortitude, hardiness and force of which, perhaps were never equaled. This beast had ten horns. These are declared in verse 24 to be ten kingdoms. The ten kingdoms are enumerated by Marchiaval, Bishop Lloyd, and Dr. Hales, as follows: 1. The Huns, A. D.

356. 2. The Ostrogoths, A. D. 377. 3. The Vis-
goths, A. D. 378. 4. The Franks, A. D. 407. 5. The
Vandals, A. D. 407. 6. The Suevi, A. D. 407. 7. The
Burgundians, A. D. 407. 8. The Heruli and Rugii,
or Thuringi, A. D. 476. 9. The Anglo-Saxons, A. D.
476. 10. The Lombards, A. D. 483. It is certain
that the Roman Empire was divided into ten kingdoms; and though they might be sometimes more
and sometimes fewer, yet they were still known by
the name of the ten kingdoms of the western empire.
—*Scott.*

I considered the horns, and behold there came up
among them another little horn, before whom there
were three of the first horns plucked up by the roots.
In this horn were eyes like the eyes of man, and a
mouth speaking great things. Verse 8. This little
horn is by all Protestants acknowledged to be a symbol of the Papacy. Said the angel, speaking of this
horn, "He shall subdue three kings." Verse 24.
The three kingdoms that were plucked up to make
way for the Papacy were, 1. The Heruli, in 493. 2.
The Vandals, in 534. And 3. The Ostrogoths, in 538.
*Gibbon's Decline and Fall.* Into the hands of this
power the saints, times, and laws, were to be given
for a time, times, and the dividing of time (1260
years; see Rev. 12:6, 14). From 538, when the
Papacy was set up, 1260 years extend to 1798; and
it is a notable fact of history, that on the 10th of
February, 1798, Berthier, a general of Bonaparte's,
at the head of the Republican army of France,
entered Rome and took it. The papal government
was abolished, and the Pope died in exile in 1799.
(See *Croley* on the Apocalypse, *Thier's History of
the French Revolution, Clarke* on Dan. 7:25.) The
Papacy has never been restored to its former power.
We are by this chain of prophecy brought down to
the eighteenth century. And the prophet does not
see this beast gradually changing his wild and fero-

cious nature to the innocence and gentleness of the lamb, to make way for a temporal millennium; but he looks only a step further, and says:—

"*I beheld even till the beast was slain, and his body destroyed, and given to the burning flame.*" Dan. 7:11.

It is characteristic of the different chains of prophecy that each succeeding one introduces particulars not furnished in any previously given. The seventh of Daniel, after covering the general field symbolized by the image of chapter 2, instructs us more particularly concerning the development of the little horn, or man of sin. In the eighth chapter we are again conducted over a portion of the world's great highway, with additional particulars concerning the mighty kingdoms that stand as waymarks along our journey. On the symbols of this chapter, the ram, he-goat, and horn which waxed exceeding great, the prophet received the following instruction :—

The ram which thou sawest having two horns are the kings of Media and Persia. Verse 20. The Persian division of the empire was the highest and came up last. The ram with the two horns was the well-known emblem of the Medes and Persians. It was usual for the Persian kings to wear a diadem made like a ram's head of gold.—*Scott.*

And the rough goat is the king of Grecia; and the great horn that is between his eyes, is the first king. Verse 21. This was Alexander, who was born B. C. 356, decided the fate of Persia at the battle of Arbela, B. C. 331, and died eight years thereafter in a drunken fit, at the age of 33, B. C. 323.

And whereas the great horn being broken, four came up in its stead, four kingdoms, said the angel, shall stand up out of the nation. Verse 22. These were Macedonia, Thrace, Syria, and Egypt, into which the empire was divided shortly after Alexander's death, governed respectively by Cassander, Lysimachus, Seleucus, and Ptolemy.

And out of one of them came forth a little horn. Verses 9, 23–27. Rome was not connected with the people of God, and hence is not introduced into prophecy, till after its conquest of Macedonia, one of the horns of the goat; hence it is represented as coming forth from one of those horns. That this little horn which waxed exceeding great was Rome, the following considerations prove :—

1. It was to rise in the latter part of their kingdom, that is, of the four kingdoms. So did Rome, so far as its place in the prophecy is concerned. Its connection with the Jews commenced B. C. 161.—1 Mac. 8. *Josephus' Antiq.*, B. xii, c. x, sec. 6. *Prideaux*, Vol. II., p. 166.

2. It was little at first. So was Rome.

3. It waxed "exceeding great, towards the east and towards the south." So did Rome. It conquered Macedonia, B. C. 168; Syria, etc., to the river Tigris, B. C. 65; Egypt, B. C. 30. From this horn's increasing toward the *south* and *east* particularly, Sir Isaac Newton infers that it arose in the northwest corner of the goat's dominion, *i. e.*, in Italy; which points directly to the Romans.

4. It cast down some of the host and of the stars to the ground. So did Rome; persecuting the disciples and ministers of Jesus as no other power ever did.

5. He magnified himself even to the Prince of the host. Thus did Rome, when both Herod and Pontius Pilate conspired against Jesus.

6. He shall destroy, wonderfully, the mighty and the holy people. Let from 50 to 100 millions of martyrs make good this charge against persecuting Rome. See *Religious Encyclopedia.*

7. It was the only power that succeeded the four kingdoms which waxed EXCEEDING GREAT.

8. In this vision Grecia succeeds Medo-Persia, just as it had been seen *twice before*; and it is absurd to

suppose that the power which follows them in this vision is a *different* power from the one which *twice before* had been seen *succeeding them,* in chapters 2 and 7; and that power was Rome.

9. He shall be broken without hand. How clear a reference to the stone cut out without hand, which smites the image upon its feet. Chap. 2:34.

Besides the symbols of governments contained in Dan. 8, there is a definite period of time brought to view, which claims attention. As recorded in verse 13, Daniel heard one saint ask another the question, how long the vision should be concerning the daily [sacrifice] and the transgression of desolation to give both the sanctuary and the host to be trodden under foot. The angel then addressed himself to Daniel and said, "Unto two thousand and three hundred days, then shall the sanctuary be cleansed." Waiving for the present the question as to what may constitute the sanctuary, we wish to ascertain if possible the nature, the commencement, and termination of this period of time. There are two kinds of time to be met with in the Bible; literal and symbolic. In symbolic time, a day signifies a year. Num. 14:34; Eze. 4:6. To which class do the 2300 days belong? Being brought in connection with acknowledged symbols, it would be both easy and natural to infer that they partook of the nature of the rest of the vision and were symbolic, presenting us with a period of 2300 years. And that such is the case is further evident from the fact, as is shown in the investigation of Dan. 8, that the field of the prophet's vision, was the empires of Persia, Greece and Rome. The 2300 days there given cannot therefore be literal days; for literal days (scarcely six years and a half) would by no means cover the duration of any one of these empires singly, much less embrace so nearly the whole of their existence put together, as they evidently do. They must consequently denote 2300 years. Can we now ascertain the commencement of this period? We answer, Yes, the key to the matter being in the ninth chapter of Daniel, between which and the eighth there is an unmistakable connection, as we shall now endeavor to show.

After their mention in verse 14, the 2300 days are not again spoken of in chapter 8. All the other parts of the vision are there fully explained; it must have been, therefore, this point concerning the time, that troubled the mind of the prophet, and in reference to which, solely, that he exclaims at the end of the chapter, I was astonished at the vision, but none understood it.

It was in the third year of Belshazzar, B. C. 553, that Daniel had this vision of chapter 8. Fifty-three years previous to this time, Jerusalem had been taken by Nebuchadnezzar, and the seventy years' captivity commenced; and thirty-five years before this, the Chaldeans had utterly demolished the city, broken down its walls and burnt the house of God with fire. 2 Chron. 36: 19. Daniel had learned from the prophecy of Jeremiah [chapter 25], that the seventy years of captivity were drawing near their close, in the first year of Darius, B. C., 538, as we read in the first verses of Daniel 9; and it is evident that he so far misunderstood the period of the 2300 days as to suppose that they ended with the seventy years of Israel's servitude; therefore, turning his face toward the prostrate city and the ruined temple of his fathers, he prays God to cause his face to shine upon his sanctuary which is desolate. Verse 17.

" While I was speaking in prayer," says he [chapter 9: 20-23], " even the man Gabriel, whom I had seen in the vision at the beginning, being caused to fly swiftly, touched me about the time of the evening oblation. And he informed me and talked with me, and said, O, Daniel, I am now come forth to give thee skill and understanding. At the beginning of thy supplications the commandment came forth, and I am come to show thee; for thou art greatly beloved; therefore understand the matter, and consider the vision. *Seventy weeks* are determined upon thy people and upon thy holy city."

That this is a continuation of the explanation of the vision of chapter 8, would seem sufficiently evident without the aid of any special argument to prove it so. But as there is a vital point that hinges upon this fact, we will offer a few reasons which place it beyond the limits of contradiction.

1. Gabriel had received a charge [chapter 8: 16], to make Daniel understand the vision; but at the end of that chapter, Daniel says he was astonished at the vision, but none understood it. Gabriel therefore did not complete his mission in chapter 8; the charge still rested upon him, Make this man to understand the vision.

2. The being who came to Daniel at the time of the supplication, was the very same who had appeared to him in the vision at the beginning; namely, Gabriel. And that he had now come to undeceive him concerning his application of the time, is evident in that he says, I am *now* come forth to give the skill and understanding. Why did he not give him a full understanding of the vision at first? We answer, because he revealed to him all that he was then able to bear. He fainted and was sick certain days.

3. Direct reference is made to *the* vision at the beginning. And if that is not the vision of chapter 8, it is impossible to find it. And again, if Gabriel does not explain in chapter 9 what he omitted in chapter 8, it is impossible for any man to show wherein Gabriel fulfilled his commission to make this man understand the vision.

4. When Gabriel commenced his further explanation, he did not explain the symbol of the ram; for that he had already explained. He did not explain the goat; for he had likewise explained that. Neither did he commence about the little horn; for he had made that plain also in chapter 8. What then did he explain? The very point there omitted; namely, the time: *Seventy weeks* are determined upon thy people, &c. These facts are sufficient to show the connection of Dan. 9 with the vision of chapter 8. But how do the words of Gabriel, Seventy weeks are determined upon thy people, &c., explain the period of the 2300 days? The answer is, The word rendered determined, signifies literally, *cut off*. Gesenius, in his Hebrew Lexicon, thus defines it: Properly, to *cut off*; tropically, to divide, and so to determine, to decree. The Englishman's Hebrew Concordance says, Determined, literally divided. From what period are the seventy weeks divided, or cut off? From the 2300 days; for there is no other period given from which they can be taken; and this is placed beyond a doubt by the connection of the two chapters, which has already been proved.

Having now ascertained that the 70 weeks of Dan. 9 are the first 490 years of the 2300 days; and that consequently the two periods commence together, we further learn that this period of weeks dates from the going forth of a commandment to restore and build Jerusalem. Daniel 9 : 25. If then we can definitely locate this commandment, we have the starting point for the great period of the 2300 years. The Bible furnishes us with four tests by which to determine when the true date is found :—

1. From the time the commandment, 49 years were to witness the completion of the street and wall of Jerusalem. Dan. 9 : 25.

2. Threescore and two weeks from this time, or, in all, 69 weeks, 483 years, were to extend to Messiah the Prince.

3. Sixty-nine and a half weeks were to extend to the crucifixion—the cessation of sacrifice and oblation in the midst of the week. Verse 27.

4. The full period of 70 weeks was to witness the complete confirmation of the covenant with Daniel's people.

In the seventh of Ezra, we find the decree for which we seek. It went forth in b. c. 457. Much concerning this decree, and the date of its promulgation, might here be said. But a more full explanation of it may more properly be given in another place. I will say, however, that, admitting that b. c. 457, is the correct date for the commencement of the 2300 years, which is susceptible of the clearest proof, none will fail to see how William Miller came to the conclusion that this prophetic period would close in the year 1843.

From.......... .................... 2300
Take............................. 457
                                   ———
And there remains................1843

## CHAPTER III.

### MY PUBLIC LABORS.

On returning from the great camp-meeting in Eastern Maine, where I heard with deepest interest such men as Miller, Himes, and Preble, I found myself happy in the faith that Christ would come about the year 1843. I had given up all to teach the doctrine to others, and to prepare myself to do this was the great object before me. I had purchased the chart illustrating the prophecies of Daniel and John, used by lecturers at that time, and had a good assortment of publications upon the manner, object, and time of the second advent. And with this chart hung before me, and these books and the Bible in my hands, I spent several weeks in close study, which gave me a clearer view of the subject.

In October, 1842, an Advent camp-meeting was held in Exeter, Me., which I attended. The meeting was large, tents numerous, preaching clear and powerful, and the singing of Second Advent melodies possessed a power such as I had never before witnessed in sacred songs. My Second Advent experience was greatly deepened at this meeting, and at its close I felt that I must immediately go out into the great harvest-field, and do what I could in sounding the warning. I therefore prepared three lectures, one to remove such objections as the time of the advent not to be known, and the temporal millennium, one on the signs of the times, and one on the prophecy of Daniel.

I had neither horse, saddle, bridle, nor money, yet felt that I must go. I had used my past winter's earnings in necessary clothing, in attending Second Advent meetings, and in the purchase of books and the chart. But my father offered me the use of a horse for the winter, and Elder Polley gave me a saddle with both pads torn off, and several pieces of an old bridle. I gladly accepted these, and cheerfully placed the saddle on a beech log and nailed on the pads, fastened the pieces of the bridle together with malleable nails, folded my chart, with a few pamphlets on the subject of the advent, over my breast, snugly buttoned up in my coat, and left my father's house on horseback.

I gave from three to six lectures in four different towns around Palmyra. Speaking, with the blessing of God, gave me freedom and confidence, and as the subject opened to me by study, reflection, and in speaking, I found it necessary to divide subjects, so that I added one discourse, at least, to the little series, at each place. I had a good hearing at all these places, but saw no special results.

A school-mate of mine had engaged to teach school in the town of Burnham; but by accident had lost an eye, and was told by his physician that he should rest at least one week before teaching. He urged me to teach for him one week. I consented, and on the first day of school gave an appointment for evening lectures. The schoolhouse was crowded. I gave seven lectures, which were listened to with interest and deep feeling.

At this place I began to feel the burden of the work, the condition of the people, and love for precious souls, as I had not before. Previous to this time I had taken great delight in dwelling upon the evidences of the Advent hope and faith. But now I realized that there was a solemn power in these evidences, to convict the people, such as I did not expect to realize. At the close of my last lecture, sixty arose for prayers. I felt deeply the condition of the people. But what could I do for them? I had not anticipated that I should ever have upon my hands sixty repenting sinners, and was wholly unprepared to lead them any farther. My little pond of thought, in the course of seven lectures, had run out, and I dared not undertake to preach a practical discourse for fear it would prove a failure, and injure the well-begun work. In this state of things it occurred to me to send for my brother, who had been in the ministry five years before me, and was favorable to the Advent doctrine. He came and labored six weeks, baptized, and organized a large church, for which they paid him sixty dollars. I paid, at the close of my week's teaching and lecturing, one dollar for horse-keeping, and left for the Kennebeck. My brother afterward told me that every one he baptized dated their experience from my lectures.

At one of the places near my native town, where I had given lectures, I met a gentleman who seemed much interested in the soon-coming of the Lord, who gave me an urgent invitation to visit Brunswick, Me. He stated that there had been no preaching on the subject in that part of the State, and that the Freewill Baptists, who were very numerous on the west side of the Kennebec river, from Augusta to Brunswick, would willingly give me a hearing. From that moment I felt inclined to make my course toward Brunswick. So, in January, 1843, I left on horseback, thinly clad, and without money, to go more than a hundred miles among strangers.

Night came on as I drew near Augusta, the capital of the State, and I inquired at a humble cottage for entertainment, stating that I was a penniless preacher, and wished to find rest with some Christian, who would willingly care for me and my tired horse without charge. "I am a member of the Christian church of this place," said he, "please stop with me." I gladly accepted the cordial invitation.

During the evening my friend stated that Elder Pearl, a Christian minister, was to preach on the next Sunday, and invited me to stop and give evening lectures in the school-house, and spend the Sunday with my old friend and acquaintance, Elder Pearl. I did so, and had a good hearing, and was kindly received by Elder Pearl, who loved the doctrine of Christ's soon coming. I was also invited to speak in the school district east of that, near the Kennebec river. The house was filled, and many stood outside at the open windows. A Universalist opposed the doctrine I was presenting to the people, and finding he could prevail nothing, brought a

Mr. Western, the editor of the Augusta *Age*, a noted Universalist, to oppose me, and, at the close of my lecture, introduced him to the people, and invited them to stop and hear what he had to say. I was too hoarse to reply, and stated that I had no further claims on the congregation. A dozen voices cried, " Clear the way, and let us pass out." Only about twenty-five, and those of the baser sort, remained to hear Mr. W. They were, of course, ready to receive what the speaker chose to say, who, being grieved and angry with the youthful lecturer for leaving, and with the people for following me, was in a state of mind to excite in them a mob spirit.

The reader may think me rash in depriving the editor of the *Age* of a hearing. But I was an inexperienced youth, and feared a battle, and took this course to avoid it. But a battle came the next evening of a different kind. Mr. W.'s hearers decided before leaving the school-house to get all to join them who would, and on the next evening break up the meeting.

As I was about to go to the house the next evening, several of my friends came to me and stated that a mob of at least three hundred was around the school-house. They warned me, as I regarded my life, to remain away from the meeting. I went before the Lord with the matter, then told my friends that I should go to the school-house, trusting in God to defend me. And as I drew near the house I heard the shouting of the mob, and was again warned by the friends who accompanied me to take their advice, and go no further lest I lose my life. I then stated to them that I believed the Lord would in some way defend me, and pressed forward. My friends had resolved that if I went to the place of meeting they would go with me, and stand by me to the last. We found the school-house filled with women, all the windows taken out, and the house surrounded by men enough to fill three such houses. I pressed through the crowd and made my way to the desk. The greatest fear prevailed within the house, while unearthly yells seemed to be the delight of the mob without. The Universalist, who had taken the trouble to get Mr. W. to the place to oppose me, stood close to the desk, and, as I entered it, said to me :—

"This, sir, is the result of your conduct last evening, in refusing to hear the gentleman I brought here to reply to you. Your meetings will be broken up."

I replied, "Very well, sir, if it is the will of God, let it be so." I then called the meeting to order, and prayed, standing upon my feet. This I did for two reasons. First, want of room to kneel, and, second, it was safer for me to stand with my eyes open and watch this infuriated Universalist, who seemed to have all he could do to keep from striking me.

While praying, a snow-ball whistled by my head and struck on the ceiling behind me. I read my text from Peter, relative to the burning day of God, and commenced commenting upon it, but could be heard by only a few near me, in consequence of the shouting of the mob. Many snow-balls were thrown at me through the open windows, but none hit me. I raised my voice above the noise of the mob, but while turning for my proof-texts they seemed to gain advantage over me. And there was too much excitement and fear for my proofs to tell on any mind.

My clothing and also my Bible were wet from the melted fragments of a hundred snow-balls which had broken upon the ceiling behind me, and had spattered over me and it. That was no time for logic, so I closed my Bible and entered into a description of the terrors of the day of God, and the awful end of the ungodly. These opened before me wonderfully. Language and power of voice seemed to be given me for the occasion. I was nearly lost to all around me, while the naked glare of the fires of the day of God seemed to light up the field of slaughter of the ungodly men before me. I cried, "Repent and be converted, that your sins may be blotted out, or you will drink of the wrath of God. Repent, and call on God for mercy and pardon. Turn to Christ and get ready for his coming, or in a little from this, on rocks and mountains you will call in vain. You scoff now, but you will pray then."

The mob seemed more quiet. The night before, a spike was thrown at me and hit me on the forehead, and fell into my Bible, and I put it into my pocket. Inexpressible pity and love for the crowd came over me, and as I was pointing sinners to the Lamb of God, with tears, I held up the spike, saying: "Some poor sinner cast this spike at me last evening. God pity him. The worst wish I have for him is, that he is at this moment as happy as I am. Why should I resent this insult when my Master had them driven through his hands," and at the moment raising my arms and placing my hands upon the ceiling behind me, in the position of Christ on the cross.

The Spirit of God accompanied the words and the gesture to the hearts of the crowd. Some shrieked, and a general groan was heard. "Hark! hark!" cried a score of voices. In a moment all was silent. In tears I was calling on sinners to turn and live. I spoke of the love of God, the sacrifice of Christ; his undying pity for vile sinners. I then spoke of his coming in glory to save all who would seek him now. More than a hundred were in tears. "Do you want to see a happy man?" said I, "please look at me." Many were weeping aloud, and I was getting so hoarse that I could hardly be heard for the penitent cries and sobs of those around me. "Who are willing to seek Christ," said I, "and with me suffer persecution, and be ready for his coming? Who in this crowd wish me to pray for them, that this may be their happy portion? As many as do, please rise up." Nearly one hundred arose. It was nine in the evening, and I was hoarse and weary. I closed with benediction, took my chart and Bible, and made my way out through the subdued crowd. Some one locked arms with me to assist and guard me. His countenance seemed impressively familiar, yet I did not know him. When I had passed the crowd, I missed him, and, from that evening, who he was, or how he left me, and where he went, have been mysteries. Was it an angel of God, sent to stand by me in the perils of that evening? Who can say it was not?

My lectures continued in this place three or four evenings without the least opposition, and a general reformation followed. In about eight weeks I returned to the place again, and as I entered the door of an especial friend, near the old scene of battle, I recognized my Universalist friend. He had been driving some exciting conversation with the lady of the house about me. Both appeared greatly agitated as I entered. The lady greeted me cordially, but with expressions of astonishment that I was in her house again. The Universalist made for the door, and left in a most abrupt manner. The lady then stated that this man had been talking of me to her in a most abusive manner, and that the last statement he made as I came to her door was as follows: "White is a rascal. He has been overtaken in crime, and is safe in jail. One of my neighbors told me that he saw him yesterday in Augusta jail."

This man was overtaken in his guilty folly in a

manner he little expected. He had certainly succeeded poorly in his war against me. I did not see
this Universalist, neither did I hear of him after his
hasty retreat homeward, showing as much shame as
the face of a guilty man is capable of silently
expressing. But let the reader go back with me
.er these eight weeks to the time I closed my labors
in this place.

An invitation came for me to visit Sidney, and
lecture in the Methodist meeting-house. Cheerfully
I accepted, and found a large house filled with
attentive hearers. The first evening I spoke on the
millennium with freedom. And as I entered the
house the second evening, I was told that Elder
Nickerson, the presiding elder, would be present that
evening. I felt my youth, my lack of general knowledge of the Scriptures, and my brief experience in
the things of God. I trembled for the result of that
meeting, as I learned that this presiding elder was
opposed to the doctrine I was teaching. I was on
Methodist ground. This led me to pray most earnestly to God for help. My confidence that the Lord
would be with me grew firm as I entered the pulpit.

" I learn," said I. " that Elder Nickerson is in the
congregation . Will he please take a seat with me,
and join in the services of the evening ?" He cheerfully came forward, and I gave him an Advent hymn
from the Methodist book to read, and found him
willing to pray. I then sung an Advent melody,
and took the text : " But of that day and hour
knoweth no man, no, not the angels of Heaven, but
my Father only." Matt. 24 : 36. I stated :—

1. That the subject was the second advent.

2. That God had not revealed the day nor the
hour of that event.

3. That Christ did say, in this connection, that
when his people should see the signs in the sun,
moon, and stars, that they should know that his

coming was near, even at the doors, as truly as men
know that summer is near when they see the trees
of the field send forth their buds and unfold their
leaves.

4. That, as it was in the days of Noah, so should
it be at the coming of the Son of man.

The work of warning the people of the coming
flood was given to righteous Noah. And in order
for him to know when to build the ark, and when to
raise his warning voice, the year of the flood was
given to him. So shall it be at the coming of the
Son of man. The world is to be warned of its approaching doom. And to this end the prophecies of
Daniel and John especially point to this time. The
signs in the heavens, on earth, in the church, and a
wicked world, all show that Christ and the day of
vengeance are at hand.

The people of that place were divided between
Methodism and Universalism, and it seemed a favorable time to show up from Matt. 24 the view held
by Universalists that Christ came at the destruction
of Jerusalem. In this I had had some experience,
and succeeded in pleasing Elder Nickerson, who
made a few general remarks, not directly opposing
me, for fear, as I supposed of pleasing the Universalists, who evidently felt stirred at my discourse. The
meeting closed with good feelings between us. But
as I left the house, I received an urgent request by
several gentlemen to call at the hotel the next morning, at nine, to answer some questions relative to
what I had said of Universalism.

At the hour appointed, I found myself surrounded
by several Universalists, who were evidently in an
unfriendly mood, and as many Methodists, who had
come to see that the young stripling should be well
treated. This was kind in my Methodist friends.
The interview lasted till the clock struck twelve.
My Methodist friends expressed themselves satisfied

with my answers. The landlord, who was the leading spirit among those professing Universalism, then arose and said to me:—

"Mr. White, please walk out to dinner. This afternoon I wish to show you that there is no connection between the Old and New Testaments."

I was surprised to find that this professed champion of Universalism was really an infidel, and declined dining with him, stating that my mission was to those who received the sacred Scriptures of both Testaments as a harmonious revelation from God. This closed our interview.

My Methodist friends charged me to be on my guard lest the Universalists take advantage of some unguarded expression, and hurt my influence. This was indeed kind in them, and for which I have ever felt to respect them. I gave a few more lectures, and parted with the Christian people of that place, with their thanks for my labors among them, and their expressions of joy that Universalism had been fearlessly exposed without giving its adherents a chance to hurt me.

My mind was still on the field of labor farther down the river toward Brunswick. My labors thus far in Augusta and Sidney, seemed more accidental, or providential, than in accordance with my design when I left home. And now, with the peace of God ruling in my heart, I journeyed on. As I passed a neat cottage in the town of Richmond, the impression came upon me powerfully, as distinctly as if a voice said unto me, "Call into this house." I obeyed, and asked for a drink of water. A middle-aged lady laid dawn the paper she was reading, and upon it placed her glasses, and gravely said to me: "Please be seated." As she stepped to another room to wait upon me, I took up her paper, and to my joyful surprise, saw that it was the *Signs of the Times*, published by J. V. Himes, No. 14, Devonshire street,

Boston. And as I took the water, the following conversation, in substance, commenced :—

"I see you have the *Signs of the Times*, which teaches the peculiar sentiments of one William Miller. Are you a subscriber for it ?"

"I am, and I think it an excellent periodical. Would you like to read it ?"

I took the paper from her hand, and enjoyed reading several stirring articles from able pens, then passed it to her, and, with an air of indifference, asked : "What do you do with the long-cherished opinion of nearly all great and good men, of all denominations, that the temporal millennium, in which the conversion of the whole world and the complete triumph of the church is to take place prior to the second advent ?"

"I reject the doctrine. And you are mistaken, sir, as to the millennium being a long-cherished sentiment. It is an unscriptural fable of recent date. It has not been the faith of the church until the last century. The parable of the wheat and tares, as explained by our Lord, and his declaration that as it was in the days of Noah so should it be at the coming of the Son of man, forbids the idea. In fact, the prophets of the Old Testament, and the apostles of the New, describe the last days as dark, gloomy and perilous, with the church fallen, and far from God, and the world filled with crime and violence."

"Admitting that you are right on this point, is it not very wrong to set the time, as Mr. Miller has done ?"

"Brother Miller, in searching the Scriptures, has found by the prophetic periods, as he thinks, the time of the end, and, as an honest man, has taken the cross to teach it to the world. He also sees by the signs of the times that Christ's coming is near, even at the doors, and takes the safe side of the question to be ready, and to warn others to get ready.

And all these texts usually quoted to show that men are to know nothing of the period of the second advent, do not prove what they are said to prove."

It was evident that this woman was mistress of the subject, and as she proceeded to give the proofs in support of definite time, I interrupted her, stating that I would no longer conceal from her my faith and mission. " I am," said I, " a full believer in the second advent of Christ as taught by William Miller, and have left all to proclaim it."

" Thank the Lord !" she exclaimed, " my prayer is answered in sending you here. My husband is a Freewill Baptist minister, and will be glad to have you speak to the people of his charge here upon the coming of Christ. Let me have your coat and hat. I will send for some one to care for your horse, and will send an appointment to the school for you to lecture this evening."

" What is your husband's name ?" I inquired.

" Andrew Rollins," was the reply.

" Is he a believer in the Advent doctrine ?"

" He does not oppose, and is favorable."

Soon Elder Rollins came in, and his wife introduced me to him as a Second Advent lecturer. He asked me a few questions in a grave manner, and looked me over closely, as much as to say, " You are a young stripling to go abroad to lecture upon the prophecies." I saw that he was a strong man, watching all my words ; therefore thought it best for me to be guarded.

The appointment flew through that portion of the town, and, at the time appointed, what has ever been known as the Reed meeting-house, was filled with both the pious and the curious. And as I sung an Advent melody, all listened with solemn silence, and some wept. Elder Rollins then prayed in a most solemn and fervent manner for the blessing of God to rest upon the youthful stranger who was about to speak to the people. This prayer drew me nearer to him, and I began to feel that in this minister I had found a true friend. And so it proved.

At the close of my lectures, there was a general interest and deep conviction upon all minds. The school children committed to memory all my texts, and almost everywhere you might hear them repeating this one from Dan. 8: "Then I heard one saint speaking, and another saint said unto that certain saint which spake, How long shall be the vision concerning the daily sacrifice, and the transgression of desolation, to give both the sanctuary and the host to be trodden under foot? And he said unto me, Unto two thousand and three hundred days, then shall the sanctuary be cleansed."

As I was about to leave, Elder Rollins said to me, " In two weeks our quarterly meeting, embracing about thirty churches in this locality, will hold its session at Richmond village. I would like to have you give some lectures before the preachers, delegates, and brethren who will be present. I will call the matter up in a business session, and they will probably vote you room, if you will decide to be present and speak to us." " Certainly, I shall be glad of the opportunity to speak what I regard important truth to the heads of your denomination in this part of the State, and will, Providence permitting, be at the meeting in season." This said, I rode off on horseback to fill appointments in Gardiner and Bowdoinham.

After filling these appointments, I returned to the quarterly meeting in Richmond. And as I entered the place of worship, Elder Rollins, who was seated beside the pulpit at the further end of the house, arose and said: "Brother White, you will find a seat here by me." After the sermon, liberty was given for remarks, and I spoke with freedom upon the Christian life, and the triumphs of the just at the second advent of Christ. Many voices cried, "Amen! amen!" and most in that large congregation were in tears.

The Freewill Baptists in those days were indeed a free people, and many in that congregation were exceedingly anxious to hear upon the subject of the advent. And as I spoke, they seemed to be finding relief from their pent-up feelings in hearty responses and tears. A portion, however, seemed unmoved, unless it was to show in their countenances that they were displeased. Elder Rollins then informed me that his brethren had voted in favor of a lecture at that meeting, and the next day rescinded the vote. This displeased him much, and his statement to me relative to the action of his people as to my speaking to them explained to me the existing state of things. Near the close of that meeting, after getting my consent, Elder Rollins arose and said :—

"Brother White, who sits at my right side, will speak at the Reed meeting-house this evening, upon the second coming of our Lord Jesus Christ. Come up, brethren, and hear for yourselves. We have sufficient room to entertain you all. Come up, brethren—it will not harm any of you to hear upon this subject."

He had as much influence as any minister in that quarterly meeting, and, being disappointed and hurt that his brethren should vote against my lectures, and shut the Advent doctrine out of their meeting, was willing they should feel it. He very well knew that most of his brethren would leave their meeting in the village, and go three miles to hear me, and that their appointed business session would be broken up. And so it was. Three-fourths of the ministers, and nearly every delegate, left, and the Reed meeting-house at an early hour was crowded. My subject was Matt. 24. The Spirit of God gave me great freedom. The interest was wonderful.

As I closed with an exhortation to Christians to fully consecrate themselves, and be ready, and to sinners to seek Christ, and get ready for the coming of the Son of man, the power of God came upon me to that degree that I had to support myself with both hands hold of the pulpit. It was a solemn hour. As I viewed the condition of sinners, lost without Christ, I called on them with weeping, repeating several times : " Come to Christ, sinner, and be saved when he shall appear in his glory. Come, poor sinner, before it shall be too late. Come, sinner, poor sinner, come."

The place was awfully solemn. Ministers and people wept—some aloud. At the close of every call to the sinner, a general groan was heard throughout the entire assembly. I had stood upon my feet explaining the chapter and exhorting for more than two hours, and was getting hoarse. I ceased speaking, and wept aloud over that dear people with depth of feeling such as he only knows whom God has called to preach his truth to sinners. It was nine o'clock, and to give liberty to others to speak, would be to continue the meeting till midnight. It was best to close with the deep feeling of the present, but not till all had a chance to vote on the Lord's side. I then called on all in the congregation who would join me in prayer, and those that wished to be presented to the throne of mercy, that they might be ready to meet the Saviour with joy at his second coming, to rise up. Every soul in that large house, as I was afterward informed by persons in different parts of it, stood up. After a brief season of prayer, the meeting closed.

The next morning I returned to the village, accompanied by at least seven-eighths of that Freewill Baptist quarterly meeting. Every one was telling what a glorious meeting they attended the evening before. This did not help the feelings of the few

who remained away, who had been instrumental in
closing the pulpit at the village against the doctrine
of the soon coming of Christ. Their course only
increased the interest to hear me. The independent
stand taken by Elder Rollins resulted in their having a taste of that spiritual food for which they hun-
gered.

At intermission, delegates and ministers invited
me to join them in making arrangements as to time
when I could lecture to the several congregations in
that quarterly meeting who had commodious houses
of worship. It was then in the middle of February,
and it was decided that there remained not
more than six weeks of firm sleighing, giving the
people a good chance to attend meetings. Twelve
of the most important places were selected for my
labors in six weeks. I was to give ten lectures,
which would require of me to speak twenty times a
week. This gave me only half a day each week,
which I generally found very necessary to travel
fifteen or twenty miles to the next place of meeting.

At Gardiner, near the river, Elders Purington and
Bush were holding a protracted meeting with poor
success, and were ready to hear me. So were most
of the church. Some opposed, stating their fears
that the Advent doctrine would destroy their reformation. They had, after tugging at the wheel several days, on the third or fourth evening of their
meeting, after inviting and coaxing for half an hour,
prevailed on two persons to take what was called
the anxious seat. In this, however, I saw no reformation to spoil. I told these ministers I was
ready to commence my work. They hesitated. I
proposed to go where the people were all anxious to
hear me. They would not consent to have me leave.
I waited one day longer, and spoke several times in
social meeting. Many urged me to lecture. I sent
them to the ministers. They labored with the

opposition privately. Their meeting was becoming divided. I decided to bring the matter to the point of decision, so that I might at once enter upon my work, or leave the place. The ministers held on to me, and also labored with the opposition.

I finally stated before the entire congregation that I had been invited to the place, and had been held there one day by their ministers and most of the congregation, waiting for a few individuals to consent to have me lecture; that I should wait no longer; that if I could not commence lectures that evening, I should go where they wanted to hear. I called for a vote of the congregation. Nearly all voted for me to remain and commence that evening. The ministers said, "Go on with your lectures, and we will stand by you."

As I took the stand that evening, I requested all who loved Christ, and the doctrine of his soon coming, to pray for me, and stated that I would excuse those who did not love him enough to wish to see him come in glory from praying for me, as I thought they could to better advantage and profit pray for themselves. Every ear was open, and every heart felt. The Lord gave perfect freedom in presenting proofs of the advent near, and in exhorting the people to prepare for that day. Many were in tears. I left the pulpit, exhorting the people, and calling on them to come forward to the front slips. About thirty came forward. Many of them wept aloud. I then turned to the ministers in the stand, saying:—

"These fears, expressed by some unconsecrated ones, that the glorious doctrine of the second coming of Jesus would kill a reformation, are without foundation. Do you think the work of reform has been injured here this evening?"

"No! no! Go on, Brother White; go on. The Lord is here."

This meeting, apparently swept away all opposition, and the way was prepared for a good work. But other appointments would not allow me to remain longer than to give three or four lectures more. The protracted meeting then progressed with success.

At Richmond Corners I gave seven lectures in their new meeting-house, just dedicated, and at the close, two hundred arose for prayers. During the progress of the meetings, a Baptist deacon opposed. When I was commenting upon Daniel 7, I stated that it was a historical fact that on February 10, 1798, at the close of the 1260 days, Berthier, a French general, entered the city of Rome and took it, and that on the 15th of the same month the Pope was taken prisoner and shut up in the Vatican; and gave Dr. Adam Clarke as one of my authorities. An educated Catholic broke in upon me, charging me with falsehood, and offered me five dollars if I would read such a statement from Clarke's comments on Daniel. With the promise that I would read Clarke the next evening, and by the entreaties and threats of his neighbors, this enraged Irishman was kept quiet.

The next evening I entered the pulpit with Clarke's Commentary under my arm, and, after calling the people to order by singing an Advent melody, read what Clarke had said upon taking away the dominion of the little horn, which fully sustained what I had stated the previous evening. I then offered the volume to any one who would see if I had read correctly, stating that I had not been to the trouble of going five miles for the Commentary in order to claim the five dollars. That I chose to let the gentleman keep his money, and have the truth on the subject besides. There was no reply. A gentleman of fine feelings and good influence in the community, who made no pretensions to piety, arose and said :—

" I wish to call the attention of this congregation to this one fact, that no persons in this community have manifested opposition to the lectures of Mr. White but a Baptist deacon and a Roman Catholic."

Many were converted in the vicinity, a strong company of believers was raised up, and a Second Advent camp-meeting was held there in the autumn of 1844.

At Bowdoinham Ridge my labors were well received. A protracted meeting was being held with that church by Elders Quinnum and Hathern. They and the church fully co-operated with me, and a good work followed. On the last day I spent in this place I spoke forenoon and afternoon, then invited sinners to come forward for prayers, and joined in prayer for them. When we arose from our knees the sun was just setting, and I had sixteen miles to go to my next appointment, which was that evening. A friend held my horse at the door. I had labored excessively, and was so hoarse that I could hardly speak above a whisper, and my clothes were wet with sweat. I needed rest. But there was my next appointment. The people would be together in about an hour, and I had sixteen miles to go. So I hastily said farewell to the friends with whom and for whom I had labored, mounted my horse and galloped away toward Lisbon Plains, in a stinging cold February evening. I was chilled, but there was no time to call and warm. My damp clothing nearly froze to me, but I galloped on. As I rode up to the door of the house of worship, an aged Freewill Baptist minister was saying to the crowd :—

" I am sorry to say to the congregation that we are disappointed. The speaker we expected to hear this evening has not come."

As this minister raised his hands to dismiss the

people with the benediction, I cried : " Hold ! I am here !"

" Good !" cried the minister ; and the people sat down. They had been waiting for me more than an hour. With a few words of explanation of my late arrival, I commenced to speak ; but I was so thoroughly chilled that my chattering teeth would cut off some of my words. However, I soon warmed up, and felt freedom in speaking.

But where was my poor horse. His turn had come to be wet with sweat, and to shake with cold. A friend had stood at the door watching for my arrival, who took the poor creature, and, as I supposed, took care of it. But he simply tied it to the fence with a rope. Heated, wet, and without blanket, it had to stand in the keen wind one hour and a half, trembling with cold until it was ruined. The next morning there was seen in the poor creature a clear case of chest-founder. It is a shame to treat God's poor creatures thus. I learned from this sad circumstance never to leave my horse without full directions as to its wants.

The large house of worship was crowded with attentive hearers three times each day, till my time came to hasten to the next place. On Sunday, the Presbyterian minister had thirteen hearers. On Monday he came to hear me, and as I passed down the symbols of Daniel 8, and began to apply the specifications of the little horn of that chapter to the historical facts of Rome, he broke in upon me, saying :—

" You mislead your hearers. Antiochus, and not Rome, is the subject of this prophecy."

" Please wait, sir," was my reply, " till I have finished speaking, then you can talk as long as the people wish to hear you. Be patient, and hear me while I show that Rome, and not Antiochus Epiphanes, is the subject of the prophecy."

The matter was made quite plain, and the minister was told that he could speak. He rose, but his subject was the temporal millennium. All his propositions and proof-texts, which he tediously brought forward, had been examined in my first lecture. But it seemed necessary to briefly reply, notwithstanding it was little more than to repeat the same in the ears of nearly the same congregation. As I closed, a tall, rough-looking, red-shirted lumberman rose up in the house and said : —

"The difficulty with Elder Merrill is that he is not ready, and is afraid the Lord will come."

The benediction repeated, the meeting closed. Good fruits followed in this place.

At Brunswick, I had a candid hearing in what was called Elder Lamb's meeting-house, a very large house of worship. My stay was brief, and most of the members of that numerous church were rich and worldly. They had not sufficient interest to even oppose me. So they heard me with a degree of apparent interest, amounting to little more than curiosity, and let me go.

At Bowdoin, Elder Purington received me as a brother, and stood by me till my work was done in that place. The large house of worship was crowded. The people listened with deep interest and feeling. The Universalists sent a few questions to the desk in writing, which I enjoyed answering. Sinners manifested their desire for salvation, and those who loved Christ and his appearing rejoiced in the Advent hope and faith.

Litchfield Plains was my next place of labor. The house was crowded the first evening. In fact, it was with difficulty that I found my way to the pulpit. To call the people to order, the first words they heard from me were in singing,—

"You will see your Lord a coming,
You will see your Lord a coming,
You will see your Lord a coming,

In a few more days,
　　While a band of music,
　　While a band of music,
　　While a band of music,
　Shall be chanting through the air."

The reader certainly cannot see poetic merit in
the repetition of these simple lines. And if he has
never heard the sweet melody to which they were
attached, he will be at a loss to see how one voice
could employ them so as to hold nearly a thousand
persons in almost breathless silence. But it is a fact
that there was in those days a power in what was
called Advent singing, such as was felt in no other.
It seemed to me that not a hand or foot moved in
all the crowd before me till I had finished all the
words of this lengthy melody. Many wept, and the
state of feeling was most favorable for the introduction of the grave subject for the evening. The
house was crowded three times each day, and a deep
impression was made upon the entire community.

West Gardiner was my next point. Elder Getchel
received me like a brother, and seemed to have a
good interest in the subject. The people in this
part of the town were nearly all Freewill Baptists.
There had been one large church in the place, composed mostly of farmers possessing more wealth than
piety. A part of the church had wanted a popular
minister, and because they were opposed in this by
a more humble portion, drew off in a church by themselves, built a fine house, and employed a preacher
that pleased them. Here stood in full view two
Freewill Baptist meeting-houses, each occupied every
Sunday by two ministers of the same denomination,
not always on friendly terms. It was a hard place
to labor.

While the members of these churches had been
occupied with the division in their midst, they had
been destitute of the spirit of reformation, and their
children had grown nearly to manhood without con-

version. These were much affected by my lectures,
and sought the Lord, while their parents seemed
unmoved. I will leave this place in my narrative,
for the present, to return again, as I have something
more to relate of the good work here in its proper
place.

According to arrangements at the quarterly meeting at Richmond village, I filled all my appointments,
and saw in every place more or less of the work of
God before I left. But the lectures were usually
followed by protracted meetings, and large acces-
sions were made to these churches. At the next
quarterly meeting it was publicly stated that within
the limits of that quarterly meeting, one thousand
souls dated their experience from my lectures during that six weeks.

The second day of April, 1843, I mounted my poor,
chest-foundered horse, and started for my native
town, much worn by the labors of the winter. The
snow was very deep. My horse's feet were much of
the time, while passing over the drifts, higher than
the tops of the fence posts. My only suit of clothes
was much worn, and I had no money. I had not
received the value of five dollars for my labors.
Yet I was happy in hope. As I journeyed homeward, my horse became very much irritated with
frequent turning out into the deep snow and sharp
crust in passing teams. Several times while passing women and children he crowded nearly into the
sleighs where they were. And fearing that he might
seriously injure some one, I decided that it was safest,
as teams approached, to dismount, crowd the horse
out of the road, and hold him with a firm hand till
they passed.

As I was entering the city of Augusta, a farmer
was returning home with an empty hay-sled, drawn
by six oxen. I chose to ride past this team. The
driver sat on the fore part of the sled, and the oxen

kept the middle of the road. On being crowded out of the road, my horse became very angry, and as the sled was passing, threw himself over the first set of stakes on to the sled. Seeing strong probabilities that I should be thrown on some one of the second set of sharp stakes and killed, I sprang from the horse, quite over the stakes, into the snow on the other side. The team continued to move along with my horse fairly loaded upon the sled; and, by the time I had rescued myself from the snow, was several rods from me.

"Halloo!" cried I. "Please stop your team and let me have my horse."

The good farmer stopped his oxen, and assisted me in unloading my horse, which, when I had mounted, galloped off as well as before.

Rain came on, and the firmly trodden drifts became soft, so that my horse with my weight upon him would frequently sink to his body in the snow. I rode all day with my feet out of the stirrups, and as he would plunge into the snow, I would instantly slide off and relieve him of my weight, that he might better struggle out, or if he could not do this alone, assist him by lifting where most needed.

April 5, I reached my father's house, and, after resting a few weeks till the ground settled, returned to my field of labor, and was rejoiced to learn that the spirit of reformation had swept over the entire field. But the time had fully come for the people in farming districts to hasten out upon their lands, and I found but little chance to get a general hearing excepting on Sunday. However, I soon had a call to labor in East Augusta.

But before going to this place I dreamed that an ox, with very high horns was pursuing me with very great fury, and that I was fleeing before him for my life. He followed me so closely that I sprang into a house near by and bolted the door.

The ox broke down the door and entered. I left the house through an open window, and escaped to the barn. The ox broke down the barn door and entered. I escaped by another door, and as my last resort for safety, crept under the barn floor. The ox tore up the planks with his horns, and drove me from under the barn. And as he was pursuing me in the open field, I felt his horns goading my back. At that moment wings were given me, and I arose and flew with ease to the roof of the house. The disappointed ox stood looking at me, frequently shaking his horns, and appeared wild with rage. My deliverance was complete, and exultingly I flew from the house near the head of the ox, then quickly arose to the roof of the barn. This repeated several times, I awoke. This dream made quite an impression upon my mind, but soon passed from me, and I thought no more of it until brought to my mind by what occurred in connection with my labors at East Augusta.

As I entered the school-house to meet my first appointment, the only person present, was a tall, athletic man, in the middle age of life. As it was a cool evening, he was kindling a fire. He spoke to me in a tone of kindness, but eyed me closely. I was afterward told that Walter Bolton, for this was his name, was an infidel. He was regarded as a good citizen, but had never before been known to take any interest in religious meetings. He attended all my lectures, and seemed deeply interested, and I often heard remarks from his neighbors like this: "What has got hold of Walter Bolton to call him out to these meetings? I never saw him out to a religious meeting before, only at a funeral." We will leave Mr. Bolton for the present, and pass to other features of this series of meetings.

During the week I gave lectures each evening to

small congregations. But Sunday morning, at an early hour, the house was crowded. My subject was the millennium. I labored to show,

1. That those texts usually quoted to prove the conversion of the entire world, did not prove what they are said to prove.

2. What those texts do teach. In speaking upon Isa. 65, I showed that it was not in this mortal state, upon this old sin-cursed earth, that the leopard would lie down with the kid, and the lion eat straw like the ox, but in the new earth, as plainly declared by the prophet. That beasts, restored from the effects of the curse, would be no more out of their proper places in the earth restored, than when created upon it before the fall.

3. That certain texts in the Old and New Testaments, in most distinct and emphatic language, teach that at no period of man's fallen condition will all men be holy.

At the close of this discourse, a Universalist preacher present arose and said:—

"I want five minutes to show that this doctrine has no foundation in the Bible, or in common sense."

He had been a regular Baptist minister, had engaged in trade, and in the sale of liquor, had backslidden, and was preaching the unconditional salvation of all men.

"You will want more than five minutes, sir, to do that," I replied. "It is already half past twelve, and the people need rest and refreshment. When I have closed this afternoon, you can speak as long as they wish to hear you."

"No; this is just the place and time for me to speak, and the people want to hear me."

"We will submit the matter to the congregation, and let them decide it for us," was my reply. I then asked those who agreed with me that the gentleman had better wait till afternoon, to rise up.

Nearly the entire congregation were at once on their feet. I then asked those who chose to have him speak immediately to arise. Ten or twelve young men, who looked like finished ruffians, arose. The congregation was immediately dismissed for one hour.

In the afternoon I spoke upon Matt. 24, and, expecting a battle with the Universalist preacher, gave some time to the examination of the view that Christ came the second time at the destruction of Jerusalem. My arguments told on the congregation, and the minister felt it. When I had closed my discourse, I said, "There is now room for that gentleman to speak as long as the people wish to hear him." He arose embarrassed, and said in substance :—

"I do not want to act the part of the scoffer, or fall under the denunciation of him who says, 'My Lord delayeth his coming, and smites his fellow servant;' but I wish to make a few remarks relative to a portion of scripture commented upon by the speaker this forenoon, which you will find in the sixty-fifth chapter of Daniel."

He immediately commenced to ridicule the idea of beasts in Heaven. I saw at once that it was Isa. 65, and not Daniel, that he referred to. And after he had gotten fairly under way, I called his attention to the fact that he had made a mistake in giving the prophet Daniel credit for speaking of the lion and the ox both feeding on straw, and the leopard and the kid lodging together. It was not Daniel, but another prophet who had thus spoken. He rebuked me for interrupting him. I stated that as he should proceed to show in five minutes that the doctrine I preached had no foundation in scripture, or in common sense, I should see that his reference was all correct. But he affirmed that he was right in quoting Daniel, and went on with his remarks in a style well calculated to disgust the people, and turn them in strong sympathy with me. And when his unsanctified tongue was moving off at full speed, I called to him again, saying, "I am not willing the gentleman shall proceed any further till he reads from Dan. 65, the scripture from which he is speaking. Please turn and read, sir, and satisfy us all that you are correct, and I will consent for you to go on."

He took up his Bible and turned from one side of it to the other, colored up, appeared greatly agitated, and said, "The book of Daniel is torn out of my Bible." "Here, sir, is mine," said I, and reaching it toward him, said to those seated near me, "Please pass it to him. Mine has the book of Daniel in it." As my Bible was being passed from seat to seat toward this man, he looked distressed. He could not readily find the book of Daniel, not being familiar with his Bible, and evidently made the false statement for the occasion, that this book was torn from his Bible.

He took my Bible and searched from one lid to the other several times for the book of Daniel, but was so agitated that he could not find it. The people fixed their eyes upon him, some with pity, others with apparent anger, while still another class laughed at him. My pity was moved toward him, and I stated that I could help the gentleman. That it was Isaiah, and not Daniel, that he wished to quote. That there were but twelve chapters in all the book of Daniel, and that he wished to speak upon Isa. 65 : 17–25. I then quoted these nine verses from memory, and said, "This is what you want, is it not?" "Yes," was his reply, and after a few broken remarks which showed his complete confusion, he sat down and covered his face with his hands. The people were ashamed of him, and seemed astonished that I should know from his remarks what chapter and verses he wanted, and that, without my Bible, I could repeat nearly half a chapter.

If the dream of the ox applied to the effort on the part of this Universalist minister to crush me, then by this time I had all that victory over him represented by my soaring above him on wings. I then exhorted this poor apostate to turn from his sins, and seek a preparation for the coming of Christ. And as I felt the condition of the people, as there was scarcely a praying man or woman present, I exhorted them for half an hour. Nearly all wept. The minister did not raise his head.

I gave an appointment for another evening meeting. Seventy men and women were present. At the close of the lecture I asked those who felt the need of Christ and desired my prayers, that they might become Christians, to rise up. Every one arose, the Universalist minister and all. He then stated as follows :—

" I was once a Christian, and was called of God to preach, and if at last I wail in hell, I shall have this to comfort me, that I have been a means in the hands of God of the salvation of sinners."

The reader may judge that by this time this man's faith in universal salvation had become very much shaken. I then asked all among those who had risen, who would esteem it a privilege to come forward and bow with me, to come to the front seats. All seventy started, and soon the floor in front of the seats was crowded so as to give no one a chance to kneel down. I then told them to go back to their seats and kneel down there as best they could, and give their hearts to the Lord. As I knelt every soul present bowed with me. There was no one in all that congregation to join me in vocal prayer, for not one of them enjoyed communion with God.

The next day I called at the house of Walter Bolton. He and his family received me kindly, and conversed with me freely relative to the meetings, and upon the subject of religion in general. Before I left, Mr. Bolton said:—

"Mr. White, when you rode into this place I knew you by sight as if I had been acquainted with you for years. Your countenance, hat, coat, horse, saddle and bridle, looked familiar to me. Just before you came here to lecture, I dreamed that a young man rode into this place on horseback, to speak upon the second coming of Christ. I noticed particularly his appearance and dress. The people asked him many questions, which he readily answered in a manner that carried strong conviction to their minds that the doctrine was true. Among these questions were those upon the millennium, suggesting the view that there was to be a thousand years of peace and prosperity to the church, during which time all men were to be holy. They were the very points you examined in your discourse last Sunday forenoon, which called out that Universalist minister. When I saw you, as you rode to this place, my dream came to my mind with such force that I felt that I must hear you speak. This is the reason why I have attended all your meetings, and have watched their progress with interest. Especially when you quoted the very texts which I heard you quote in my dream, and when you made the very remarks upon those texts which I distinctly remember of hearing you make, my feelings were beyond description."

From anything Mr. Bolton said during this interview with him and family, no one would receive the idea that he had been troubled with infidelity. He was under deep conviction, and seemed to choose the religion of the Bible as the theme of conversation. I bowed with this dear family in prayer, and parted with them in tears. The case of Walter Bolton furnishes an illustration of the simple means by which the Lord sometimes softens the hearts and enlightens the minds of those shut up to the hardness and blindness of infidelity, and prepares them for the reception of light and truth.

In a few days I returned to Palmyra, where I received ordination to the work of the ministry from the hands of ministers of the Christian denomination, of which I was a member. But I soon returned back to East Augusta and baptized three persons. A fourth candidate stood ready to go into the water, but not being satisfied that she was sincere, I refused to baptize her in the presence of a large congregation at the water. This young woman was disappointed, and joined her parents in expressions and manifestations of anger. They sent for Elder Hermon Stinson, an educated Freewill Baptist minister of note, who came to the place, baptized the young woman, and organized a small church. And in just four weeks from that time, Elder Stinson was again called to the place to sit in counsel in the case of this woman, when she was dismissed from the church for bad conduct.

During the summer of 1843, I was not able to awaken especial interest at any new place upon the subject of the second advent. I visited the congregation of believers in Portland and Boston, labored in the hay-field to earn clothing for the winter, and preached in different places where I had the previous winter given lectures.

In the autumn of that year, in company with my father and two sisters, I attended the Maine Eastern Christian Conference, of which I was a member, held in the town of Knox. Before we reached the place, as night drew on, a heavy shower of rain compelled us to call at a hotel. In those days singing was our delight. My father had been a teacher of vocal music, and my sisters were first-class singers. And as time began to hang heavily upon our hands, we found relief in singing some of the most stirring revival melodies of those times.

The landlord, his family, and many who had been driven in by the rain as we had been, seemed to enjoy our singing, and when we had finished one piece, they would call for another. In this way the evening passed off pleasantly. And when my father called for our bill the next morning, the landlord told him there was none for him to settle, as we had paid him the evening before in singing. He also stated that at any time we would put up with him he would entertain us, and take his pay in singing.

The Christian denomination in Maine, as well as in other States, had been deeply imbued with the spirit of the Advent hope and faith. But it was evident before that Conference closed, that many, especially among the ministers, were drawing back, and were partaking of the spirit of opposition. The religious meetings and business sessions, however, passed off with a good degree of apparent harmony. No one preached or spoke in favor of the soon advent of Christ in a manner to offend any, and no one directly opposed. But a lack of freedom of spirit was felt by that portion of the Conference who were decided believers. This class constituted a majority, and on Sunday, the last day of the meeting, I was urged to preach. But I was young, and well knew that according to custom the ablest men present were already selected to preach to the crowd on that day, yet I felt assured by the Spirit of God, that I had the word of the Lord to speak to the people on that occasion.

Just as the afternoon service was to commence, I felt so deeply impressed with duty to preach, that several ministers noticed it in my appearance, and came to me, saying: " It is your duty to speak, and we will try and secure the time to you this afternoon." I then retired from the crowd in and around the house, to pray over the matter, and while bowed before the Lord, decided that I would press my way directly toward the pulpit, and if the ministers gave me room, and the time, I would speak. As I came toward the pulpit, I saw that the sofa was filled with ministers, and that one of experience in the ministry sat in the center, directly behind the large Bible. This man had been selected to give the last discourse. He had opposed me when lecturing in the west part of the State, and I concluded that he would not consent to give me the time.

But as I drew near the pulpit, my brother Samuel, who was then a member of the Conference, and a Brother Chalmers, stepped down from the pulpit, took hold of my arms, and urged me to take a seat upon the sofa, stating to me that if I wished to preach I should have a chance. I replied that if one of them would read Advent hymns, the other pray, and I could get hold of the large Bible, I would speak. My brother read a hymn, and while Brother Chalmers was praying, I took the Bible from the stand and turned leaves to certain proof texts. When the prayer was finished, some uneasiness was manifested by several ministers as they saw me in possession of the Bible. The second hymn was read and sung, while I held fast the Bible. My intentions to preach were by this time well known to all the ministers, yet no one offered to take the Bible, or to speak to me in reference to occupying the time. The way seemed fully open, and I moved forward with freedom, while responses of "Amen," were heard in different parts of the house from those who cherished the blessed hope of the soon coming of Jesus.

At the close of this service, the Lord's supper was to be celebrated, and while the friends of Jesus were gathering around this table, I joined with my sisters in singing :—

" You will see your Lord a coming," &c.

Our voices in those days were clear and powerful, and our spirits triumphant in the Lord. And as we would strike the chorus of each verse—" With a band of music,"—a good Brother Clark, who ever seemed to have resting upon him a solemn sense of the great day of God near at hand, would rise, strike his hands together over his head, shout " Glory !" and immediately sit down. A more solemn appearing man I never saw. Each repetition of this chorus would bring Brother Clark to his feet, and call from him the same shout of glory. The Spirit of God came upon the brethren, who by this time were seated ready to receive the emblems of our dying Lord. The influence of the melody, accompanied by Brother Clark's solemn appearance and sweet shouts, seemed electrifying. Many were in tears, while responses of " Amen," and " Praise the Lord," were heard from almost every one who loved the Advent hope. The emblems were passed, and that yearly meeting closed.

In a few weeks I returned to my old field of labor, and gave lectures at Brunswick and Harpswell, where a good degree of interest was manifested. The field of labor seemed to open before me as winter drew near. I had become acquainted with Brother John Pearson, Jr., of Portland, who had been laboring a portion of his time giving lectures upon the near advent, and I invited him to join me. We labored together in different parts of Maine much of the time for nearly one year. At the Reed neighborhood, in Richmond, we saw a good work. Elder E. Cromwell, the pastor of the church, embraced the faith in full. I there baptized several.

We labored at Litchfield and saw a good work. Many professed Christians embraced the faith, and sinners were converted. The Congregationalist minister felt that the work was against his interests, and in private circles opposed. On returning to the place, after an absence of some weeks, I met this minister in the road, and as we passed he seemed to be surprised to meet me again, and said :—

" Why, Mr. White, are you yet in the land of the living ?"

" No, sir," was the reply, " I am in the land of the dying, but at the soon coming of the Lord I expect to go to the land of the living." We each went our way.

The year 1843, Jewish time, which was supposed to reach, as stated by Mr. Miller, from March 21, 1843, to March 21, 1844, passed, and many were sadly disappointed in not witnessing the coming of the Lord in that year. But these soon found relief in the clear and forcible application to the existing disappointment of those scriptures which set forth the tarrying time.

It was as early as 1842 that the prophecy of Habakkuk suggested the idea of the prophetic chart to the mind of that holy man of God, Charles Fitch. No one, however, then saw in this prophecy the tarrying time. Afterward they could see both the chart and the tarry. Here is the prophecy :—

" Write the vision, and make it plain upon tables, that he may run that readeth it. For the vision is yet for an appointed time, but at the end it shall speak and not lie. Though it tarry, wait for it ; because it will surely come, it will not tarry." Chap. 2 : 2, 3.

True believers were also much comforted and strengthened by that portion of the prophecy of Ezekiel which seemed exactly to the point, as follows :—

" And the word of the Lord came unto me, saying, Son of man, what is that proverb that ye have in the land of Israel, saying, The days are prolonged and every vision faileth ? Tell them, therefore, Thus saith the Lord God, I will make this proverb to cease; and they shall no more use it as a proverb in Israel; but say unto them, The days are at hand, and the effect of every vision.  For there shall be no more any vain vision, nor flattering divination within the house of Israel.  For I am the Lord, I will speak, and the word that I shall speak shall come to pass. It shall be no more prolonged, for in your days, O rebellious house, will I say the word, and will perform it, saith the Lord God.  Again the word of the Lord came to me saying, Son of man, behold, they of the house of Israel say, The vision that he seeth is for many days to come, and he prophesieth of the times that are far off.  Therefore, say unto them, thus saith the Lord God, There shall none of my words be prolonged any more, but the word which I have spoken shall be done, saith the Lord God." Chap. 12 : 21–28.

There was a general agreement with those who taught the immediate coming of Christ, in applying the parable of the ten virgins of Matt. 25 to the events connected with the second advent.  And the passing of the time of expectation, the disappointment and the delay, seemed to be forcibly illustrated by the tarrying of the bridegroom in the parable. The definite time had passed, yet believers were united in the faith that the event was near.  It soon became evident that they were losing a degree of their zeal and devotion to the cause, and were falling into that state illustrated by the slumbering of the ten virgins of the parable, following the tarrying of the bridegroom.

The first of May I received an urgent call to visit West Gardiner, and baptize.  A messenger was sent twenty miles for me.  He stated that there were ten or twelve children there, who were convicted by my lectures, who had held their little meetings by themselves, and sought and found the Lord, and who had decided to have me baptize them.  Their parents opposed the idea, and told them that Elder Getchel, the pastor of the church, would baptize them. They held a little counsel and decided that they would not go into the water unless they could have me to immerse them. Their parents yielded and sent for me. But before I reached the place, an effort was made to intimidate these dear children, and, if possible, to frighten them, and thus keep them from doing their duty. "What kind of an experience does Mr. White suppose those babies can tell ?" said a Baptist minister of the most rigid stamp of past times.

The large school-house was crowded at the time appointed, and there were three unfriendly ministers present to watch the proceedings. " Please vacate these front seats," said I, "and give those who are to be baptized a chance to come forward." Twelve boys and girls, from seven to fifteen years of age, came forward. It was a beautiful sight, which stirred the very depths of my soul, and I felt like taking charge of them as I would of a class in school. I was determined to help the feelings of those dear children as much as possible, and rebuke their persecutors.

After taking my text, " Fear not little flock, it is your Father's good pleasure to give you the kingdom," Luke 12:32, a text quite applicable to the occasion, I stated that I should not require the children before me to relate their experiences before the congregation. That it would be cruel to decide their fitness to follow the Lord in the ordinance of baptism by the confidence and freedom they might have in speaking before those professed Christians present who felt unfriendly toward them, and that I should, at the close of my discourse, ask them a few questions. The children were much comforted and cheered by the discourse. In fact I was enjoying decidedly a good time with those lambs of the flock.

They then arose in their turn and answered some questions, and related particulars as to their conviction of sin, the change they had experienced, and the love of Jesus they felt, until the congregation heard twelve intelligent and sweet experiences. It may be proper for me here to state that questions asked these children at the very point in the relation of their experiences when they were becoming confused, and were about to cut their story short, gave them confidence, and helped them to enter into all parts of their experiences.

I then called upon all present who felt opposed to the baptism of the little flock before me, to rise up. Not one arose. I stated to them that the present was the time to object if they had objections. But if they did not then and there object, to forever be silent. I then said to the children that no one objected, and that the way was fully open before them, and no person from that day had any right to object to their baptism. We went to a beautiful body of water, where I led those dear children down into the liquid grave, and buried them with their divine Lord. Not one of them strangled or seemed the least agitated. And as I led them out of the water and presented them to their parents, the children met them with a heavenly smile of joy, and I praised the Lord with the voice of triumph. This meeting, and that sweet baptism, has lived among the most pleasing memories of the past, and when laboring for the youth in different States, I have probably rehearsed more or less of the particulars of that sweet meeting, and that happy baptism, a hundred times.

In the month of June, 1844, a Second Advent Conference was held at Portland, Me., which I attended in company with Elder Pearson. I had traveled extensively in the heat and dust of summer, until my plain clothing was much soiled and worn.

And not enjoying my usual freedom of spirits, I chose to remain silent and give others the time. I enjoyed the preaching, however, and the social seasons of this excellent Conference, and at its close felt my usual spiritual strength and freedom.

There was present at this Conference an Elder H., from Eastern Maine, who had much to say in his peculiar, noisy style. He professed to be a man of great faith, and wonderfully filled with the Holy Spirit. If noise, harsh expressions, rough language generally, and frequent empty shouts of " Glory, hallelujah," constitute the sum total of the fruits of the Spirit, then this Elder H. was an exceedingly good man. But if love, peace, long-suffering, gentleness, goodness, meekness, and temperance, are among the fruits of the Spirit, this poor man was sadly deficient. In fact, these precious fruits were not exhibited in him. He enjoyed a shout with those who would join with him, and ever appeared to feel strong and sure of Heaven. Self appeared in this man, and not Christ. He had much to say of humility ; but his was evidently on the outside. His style of worship, and pretended humility, are well described by the apostle as " voluntary humility and will-worship." At times he was so very humble (?) that he chose not to seat himself at the table with others to take food ; but, forgetting the words of the apostle, " Let all things be done decently and in order," he would take food from the table, and go behind the door and eat it, attracting attention to his wonderful humility by shouts. But if corrected for his faults, however carefully, the demon in him was aroused at once. This man had no words of tenderness and comfort for the weak and fainting. So far from this, he even boasted of running over, as he expressed it, this one and the other. He spoke and acted as if he regarded himself as being on exhibition at that meeting as a wonderful specimen of faith and goodness.

His career since that time, in following the spirit that seemed to possess him at that Conference, has proved that the man was laboring under the sad mistake of supposing himself led by the Spirit of God, while being controlled by Satan.

The reader may be disappointed at the introduction of this unpleasant matter, choosing to read only of those incidents with which are connected the victories of the work and power of God. But it may be for the safety and sure advancement of young disciples, and those of little experience in the conflicts of the Christian life, to learn of the trials of the way, and of the wiles of the devil, as to know only of the power and love of God, and the triumphant victories of his truth and people. The various attacks of Satan, in order to mislead and finally destroy even honest men and women, may with propriety, in consequence of their numbers, bear the name of legion. And the duty of all is, as stated by our Lord, " Watch and pray, lest ye enter into temptation."

But he who is filled with pride in spiritual things, and is unteachable—thinks himself especially led by the Spirit, and understands all about the work of the Lord, who regards himself as an eminent Christian, yet is easily tempted, and becomes jealous of being slighted, and even ugly if he does not receive a large share of attention—is a tool for the devil, and an exceedingly dangerous man. He is a medium in the hands of Satan through which to effect and mislead the precious flock of Christ. Let all beware lest they, in some way, be brought more or less under the influence of such, and, in consequence, weave into their experience uncomely stripes of vain religion.

Such things ever have existed, and ever will exist during the entire period of Satan's efforts to wrest precious souls from the hands of Jesus Christ. "For there must be also heresies among you," says Paul, "that they which are approved may be made manifest among you." These, in the Lord's providence, constitute a portion of the fuel to heat the furnace of affliction in which the true Christian loses his dross and is refined, so as to reflect in his life the meekness and purity of the loving Lamb of God. Therefore let not the beloved of the Lord think it strange concerning the fiery trial which is to try them, as though some strange thing had happened unto them. But rejoice, inasmuch as they are partakers of Christ's sufferings, that when his glory shall be revealed, they may be glad with exceeding joy. 1 Pet. 4 : 12, 13.

The reader will please return to Poland Conference. One morning about forty brethren and sisters bowed at the family altar, at the house of Brother Jordan, while Elder H. led in prayer. A portion of that strange prayer was in substance as follows :—

"O Lord, have mercy on Brother White. He is proud, and will be damned unless he gets rid of his pride. Have mercy upon him, O Lord, and save him from pride. O Lord have mercy, and wean him from the pride of life. Break him down, Lord, and make him humble. Have mercy upon him. Have mercy."

He went on telling a long story about me, informing the Lord of my pride, and how sure I was of destruction unless I should speedily repent, and closed up with vehement cries of, " Have mercy ! Have mercy ! Mercy ! Mercy !" This was his way of treating those who did not seem to receive him with feelings of great reverence for his special humility and extra holiness. His object in this was to cast fear upon those around him, and thus bring them directly under his influence, that they might show him all that respect which his especial endowments demanded.

But he did not succeed in my case. After the company had arisen to their seats, and had for awhile painfully pondered in silence what these things could mean, I drew my chair near Elder H., and in a kind manner said to him :—

"Brother H., I fear you have told the Lord a wrong story. You say I am proud. This I think is not true. But why tell this to the Lord? He knows more about me than you do. He does not need to be instructed in my case. But this was not your object. You wished to represent me before these brethren and sisters as proud, and have chosen to do so through the medium of prayer to God. Now, sir, if I am proud, so much so that you are able to give the Lord information on the subject, you can tell me before these present in what I am proud. Is it in my general appearance, or my manner of speaking, praying, or singing?"

"No, Brother White, it is not in those things."

"Well, is it manifested by these worn and soiled clothes? Please look me over. Is it in my patched boots? my rusty coat? this nearly worn-out vest? these soiled pants? or that old hat I wear?"

"No; I do not see pride in any of these things you mention. But, Brother White, when I saw that starched collar on you, God only knows how I felt."

And here the man wept as though his heart would break. This was for effect. It was his usual resort when he had points to carry in a difficult case. In an extremity, tears are not unfrequently woman's closing and most powerful argument. In her, if her cause be just, they are excusable, and even appropriate and beautiful. But to see a coarse, hard-hearted man, possessing in his very nature but little more tenderness than a crocodile, and nearly as destitute of moral and religious training as a hyena, shedding hypocritical tears for effect, is enough to stir the mirthfulness of the gravest saint.

"But let me explain to you, Brother H., about this starched collar. I may be able to help you. When

I came to this Conference, Sister Rounds offered to do my washing, and as I had no clean change, she kindly lent me her husband's shirt, which unfortunately has a starched collar. Mine have only a narrow binding round the neck. I wear no collars only in cases of necessity like the present. It is this, sir, that has given rise to all your ado this morning. I usually wear a black alpaca bosom, but am not the owner of a single collar. You have certainly told the Lord a wrong story about me, under circumstances the most inexcusable. And I think your first and most important work is to settle this matter with him."

Elder H. dropped upon his knees, and said, in substance :—

"O Lord, I have prayed for Brother White, and he is displeased with me for it. Have mercy upon him! Have mercy! Mercy! Mercy!"

And seeing that none joined with him, not even so much as to kneel, he felt that his effort was proving a failure, and in a subdued tone came to me and said :—

"Why did you not kneel with me? O Brother White, I have felt for you, prayed for you, and have wept over you, and I hope you will not be offended."

"Certainly, I am not offended. There is nothing in all this to offend any one. I pity you. You are suffering from unsanctified feelings arising from an unfortunate application of false ideas. Your prayers are no more to me than the howling of the winds. And when you, under such circumstances, plead your tears, feelings of shame and inexpressible disgust and pity for you come over me. I advise you to carry this matter no further; and I hope you will learn a good lesson from the folly you have manifested this morning."

By this time I seemed to lose sight of that gloom and despondency under which I had been suffering for several days, and I enjoyed the closing portion of the Conference exceedingly well, and from that time felt my usual freedom of spirits. This was my first experience in meeting and rebuking fanaticism, which served to prepare me to deal with it in its ever varying forms in after time.

That fanaticism did arise about this time, and labor to attach itself to the Advent cause, I would not deny. I, however, by no means admit the truthfulness of the highly-colored reports of bitter enemies of the cause. Not more than one in ten of the slanderous reports had the least semblance of truth in them. Men filled with prejudice and bitterness against the proclamation of the immediate second advent of Christ, mingled with fear that it might be true, were totally unfitted to fairly represent the faith, motives and actions of believers. And there are no good reasons why he who gives a faithful sketch of Advent history, should hesitate to admit all the facts relative to fanaticism which have arisen from the bigotry and blind zeal of such men as Elder H., and those more designing and shrewd, who have borne the Advent name, and have professed the Advent faith.

Is it not one of the plainest facts in sacred history, that when God has especially wrought for his people, Satan has ever improved the opportunity to make especial efforts? And, during the entire period of the controversy between Christ and his angels, and Satan and his angels, when the sons of God come to present themselves before the Lord, may they not expect that Satan will come also? Has not this ever been true in the history of the people of God? And does not the sad experience of the church of Jesus Christ, since the time where sacred history leaves it, agree with that of the patriarchs and prophets?

We read of Luther's perplexities, and of his anguish, in consequence of the conduct of fanatics, and the terrible influence the course of these men had on the great reformation, and count these things among the evidences that God was especially with Martin Luther. And there were the Wesleys, and a host of other good men, who have lifted at the great wheel of reform, and have blessed the world with the inspiring influence of their living faith. These men who kept pace with the spirit of reform, have, in their turn, been annoyed at every step by Satan close at their heels, pushing unguarded souls, over-zealous and illy-balanced ones, into fanaticism. The experiences of these men are in harmony with that of the holy men of old, and attest the fact that when and where God works for his people, just there is the time and place for Satan to practice his impositions upon those he can get under his foul influence.

Did Satan stir up fanaticism in connection with the Advent movement? This is one of the proofs of the genuineness of the work. What! He suffer the world to be warned of their and his approaching doom, and he not be stirred in consequence of it? The church be aroused to action, and to readiness for the day of God, and sinners by thousands leaving his ranks and seeking a preparation to meet the King of kings, and he remain quiet? No. He knows his time is short, hence not only his wrath, but his wiles in all their forms. This is well illustrated by what is said to be a dream. A traveler saw Satan seated upon a post, in front of a house of worship, asleep. He aroused him from his slumbers and addressed him as follows:—

"How is it that you are so quietly sleeping? This I conclude is unusual for you, considering your reputation for activity in your kind of work. Is it not?"

"Yes," was the reply, "but the people in this house of worship are asleep, and the minister is asleep, and I thought this a good time for me to take a nap."

Let the people be aroused to the living truths of the word of God, and to a life of faith and holiness; let them with gladness receive the news of the return and peaceful reign of the Just One; let them consecrate themselves and all they have to the Lord, and with one united voice swell the note, " Behold he cometh," and you will have good evidence that the powers of darkness are all astir. Satan will not sleep then. With vigilance will he manifest his wrath, and, calling to his aid all the fallen angels of his realm, his wiles will be imposed upon all connected with the people of God who are not properly instructed and guarded.

But it should be distinctly understood that the proclamation of time in the message symbolized by the first angel of Rev. 14:6, 7, and in the cry " Behold the Bridegroom cometh," given in great power in the autumn of 1844, did not produce fanaticism. In those solemn movements, believers were sweetly united in the one blessed hope, and the one living faith. It was when they were left without definite time, during the summer of 1844, that extravagant views of being led by the Spirit prevailed, and to some extent brought in fanaticism, division and wild-fire, with their blighting results, among the happy expectants of the King of glory. But when the proclamation of definite time came in the autumn of 1844, fanaticism, ultra holiness, unhappy divisions, and their results, melted away before it like an early autumn frost before the rising sun.

# CHAPTER IV.

### THE TENTH DAY OF THE JEWISH SEVENTH MONTH.

As to the character of the work which resulted from giving what was called the midnight cry, it evidently was the special work of God. It was not, as many suppose, the result of fanaticism.

1. Because it bore the marks of the especial providence of God. It was not characterized by those extremes ever manifested where human excitement. and not the word and Spirit of God, has the controlling influence. It was in harmony with those seasons of humiliation, rending of heart. confession and complete consecration of all, which are matters of history in the Old Testament, and are made matters of duty in the New.

2. Because it was subversive of all those forms of fanaticism which had made their appearance somewhat in connection with the Second Advent cause. And it is a fact, that Satan had crowded upon some who bore the Advent name, almost every stripe of fanaticism he had ever invented. But these were at once swallowed up by the solemn power of the midnight cry, as the rods of the magicians were by the rod of Aaron.

3. Because the work was marked with sobriety, humility, solemnity, reverence, self-examination, repentance, confessions and tears, instead of lightness, exaltation, trifling, irreverent expressions, self-justification, pride in spiritual things, voluntary humility and will-worship, which generally characterize the conduct of fanatics.

4. Because the work bore the fruit of the Spirit of God, as set forth in the New Testament. It was evidently guided by wisdom from above. The apostle James declares this wisdom to be " first pure, then peaceable, gentle, and easy to be entreated, full of

mercy and good fruits, without partiality, and without hypocrisy." Chap. 3 : 17. Paul says that the fruit of the Spirit is love, joy, peace, long-suffering, gentleness, goodness, faith, meekness, temperance. Gal. 5 : 22, 23. These are the good fruits of the work and Spirit of God, and these did all appear in an eminent sense as the results of the midnight cry.

But fanaticisms are the works of the flesh, the power of Satan being brought to bear upon the carnal mind.

It is true that Satan seeks to clothe his work, as far as possible, with that which may resemble garments of truth and righteousness. But the experienced observer will not fail to see that he, and those who are brought under his influence, come infinitely short of counterfeiting the work of God. He may succeed in blinding the eyes of men, so that they may not be able to discern the difference between the work of God and his imperfect mimicry. But the work of high Heaven he cannot imitate. And when the work of Satan in fanaticism is carried out, and its terrible fruit is ripened into bitterness, its contrast with the fruit of the work and Spirit of God will be seen as wide as Beelzebub with Christ, perdition with all its terror and blackness of despair with the matchless glories of the kingdom of God.

There is a difference between the road to life, and that leading to death. And these do not lie side by side. They are in opposite directions. Do not be deceived by those who mix fanaticism with the work of God, and affirm that the compound all came from heaven. Neither be deceived by those who, seeing evidence of fanaticism in some who have been connected with the Advent cause, denounce the entire movement as being the work of men, or of Satan. I here enter my solemn protest against making one grand Second Advent chowder of all that in any way has been connected with the great Advent movement, of truth and error, of wisdom from heaven, and the spirit and work of fanaticism, and then presenting it to the people as being all the work of Satan, or all the work of God. Such insult God by making him the author of fanaticism and confusion. They also please the devil, by attributing the work of God which he has tried to mar, to his Satanic power. That they might do this, and make no difference between the pure work of God and the results of his miserable efforts at counterfeiting, is the spur of his ambition.

But of all the great religious movements since the days of the first apostles of our Lord, none stand out more pure and free from the imperfections of human nature, and the wiles of Satan, than that of the autumn of 1844. In fact, after looking back upon it for more than twenty years as the greenest spot on all the way in which God has led his people, I do not see how it could have been better, at least so far as the direct providence and work of God is concerned. It was beyond the control of human hands, or human minds. Men and demons sought to hinder and to mar this work, but the power that attended it brushed away their influence, as you would remove a spider's web, and there stood the work of God free from the print of a man's hand.

But as the reader will be better edified by reading the statements and experience of those ministers who had the burden of the work upon them, and were imbued with the spirit of that solemn message, I will here let them speak in confirmation of the foregoing statements.

Elder George Storrs, New York, September 24, 1844, says:—

"I take up my pen with feelings such as I never before experienced. *Beyond a doubt*, in my mind, the *tenth day* of the *seventh month* will witness the revelation of our Lord Jesus Christ in the clouds of heaven. We are then within a *few days* of that event. Awful moment to those who are unprepared, but glorious to those who are ready. I feel that I am making the *last appeal* that I shall ever make through the press. My heart is full. I see the ungodly and sinner disappearing from my view, and there now stands before my mind the *professed believers* in the Lord's near approach. But what shall I say to them? Alas! we have been *slumbering* and *sleeping*, both the *wise* and the *foolish*; but so our Saviour told us it would be; and 'thus the Scriptures are fulfilled,' and it is the last prophecy relating to the events to precede the personal advent of our Lord; now comes the true midnight cry; the previous was but the alarm. Now the real one is sounding; and oh, how solemn the hour! The 'virgins' have been asleep or slumbering; yes, all of us. Asleep on the time; that is the point. Some have indeed preached the seventh month, but it was with doubt whether it is this year or some other; and that doubt is now removed from my mind. 'Behold the Bridegroom cometh,' this year, 'go ye out to meet him.' We have done with the nominal churches and all the wicked, except so far as this cry may effect them; our work is now to wake up the 'virgins' who 'took their lamps and went forth to meet the bridegroom.' Where are we now? 'If the vision tarry, wait for it.' Is not that our answer since March and April? Yes. What happened while the bridegroom tarried? The virgins all slumbered and slept, did they not? Christ's words have not failed, and 'the Scriptures cannot be broken,' and it is of no use for us to pretend that we have been awake. We have been slumbering; not on the fact of Christ's coming, but on the time. We came into the tarrying time; we did not know 'how long' it would tarry, and on that point we have slumbered. Some of us have said in our sleep, 'Don't fix another time;'

so we slept. Now the trouble is to wake us up.
Lord, help, for vain is the help of man. Speak thyself, Lord. Oh! that the 'Father' may now 'make
known' the time.

"To illustrate the position we have occupied:
Time, the preaching of definite time for the coming
of our Lord, was what led us to take our lamps, and
go forth to meet the Bridegroom. The great truth,
our Lord Jesus Christ is coming again, personally,
to this earth, was, so to speak, the rope let down
from heaven, made fast to the throne of God, equally
as immovable as that throne; by faith, as with both
hands, we took hold of that rope; under our feet we
had solid platform, time, where we stood, and all
opponents could not remove it, nor make us let go
of the rope. There we stood, and rejoiced in the
'blessed hope.' What our opponents never could and
never did do, the end of the supposed Jewish year
1843 effected, viz: swept away our platform from
under us, and left us with nothing but the rope to hold
on by. Did we let go? Some have, and drawn back
to perdition. But many have continued to hold by
the rope. The scoffing winds have beaten against us
severely, and we have swung in the air, the sport of
our opponents. They told us we were now with
them, looking for the Lord's coming, but without any
definite time; and we have been compelled to admit
it, but have refused to let go the rope, saying: 'If
the vision tarry, wait for it.' But we have not known
how long we were thus to swing upon the rope, without a foundation for our feet; and we have not felt
the same joy and glory that we did when we stood
on definite time. God has been trying our faith, to
see if we would hold on. Now, once more, he offers
us a platform on which to stand. It is in the twenty-fifth chapter of Matthew. Here we have the
chronology of the tarrying time, and its duration.
'If ye shall receive it,' you will find once more your

feet upon a rock, and the glory that the first belief in time produced in our breast, returns with a large addition to it, even a 'joy unspeakable and full of glory.'

"The present strong cry of time commenced about the middle of July, and has spread with great rapidity and power, and is attended with a demonstration of the Spirit, such as I never witnessed when the cry was '1843.' It is now literally, 'Go ye out to meet him.' There is a leaving all, that I never dreamed could be seen. Where this cry gets hold of the heart, farmers leave their farms, with their crops standing, to go out and sound the alarm, and mechanics their shops. There is a strong crying with tears, and a consecration of all to God, such as I never witnessed. There is a confidence in this truth such as was never felt in the previous cry, in the same degree; and a weeping or melting glory in it that passes all understanding, except to those who have felt it.

"On this present truth, I, through grace, dare venture all, and feel that to indulge in doubt about it would be to offend God, and bring upon myself 'swift destruction.' I am satisfied that now, 'whosoever shall seek to save his life,' where this cry has been fairly made, by indulging in an 'if it don't come,' or by a fear to venture out on this truth, 'shall lose' his life. It requires the faith that led Abraham to offer up Isaac, or Noah to build the ark, or Lot to leave Sodom, or the children of Israel to stand all night waiting for their departure out of Egypt, or for Daniel to go into the lion's den, or the three Hebrews to go into the fiery furnace. We have fancied we were going into the kingdom without such a test of faith; but I am satisfied we are not. This last truth brings such a test, and none will venture upon it but such as dare be accounted fools, madmen, or anything else that Antediluvians, Sodomites, a lukewarm church, or sleeping virgins, are disposed to heap upon them. Once more would I cry, 'Escape for thy life;' look not behind you; 'remember Lot's wife.'"

N. Southard, editor of the *Midnight Cry*, September 26, 1844, says:—

"Before God, whose swift, approaching judgment will bring every secret thing to light, I wish to say, that up to this hour my professed consecration to him has not been complete. If this fact makes me a hypocrite, I have been one. I have not been dead to the world. If all Christians are dead to the world, I have not been a Christian. But I now say, let Christ be all, and let me be nothing. He has a balm for every wound, for his blood cleanseth from all sin; and I, even I, can stand complete in him.

"After writing thus far, I kneeled and asked God for direction as to what I should say next. I arose and took my Bible, and opening it, read Rev. 7:9–17: 'After this I beheld, and lo, a great multitude, which no man could number, of all nations, and kindreds, and people, and tongues, stood before the throne and before the Lamb, clothed with white robes, and palms in their hands; and cried with a loud voice, saying, Salvation to our God, which sitteth upon the throne, and unto the Lamb,' &c. If this great multitude is admitted before the throne, is there anything to keep me from being there? They differ in every conceivable particular from each other, except in two. They have all washed their robes in the blood of the Lamb, and have all suffered great tribulation for his sake. Here, then, is the touchstone. Is your robe all washed clean in the blood of Christ? or have you been insulting him, by trying to patch up a robe out of the filthy rags of your own righteousness? Alas! I have thought that I could rest partly upon myself and partly on Christ. I now cast myself naked and helpless upon that mercy which saved the thief on the cross, which received denying Peter, which honored Mary Magdalene as the first witness of his resurrection, and which changed a persecuting Saul into a chief apostle.

"But can I bear the second mark? Can I joyfully endure tribulation for Jesus? Not in my own strength, but his grace is sufficient for me. In that grace I believe; Lord, help mine unbelief.

"One of my besetting sins has been a desire to please those around me, instead of inquiring simply, what would the Lord have me to do, to be, and to say. I confess this before the world, but I cannot confess that I have not thought I was doing right in publishing the evidence of Christ's near coming. I have not been half enough awake to the greatness of the subject. May God forgive me in this thing, and grant me grace to be wide awake till he comes. Dear reader, are you awake? If not, it is high time to awake out of sleep."

Elder F. G. Brown, October 2, 1844, says :—

" I wish to say to all my dear brethren and sisters, who with me have been waiting for the kingdom of heaven, that I am thoroughly convinced that we are now in that portion of the parable of the ten virgins, represented by the cry at midnight, 'Behold the Bridegroom cometh, go ye out to meet him.' I fully respond to the cry; my expiring lamp has been re-kindled, and I am now permitted, by God's grace, to see additional light blazing from the Scriptures, and all converging to one glorious point, the advent of our blessed Lord this very month! My dear friends, I have been in an awful, slumbering, sleeping state. I have been on the verge of perdition; though I have never ceased to cherish in my heart the great and leading doctrines of the Lord's coming. I thought a few weeks ago that I was in a pretty good state; awful delusion! Look out for deception! Awake, and trim your lamps, or you will be lost after all!'"

Elder J. Litch, late editor of the *Advent Herald*, Boston, October, 1844, says:—

" I wish to say to my dear brethren and sisters, who are looking for the coming of the Lord on the tenth day of the seventh month, but especially to those who have hesitated on the question, that the strong objections which have existed in my mind against it, are passed away, and I am now convinced that the types, together with the signs of the times, are sufficient authority for believing in the Lord's coming at that time ; and henceforth I shall look to that day with the expectation of beholding the King in his beauty. I bless the name of the Lord for sending this midnight cry to arouse me to go out to meet the Bridegroom. May the Lord make us meet for the inheritance of the saints."

William Miller, Low Hampton, N. Y., October 11, 1844, says:—

" I think I have never seen among our brethren such faith as is manifested in the seventh month. 'He will come,' is the common expression. 'He will not tarry the second time,' is their general reply. There is a forsaking of the world, an unconcern for the wants of life, a general searching of heart, confession of sin, and a deep feeling in prayer for Christ to come. A preparation of heart to meet him seems to be the labor of their agonizing spirits. There is something in this present waking up different from anything I have ever before seen. There is no great expression of joy ; that is, as it were, suppressed for a future occasion, when all heaven and earth will rejoice together with joy unspeakable and full of glory. There is no shouting ; that, too, is reserved for the shout from heaven. The singers are silent ; they are waiting to join the angelic hosts, the choir from heaven. No arguments are used or needed ; all seem convinced that they have the truth. There

is no clashing of sentiments; all are of one heart and
of one mind. Our meetings are all occupied with
prayer and exhortation to love and obedience. The
general expression is, ' Behold the Bridegroom cometh, go ye out to meet him.' Amen. Even so come,
Lord Jesus."

I will here give, as the closing testimony relative
to the character of the seventh-month movement,
one from the *Advent Shield*, published January,
1845. And let it be borne in mind that the *Shield*
was a standard work, of 440 pages, for all Adventists at that time, and that the following testimony
from it was not published till about three months
after the seventh-month movement, when Adventists had taken time to review the past, and settle, as
was supposed, upon a firm, united position.

" It produced everywhere the most deep searching
of heart and humiliation of soul before the God of
high Heaven. It caused a weaning of affections
from the things of this world, a healing of the con-
troversies and animosities, a confession of wrongs,
a breaking down before God, and penitent, broken-
hearted supplications to him for pardon and acceptance. It caused self-abasement and prostration of
soul, such as we never before witnessed. As God,
by Joel, commanded, when the great day of God
should be at hand, it produced a rending of hearts
and not of garments, and a turning unto the Lord
with fasting, and weeping; and mourning. As God
said by Zechariah, a spirit of grace and supplication
was poured out upon his children; they looked to
him whom they had pierced, there was a great
mourning in the land, every family apart and their
wives apart, and those who were looking for the
Lord afflicted their souls before him. Such was its
effect upon the children of God.

" While none could deny the possibility of the
Lord's then coming; and as the fulfillment of some of

the types chronologically at Christ's first advent rendered it highly probable that those which typified the second advent, would also be chronologically fulfilled, so general an awakening, and with such blessed fruits, could not but impress many minds ; and those who were not convinced of the soundness of the typical argument, were led to regard it as a fulfillment of the parable of the ten virgins, in the twenty-fifth of Matthew,—as their arising to trim their lamps, after having gone forth to meet the bridegroom, and slumbering while he tarried ; so that the definite time was finally embraced by nearly all of the Advent faith. So universal a movement among those who a short time before were comparatively asleep on this question, could not be unnoticed by the world.

" The wicked, consequently, flocked to the various places of meeting, some out of idle curiosity to hear, others out of concern for their spiritual interests, and others still to scoff at solemn things. Those who believed they should so shortly stand in their Saviour's presence, and whose works corresponded with their faith, could not but feel a nearness of access to God, and sweet communion with him ; and the souls of such were greatly blessed. With a realizing sense of such a nearness of the greatest of all events, as we came up to that point of time, all other unnecessary cares were laid aside, and the whole soul was devoted to a preparation for the great event. God being more ready to give than we are to receive, does not permit any thus to plead in vain; and his Holy Spirit came down like copious showers upon the parched earth. It was then evident that there was faith upon the earth, such faith as is ever ready to act in accordance with what the soul believes that God has spoken ; such faith as would, in obedience to a supposed command, bid all the pleasures of this world adieu, having respect to the recompense of reward. Such was a faith like that of Abraham's when, at the command of God, he went out, ' not knowing whither he went,' nor withheld his only son ; and here were those all ready to join the multitude, who through faith will inherit the promises."

It was our privilege to take part in giving the cry, Behold he cometh ! Our field of labor was eastern Maine. The time for giving the message was brief, and the work moved with great power. Every house of worship, whether large or small, was crowded. All who came under the influence of the cry were moved. Nearly the entire congregation at each place would request prayers. And was there fanaticism in eastern Maine before, the solemn message, " Behold the Bridegroom cometh," swept it from the field.

The tenth day of the seventh month of the Jewish year 1844, came and passed, and left impressions upon the minds of believers not easily effaced ; and although more than a quarter of a century has passed since that memorable period, that work has not lost its interest and force upon the minds of those who participated in it. Even now, when one who shared in that blessed work, and who feels its hallowed influence rekindling upon his mind shall speak of that solemn work, of that consecration of all, made in full view of eternal scenes, and of that sweet peace and holy joy which filled the minds of the waiting ones, his words will not fail to touch the feelings of all who shared the blessings of that work and have held fast.

And those who participated in that movement are not the only ones who can now go back in their experience, and feast upon the faith-reviving, soul-inspiring realities of the past. Those who have since embraced the Advent faith and hope, and who have seen in the three messages of Rev. 14, the past con-

secration and blessedness, the present work of preparation, and the future glory, may go back with us
to the autumn of 1844, and with us share the rekindling of the heavenly illumination. Was that our
Jerusalem, where we waited for, and enjoyed, the
outpouring of the Holy Spirit? Then as all Christians, as well as Christ's first disciples who were
present on the occasion, have looked back to the day
of Pentecost with pleasure and profit, so may these
who have embraced the doctrine of the Second
Advent since the memorable seventh-month movement, look back to that period with all that interest
those can who participated in it.

The impressions made and left upon the minds of
believers were deep and lasting. However far one
has since departed from God and his truth, there
still remains upon the soul of the apostate, traces of
the work. Let him hear the subject afresh; let the
simple facts be again brought before his mind, and
he will feel upon this subject as he can feel upon no
other. And those who took part in that work, who
are far backslidden from God, yet cherish regard for
the word of God and Christian experience, will yet
feel deeply over this subject, and the faith of many
of them will be resurrected to new life. God grant
that these pages may prove a blessing to many such.

The disappointment at the passing of the time
was a bitter one. True believers had given up all
for Christ, and had shared his presence as never before. They had, as they supposed, given their last
warning to the world, and had separated themselves,
more or less, from the unbelieving, scoffing multitude. And with the divine blessing upon them,
they felt more like associating with their soon-ex-
pected Master and the holy angels, than with those
from whom they had separated themselves. The
love of Jesus filled every soul, and beamed from
every face, and with inexpressible desires they

prayed, "Come Lord Jesus, and come quickly." But he did not come. And now to turn again to the cares, perplexities, and dangers of life, in full view of the jeers and revilings of unbelievers who now scoffed as never before, was a terrible trial of faith and patience. When Elder Himes visited Portland, Me., a few days after the passing of the time, and stated that the brethren should prepare for another cold winter, my feelings were almost uncontrollable. I left the place of meeting and wept like a child.

But God did not forsake his people. His Spirit upon them still abode, with all who did not rashly deny and denounce the good work in the Advent movement up to that time. And with especial force and comfort did such passages as the following, to the Hebrews, come home to the minds and hearts of the tried, waiting ones: "Cast not away therefore your confidence, which hath great recompense of reward. For ye have need of patience, that, after ye have done the will of God, ye might receive the promise. For yet a little while, and He that shall come will come, and will not tarry. Now the just shall live by faith; but if any man draw back, my soul shall have no pleasure in him. But we are not of them who draw back unto perdition; but of them that believe to the saving of the soul." Chapter 10: 35-39. The points of interest in this portion of Scripture are:—

1. Those addressed are in danger of casting away their confidence in that in which they had done right.

2. They had done the will of God, and were brought into that state of trial where patience was necessary.

3. The just at this time are to live by faith, not by doubting whether they had done the will of God, but faith, in that in which they had done the will of God.

4. Those who should not endure the trial of faith, but should cast away their confidence in the work in which they did the will of God, and draw back, would take the direct road to perdition.

But why apply all this to the subject of the second advent? Answer: Because Paul applies it there. His words, in the very center of the foregoing quotation from his epistle to the Hebrews, forbid any other application: "For yet a little while, and he that shall come will come, and will not tarry." No one will for a moment question that the second advent is the subject upon which the apostle treats. The peculiar situation of those who should be looking for the second appearing of Jesus, is the burden of his exhortation. And how wonderfully applicable to those who were sadly disappointed, tempted and tried, in the autumn of 1844, are his words. With great confidence had they proclaimed the coming of the Lord, with the assurance that they were doing the will of God. But as the time passed, they were brought into a position exceedingly trying to faith and patience. Hence the words of Paul to them, just then, and just there: "Cast not away therefore your confidence." "Ye have need of patience." "Ye have done the will of God." To this decision of the apostle every true Adventist, who tasted the good word of God and the powers of the world to come, in the movement of 1844, will respond, Amen.

But how fearful the words which follow: "Now the just shall live by faith; but if any man draw back my soul shall have no pleasure in him." As Adventists came up to the point of expectation in the blazing light of unsealed prophecy, and the rapidly-fulfilling signs that Christ's coming was at the doors, they walked, as it were, by sight. But now they stand with disappointed hopes, and stricken hearts, and live by faith in the sure word, and the work of God in their Second Advent experience.

With these who hold fast, God is well pleased; but in those who draw back he has no pleasure. These believe to the saving of the soul; while those who become impatient, cast away their confidence in the way God has led them, and give it up as the work of man, or of Satan, and draw back to perdition.

This and many other portions of Scripture of like import, having a direct application to the condition of believers at that time, served not only as an encouragement to them to hold fast their faith, but as a warning to them not to apostatize.

In the providence of God, in the seventh-month movement the attention of the people was turned to the types of the law of Moses. The argument which had been given, that as the vernal types, namely, the passover, the wave sheaf, and the meat-offering, were fulfilled in their order and time in the crucifixion, the resurrection of Christ, and the descent of the Holy Spirit on the day of Pentecost, so would the autumnal types be fulfilled as to time, in the events connected with the second advent, seemed to be conclusive and satisfactory. The position taken was, that as the high priest came out of the typical sanctuary on the tenth day of the seventh month and blessed the people, so Christ, our great High Priest, would on that day come out of heaven to bless his waiting people.

But it should be borne in mind that at that time those types which point to the work in the heavenly sanctuary were not understood. In fact, no one had any definite idea of the tabernacle of God in heaven. We now see that the two holies of the typical sanctuary, made by the direction of the Lord to Moses, with their two distinct ministrations—the daily and the yearly services—were, in the language of Paul to the Hebrews, " patterns of things in the heavens," " figures of the true," chapter 9. He also says of the work of the Jewish priests in chapter 8,

" Who serve unto the example and shadow of
heavenly things." His words mean simply this : In
heaven there is a sanctuary where Christ ministers,
and that sanctuary has two holies, and two distinct
ministrations, as truly as the earthly sanctuary had.
If his words do not mean this, they have no meaning at all. How natural, then, the conclusion, that
as the Jewish priests ministered daily in connection
with the holy place of the sanctuary, and on the
tenth day of the seventh month, at the close of their
yearly round of service, the high priest entered the
most holy place to make atonement for the cleansing of the sanctuary, so Christ ministered in connection with the holy place of the heavenly sanctuary from the time of his ascension to the ending of
the 2300 days of Dan. 8, in 1844, when on the tenth
day of the seventh month of that year he entered
the most holy place of the heavenly tabernacle to
make a special atonement for the blotting out of the
sins of his people, or, which is the same thing, for
the cleansing of the sanctuary. " Unto two thousand three hundred days," said the angel to the
prophet, " then shall the sanctuary be cleansed."

The typical sanctuary was cleansed from the sins
of the people with the offering of blood. The nature
of the cleansing of the heavenly sanctuary may be
learned from the type. By virtue of his own blood,
Christ entered the most holy place to make a special
atonement for the cleansing of the heavenly tabernacle. For clear and full expositions of the sanctuary and the nature of its cleansing, see works upon
the subject by J. N. Andrews and U. Smith, for sale
at the *Review* Office, Battle Creek, Mich., or *Signs
of the Times* Office, Oakland, Cal.

With this view of the heavenly sanctuary before
the reader, he can see the defect in the seventh-
month theory. It now appears evident that the
conclusion that Christ would come out of heaven

on that day is not justified by the premises in the case. But if Christ's ministry in the heavenly sanctuary was to last but one year, on the last day of which he would make an atonement for the cleansing of the heavenly tabernacle, according to the type, then the conclusion that he would on that day come out and bless his waiting people, would be irresistible.

But let it be remembered that "the law having a shadow of good things to come," was "not the very image of the things." In the shadow, the round of service, first in the holy place for the entire year, save one day, and second, in the most holy place on the last day of that year, was repeated each successive year. But not so in the ministry of Christ. He entered the holy place of that heavenly sanctuary at his ascension once for all. There he ministered till the time for the cleansing of the sanctuary at the close of the 2300 days in the autumn of 1844. To accomplish this work, he then entered the most holy place once for all. Christ suffered upon the cross—not often—but once for all. He entered upon his work in the holy place once for all. And he cleanses the heavenly sanctuary for the sins of his people once for all. His ministry in the holy, from his ascension in the spring of A. D. 31 to the autumn of 1844, was eighteen hundred and thirteen years and six months. The period of his ministry in the most holy can no more be defined before its close, than the time of his ministry in the holy could be defined before it terminated. Therefore, however much the tenth-day atonement for the cleansing of the typical sanctuary proved that our great High Priest would enter the most holy of the heavenly tabernacle on the tenth day of the seventh month, it proved nothing to the point that he would on that day come out of the most holy place.

But just what was accomplished on the tenth day

of the seventh month became a matter of discussion.
Some took the rash position that the movement had
not been directed by the providence of God. They
cast away their confidence in that work, not having
sufficient faith and patience to " wait " and " watch,"
until it should be explained by the light of the sanctuary and the three messages of Rev. 14, and they
drew back, to say the least, toward perdition.

Others trembled for this fearful step, and felt the
deepest solicitude for the welfare of the flock,
and exhorted the brethren to patiently wait and
watch for the coming of the Lord, in full faith that
God had been in the work. Among these was William Miller. In a letter published in the *Advent
Herald* for December 11, 1844, he says :—

" MY DEAR BRETHREN : Be patient, establish your
heart, for the coming of the Lord draweth nigh.
For ye have need of patience, that after ye have done
the will of God, ye might receive the promise. For
yet a little while and he that shall come will come,
and will not tarry."

The following is from the cheering pen of Elder
F. G. Brown, who was not only a man of ability, but
one who drank deeply at the fountain of Advent
experience. He saw and felt the danger of drawing
back, and wrote the following letter to encourage his
brethren to hold fast and believe to the saving of
the soul. It was written November 11, 1844, and
published in the *Advent Herald* :—

" MY DEAR BRETHREN AND SISTERS : The great
God has dealt wonderfully with us. When we were
in a state of alarming blindness in relation to the
coming of the great and terrible day of the Lord, he
saw fit to awaken us from our death-like slumbers,
to a knowledge of these things. How little of our
own or man's agency was employed in this work,
you know. Our prejudices, education, tastes, both
intellectual and moral, were all opposed to the doc-

trine of the Lord's coming. We know that it was
the Almighty's arm that disposed us to receive this
grace. The Holy Ghost wrought it in our inmost
souls, yea, incorporated it into our very being, so
that it is now a part of us, and no man can take it
from us. It is our hope, our joy, our all. The Bible
reads it, every page is full of the Lord's immediate
coming, and much from without strengthens us in
the belief that the Judge standeth at the door! At
present everything tries us. Well, we have heretofore had almost uninterrupted peace and exceeding
great joy. True, we have had some trials formerly,
but what were they in comparison with the glory to
be revealed? We are permitted to live in the days
of the Son of man, which Jesus spake of as a desirable day. How special the honor! How unspeakable the privilege!

"And shall we be so selfish as not to be willing to
endure a little trial for such a day, when all our
worthy and honored predecessors have so patiently
submitted to the toils and sufferings incident to their
pilgrimage and to their times? Let it never be!
We know that God has been with us. Perhaps never
before this has he for a moment seemed to depart
from us. Shall we now begin like the children of
Israel to doubt, and to fear, and repine, after he has
so frequently and signally shown us his hand in
effecting for us one deliverance after another? Has
God blessed us with sanctification, and salvation,
and glory, now to rebuke and destroy us? The
thought is almost blasphemous. Away with it!
Have we been so long with our Lord and yet not
known him? Have we read our Bibles in vain?
Have we forgotten the record of his wonderful dealings unto his people in all past ages? Let us pause,
and wait, and read, and pray, before we act rashly
or pronounce a hasty judgment upon the ways and
works of God. If we are in darkness, and see not as

clearly as heretofore, let us not be impatient. We
shall have light just as soon as God sees it will be
for our good. Mark it, dearly beloved, our great
Joshua will surely bring us unto the goodly land. I
have no kind of fears of it, and I will not desert
him before he does me.

"He is doing the work just right. Glory to his
name! Remember, you have been sailing a long,
long voyage, and you began to think yourselves
pretty skillful sailors until you approached the home
coast, when the Pilot coming on board, you had to
relinquish the charge to him, and oh! how hard it
is to commit all your precious cargo and your
noble vessel into his hands. You fear, you tremble,
lest the gallant ship shall become a wreck, and the
dearly-bought freight be emptied into the ocean!
But do n't fear. Throw off the master, and like a
good, social, relieved officer, go and take your place
with the humble, yet sturdy crew, and talk over
home scenes and endearments. Cheer up, 'all's
well.' You have done the will of God, and now be
patient, and you shall have the reward.

"It was necessary that our faith and patience
should be tried before our work could be completed.
We closed up our work with the world some time
ago. This is my conviction. And now God has
given us a little season of self-preparation, to prove
us before the world. Who now will abide the test?
Who is resolved to see the end of his faith, live or die?
Who will go to heaven if he has to go alone? Who
will fight the battle through, though the armor-
bearers faint, and fear, and fail? Who will keep
his eye alone on the floating flag of his King, and,
if need be, sacrifice his last drop of blood for it?
Such only are worthy to be crowned, and such only
will reap the glorious laurels.

"We must be in speaking distance of port. God's
recent work for us proves it. We needed just such

a work if Christ is coming forthwith. I bless God for such glorious manifestations of himself to his people. Do n't dishonor him, questioning whether it might not have been the work of man, for he will vindicate that, and his word, too, very shortly, is my solemn belief. Do not be allured by the baits that may be flung out to draw you back from your confidence in God. The world and the nominal church know nothing at all of your hope. They cannot be made to understand us. Let them alone. You have buried your name and reputation once, and now do not go to digging it up again, when all manner of evil is spoken of you, falsely, for Christ's sake. Pray for your enemies. Do look straight ahead, lest your minds again become occupied with earth—its business, cares, labors, pleasures, friends. The Bible, the Bible, is the best teacher now. Prayer, prayer, is the best helper. The next signal we have will be the final one. Oh! shall any of us be found with our lamps going out when the Master comes? Oh! how impressive the Saviour's repeated admonition, *Watch, watch, watch!*"

The *Voice of Truth* for November 7, 1844, says: "We did believe that he would come at that time, and now, though we sorrow on account of our disappointment, yet we rejoice that we have acted according to our faith. We have had, and still have, a conscience void of offense in this matter, toward God and man. God has blessed us abundantly, and we have not a doubt but that all will soon be made to work together for the good of his dear people, and his glory. We cheerfully admit that we have been mistaken in the nature of the event we expected would occur on the tenth day of the seventh month; but we cannot yet admit that our great High Priest did not on that very day accomplish all that the type would justify us to expect. We now believe he did."

The hour was a most trying one. There seemed to be a strong inclination with many to draw back, which ripened in them into a general stampede in the direction of Egypt. Finally, not a few settled, with more or less clearness, upon a position embracing the following points :—

1. That the parable of the ten virgins represented the great Advent movement, each specification illustrating a corresponding event connected with Second Advent history.

2. That, in answer to the inquiry, Where are we ? the point of time was reached when the words of our Lord, following the parable, were applicable, " Watch, therefore, for ye know neither the day nor the hour wherein the Son of man cometh." Matt. 25 : 13.

3. That the time had come to liken, or to compare, the experience of those who were looking for the kingdom, here called the kingdom of heaven, with an eastern marriage, and that in order to do this, both must be matters of history, showing that each specification in the parable was already fulfilled.

4. That the time when to compare Second Advent experience with the events in the marriage was definitely pointed out by our Lord when he says, "*Then* shall the kingdom of Heaven be likened unto ten virgins." When ? He had just closed a description of two kinds of servants in chapter 24, one servant giving meat to his master's household in due season, the other smiting this good and faithful servant, and in his heart saying, " My Lord delayeth his coming." Just then may the events connected with Advent history be compared with the specifications of the parable. These two servants had been engaged in the same work. But by some means one begins to say in his heart, My Lord delayeth his coming, and smites his fellow. No one who

wished to see, could fail to see a clear fulfillment of this illustration in the labors and general course of Advent ministers soon after the passing of the time. All came up to that time apparently a band of brothers. The time passed. Some became impatient and cast away their confidence in the work, confessed to a scoffing church and world, and because others would not confess as they had done, that a human or satanic influence had controlled them, they were ready to smite those who were strengthening the Master's household with the bread of heaven.

The spiritual food for that time was by no means that teaching which would let them down from the position they had taken, and send them weeping and mourning back to Egypt. But meat in due season was those expositions of God's word which showed his hand in the movement, and such cheering testimonies as are quoted in the foregoing pages in vindication of the Advent movement. How humiliating and painful the fact that Satan is permitted to bring the spiritual warfare within the Second Advent ranks.

5. That in the sense of the parable the Bridegroom had come. Come where? Answer, To the marriage. Was the marriage of the Lamb to take place in this world at the second appearing of Christ? The Bridegroom had not come. But if the marriage of the Lamb was to take place in heaven, the position might be correct. And right here the charge of our Lord to the waiting ones comes in with peculiar force : " Let your loins be girded about, and your lights burning, and ye yourselves like unto men that wait for their Lord when he will return from the wedding." Luke 12 : 35, 36. If our Lord at his second appearing returns from the wedding, then the marriage of the Lamb must take place in heaven prior to his return. Therefore, the coming of the bridegroom in the parable illustrated some change

in the position and work of our great High Priest in heaven in reference to the marriage of the Lamb.

6. That the established view, that in the marriage of the Lamb the church is the bride of Christ, was among the errors of past times. By investigation it was clearly seen that there were two things which the Scriptures of the Old and New Testaments illustrate by marriage. First, the union of God's people in all past ages, as well as at the present time, with their Lord. Second, Christ's reception of the throne of David, which is in the New Jerusalem. But union of believers with their Lord has existed since the days of Adam, and cannot be regarded as the marriage of the Lamb. It is supposed that Isaiah 54:5, speaks of the church when he says, "Thy Maker is thine husband;" but Paul in Gal. 4, applies this prophecy to the New Jerusalem.

Says John, speaking of Christ, "He that hath the bride is the bridegroom." John 3:29. That Christ is here represented in his relation to his followers by a bridegroom, and his followers by a bride, is true; but that he and they are here called the bridegroom and bride, is not true. No one believes that the event called the marriage of the Lamb took place eighteen hundred years since.

Paul, in writing to the church, 2 Cor. 11:2, says, "I have espoused you to one husband, that I may present you a chaste virgin to Christ." But does this prove that the marriage of the Lamb took place in Corinth? Or, did Paul only wish to represent by marriage, the union which he had effected, through the gospel, between Christ and the church at Corinth? He also says, Eph. 5:23, "For the husband is the head of the wife, even as Christ is the head of the church." But please turn and read from verse 22, and it will be seen that Paul's subject is the relation and duty of man and wife to each other. This is illustrated and enforced by the relation of Christ and the church. Those who suppose that Paul is here defining who the Lamb's wife is, are greatly mistaken. That is not his subject. He commences, "Wives, submit yourselves unto your own husbands." Verse 22. "Husbands, love your wives." Verse 25. It is, indeed, an excellent subject, but has nothing to do in determining what the bride is.

The marriage of the Lamb does not cover the entire period of probation, in which believers are united to their Lord, from Adam to the close of probation. It is one event, to take place at one point of time, and that is just prior to the resurrection of the just.

Then what is the bride in the marriage of the Lamb? Said the angel to John, " Come hither, I will show thee the bride, the Lamb's wife." Rev. 21 : 9. Did the angel show John the church? Let John testify. "And he carried me away in the Spirit to a great and high mountain, and showed me that great city, the holy Jerusalem, descending out of heaven from God." Verse 10.

The New Jerusalem is also represented as the mother. "But Jerusalem which is above is free, which is the mother of us all." Gal. 4 : 26. Christ is represented (Isa. 9 : 6,) as the "everlasting Father" of his people; the New Jerusalem, the mother, and the subjects of the first resurrection, the children. And, beyond all doubt, the resurrection of the just is represented by birth. How appropriate, then, is the view that the marriage of the Lamb takes place in heaven, before the Lord comes, and before the children of the great family of heaven are brought forth at the resurrection of the just.

Let those who are disposed to cling to the old view that the church is the bride, and that the marriage is after Christ comes, and the saints are caught up to heaven, answer the following questions :—

1. Who are illustrated by the man found at the

marriage, Matt. 22, not having on the wedding garment ?

2. Will any be caught up by mistake, to be bound hand and foot, and be cast down to the earth again ?

3. If the church is the wife, who are they that are called to the marriage as guests ?

4. Jerusalem above is the mother of the children of promise ; but if the church is the Lamb's wife, who are the children ?

5. That the door was shut. The clear light from the heavenly sanctuary that a door, or ministration, was opened at the close of the 2300 days, while another was closed at that time, had not yet been seen. And in the absence of light in reference to the shut and open door of the heavenly sanctuary, the reader can hardly see how those who held fast their Advent experience, as illustrated by the parable of the ten virgins, could fail to come to the conclusion that probation for sinners had closed.

But light on the subject soon came, and then it was seen that although Christ closed one ministration at the termination of the 2300 days, he had opened another in the most holy place, and still presented his blood before the Father for sinners. As the high priest, in the type, on the tenth day of the seventh month, entered the most holy place, and offered blood for the sins of the people, before the ark of the testament and the mercy-seat, so Christ, at the close of the 2300 days, came before the ark of God and the mercy-seat to plead his blood in behalf of sinners. Mark this: The great Redeemer then approached the mercy-seat in behalf of sinners. Was the door of mercy closed ? This is an unscriptural expression, but, if I may be allowed to use it, may I not say that in the fullest sense of the expression the door of mercy was opened on the tenth day of the seventh month, 1844 ?

Beside the ark of God containing the ten precepts

of his holy law, over which was the mercy-seat, did
the trusting ones now behold their merciful High
Priest. They had stood in harmony with the whole
Advent host at the passing of the time, then represented as "the church in Philadelphia," meaning brotherly love. And with what inexpressible
sweetness did the following words addressed to that
church come home to their stricken hearts: "These
things saith he that is holy, he that is true, he that
hath the key of David, he that openeth, and no man
shutteth; and shutteth, and no man openeth. I
know thy works. Behold, I have set before thee an
open door, and no man can shut it." Rev. 3:7, 8.

Adventists were agreed that the seven churches
of Rev. 2 and 3, symbolized seven states of the Christian church, covering the entire period from the first
advent of Christ to his second appearing, and that
the sixth state addressed represented those who with
one united voice proclaimed the coming of Jesus, in
the autumn of 1844. This church was about to
enter upon a period of great trial. And they were
to find relief from it, so far as ascertaining their true
position is concerned, by light from the heavenly
sanctuary. After the light should come, then would
also come the battle upon the shut and open door.
Here was seen the connecting link between the work
of God in the past Advent movement, present duty
to keep the commandments of God, and the future
glory and reward. And as these views were taught
in vindication of the Advent movement, in connection with the claims of the Sabbath of the fourth
commandment, these men, especially those who had
given up their Advent experience, felt called upon
to oppose. And their opposition, as a general thing,
was most violent, bitter, and wicked.

The shut and open door of the heavenly sanctuary
constituted the strong point upon which the matter
turned. If we were right on the subject of the

cleansing of the sanctuary, then the door or ministration of the holy place was shut, and the door or
ministration of the most holy place was opened, the
2300 days had ended, the preaching of time was correct, and the entire movement was right. But let
our opponents show that we were in error upon the
sanctuary question, that Christ had not entered the
most holy place to cleanse the sanctuary, then the
2300 days had not ended, the preaching of the time
was an error, and the entire movement was wrong.
And, again, if the door or ministration of the most holy
place was opened, and the faith of the waiting ones
was to view Jesus standing before the mercy-seat
and the ark of the ten commandments in heaven,
how forcible the arguments for the perpetuity and
claims of the entire law of God, the fourth precept
not excepted. The hand of the Lord was with those
who took a firm position that the great Advent
movement had been in his direct providence, and
that the time had come for the Sabbath reform, and
many embraced these views. Then it was that our
opponents arose in the spirit of persecution, mani-
festing the wrath of the dragon against those who
kept the commandments of God, and labored to open
the door that had been shut, and to shut that door
which had been opened, and thus put an end to the
matter. Hence the strong expressions quoted above
—" He that openeth and no *man* shutteth, and shutteth and no *man* openeth." " Behold, I have set
before thee an open door, and no *man* can shut it."
Nothing can be plainer than that man, or a set of
men, near the close of the history of the church,
would war against the truth of God in reference to
the shut and open door.

And to this day those who retain the spirit of war
upon those who keep the commandments of God,
make the belief in the shut and open door odious,
and charge it all upon Seventh-day Adventists,

Many of them, however, are not unaware of the injustice of this.

And it may be worthy of notice that although the belief in, and abandonment of, the shut-door position has been general, there have been two distinct and opposite ways of getting out of it. One class did this by casting away their confidence in the Advent movement, by confessions to those who had opposed and had scoffed at them, and by ascribing the powerful work of the Holy Spirit to human or satanic influences. These got out of the position on the side of perdition.

Another class heeded the many exhortations of Christ and his apostles, applicable to their position, with its trials, dangers, and duties—Watch—Be ye therefore patient—Cast not away therefore your confidence—For ye have need of patience—Hold fast. They waited, watched, and prayed, till light came, and they by faith in the word saw the open door of the heavenly sanctuary, and Jesus there pleading his precious blood before the ark of the most holy place.

But what was that ark? It was the ark of God's testimony, the ten commandments. Reader, please follow these trusting, waiting ones, as they by faith enter the heavenly sanctuary. They take you into the holy place and show you "the candlestick, and the table, and the shewbread," and other articles of furniture. Then they lead you into the most holy where stands Jesus, clad in priestly garments, before the mercy-seat which is upon, and but the cover of, the ark containing the law of God. They lift the cover and bid you look into the sacred ark, and there you behold the ten commandments, a copy of which God gave to Moses. Yes, dear reader, there, safe from the wrath of man and the rage of demons, beside his own holiness, are the ten precepts of God's holy law.

The waiting, watching, praying ones, embraced the fourth precept of that law, and with fresh courage took their onward course to the golden gates of the city of God, cheered by the closing benediction of the Son of God: "Blessed are they that do his commandments, that they may have right to the tree of life, and may enter in through the gates into the city." Thus they came out of the position of the shut door on the side of loyalty to the God of high heaven, the tree of life, and the eternal city of the redeemed. The reader will not fail to see the difference between their course and getting out of the shut door on the side of perdition. God pity the apostate.

## CHAPTER V.

### PARENTAGE AND EARLY LIFE.

HAVING traced my early experience up to the year 1846, when I linked life's destiny in marriage with Miss Ellen G. Harmon, we shall leave the reader here, after a few brief remarks relative to our early united labors, while we go back and trace her early life to the same point, since which time our labors at home and abroad have been so united that both should be given in one.

Marriage marks an important era in the lives of men. "Whoso findeth a wife findeth a good thing, and obtaineth favor of the Lord," is the language of wisdom. Prov. 18 : 22. This expression taken alone may be understood to convey the idea that all wives are from the Lord. But Solomon qualifies the expression by other statements. "A virtuous woman is a crown to her husband ; but she that maketh ashamed is as rottenness in his bones." Prov. 12 : 4.

We were married August 30, 1846, and from that hour to the present she has been my crown of rejoicing. I first met her in the city of Portland, in the State of Maine. She was then a Christian of the most devoted type. And although but sixteen, she was a laborer in the cause of Christ in public and from house to house. She was a decided Adventist, and yet her experience was so rich and her testimony so powerful that ministers and leading men of different churches sought her labors as an exhorter in their several congregations. But at that time she was very timid, and little thought that she was to be brought before the public to speak to thousands.

We both viewed the coming of Christ near, even at the doors, and when we first met had no idea of marriage at any future time. But God had a great work for both of us to do, and he saw that we could greatly assist each other in that work. As she should come before the public she needed a lawful protector, and God having chosen her as a channel of light and truth to the people in a special sense, she could be of great help to me. But it was not until the matter of marriage was taken to the Lord by both, and we obtained an experience that placed the matter beyond the reach of doubt, that we took this important step. Most of our brethren who believed with us that the second advent movement was the work of God were opposed to marriage in the sense that as time was very short it was a denial of faith, as such a union contemplated long years of married life. We state the fact as it existed without pleading the correctness of the position.

It had been in the good providence of God that both of us had enjoyed a deep experience in the Advent movement. Mine has been given in the preceding pages, that of Mrs. White is to be given in succeeding pages. This experience was now needed as we should join our forces and, united, labor extensively from the Atlantic ocean to the Pacific, to build up churches and establish that discipline which the New Testament recognizes, and establish those institutions which should be of great service to the cause of truth. We mention as first in importance our houses of publication at Battle Creek, Michigan, and at Oakland, California. Next in importance is our denominational College, located at Battle Creek, and also the Sanitarium, as important to a good hold on health and life which has a decided bearing on usefulness here to be rewarded in the life to come.

We entered upon this work penniless, with few friends, and broken in health. Mrs. W. has suffered ill health from a child, as will be seen in succeeding pages, and although I had inherited a powerful constitution, imprudence in study at school, and in lecturing, as narrated in preceding pages had made me a dyspeptic. In this condition, without means, with very few who sympathized with us in our views, without a paper, and without books, we entered upon our work. We had no houses of worship at that time. And the idea of using a tent had not then occurred to us. Most of our meetings were held in private houses. Our congregations were small. It was seldom that any came into our meetings excepting Adventists, unless they were attracted by curiosity to hear a woman speak.

Mrs. W. at first moved out in the work of public speaking timidly. If she had confidence it was given her by the Holy Spirit. If she spoke with freedom and power it was given her of God. Our meetings were usually conducted in a manner so that both of us took part. I would give a doctrinal discourse, then Mrs. W. would give an exhortation of considerable length melting her way into the tenderest feelings of the congregation. Was my part of the work important, hers was no less important. While I presented the evidences, and sowed the seed, hers was to water it.   And God did give the increase.

It was in the autumn of 1846 that we commenced to observe the Bible Sabbath, and teach and defend it.   There were at that time about twenty-five in Maine who observed the Sabbath ; but these were so scattered in point of location and diverse in sentiment upon other points of doctrine that their influence was very small.   There was about the same number, in similar condition in other parts of New England.   It seemed to be our duty to visit these frequently at their homes, and strengthen them in the Lord and in his truth, and as they were very much scattered, it was necessary for us to be on the road much of the time.   For want of means we took the cheapest private conveyance, second-class cars, and lower deck passage on steamers.   Private conveyance was the most comfortable for Mrs. W. who was feeble.   I could then endure hardships, labors and privations to almost any extent for the sake of the truth of God and his precious, scattered people. When on second-class cars we were usually enveloped in tobacco smoke.   This I could endure, but Mrs. W. would frequently faint.   When on steamers, on lower deck, we suffered the same from the smoke of tobacco, besides the swearing and vulgar conversation of the ship hands and the baser portion of the traveling public.   Sleeping conveniences are summed up as follows : We lie down on the hard floor, dry-goods boxes, or sacks of grain, with carpetbags for pillows, without covering only overcoats and shawls.   If suffering from the winter's cold, we would walk the deck to keep warm.   If suffering the heat of summer we would go upon the upper deck to secure the cool night air.   This was fatiguing to Mrs. W., especially so with an infant in her arms. This manner of life was by no means one of our choosing. God called us in our poverty, and led us through the furnace of affliction, to give us an experience which should be of great worth to us, and an example to others who should afterwards join us in labor.

Our Master was a man of sorrows. He was acquainted with grief. And those who suffer with him will reign with him. When the Lord appeared to Saul in his conversion he did not purpose to show him how much good he should enjoy, but what great things he should suffer for his name. Suffering has been the portion of the people of God from the days of the martyr Abel. The patriarchs suffered for being true to God, and obedient to his commandments. The great Head of the church suffered for our sake. His first apostles and the primative church suffered, the millions of martyrs suffered, and the reformers suffered. And why should we, who have the blessed hope of immortality, to be consummated at the soon appearing of Christ, shrink from a life of suffering? Were it possible to reach the tree of life in the midst of the Paradise of God without suffering we would not enjoy so rich a reward for which we had not suffered. We would shrink back from the glory, and shame would seize us in the presence of those who had fought the good fight, had run the race with patience, and had laid hold on eternal life. But none will be there who have not chosen to suffer affliction with the people of God as did Moses. The prophet John saw the multitude of the redeemed and inquired who they were. The prompt answer came : " These are they which came out of great tribulation and have washed their robes and made them white in the blood of the Lamb." Rev. 7 : 13, 14.

At that time we had no clearly defined idea of the third angel's message. The burden of our testimony as we came before the people was that the great

second advent movement was of God, that the first
and second messages had gone forth, and that the
third was to be given. We saw that the third message closed with the words : " Here is the patience
of the saints, here are they that keep the commandments of God and the faith of Jesus." And we as
clearly saw as we now see that these prophetic words
suggested a Sabbath reform. We were not observ-
ing all ten of the precepts of the law of God. And
before it could be said of those who had reached the
waiting time demanding patience in a special sense,
we must observe the day commanded and guarded
by the fourth commandment. But what the worship of the beast mentioned in the message was, what
the image, and what the mark of the beast were we
had no defined position.

God, however, by his holy Spirit, let light shine
forth upon his servants, and the subject opened,
and precious truth, link after link, was brought out
and published to the world until now the message
in its strength is given to the world by ministers
whom he has raised up to declare it, and by millions
of pages of tracts and other publications which have
been written and printed in the most careful manner. Our publications have proved the right arm
of our strength in giving the light to the world.

Mrs. White's parents, Robert and Eunice Harmon,
were residents of Maine. In early life they were
earnest and devoted members of the Methodist Episcopal church. In that church they held prominent
connection, and labored for the conversion of sinners,
and to build up the cause of God for a period of forty
years. During this time they had the joy of seeing
their children, eight in number, all converted and
gathered into the fold of Christ. Their decided Second Advent views, however, severed the connection
of the family from the Methodist church in the year
1843, after which meetings were held in their house

in the city of Portland much of the time for several years. Of her early life and Christian experience we will let Mrs. White speak for herself, as taken from her second volume of Spiritual Gifts.

"At the age of nine years an accident happened to me which was to affect my whole life. In company with my twin sister and one of our school-mates, I was crossing a common in the city of Portland, Maine, when a girl about thirteen years of age, also a member of our school, becoming angry at some trifle, followed us, threatening to strike us. Our parents had taught us never to contend with any one, but if we were in danger of being abused or injured, to hasten home at once. We were doing this with all speed, but the girl followed us as rapidly, with a stone in her hand. I turned my head to see how far she was behind me, and as I did so, she threw the stone and it hit me on the nose. A blinding, stunning sensation overpowered me, and I fell senseless.

"When consciousness again returned, I found myself in a merchant's store; my garments were covered with blood which was pouring from my nose and streaming over the floor. A kind stranger offered to take me home in his carriage, but I, not realizing my weakness told him that I preferred to walk home rather than soil his carriage with blood. Those present were not aware that my injury was so serious and allowed me to have my own way; but after walking only a few rods I grew faint and dizzy. My twin sister and my school-mate carried me home.

"I have no recollection of anything further for some time after the accident. My mother said that I noticed nothing but lay in a stupor for three weeks; no one but herself thought it possible for me to recover. For some reason she felt that I would live. A kind neighbor, who had been very much interested in my behalf, at one time thought me to be dying. She wished to purchase a burial robe for me, but my mother said, ' Not yet,' for something told her that I would not die.

" When I again aroused to consciousness, it seemed to me that I had been asleep. I did not remember the accident and was ignorant of the cause of my illness. As I began to gain a little strength, my curiosity was aroused by overhearing those who came to visit me say: ' What a pity!' ' I should not have known her,' etc. I asked for a looking-glass, and upon gazing into it, was shocked at the change in my appearance. Every feature of my face seemed changed. The bones of my nose had been broken which caused this disfigurement.

" The idea of carrying my misfortune through life was insupportable. I could see no pleasure in my existence. I did not wish to live, and yet dared not die for I was unprepared. Friends often visited my parents and looked with pity upon me, and advised them to prosecute the father of the girl who had, as they said, ruined me. But my mother was for peace; she said that if such a course could bring me back my health and natural looks there would be something gained, but as this was impossible, it was best not to make enemies by following such advice.

" Physicians thought that a silver wire might be put in my nose to hold it in shape. This would have been very painful, and they feared it would be of little use, as I had lost so much blood and sustained such a nervous shock that my recovery was very doubtful. Even if I revived it was their opinion I could live but a short time. I was reduced almost to a skeleton.

" At this time I began to pray the Lord to prepare me for death. When Christian friends visited the family, they would ask my mother if she had talked to me about dying. I overheard this and it roused me. I desired to become a Christian and prayed earnestly for the forgiveness of my sins. I felt a peace of mind resulting, and loved every one, feeling desirous that all should have their sins forgiven and love Jesus as I did.

"I well remember one night in winter when the snow was on the ground, the heavens were lighted up, the sky looked red and angry, and seemed to open and shut, while the snow looked like blood. The neighbors were very much frightened. Mother took me out of bed in her arms and carried me to the window. I was happy; I thought Jesus was coming, and I longed to see him. My heart was full, I clapped my hands for joy, and thought my sufferings were ended. But I was disappointed; the singular appearance faded away from the heavens, and the next morning the sun arose the same as usual.

"I gained strength very slowly. As I became able to join in play with my young friends, I was forced to learn the bitter lesson that one's personal appearance makes a difference in the treatment they receive from the majority of their companions. At the time of my misfortune, my father was absent in Georgia. When he returned he embraced my brother and sisters and then inquired for me. I, timidly shrinking back, was pointed out by my mother, but my own father did not recognize me. It was hard for him to believe that I was his little Ellen, whom he had left only a few months before a healthy, happy child. This cut my feelings deeply, but I tried to appear cheerful though my heart seemed breaking.

"Many times in those childish days, I was made to feel my misfortune keenly. My feelings were unusually sensitive and caused me great unhappiness. Often with wounded pride, mortified and wretched in spirit, have I sought a lonely place and gloomily contemplated the trials I was daily doomed to bear.

"The relief of tears was denied me. I could not weep readily as could my twin sister, so, though my heart was heavy and ached as if it were breaking, I could not shed a tear. I often felt that it would greatly relieve me to weep away my overcharged feelings. Sometimes the kindly sympathy of friends banished my gloom and removed, for a time, the leaden weight that oppressed my heart. How vain and empty seemed the pleasures of earth to me then! How changeable the friendships of my young companions yet these little school-mates were not unlike a majority of the great world's people. A pretty face, a handsome dress attracts them, but let misfortune take these away and the fragile friendship grows cold or is broken. But when I turned to my Saviour, he comforted me. I sought the Lord earnestly in my trouble and received consolation, believed that Jesus loved even me.

"My health seemed to be completely shattered. For two years I could not breathe through my nose, and was able to attend school but little. It seemed impossible for me to study and retain what I learned. The same girl who was the cause of my misfortune, was appointed monitor by our teacher, and it was among her duties to assist me in my writing and other lessons. She always seemed sincerely sorry for the great injury she had done me, although I was careful not to remind her of it. She was tender and patient with me, and seemed sad and thoughtful as she saw me laboring, under serious disadvantages, to get an education.

"My nervous system was prostrated, and my hand trembled so that I made but little progress in writing and could get no fa:ther than the simple copies in coarse hand. As I endeavored to bend my mind to my studies, the letters on the page would run together, great drops of perspiration would stand upon my brow, and a faintness and giddiness would seize me. I had a bad cough, and my whole system seemed debilitated. My teachers advised me to leave school and not pursue my studies further till my health would warrant it. It was the hardest struggle of my young life to yield to my feebleness, and decide that I must give up my studies and relinquish the cherished hope of acquiring an education.

" My ambition to become a scholar had been very great, and when I pondered over my disappointed hopes, and the thought that I was to be an invalid for life, despair seized me. The future stretched out before me dark and cheerless, without one ray of light. I was unreconciled to my lot, and at times murmured against the providence of God in thus afflicting me. I concealed my troubled feelings from my family and friends, fearing that they could not understand me. This was a mistaken course. Had I opened my mind to my mother, she might have instructed, soothed, and encouraged me.

" After I had struggled with this unreconciled spirit for days the tempter came under a new guise and increased my distress by condemning me for having allowed such rebellious thoughts to take possession of my mind. My conscience was perplexed, and I knew no way to extricate myself from the labyrinth in which I was wandering.

" The happy confidence in the Saviour's love that I had enjoyed during my illness, was gone. I had lost the blessed consciousness that I was a child of God, and felt that the hopes of my heart had deceived me. It was my determination not to again put confidence in my feelings, until I knew for a certainty that the Lord had pardoned my sins.

" At times my sense of guilt and responsibility to God lay so heavy upon my soul, that I could not sleep but lay awake for hours, thinking of my lost condition and what was best for me to do. The consequences of my unfortunate accident again assumed gigantic proportions in my mind. I seemed to be cut off from all chance of earthly happiness, and doomed to continual disappointment and mortification. Even the tender sympathy of my friends pained me, for my pride rebelled against being in a condition to excite their pity. My prospect of worldly enjoyment was blighted, and heaven seemed closed against me.

"I had the highest reverence for Christians and ministers of the gospel, but religion seemed too holy and sacred for me to obtain. An inconceivable anguish bore me down until it seemed impossible for me to longer live beneath the burden. I locked my secret agony within my heart, and did not seek the advice of experienced Christians as I should have done.

"No one conversed with me on the subject of my soul's salvation, and no one prayed with me. I felt that Christians were so far removed from me, so much nobler and purer than myself, that I dared not approach them on the subject that engrossed my thoughts, and was ashamed to reveal the lost and wretched condition of my heart.

"In March, 1840, William Miller visited Portland, Me., and gave his first course of lectures on the second coming of Christ. These lectures produced a great sensation, and the Christian church, on Casco street, that Mr. Miller occupied, was crowded day and night. No wild excitement attended these meetings, but a deep solemnity pervaded the minds of those who heard his discourses. Not only was there manifested a great interest in the city, but the country people flocked in day after day, bringing their lunch baskets, and remaining from morning until the close of the evening meeting.

"Mr. Miller dwelt upon the prophecies, comparing them with Bible history, that the end of the world was near. I attended these meetings in company with my friends and listened to the strange doctrines of the preacher. Four years previous to this, on my way to school, I had picked up a scrap of paper containing an account of a man in England, who was preaching that the earth would be consumed in about thirty years from that time. I took this paper home and read it to the family.

"In contemplating the event predicted, a great terror seized me; for the time seemed so short for the conversion and salvation of the world. I had been taught that a temporal millennium would take place prior to the coming of Christ in the clouds of heaven. Such a deep impression was made upon my mind by the little paragraph on the waste scrap of paper, that I could scarcely sleep for several nights, and prayed continually to be ready when Jesus came.

"But now I was listening to the most solemn and powerful sermons to the effect that Christ was coming in 1843, only a few short years in the future. The preacher traced down the prophecies with a keen exactitude that struck conviction to the hearts of his hearers. He dwelt upon the prophetic periods, and piled up proof to strengthen his position. Then his solemn and powerful appeals and admonitions to those who were unprepared, held the crowds as if spell-bound.

"Special meetings were appointed where sinners might have an opportunity to seek their Saviour and prepare for the fearful events soon to take place. Terrible conviction spread through the entire city. Prayer-meetings were established, and there was a general awakening among the various denominations, for they all felt more or less the influence that proceeded from the teaching of the near coming of Christ.

"When sinners were invited forward to the anxious seat, hundreds responded to the call, and I, among the rest, pressed through the crowd and took

my humble place with the seekers. But there was
a hopeless feeling in my heart that I could never
become worthy to be called a child of God. A lack
of confidence in myself and a conviction that it
would be impossible to make any one understand
my feelings, prevented me from seeking advice and
aid from my Christian friends. Thus I wandered
needlessly in darkness and despair, while they, not
penetrating my peculiar reserve, were entirely ignorant of my true state.

"One evening my brother Robert and myself were
returning home from a meeting where we had listened to a most impressive discourse on the approaching reign of Christ upon the earth, followed by an
earnest and solemn appeal to Christians and sinners,
urging them to prepare for the Judgment and the
coming of the Lord. My soul had been stirred
within me by what I had heard. And so deep was
the sense of conviction in my heart, that I feared
the Lord would not spare me to reach home.

"These words kept ringing in my ears, The great
day of the Lord is at hand! Who shall be able to
stand when he appeareth! The language of my
heart was, 'Spare me, O Lord, through the night!
Take me not away in my sins, pity me, save me!'
For the first time, I tried to explain my feelings to
my brother Robert, who was two years older than
myself; I told him that I dared not rest nor sleep
until I knew that God had pardoned my sins.

"My brother made no immediate response, but
the cause of his silence was soon apparent to me: he
was weeping in sympathy with my distress. This
encouraged me to confide in him still more, to tell
him that I had coveted death in the days when life
seemed so heavy a burden for me to bear; but now
the thought that I might die in my present sinful
state and be eternally lost, filled me with inexpressible terror. I asked him if he thought God would

spare my life through that one night, if I spent it agonizing in prayer to him. He answered, ' I think he will if you ask him with faith, and I will pray for you and for myself. Ellen. we must never forget the words we have heard this night.'

„Arriving at home, I spent most of the long hours of darkness in prayer and tears. One special reason that prompted me to conceal my feelings from my friends, was the dread of hearing a word of discouragement. My hope was so small, and my faith so weak, that I feared if another took a similar view of my condition, it would plunge me into absolute despair. Yet my heart longed for some one to tell me what I should do to be saved, what steps to take to meet my Saviour and give myself entirely up to the Lord. I regarded it a great thing to be a Christian, and felt that it required some peculiar effort on my part.

" My mind remained in this condition for months. I had usually attended the Methodist meetings with my parents; but since becoming interested in the soon appearing of Christ, I had attended the meetings on Casco street. The following summer my parents went to the Methodist camp-meeting at Buxton, Me., taking me with them. I was fully resolved to seek the Lord in earnest there, and obtain, if possible, the pardon of my sins. There was a great longing in my heart for the Christian's hope and the peace that comes of believing.

" Some things at this camp-meeting perplexed me exceedingly. I could not understand the exercises of many persons during the conference meetings at the stand and in the tents. They shouted at the top of their voices, clapped their hands, and appeared greatly excited. Quite a number fell, through exhaustion it appeared to me, but those present said they were sanctified to God, and this wonderful manifestation was the power of the Almighty upon them

After lying motionless for a time, these persons would rise and again talk and shout as before.

" In some of the tents, meetings were continued through the night, by those who were praying for freedom from sin, and the sanctification of the Spirit of God. Quite a number became sick in consequence of the excitement and loss of sleep, and were obliged to leave the ground. These singular manifestations brought no relief to me, but rather increased my discouragement. I despaired of ever becoming a Christian if, in order to obtain the blessing, it was necessary for me to be exercised as these people were. I was terrified by such peculiar demonstrations, and at a loss to understand them.

" At length I was greatly relieved while listening to a discourse from the words: ' I will go in unto the king,' 'and if I perish, I perish.' In his remarks the speaker referred to those who were wavering between hope and fear, longing to be saved from their sins and receive the pardoning love of Christ, yet held in doubt and bondage by timidity and fear of failure. He counseled such ones to surrender themselves to God and venture upon his mercy without delay. They would find a gracious Saviour ready to present to them the scepter of mercy even as Ahasuerus offered to Esther the signal of his favor. All that was required of the sinner, trembling in the presence of his Lord, was to put forth the hand of faith and touch the scepter of his grace. That touch insured pardon and peace.

" Those who were waiting to make themselves more worthy of divine favor, before they dared venture to claim the promises, were making a fatal mistake. Jesus alone cleanses from sin ; he only can forgive our transgressions. He has pledged himself to listen to the petition and grant the prayer of those who come to him in faith. Many had a vague idea that they must make some wonderful effort in order to gain the favor of God. But all self-dependence is vain. It is only by connecting with Jesus through faith that the sinner becomes a hopeful, believing child of God.

"These words comforted me and gave me views of what I must do to be saved. Soon after this I passed into a tent where the people were praying and shouting, some confessing their sins and crying for mercy, while others were rejoicing in their newfound happiness. My attention was attracted to a little girl who seemed to be in great distress. Her face would pale and flush by turns, as though she were passing through a severe conflict.

"Tightly clasped in her arms was a pretty little parasol. Occasionally she would loosen her hold on it for a moment as if about to let it fall, then her grasp would tighten upon it again; all the time she seemed to be regarding it with a peculiar fascination. At last she cried out: 'Dear Jesus, I want to love thee and go to heaven! Take away my sins! I give myself to thee, parasol and all.' She threw herself into her mother's arms weeping and exclaiming: 'Ma, I am so happy, for Jesus loves me, and I love him better than my parasol or anything else!'

"The face of the child was fairly radiant, she had surrendered her little all. In her childish experience she had fought the battle and won the victory. There was much weeping and rejoicing in the tent. The mother was deeply moved and very joyful that the Lord had added her dear child as a lamb to his fold. She explained to those present that her little daughter had received the parasol as a present not long before. She was very much delighted with it, and had kept it in her hands most of the time, even taking it to bed with her.

"During the meeting her tender heart had been moved to seek the Saviour. She had heard that nothing must be withheld from Jesus; that nothing short of an entire surrender of ourselves and all we have would be acceptable with him. The little parasol was the child's earthly treasure upon which her heart was set, and, in the struggle to give it up to the Lord, she had passed through a trial keener perhaps than that of the mature Christian, who sacrifices this world's treasures for the sake of Christ.

"It was afterwards explained to the little girl, that since she had relinquished her parasol to Jesus, and it no longer stood between herself and her love for him, it was right for her to retain it and use it in a proper manner.

"Many times in after life that little incident had been brought to my mind. When I saw men and women holding desperately to the riches and vanity of earth, yet anxiously praying for the love of Christ, I would think: 'How hard it is to give up the parasol!' Yet Jesus gave up heaven for our sake, and became poor that we, through his poverty and humiliation, might secure eternal riches.

"I now began to see my way more clearly, and the darkness began to pass away. I saw that, in my despair of at once attaining to the perfection of Christian character, I had scarcely dared to make the trial of serving God. I now earnestly sought the pardon of my sins and strove to give myself entirely to the Lord. But my mind was often in great distress, for I did not experience the spiritual ecstasy that I considered would be the evidence of my acceptance with God, and dared not believe myself converted without it. How much I needed instruction concerning the simplicity of faith.

"While bowed at the altar with others who were seeking the Lord, all the language of my heart was: 'Help, Jesus, save me or I perish!' I will never cease to entreat till my prayer is heard and my sins forgiven.' I felt my needy, helpless condition as

never before. As I knelt and prayed, suddenly my
burden left me and my heart was light. At first a
feeling of alarm came over me and I tried to resume
my load of distress again. It seemed to me that I
had no right to feel joyous and happy. But Jesus
seemed very near me; I felt able to come to him
with all my griefs, misfortunes and trials, even as
the needy ones came to him for relief when he was
upon earth. There was a surety in my heart that
he understood my peculiar trials and sympathized
with me. I can never forget this precious assurance
of the pitying tenderness of Jesus toward one so
unworthy of his notice. I learned more of the
divine character of Christ in the short period when
bowed among the praying ones than ever before.

"One of the mothers in Israel came to me and
said: 'Dear child, have you found Jesus?' I was
about to answer, 'Yes,' when she exclaimed: 'Indeed you have, his peace is with you, I see it in
your face!' Again and again I said to myself, 'Can
this be religion? Am I not mistaken?' It seemed
too much for me to claim, too exalted a privilege.
Though too timid to openly confess it, I felt that
the Saviour had blessed me and pardoned my sins.

"Soon after this the meeting came to a close and
we started for home. My mind was full of the sermons, exhortations and prayers we had heard.
Everything in nature seemed changed. During the
meeting, clouds and rain prevailed a greater part of
the time and my feelings had been in harmony with
the weather. Now the sun shone bright and clear
and flooded the earth with light and warmth. The
trees and grass were a fresher green, the sky a
deeper blue. The earth seemed to smile under the
peace of God. So the rays of the Sun of Righteousness had penetrated the clouds and darkness of my
mind, and dispelled its gloom.

"It seemed to me that every one must be at peace

with God and animated by his Spirit. Everything my eyes rested upon seemed to have undergone a change. The trees were more beautiful, and the birds sang sweeter than ever before; they seemed to be praising the Creator in their songs. I did not care to talk, for fear this happiness might pass away, and I should lose the precious evidence of Jesus' love for me.

"As we neared our home in Portland, we passed men at work upon the street. They were conversing upon ordinary topics with each other, but my ears were deaf to everything but the praise of God, and their words came to me as grateful thanks and glad hosannas. Turning to my mother, I said: 'Why, these men are all praising God, and *they* haven't been to the camp-meeting.' I did not then understand why the tears gathered in my mother's eyes, and a tender smile lit up her face, as she listened to my simple words,· that recalled a similar experience of her own.

"My mother was a great lover of flowers, and took much pleasure in cultivating them, and thus making her home attractive and pleasant for her children. But our garden had never before looked so lovely to me as upon the day of our return. I recognized an expression of the love of Jesus in every shrub, bud, and flower. These things of beauty seemed to speak in mute language of the love of God.

"There was a beautiful pink flower in the garden called the rose of Sharon. I remember approaching it and touching the delicate petals reverently; they seemed to possess a sacredness in my eyes. My heart overflowed with tenderness and love for these beautiful creations of God. I could see divine perfection in the flowers that adorned the earth. God tended them, and his all-seeing eye was upon them. He had made them and called them good.

'Ah,' thought I, 'If he so loves and cares for the flowers that he has decked with beauty, how much more tenderly will he guard the children who are formed in his image.' I repeated softly to myself, 'I am a child of God, his loving care is around me, I will be obedient and in no way displease him, but will praise his dear name and love him always.'

"My life appeared to me in a different light The affliction that had darkened my childhood seemed to have been dealt me in mercy for my good, to turn my heart away from the world and its unsatisfying pleasures and incline it towards the enduring attractions of heaven.

"Soon after our return from the camp-meeting, I, with several others, was taken into the church on probation. My mind was very much exercised on the subject of baptism. Young as I was, I could see but one mode of baptism authorized by the Scriptures, and that was immersion. My sisters tried in vain to convince me that sprinkling was Bible baptism. The Methodist minister consented to immerse the candidates if they conscientiously preferred that method, although he intimated that sprinkling would be equally acceptable with God.

"Finally the day was appointed for us to receive this solemn ordinance. Although usually enjoying, at this time, great peace, I frequently feared that I was not a true Christian, and was harrassed by perplexing doubts as to my conversion. It was a windy day when we, twelve in number, were baptized, walking down into the sea. The waves ran high and dashed upon the shore, but in taking up this heavy cross, my peace was like a river. When I arose from the water, my strength was nearly gone for the power of the Lord rested upon me. I felt that henceforth I was not of this world, but had risen from the watery grave into a newness of life.

"My cousin Hannah made confession of her faith

at the same time that I did. She wished to be baptized by immersion, but her father, who was not a
Christian, would not consent to this although we
urged him to do so. So she knelt before the altar
and had a few drops of water sprinkled upon her
head. As I witnessed the ceremony, my heart
rejoiced that I had not submitted to receive sprinkling for baptism, feeling confident that there was no
Scripture to sustain it.

"The same day in the afternoon, I was received
into the church in full membership. A young
woman, arrived at the age of maturity, stood by my
side and was also a candidate for admission to the
church with myself. My mind was peaceful and
happy till I noticed the gold rings glittering upon
this sister's fingers, and the large showy ear-rings
in her ears. I then observed that her bonnet was
adorned with artificial flowers and trimmed with
costly ribbons, arranged in bows and puffs. My joy
was dampened by this display of vanity in one who
professed to be a follower of the meek and lowly
Jesus.

" I expected that the minister would give some
whispered reproof or advice to this sister, but he
was apparently regardless of her showy apparel
and no rebuke was administered. We both received
the right hand of fellowship. The hand decorated
with jewels was clasped by the representative of
Christ, and both our names were registered upon
the church book.

"I can now look back upon my youthful experience and see how near I came to making a fatal
mistake. I had read many of the religious biographies of children who had possessed numberless virtues and lived faultless lives. I had conceived a
great admiration for the paragons of perfection there
represented. But far from encouraging me in my
efforts to become a Christian, these books were as

stumbling-blocks to my feet. I despaired of ever attaining to the perfection of the youthful characters in those stories who lived the lives of saints and were free from all the doubts, and sins, and weaknesses under which I staggered.

"Their faultless lives were followed by a premature but happy death, and the biographers tacitly intimated that they were too pure and good for earth, therefore, God in his divine pity had removed them from its uncongenial atmosphere. The similarity of these avowedly true histories seemed to point the fact to my youthful mind, that they really presented a correct picture of a child's Christian life.

"I repeated to myself again and again, 'If that is true, I can never be a Christian. I can never hope to be like those children,' and was driven by this thought to discouragement and almost to despair. But when I learned that I could come to Jesus just as I was, that the Saviour had come to ransom just such unworthy sinners, then light broke upon my darkness, and I could claim the promises of God.

"Later experience has convinced me that these biographies of immaculate children mislead the youth. They extol the amiable qualities of their characters, and suppress their faults and failures. If they were represented as struggling with temptations, occasionally vanquished, yet triumphing over their trials in the end, if they were represented as subject to human frailties, and beset by ordinary temptations, *then* children would see that they had experienced like trials with themselves, yet had conquered through the grace of God. Such examples would give them fresh courage to renew their efforts to serve the Lord, hoping to triumph as those before them had done.

"But the sober realities and errors of the young Christian's life were vigorously kept out of sight, while the virtues were so exaggerated as to lift them from above the common level of ordinary children, who naturally despair of ever reaching such excellence and therefore give up the effort, in many cases, and gradually sink into a state of indifference.

"I again became very anxious to attend school and make another trial to obtain an education. But upon attempting to resume my studies my health rapidly failed, and it became apparent that if I persisted in attending school it would be at the expense of my life. I had found it difficult to enjoy religion in a large female seminary, surrounded by influences calculated to attract the mind and lead it from God.

"I felt a constant dissatisfaction with myself and my Christian attainments, and did not continually realize a lively sense of the mercy and love of God. Feelings of discouragement would come over me, and this caused me great anxiety of mind. I heard much in regard to sanctification, but had no defined idea in regard to it. This blessing seemed away beyond my reach, a state of purity my heart could never know. The manner in which it was preached and taught made it appear a human impossibility.

"In June, 1842, Mr. Miller gave his second course of lectures in the Casco street church, in Portland. I felt it a great privilege to attend these lectures, for I had fallen under discouragements and did not feel prepared to meet my Saviour. This second course created much more excitement in the city than the first. The different denominations, with a very few exceptions, closed the doors of their churches against Mr. Miller. Many discourses from the various pulpits sought to expose the alleged fanatical errors of the lecturer. But crowds of anxious listeners attended his meetings, while many were unable to enter the house, which was literally packed.

"The congregations were unusually quiet and attentive. His manner of preaching was not flowery or oratorical, but he dealt in plain and startling facts that roused his hearers from the apathy in which they had been locked. He substantiated his statements and theories by Scripture as he progressed. A convincing power attended his words that seemed to stamp them as the language of truth.

"He was courteous and sympathetic. When every seat in the house was full, and the platform and places about the pulpit seemed crowded, I have seen him leave the desk and walk down the aisle, and take some feeble old man or woman by the hand and find a seat for them, then return and resume his discourse. He was indeed rightly called Father Miller, for he had a watchful care over those who came under his ministrations, was affectionate in his manner, of genial and tender heart.

"He was a very interesting speaker, and his exhortations, both to professed Christians and the impenitent, were appropriate and powerful. Sometimes a solemnity so marked as to be painful, pervaded his meetings. A sense of the impending crisis of human events impressed the minds of the listening crowds. Many yielded to the conviction of the Spirit of God. Gray-haired men and aged women, with trembling steps, sought the anxious-seats. Those in the strength of maturity, the youth and children, were deeply stirred. Groans and the voice of weeping and of praising God were mingled together at the altar of prayer.

"I believed the solemn words spoken by the servant of God, and my heart was aggrieved when they were opposed or made the subject of jest. I attended the meetings on Casco street quite frequently, and believed that Jesus was soon to come in the clouds of heaven; but my great anxiety was to be ready to meet him. My mind constantly dwelt upon the subject of holiness of heart. I longed above all things to obtain this great blessing, and feel that I was entirely accepted of God.

"Among the Methodists I had heard much in regard to sanctification. I had seen people lose their physical strength under the influence of strong mental excitement, and had heard this pronounced to be the evidence of sanctification. But I could not comprehend what was necessary in order to be fully consecrated to God. My Christian friends said to me: 'Believe in Jesus *now!* Believe that he accepts you *now!*' This I tried to do but found it impossible to believe that I had received a blessing which, it seemed to me, should electrify my whole being. I wondered at my own hardness of heart in being unable to experience the exaltation of spirit that others manifested. It seemed to me that I was different from them, and forever shut out from the perfect joy of holiness of heart.

"My ideas concerning justification and sanctification were confused. These two states were presented to my mind as separate and distinct from each other. Yet I failed to comprehend the difference or understand the meaning of the terms, and all the explanations of the preachers increased my difficulties. I was unable to claim the blessing for myself, and wondered if it was only to be found among the Methodists, and if, in attending the Advent meetings, I was not shutting myself away from that which I desired above all else, the sanctifying Spirit of God.

"Still, I observed that some of those who pretended to be sanctified, manifested a bitter spirit when the subject of the soon coming of Christ was introduced; this did not seem to me a manifestation of the holiness which they professed. I could not understand why ministers from the pulpit should so oppose the doctrine that Christ's second coming was near at hand. Reformation had followed the preaching of this belief and many of the most devoted ministers and laymen had received it as the truth. It seemed to me that those who sincerely loved Jesus would be ready to accept the tidings of his coming, and rejoice that it was near at hand.

" I felt that I could only claim what they called justification. In the word of God I read that without holiness no man should see God. Then there was some higher attainment that I must reach before I could be sure of eternal life. I studied over the subject continually, for I believed that Christ was soon to come, and feared he would find me unprepared to meet him. Words of condemnation rang in my ears day and night, and my constant cry to God was, What shall I do to be saved? In my mind the justice of God eclipsed his mercy and love.

" I had been taught to believe in an eternally burning hell, and the horrifying thought was ever before me that my sins were too great to be forgiven, and that I should be forever lost. The frightful descriptions that I had heard of souls lost in perdition sank deep into my mind. Ministers in the pulpit drew vivid pictures of the condition of the damned. They taught that God never proposed to save any but the sanctified. The eye of God was upon us always; every sin was registered and would meet its just punishment. God himself was keeping the books with the exactitude of infinite wisdom, and every sin we committed was faithfully recorded against us.

" The devil was represented as eager to seize upon his prey and bear us to the lowest depths of anguish, there to exult over our sufferings in the horrors of an eternally burning hell, where, after the tortures of thousands upon thousands of years, the fiery billows would roll to the surface the writhing victims,

who would shriek, ' How long, O Lord, how long?'
Then the answer would thunder down the abyss,
' Through all eternity!'  Again the molten waves
would engulf the lost, carrying them down into the
depths of an ever restless sea of fire.

"While listening to these terrible descriptions,
my imagination would be so wrought upon that the
perspiration would start from every pore, and it
was difficult to suppress a cry of anguish, for I
seemed to already feel the pains of perdition.  Then
the minister would dwell upon the uncertainty of
life.  One moment we might be here, and the next
in hell, or one moment on earth, and the next in
heaven.  Would we choose the lake of fire and the
company of demons, or the bliss of heaven with
angels for our companions.  Would we hear the
voice of wailing and the cursing of lost souls through
all eternity, or sing the songs of Jesus before the
throne.

" Our heavenly father was presented before my
mind as a tyrant, who delighted in the agonies of
the condemned ; not the tender, pitying Friend of
sinners who loves his creatures with a love past all
understanding, and desires them to be saved in his
kingdom.

" My feelings were very sensitive.  I dreaded
giving pain to any living creature.  When I saw
animals ill-treated my heart ached for them.  Perhaps my sympathies were more easily excited by
suffering, because I myself had been the victim of
thoughtless cruelty, resulting in the injury that had
darkened my childhood.  But when the thought
took possession of my mind that God delighted in
the torture of his creatures, who were formed in his
image, a wall of darkness seemed to separate me
from him.  When I reflected that the Creator of the
universe would plunge the wicked into hell, there
to burn through the ceaseless rounds of eternity,

my heart sank with fear, and I despaired that so cruel and tyrannical a being would ever condescend to save me from the doom of sin.

"I thought that the fate of the condemned sinner would be mine, to endure the flames of hell forever, even as long as God himself existed. This impression deepened upon my mind until I feared that I would lose my reason. I would look upon the dumb beasts with envy, because they had no soul to be punished after death. Many times the wish arose that I had never been born.

"Total darkness settled upon me and there seemed no way out of the shadows. Could the truth have been presented to me as I now understand it, my despondency would have taken flight at once, much perplexity and sorrow would have been spared me. If the love of God had been dwelt upon more and his stern justice less, the beauty and glory of his character would have inspired me with a deep and earnest love for my Creator.

"I have since thought that many inmates of the lunatic asylums were brought there by experiences similar to my own. Their tender consciences have been stricken with a sense of sin, and their trembling faith dared not claim the promised pardon of God. They have listened to descriptions of the orthodox hell until it has seemed to curdle the very blood in their veins, and burnt an impression upon the tablets of their memory. Waking or sleeping, the frightful picture has ever been before them, until reality has become lost in imagination, and they see only the wreathing flames of a fabulous hell and hear only the shrieking of the damned. Reason has become dethroned and the brain is filled with the wild phantasy of a terrible dream. Those who teach the doctrine of an eternal hell, would do well to look more closely after their authority for so cruel a belief.

"I had never prayed in public, and had only spoken a few timid words in prayer-meeting. It was now impressed upon me that I should seek God in prayer at our small social meetings. This I dared not do, fearful of becoming confused, and failing to express my thoughts. But the duty was impressed upon my mind so forcibly that when I attempted to pray in secret I seemed to be mocking God, because I had failed to obey his will. Despair overwhelmed me, and for three long weeks no ray of light pierced the gloom that encompassed me about.

"My sufferings of mind were intense. Sometimes for a whole night I would not dare to close my eyes, but would wait until my twin sister was fast asleep, then quietly leave my bed and kneel upon the floor, praying silently with a dumb agony that cannot be described. The horrors of an eternally burning hell were ever before me. I knew that it was impossible for me to live long in this state, and I dared not die and meet the terrible fate of the sinner. With what envy did I regard those who realized their acceptance with God. How precious did the Christian's hope seem to my agonized soul.

"I frequently remained bowed in prayer nearly all night, groaning and trembling with inexpressible anguish and a hopelessness that passes all description. Lord have mercy! was my plea, and, like the poor publican, I dared not lift my eyes to heaven but bowed my face upon the floor. I became very much reduced in flesh and strength, yet kept my suffering and despair to myself.

"While in this state of despondency, I had a dream that made a powerful impression upon my mind, but in no wise lifted the vail of melancholy that darkened my life. I dreamed of seeing a temple, to which many people were flocking. Only those who took refuge in that temple would be saved when time should close. All who remained outside would be forever lost. The multitudes without who were going about their various ways, were deriding and ridiculing those who were entering the temple, and told them that this plan of safety was a cunning deception, that in fact there was no danger whatever to avoid. They even laid hold of some to prevent them from hastening within the walls.

"Fearing to be laughed at and ridiculed, I thought best to wait until the multitude were dispersed or until I could enter unobserved by them. But the numbers increased instead of diminishing, and fearful of being too late, I hastily left my home and pressed through the crowd. In my anxiety to reach the temple I did not notice or care for the throng that surrounded me. On entering the building I saw that the vast temple was supported by one immense pillar, and to this was tied a Lamb all mangled and bleeding. We who were present seemed to know that this Lamb had been torn and bruised on our account. All who entered the temple must come before it and confess their sins.

"Just before the Lamb, were elevated seats upon which sat a company of people looking very happy. The light of heaven seemed to shine upon their faces and they praised God and sang songs of glad thanksgiving that seemed to be like the music of the angels. These were they who had come before the Lamb, confessed their sins, been pardoned, and were now waiting in glad expectation of some joyful event.

"Even after having entered the building, a fear came over me, and a sense of shame that I must humiliate myself before these people. But I seemed compelled to move forward, and was slowly making my way around the pillar in order to face the Lamb, when a trumpet sounded, the temple shook, shouts of triumph arose from the assembled saints, an awful brightness illuminated the building, then all was intense darkness. The happy people had all disappeared with the brightness, and I was left alone in the silent horror of night.

"I awoke in agony of mind and could hardly convince myself that I had been dreaming. It seemed to me that my doom was fixed, that the Spirit of the Lord had left me never to return. My despondency deepened if that were possible. Soon after this I had another dream. I seemed to be sitting in abject despair with my face in my hands, reflecting like this: If Jesus were upon earth I would go to him, throw myself at his feet and tell him all my sufferings. He would not turn away from me, he would have mercy upon me, and I should love and serve him always. Just then the door opened, and a person of beautiful form and countenance entered. He looked upon me pitifully and said : ' Do you wish to see Jesus ? He is here, and you can see him if you desire to do so. Take everything you possess and follow me.'

"I heard this with unspeakable joy, and gladly gathered up all my little possessions, every treasured trinket, and followed my guide. He led me to a steep and apparently frail stairway. As I commenced to ascend the steps, he cautioned me to keep my eyes fixed upward, lest I should grow dizzy and fall. Many others who were climbing up the steep ascent fell before gaining the top.

"Finally we reached the last step and stood before a door. Here my guide directed me to leave all the things that I had brought with me. I cheerfully laid them down ; he then opened the door and bade me enter. In a moment I stood before Jesus. There was no mistaking that beautiful countenance. Such a radiant expression of benevolence and majesty could belong to no other. As his gaze rested upon me I knew at once that he was acquainted with every circumstance of my life and all my inner thoughts and feelings.

"I tried to shield myself from his gaze, feeling unable to endure his searching eyes, but he drew near with a smile, and, laying his hand upon my head, said: 'Fear not.' The sound of his sweet voice thrilled my heart with a happiness it had never before experienced. I was too joyful to utter a word, but, overcome with ineffable happiness sank prostrate at his feet. While I was lying helpless there, scenes of beauty and glory passed before me, and I seemed to have reached the safety and peace of heaven. At length my strength returned and I arose. The loving eyes of Jesus were still upon me, and his smile filled my soul with gladness. His presence filled me with a holy reverence and an inexpressible love.

"My guide now opened the door, and we both passed out. He bade me take up again all the things I had left without. This done, he handed me a green cord coiled up closely. This he directed me to place next my heart, and when I wished to see Jesus take it from my bosom and stretch it to the utmost. He cautioned me not to let it remain coiled for any length of time, lest it should become knotted and difficult to straighten. I placed the cord near my heart and joyfully descended the narrow stairs, praising the Lord and joyfully telling all whom I met where they could find Jesus. This dream gave me hope. The green cord represented faith to my mind, and the beauty and simplicity of trusting in God began to dawn upon my benighted soul.

"I now confided all my sorrows and perplexities to my mother. She tenderly sympathized with and encouraged me, advising me to go for counsel to Elder Stockman who then preached the Advent

doctrine in Portland. I had great confidence in him,
for he was a devoted servant of Christ. Upon hearing my story, he placed his hands affectionately
upon my head, saying with tears in his eyes: ' Ellen,
you are only a child. Yours is a most singular
experience for one of your tender age. Jesus must
be preparing you for some special work.'

"He then told me that even if I were a person of
mature years and thus harrassed by doubt and
despair, he should tell me that he *knew* there was
hope for me, through the love of Jesus. The very
agony of mind I had suffered was positive evidence
that the Spirit of the Lord was striving with me.
He said that when the sinner becomes hardened
in guilt he does not realize the enormity of his transgression, but flatters himself that he is about right
and in no particular danger. The Spirit of the Lord
leaves him and he becomes careless and indifferent
or recklessly defiant. This good man told me of
the love of God for his erring children, that instead
of rejoicing in their destruction he longed to draw
them to himself in simple faith and trust. He
dwelt upon the great love of Christ and the plan of
redemption.

"He spoke of my early misfortune, and said it
was indeed a grievous one, but he bade me believe
that the hand of a loving Father had not been withdrawn from me ; that in the future life, when the
mist that then darkened my mind had vanished, I
would discern the wisdom of the providence which
had seemed so cruel and mysterious. Jesus said to
his disciples : 'What I do thou knowest not now,
but thou shalt know hereafter.' In the great future
we should no longer see as through a glass darkly,
but come face to face with the great beauties of
divine love.

"' Go free, Ellen,' said he with tears in his eyes,
' Return to your home trusting in Jesus, for he will

not withhold his love from any true seeker.' He then prayed earnestly for me, and it seemed that God would certainly regard the prayer of this saint, even if my humble petitions were unheard. My mind was much relieved, and the wretched slavery of doubt and fear departed as I listened to the wise and tender counsel of this teacher in Israel. I left his presence comforted and encouraged.

" During the few minutes in which I received instruction from Elder Stockman, I had obtained more knowledge on the subject of God's love and pitying tenderness, than from all the sermons and exhortations to which I had ever listened. I returned home and again went before the Lord, promising to do and suffer anything he might require of me, if only the smiles of Jesus might illume my heart. The same duty was presented to me that had troubled my mind before, to take up my cross among the assembled people of God. An opportunity was not long wanting; there was a prayer-meeting that evening which I attended.

" I bowed trembling during the prayers that were offered. After a few had prayed, I lifted up my voice in prayer before I was aware of it, and in that moment the promises of God appeared to me like so many precious pearls that were to be received only for the asking. As I prayed, the burden and agony of soul that I had endured so long, left me, and the blessing of the Lord descended upon me like the gentle dew. I praised God from the depths of my heart. Everything seemed shut out from me but Jesus and his glory, and I lost consciousness of what was passing around me.

" When I again awoke to realization, I found myself cared for in the house of my uncle where we had assembled for the prayer-meeting. Neither my uncle nor aunt enjoyed religion, although the former once made a profession but had since backslidden.

I was told that he had been greatly disturbed while the power of God rested upon me in so special a manner, and had walked the floor, sorely troubled and distressed in his mind. When I was first struck down, some of those present were greatly alarmed, and were about to run for a physician, thinking that some sudden and dangerous indisposition had attacked me, but my mother bade them let me alone, for it was plain to her, and to the other experienced Christians, that it was the wondrous power of God that had prostrated me.

"The next day I had recovered sufficiently to go home, but a great change had taken place in my mind. It seemed to me that I could hardly be the same person that left my father's house the previous evening. This passage was continually in my thoughts: 'The Lord is my shepherd, I shall not want.' My heart was full of happiness as I softly repeated these words.

"Faith now took possession of my heart. I felt an inexpressible love for God, and had the witness of his Spirit that my sins were pardoned. My views of the Father were changed. I now looked upon him as a kind and tender parent, rather than a stern tyrant compelling men to a blind obedience. My heart went out towards him in a deep and fervent love. Obedience to his will seemed a joy; it was a pleasure to be in his service. My path was radiant before me; no shadow clouded the light that revealed to me the perfect will of God. I felt the assurance of an indwelling Saviour, and realized the truth of what Christ had said: 'He that followeth me shall not walk in darkness, but shall have the light of life.'

"Everything in nature seemed to possess a glory, and seemed to reflect the loving smiles of God. My peace and happiness was in such marked contrast with my former gloom and anguish that it seemed to me as if my soul had been rescued from hell and transported to heaven. I could even praise God for the misfortune that had been the trial of my life, for it had been the means of concentrating my thoughts upon eternity. Naturally proud and ambitious, I might not have been inclined to give my heart to Jesus had it not been for the sore affliction that had cut me off, in a manner, from the triumphs and vanities of the world.

" For six months not a shadow clouded my mind, nor did I neglect one known duty. My whole endeavor was to do the will of God and keep Jesus and heaven continually in my mind. I was surprised and enraptured with the clear views now presented to my mind of the atonement and the work of Jesus Christ. I will not attempt to farther explain the exercises of my mind, suffice it to say that old things had passed away, all things had become new. There was not a cloud to mar my perfect bliss. I longed to tell the story of Jesus' love, but felt no disposition to engage in common conversation with any one. My heart was so filled with love to God and the peace that passeth understanding, that I loved to meditate and to pray.

" The night after receiving so great a blessing I attended the Advent meeting. When the time arrived for the followers of Christ to speak in his favor, I could not remain silent, but rose and related my experience. Not a thought had entered my mind of what I should say; but the simple story of Jesus' love to me fell from my lips with perfect freedom, and my heart was so happy to be liberated from its thralldom of dark despair that I lost sight of the people about me and seemed to be alone with God. I found no difficulty in expressing my peace and happiness, except for the tears of gratitude that choked my utterance, as I told of the wondrous love that Jesus had shown for me.

"Elder Stockman was present. He had so recently seen me in deep despair, and had endeavored to encourage and inspire me with hope, that the remarkable change in my appearance and feelings touched his heart and he wept aloud, rejoicing with me and praising God for this proof of his tender mercy and loving kindness. My heart was so over-flowing with joy that I wanted to tell others how much the Lord had done for me.

"I occasionally attended the Christian church, where Elder Brown was pastor. During a conference meeting I was invited to relate my experience, which was considered a marked one, and I felt not only great freedom of expression, but happiness in telling my simple story of the love of Jesus and the joy of being accepted of God. I told of my wonderful deliverance from the bondage of doubt and despair, and the joy that I experienced in the hope of salvation. As I spoke in simple language, with subdued heart and tearful eyes, my soul seemed drawn toward heaven in an ecstasy of thanksgiving. The melting power of the Lord came upon the assembled people. Many were weeping and others praising God.

"Sinners were invited to arise for prayers, and many responded to the call. My heart was so thankful to God for the unspeakable blessing he had given me, that I longed to have others participate in this sacred joy. My mind was deeply interested for those who might be suffering under a sense of the Lord's displeasure and the burden of sin. While relating my experience, I felt that no one could resist the evidence of God's pardoning love that had wrought such a wonderful change in me. The reality of true conversion seemed so plain to me that I felt like helping my young friends into the light, and at every opportunity exerted my influence toward this end.

"I arranged meetings with my young friends, some of whom were considerably older than myself, and a few were married persons. A number of them were vain and thoughtless, my experience sounded to them like an idle tale, and they did not heed my entreaties. But I determined that my efforts should never cease till these dear souls, for whom I had so great an interest, yielded to God. Several entire nights were spent by me in earnest prayer for those whom I had sought out and brought together for the purpose of laboring and praying with them.

"Some of these had met with us from curiosity to hear what I had to say, others thought me beside myself to be so persistent in my efforts, especially when they manifested no concern on their own part. But at every one of our little meetings I continued to exhort and pray for each one separately, until my labors were crowned with success, and every one had yielded to Jesus, acknowledging the merits of his pardoning love. Every one was converted to God.

"Night after night in my dreams I seemed to be laboring for the salvation of souls. At such times special cases were presented to my mind, which I afterwards sought out and prayed with. In every instance but one these persons yielded themselves to the Lord. Some of our more formal brethren feared that I was too zealous and solicitous for the conversion of souls, but time seemed to me so short that it behooved all who had a hope of a blessed immortality, and looked for the soon coming of Christ, to labor without ceasing for those who were still in their sins and standing on the awful brink of ruin.

"Though very young, the plan of salvation was so clear to my mind, and my personal experience had been so marked, that, upon carefully considering

the matter, I knew it was my duty to continue my
efforts for the salvation of precious souls, and to
pray and confess Christ at every opportunity. My
entire being was offered to the service of my Master.
Let come what would, I determined to please God,
and live as one who expected the Saviour to come
and reward the faithful. I felt like a little child
coming to God as to my father and asking him
what he would have me to do. Then as my duty
was made plain to me, it was my greatest happiness
to perform it. Peculiar trials sometimes beset me.
Those older in experience than myself endeavored
to hold me back and cool the ardor of my faith, but
with the smiles of Jesus brightening my life, and the
love of God in my heart, I went on my way with a
joyful spirit.

"As I recall the youthful experience of my early
life, my brother, the confidant of my hopes and
fears, the earnest sympathizer with me in my Christian experience comes to my mind with a flood of
tender memories. He was one of those to whom
sin presents but few temptations. Naturally devo-
tional, he never sought the society of the young and
gay, but chose rather the company of Christians,
whose conversation would instruct him in the way
of life. His manner was serious beyond his years.
he was gentle and peaceful, and his mind was
almost constantly filled with religious thoughts.
His life was pointed to, by those who knew him, as
a pattern to the youth, a living example of the
grace and beauty of true Christianity.

"My father's family still occasionally attended
the Methodist church and also the class-meetings
held in private houses. One evening my brother
Robert and myself went to class-meeting. The
Methodist presiding elder was present. When it
came my brother's turn, he spoke with great humility, yet with clearness, of the necessity for a com-

plete fitness to meet our Saviour, when he should come in the clouds of heaven with power and great glory. While speaking, a heavenly light irradiated his usually pale countenance. He seemed to be carried in spirit above present surroundings, and spoke as if in the presence of Jesus. When I was called upon to speak, I arose, free in spirit, with a heart full of love and peace. In my simple way I told the story of my great suffering under the conviction of sin, how that I had at length received the blessing so long sought, an entire conformity to the will of God, and expressed my joy in the tidings of the soon coming of my Redeemer to take his children home.

"In unsuspecting simplicity I expected that my Methodist brethren and sisters would understand my feelings and rejoice with me. But I was disappointed; several sisters groaned and moved their chairs noisily, turning their backs upon me. I could not think what had been said to offend them, and spoke very briefly, feeling the chilling influence of their disapprobation. When I had ceased speaking, Elder B. asked me if it would not be more pleasant to live a long life of usefulness, doing others good, than for Jesus to come speedily and destroy poor sinners. I replied that I longed for the coming of Jesus. Then sin would have an end, and we should enjoy sanctification forever, with no devil to tempt and lead us astray.

"He then inquired if I would not rather die peacefully upon my bed than to pass through the pain of being changed, while living, from mortality to immortality. My answer was that I wished for Jesus to come and take his children; that I was willing to live or die as God willed, and could easily endure all the pain that could be borne in a moment, in the twinkling of an eye; that I desired the wheels of time to roll swiftly round, and bring the welcome day when these vile bodies should be changed, and fashioned like unto Christ's most glorious body. I also stated that when I lived nearest to the Lord, then I most earnestly longed for his appearing. Here some present seemed to be greatly displeased.

"When the presiding elder addressed others in the class he expressed great joy in anticipating the temporal millennium of a thousand years, when the earth would be filled with the knowledge of the Lord as the waters cover the sea. He longed to see this glorious period ushered in, and appeared to be in an ecstasy over the expected event. After the meeting closed I was conscious of being treated with marked coldness by those who had formerly been kind and friendly to me. My brother and I returned home feeling sad that we should be so misunderstood by our brethren, and that the subject of the near coming of Jesus should awaken such bitter antagonism in their breasts.

"Yet we were thankful that we could discern the precious light, and rejoice in looking for the coming of the Lord. On the way we talked seriously concerning the evidences of our new faith and hope. 'Ellen,' said Robert, 'are we deceived? Is this hope of Christ's soon appearing upon earth a heresy, that ministers and professors of religion oppose it so bitterly? They say that Jesus will not come for thousands and thousands of years. If they even approach the truth, then the world cannot come to an end in our day.'

"I dared not give unbelief a moment's encouragement, but quickly replied, 'I have not a doubt but that the doctrine preached by Mr. Miller is the truth. What power attends his words, what conviction is carried home to the sinner's heart.'

"We talked the matter over candidly, as we walked along, and decided that it was our duty and

privilege to look for our Saviour's coming, and that
it would be safest to make ready for his appearing
and be prepared to meet him with joy. If he did
come, what would be the prospect of those who
were now saying, 'My Lord delayeth his coming,'
and had no desire for his appearance? We wondered how ministers dared to quiet the fears of sinners and backsliders by saying peace, peace, while
the message of warning was being given by a few
faithful souls all over the land. The period seemed
very solemn to us; we felt that we had no time to lose.

"Said Robert: 'A tree is known by its fruits.
What has this belief done for us? It has convinced
us that we were not ready for the coming of the
Lord, that we must become pure in heart or we
could not meet our Saviour in peace. It has
aroused us to seek for new strength and grace from
God. What has it done for you, Ellen? Would
you be what you are now if you had never heard
the doctrine of Christ's soon coming? What hope
has inspired your heart; what peace, joy, and love
has it given you. And for me, it has done everything. I love Jesus, and all Christians. I love the
prayer-meeting. I find great joy in reading my
Bible and in prayer. If this precious faith has done
so great a work for us, will it not do as much for all
those who will believe it, and earnestly long for the
appearing of the Lord.'

"We both felt strengthened by this conversation,
and resolved that we would not be turned from our
honest convictions of truth, and the blessed hope of
Christ's soon coming in the clouds of heaven. Not
long after this we again attended the class-meeting.
We really wanted an opportunity to speak of the
precious love of God that animated our souls. I
particularly wished to tell of the Lord's goodness
and mercy to me. So great a change had been
wrought in me that it seemed my duty to improve

every opportunity of testifying to the unsurpassed love of my Saviour.

"When my turn came to speak, I stated the evidences I enjoyed of Jesus' love, and that I looked forward with glad expectation to meeting my Redeemer soon. The belief that Christ's coming was near had stirred my soul to seek more earnestly for the sanctification of the Spirit of God. Here the class-leader interrupted me, saying: 'You received sanctification through Methodism, through *Methodism*, sister, not through an erroneous theory.' My heart was full of love and happiness, but 1 felt compelled to confess the truth, that it was not through Methodism my heart had received its new blessing, but by the stirring truths heard concerning the personal appearance of Jesus. Through them I had found peace, joy, and perfect love. Thus my testimony closed, the last that I was to bear in class with my Methodist brethren.

"Robert then spoke in his meek way, yet in so clear and touching a manner that some wept and were much moved; but others coughed dissentingly and seemed quite uneasy. After leaving the class-room, we again talked over our faith, and marveled that our Christian brethren and sisters could so illy endure to have a word spoken in reference to our Saviour's coming. We thought if they loved Jesus as they should, it would not be so great an annoyance to hear of his second advent, but, on the contrary, they would hail the news with great joy.

"We were convinced that we ought no longer to attend the Methodist class-meeting. The hope of the glorious appearing of Christ filled our souls, and would find expression when we rose to speak. This seemed to kindle the ire of those present against the two humble children who dared, in the face of opposition, to speak of the faith that had filled their hearts with peace and happiness. It was evident that we could have no freedom in the class-meeting, for our simple testimony provoked sneers and taunts that reached our ears at the close of the meeting from brethren and sisters whom we had respected and loved.

"The Adventists held meetings at this time in Beethoven Hall. My father, with his family, attended them quite regularly, for we greatly prized the privilege of hearing the doctrine of Christ's personal and soon appearing upon earth. The period of the second advent was thought to be in the year 1843. The time seemed so short in which souls could be saved, that I resolved to do all that was in my power to lead sinners into the light of truth. But it seemed impossible for one so young, and in feeble health, to do much in the great work.

"There were three sisters of us at home, Sarah, who was several years the oldest, my twin sister Elizabeth, and myself. We talked the matter over among ourselves, and decided to earn what money we could and spend it in buying books and tracts to distribute gratuitously among the people. This was the best we could do, and we did this little gladly. I could earn only twenty-five cents a day, but my dress was plain, nothing was spent for needless ornaments, or ribbons, for vain display appeared sinful in my eyes; so I had ever a little fund in store with which to purchase suitable books. These were placed in the hands of experienced persons to send abroad.

"Every leaf of this printed matter seemed precious in my eyes, for they were as messages of light to the world, bidding them to prepare for the great event near at hand. Day after day I sat in bed propped up with pillows, performing my allotted task with trembling fingers. How carefully would I lay aside the precious bits of silver taken in return, and which was to be expended in reading

matter that might enlighten and arouse those who
were in darkness. I had no temptation to spend
my earnings for my own personal gratification; the
salvation of souls was the burden of my mind, and
my heart ached for those who flattered themselves
they were living in security, while the message of
warning was being given to the world.

"One day I was listening to a conversation between my mother and a sister, in reference to a discourse which they had recently heard, to the effect
that the soul had not natural immortality. Some
of the minister's proof texts were repeated. Among
them I remember these impressed me very forcibly:

"'The soul that sinneth it shall die.' 'A living
dog is better than a dead lion, for the living know
that they shall die; but the dead know not anything.' 'Which in his times he shall show who is
the blessed and only Potentate, the King of kings
and Lord of lords; who *only* hath immortality,
dwelling in the light which no man can approach
unto.' 'To them who by patient continuance in
well-doing seek for glory, and honor, and immortality, eternal life.' 'Why,' said my mother, after
quoting the foregoing passage, 'should they seek
for what they already have?'

"I listened to these new ideas with an intense
and painful interest. When alone with my mother,
I inquired if she really believed that the soul was
not immortal? Her reply was she feared we had
been in error on that subject as well as upon some
others.

"'But mother,' said I, 'Do you really believe
that the soul sleeps in the grave until the resurrection? Do you think that the Christian, when he
dies, does not go immediately to heaven, nor the
sinner to hell?'

"She answered: 'The Bible gives us no proof that
there is an eternally burning hell. If there is such

a place, it should be mentioned in the Sacred Book.'

"'Why mother!' cried I, in astonishment, 'This is strange talk for you! If you believe this strange theory, do not let any one know of it, for I fear that sinners would gather security from this belief and never desire to seek the Lord.'

"'If this is sound Bible truth,' she replied, 'instead of preventing the salvation of sinners, it will be the means of winning them to Christ. If the love of God will not induce the rebel to yield, the terrors of an eternal hell will not drive him to repentance. Besides it does not seem a proper way to win souls to Jesus, by appealing to one of the lowest attributes of the mind, abject fear. The love of Jesus attracts, it will subdue the hardest heart.'

It was some months after this conversation before I heard anything farther concerning this doctrine; but during this time, my mind had been much exercised upon the subject. When I heard it preached I believed it to be the truth. From the time that light in regard to the sleep of the dead dawned upon my mind, the mystery that had enshrouded the resurrection vanished, and the great event itself assumed a new and sublime importance. My mind had often been disturbed by its efforts to reconcile the immediate reward or punishment of the dead, with the undoubted fact of a future resurrection and judgment. If the soul, at death, entered upon eternal happiness or misery, where was the need of a resurrection of the poor moldering body?

"But this new and beautiful faith taught me the reason that inspired writers had dwelt so much upon the resurrection of the body, it was because the entire being was slumbering in the grave. I could now clearly perceive the fallacy of our former position on this question. The confusion and uselessness of a final judgment, after the souls of the departed had already been judged once and appointed to their lot, was very apparent to me now. I saw that the hope of the bereaved was in looking forward to the glorious day when the Life-giver shall break the fetters of the tomb, and the righteous dead shall arise and leave their prison-house, to be clothed with glorious immortal life.

"Our family were all interested in the doctrine of the Lord's soon coming. My father had long been considered one of the pillars of the Methodist church where he lived, and the whole family had been active members, but we made no secret of our new belief, although we did not urge it upon others on inappropriate occasions, or manifest any antagonism toward our church. However, the Methodist minister made us a special visit, and took the occasion to inform us that our faith and Methodism could not agree. He did not inquire our reasons for believing as we did, nor make any reference to the Bible in order to convince us of our error; but he stated that we had adopted a new and strange belief that the Methodist church could not accept.

"My father replied that he must be mistaken in calling this a new and strange doctrine, that Christ himself had preached his second advent to his disciples. He had said, '"In my Father's house are many mansions; if it were not so, I would have told you. I go to prepare a place for you. And if I go and prepare a place for you, I will come again, and receive you unto myself; that where I am there ye may be also."

"'When he was taken up to heaven before their eyes and a cloud received him out of their sight, as his faithful followers stood gazing after their vanishing Lord, "Behold, two men stood by them in white apparel; which also said, Ye men of Galilee, why stand ye gazing up into heaven? this same Jesus which is taken up from you into heaven, shall so come in like manner as ye have seen him go into heaven."

"'And,' said my father, warming with his subject, 'the inspired Paul wrote a letter to encourage his brethren in Thessalonica, saying, "And to you who are troubled rest with us, when the Lord Jesus shall be revealed from heaven with his mighty angels, in flaming fire taking vengeance on them that know not God, and that obey not the gospel of our Lord Jesus Christ: who shall be punished with everlasting destruction from the presence of the Lord, and from the glory of his power: when he shall come to be glorified in his saints, and to be admired in all them that believe in that day." "For the Lord himself shall descend from heaven with a shout, with the voice of the archangel, and with the trump of God; and the dead in Christ shall rise first. Then we which are alive and remain shall be caught up together with them in the clouds, to meet the Lord in the air; and so shall we ever be with the Lord. Wherefore comfort one another with these words."

"'This is high authority for our faith. Jesus and his apostles dwell upon the event of the second advent with joy and triumph; and the holy angels proclaim that Christ who has ascended up into heaven shall come again. This is our offense, believing the word of Jesus and his disciples. This is a very old doctrine, and bears no taint of heresy.'

"The minister did not attempt to refer to a single text that would prove us in error, but excused himself on the plea of a want of time. He advised us to quietly withdraw from the church and avoid the publicity of a trial. We were aware that others of our brethren were meeting with similar treatment, for a like cause, and we did not wish it understood that we were ashamed to acknowledge our faith, or were unable to sustain it by Scripture; so my parents insisted that they should be acquainted with the reasons for this request.

"The only answer to this was an evasive declaration that we had walked contrary to the rules of the church, and the best course would be to voluntarily withdraw from it to save a trial. We answered that we preferred a regular trial, and demanded to know what sin was charged to us, as we were conscious of no wrong in looking for and loving the appearing of the Saviour.

"Not long after, we were notified to be present at a meeting to be held in the vestry of the church. There were but few present. The influence of my father and his family was such that our opposers had no desire to present our cases before a larger number of the congregation. The single charge preferred was that we had walked contrary to their rules. Upon our asking what rules we had violated, it was stated, after a little hesitation, that we had attended other meetings and had neglected to meet regularly with our class. We stated that a portion of the family had been in the country for some time past, that none who remained in the city had been absent from class-meeting more than a few weeks, and they were morally compelled to remain away because the testimonies they bore met with such marked disapprobation. If the hope of their Saviour's soon coming was mentioned, a feeling of displeasure was manifested against them, and they were conscious of arousing a bitter spirit of antagonism. We also reminded them that certain persons who had not attended class-meeting for a year were yet held in good standing.

"It was asked if we would confess that we had departed from their rules, and if we would also agree to conform to them in future. We answered that we dared not yield our faith nor deny the sacred truth of God; that we could not forego the hope of the soon coming of our Redeemer; that after the manner which they called heresy we must continue to worship the Lord. My father in his defense received the blessing of God, and we all left the vestry with free spirits and happy in the conscious- ness of right and the approving smile of Jesus. We felt the assurance that God was on our side, and he was stronger than all that were against us.

"The next Sunday, at the commencement of love- feast, the presiding elder read off our names, seven in number, as discontinued from the church. He stated that we were not expelled on account of any wrong or immoral conduct, that we were of unblem- ished character and enviable reputation; but we had been guilty of walking contrary to the rules of the Methodist church. He also declared that a door was now open and all who were guilty of a similar breach of the rules, would be dealt with in like manner.

"There were many in the church who waited for the appearing of the Saviour, and this implied threat was made for the purpose of frightening them into subjection. In some cases this policy brought about the desired result, and the favor of God was sold for a place in the Methodist church. Many believed, but dared not confess their faith lest they should be turned out of the synagogue. But some left soon afterward and joined the company of those who were looking for the Saviour.

"At this time the words of the prophet were ex- ceedingly precious: 'Your brethren that hated you, that cast you out for my name's sake, said, Let the Lord be glorified; but he shall appear to your joy, and they shall be ashamed.'

"For six months not a cloud intervened between me and my Saviour. Whenever there was a proper opportunity I bore my testimony, and was greatly blessed. At times the Spirit of the Lord rested upon me with such power that my strength was taken from me. This was a trial to some who had come out from the formal churches, and remarks were often made that grieved me much. Many could not believe that one could be so overpowered by the Spirit of God as to lose all strength. My position was exceedingly painful. I began to reason with myself whether I was not justified in withholding my testimony in meeting, and thus restrain my feelings when there was such an opposition in the hearts of some who were older in years and experience than myself.

"I adopted this plan of silence for a time, trying to convince myself that to repress my testimony would not hinder me from faithfully living out my religion. I often felt strongly impressed that it was my duty to speak in meeting, but refrained from doing so, and was sensible of having thereby grieved the Spirit of God. I even remained away from meetings sometimes because they were to be attended by those whom my testimony annoyed. I shrank from offending my brethren, and in this allowed the fear of man to break up that uninterrupted communion with God which had blessed my heart for so many months.

"We had appointed evening prayer-meetings in different localities of the city to accommodate all who wished to attend them. The family who had been most forward in opposing me attended one of these. Upon this occasion, while those assembled were engaged in prayer, the Spirit of the Lord came upon the meeting, and one of the members of this family was prostrated as one dead. His relatives stood weeping around him, rubbing his hands and applying restoratives. At length he gained sufficient strength to praise God, and quieted their fears by shouting with triumph over the marked evidence he had received of the power of the Lord upon him. This young man was unable to return home that night.

"This was believed by the family to be a demonstration of the Spirit of God, but did not convince them that it was the same divine power that had rested upon me at times, robbing me of my natural strength, and filling my soul with the unbounded peace and love of Jesus. They were free to say that not a doubt could be entertained of my sincerity and perfect honesty, but they considered me self-deceived in taking that for the power of the Lord which was only the result of my own over-wrought feelings.

" My mind was in great perplexity, in consequence of this opposition, and, as the time drew near for our regular meeting, I was in doubt whether or not it was best for me to attend it. For some days previous I had been in great distress on account of the feeling manifested towards me. Finally I decided not to go, and thus escape the criticism of my brethren. In trying to pray, I repeated these words again and again, ' Lord, what wilt thou have me to do ?' The answer that came to my heart seemed to bid me trust in my heavenly Father and wait patiently to know his will. I yielded myself to the Lord with the simple trust of a little child, remembering he had promised that those who follow him shall not walk in darkness.

" My duty impelled me to go to the meeting, and I went with the full assurance in my mind that all would be well. While we were bowed before the Lord, my heart was drawn out in prayer, and filled with a peace that only Christ can give. My soul rejoiced in the love of the Saviour, and physical strength left me. With child-like faith I could only say, ' Heaven is my home, and Christ my Redeemer.'

" One of the family before mentioned, as being opposed to the manifestations of the power of God upon me, on this occasion, stated his belief that I was under an excitement which he thought it my duty to resist, but instead of doing so he thought I encouraged it, as a mark of God's favor. His doubts and opposition did not affect me at this time, for I seemed shut in with the Lord, and lifted above all outward influence. But he had scarcely stopped speaking when a strong man, a devoted and humble Christian, was struck down before his eyes, by the power of God, and the room was filled with the Holy Spirit.

"Upon sufficiently recovering, I was very happy in bearing my testimony for Jesus, and in telling of his love for me. I confessed my lack of faith in the promises of God, and my error in checking the promptings of his Spirit from fear of men, but that, notwithstanding my distrust, he had bestowed upon me unlooked for evidence of his love and sustaining grace. The brother who had opposed me then rose, and with many tears confessed that his feelings in regard to me had been all wrong. He humbly asked my forgiveness, and said, 'Sister Ellen, I will never again lay a straw in your way. God has shown me the coldness and stubbornness of my heart, which he has broken by the evidence of his power. I have been very wrong.' Then, turning to the people, he said, 'When sister Ellen seemed so happy I would think, Why don't I feel like that? Why don't Brother R. receive some such evidence? for I was convinced that he was a devoted Christian, yet no such power had fallen upon him. I offered a silent prayer that, if this was the holy influence of God, Brother R. might experience it this evening.

"'Almost as the desire went up from my heart, Brother R. fell, prostrated by the power of God, crying, Let the Lord work! My heart is convinced that I have been warring against the Holy Spirit, but I will grieve it no more by stubborn unbelief. Welcome, light! Welcome, Jesus! I have been backslidden and hardened, feeling offended if any one praised God and manifested a fullness of joy in his love; but now my feelings are changed, my opposition is at an end, Jesus has opened my eyes, and I may yet shout his praises myself. I have said bitter and cutting things of Sister Ellen, that I sorrow over now, and pray for her forgiveness as well as that of all who are present.'

" Brother R. then bore his testimony. His face was lighted with the glory of heaven, as he praised the Lord for the wonders he had wrought that night. Said he, 'This place is awfully solemn because of the presence of the Most High. Sister Ellen, in future you will have our help and sustaining sympathies, instead of the cruel opposition that has been shown you. We have been blind to the manifestations of God's Holy Spirit.'

" There had never been a question as to my perfect sincerity, but many had thought me young and impressible, and that it was my duty to restrain my feelings, which they regarded as the effect of excitement. But all the opposers were now brought to see their mistake and to confess that the work was indeed of the Lord. In a prayer-meeting soon after, the brother who had confessed that he was wrong in his opposition, experienced the power of God in so great a degree that his countenance shone with a heavenly light, and he fell helpless to the floor. When his strength returned, he again acknowledged that he had been ignorantly warring against the Spirit of the Lord in cherishing the feeling he had against me.

" In another prayer-meeting still another member of the same family was exercised in a similar manner and bore the same testimony. A few weeks after, while the large family of Brother P. were engaged in prayer at their own house, the Spirit of God swept through the room and prostrated the kneeling suppliants. My father came in soon after, and found them all, both parents and children, helpless under the power of the Lord.

"Cold formality began to melt before the mighty influence of the Most High. All who had opposed me, confessed that they had grieved the Holy Spirit by so doing, and they united in sympathy with me and in love for the Saviour. My heart was glad that divine mercy had smoothed the path for my feet to tread, and rewarded my faith and trust so bounteously. Unity and peace now dwelt among our people who were looking forward toward the coming of the Lord.

"How carefully and tremblingly did we approach the time of expectation. We sought, as a people, with solemn earnestness to purify our lives that we might be ready to meet the Saviour at his coming. Notwithstanding the opposition of ministers and churches, Beethoven Hall, in the city of Portland, was nightly crowded, and especially was there a large congregation on Sundays. Elder Stockman was a man of deep piety. He was in feeble health, yet when he stood before the people he seemed to be lifted above physical infirmity, and his face was lighted with the consciousness that he was teaching the sacred truth of God.

"There was a solemn, searching power in his words that struck home to many hearts. He sometimes expressed a fervent desire to live until he should welcome the Saviour coming in the clouds of heaven. Under his ministration, the Spirit of God convicted many sinners, and brought them into the fold of Christ. Meetings were still held at private houses in different parts of the city with the best results. Believers were encouraged to work for their friends and relatives, and conversions were multiplying day by day.

"In the district where my father's family properly belonged, these evening meetings were held at the house of a sea-captain. He made no profession of religion, but his wife was a sincere lover of the truth. The captain finally became convicted through the influence of the meetings, professed Christ and embraced the belief that he was soon coming to the world.

" All classes flocked to the meetings at Beethoven Hall. Rich and poor, high and low, ministers and laymen were all, from various causes, anxious to hear for themselves the doctrine of the second advent. The crowd was such that fears were expressed that the floor might give way beneath its heavy load ; but the builder, upon being consulted, quieted such apprehensions and established confidence in regard to the strength of the building. Many came who, finding no room to stand, went away disappointed.

" The order of the meetings was simple. A short and pointed discourse was usually given, then liberty was granted for general exhortation. There was, as a rule, the most perfect stillness possible for so large a crowd. The Lord held the spirit of opposition in check, while his servants explained the reasons of their faith. Sometimes the instrument was feeble, but the Spirit of God gave weight and power to his truth. The presence of the holy angels was felt in the assembly, and numbers were daily being added to the little band of believers.

" On one occasion, while Elder Stockman was preaching, Elder Brown, a Christian Baptist minister, whose name has been mentioned before in this narrative, was sitting in the desk listening to the sermon with intense interest. He became deeply moved, and suddenly his countenance grew pale as the dead, he reeled in his chair, and Elder Stockman caught him in his arms just as he was falling to the floor, and laid him on the sofa behind the desk, where he lay powerless until the discourse was finished.

" He then arose, his face still pale, but shining

with light from the Sun of righteousness, and gave
a very impressive testimony. He seemed to receive
holy unction from above. He was usually slow of
speech, with an earnest manner, entirely free from
excitement. On this occasion, his solemn, measured
words carried with them a new power, as he warned
sinners and his brother ministers to put away
unbelief, prejudice and cold formality, and, like the
noble Bereans, searched the sacred writings, comparing scripture with scripture, to ascertain if these
things were not true. He entreated the ministers
present not to feel themselves injured by the direct
and searching manner in which Elder Stockman
had presented the solemn subject that interested all
minds.

"Said he, 'We want to reach the people, we want
sinners to be convicted and become truly repentant to God before it is too late for them to be saved,
lest they shall take up the lamentation, The harvest
is past, the summer is ended, and we are not saved.
Brethren in the ministry say that our arrows hit
them; will they please stand aside from between
us and the people, and let us reach the hearts of
sinners? If they make themselves a target for our
aim they have no reason to complain of the wounds
they receive. Stand aside brethren and you will
not get hit!'

"He related his own experience with such simplicity and candor, that many who had been greatly
prejudiced were affected to tears. The Spirit of
God was felt in his words and seen upon his countenance. With a holy exaltation he boldly declared
that he had taken the word of God as his counselor,
that his doubts had been swept away and his faith
confirmed. With sanctified earnestness he invited
his brother ministers, church members, sinners and
infidels to examine the Bible for themselves and
charged them to let no man turn them from the
purpose of ascertaining what was the truth.

"Elder Brown neither then nor afterwards severed his connection with the Christian Baptist church, but was looked upon with great reverence and respect by his people. When he had finished speaking, those who desired the prayers of the people of God were invited to rise. Hundreds responded to the call. The sea-captain who had been recently converted, sprang to his feet with tears raining down his cheeks. He was unable to express his feelings in words, and stood for a moment the picture of mute thanksgiving; then he involuntarily raised his hat, and swung it above his head with the free movement of an old sailor, and in the abandonment of his joy, shouted, 'Hurrah for God! I've enlisted in his crew, he is my captain! Hurrah for Jesus Christ!' He sat down overpowered by the intensity of his emotions, his face glowing with the radiance of love and peace. This singular testimony, so characteristic of the bluff mariner, was not received with laughter, for the Spirit of God that animated the speaker lent his extraordinary words a strange solemnity that was felt through all that dense crowd.

"Others followed with their testimonies. The voice of Brother Abbot rung through the hall in notes of warning to the world. He repeated the evidences of the soon coming of Christ, and that vast crowd listened in sacred silence to his stirring words. The Holy Spirit rested upon the assembly. Heaven and earth seemed to approach each other. The meeting lasted until a late hour of the night. The power of the Lord was felt upon young, old, and middle aged. Some Methodists and Baptists who were present seemed to fully unite with the spirit of the meeting.

"As we returned to our homes by various ways, a voice praising God would reach us from one direction, and, as if in response, voices from another and still another quarter, shouted, 'Glory to God, the Lord reigneth!' Men sought their homes with praises upon their lips, and the glad sound rang out upon the still night air. No one who attended these meetings can ever forget those scenes of deepest interest.

"Those who sincerely love Jesus can appreciate the feelings of those who watched with the most intense interest for the coming of their Saviour. The point of expectation was nearing. The time when we hoped to meet him was close at hand. We approached this hour with a calm solemnity. The true believers rested in a sweet communion with God, an earnest of the peace that was to be theirs in the bright hereafter. Those who experienced this hope and trust can never forget those precious hours of waiting.

"Worldly business was for the most part laid aside for a few weeks. We carefully scrutinized every thought and emotion of our hearts as if upon our death-beds and in a few hours to close our eyes forever upon earthly scenes. There was no making 'ascension robes' for the great event; we felt the need of internal evidence that we were prepared to meet Christ, and our white robes were purity of soul, character cleansed from sin by the atoning blood of our Saviour.

"But the time of expectation passed. This was the first close test brought to bear upon those who believed and hoped that Jesus would come in the clouds of heaven. The disappointment of God's waiting people was great. The scoffers were triumphant and won the weak and cowardly to their ranks. Some who had appeared to possess true faith seemed to have been influenced only by fear, and now their courage returned with the passing of the time, and they boldly united with the scoffers declaring they had never been duped to really believe the doctrine of Miller, who was a mad fanatic. Others, naturally yielding or vacillating, quietly deserted the cause. I thought if Christ had surely come, what would have become of those weak and changing ones? Where would have been their robes of righteousness? They professed to love and long for the coming of Jesus, but when he failed to appear they seemed greatly relieved and went back to a state of carelessness and disregard of true religion.

"We were perplexed and disappointed, yet did not renounce our faith. Many still clung to the hope that Jesus would not long delay his coming; the word of the Lord was sure, it could not fail. We felt that we had done our duty, we had lived up to our precious faith, we were disappointed but not discouraged; the signs of the times denoted that the end of all things was near at hand, we must watch and hold ourselves in readiness for the coming of the Master at any time. We must wait with hope and trust, not neglecting the assembling of ourselves together for instruction, encouragement and comfort, that our light might shine forth into the darkness of the world.

"Calculation of the time was so simple and plain that even the children could understand it. From the date of the decree of the king of Persia, found in Ezra 7, which was given in 457 before Christ, the 2300 years of Dan. 8:14 must terminate with 1843. Accordingly we looked to the end of this year for the coming of the Lord. We were sadly disappointed when the year entirely passed away and the Saviour had not come.

"It was not at first perceived that if the decree did not go forth at the beginning of the year 457 B. C., the 2300 years would not be completed at the close of 1843. But it was ascertained that the decree was given near the close of the year 457, B.

c., and therefore the prophetic period must reach to the fall of the year 1844. Therefore the vision of time did not tarry, though it had seemed to do so. We learned to rest upon the language of the prophet, 'For the vision is yet for an appointed time, but at the end it shall speak and not lie. Though it tarry, wait for it ; because it will surely come, it will not tarry.'

"God tested and proved his people by the passing of the time in 1843. The mistake made in reckoning the prophetic periods was not at once discovered even by learned men who opposed the views of those who were looking for Christ's coming. These profound scholars declared that Mr. Miller was right in his calculation of the time, though they disputed him in regard to the event that would crown that period. But they, and the waiting people of God, were in a common error on the question of time.

"We fully believe that God, in his wisdom, designed that his people should meet with a disappointment, which was well calculated to reveal hearts and develop the true characters of those who had professed to look for and rejoice in the coming of the Lord. Those who embraced the first angel's message (see Rev. 14 : 6, 7) through fear of the wrath of God's judgments, not because they loved the truth and desired an inheritance in the kingdom of heaven, now appeared in their true light. They were among the first to ridicule the disappointed ones who sincerely longed for and loved the appearing of Jesus. This most searching test of God revealed the true characters of those who would shirk responsibility and stigma by denying their faith in the hour of trial.

"Those who had been disappointed were not left in darkness ; for in searching the prophetic periods with earnest prayers, the error was discovered, and the tracing of the prophetic pencil down through the tarrying time. In the joyful expectation of the coming of Christ, the apparent tarrying of the vision had not been taken into account, and was a sad and unlooked for surprise. Yet this very trial was highly necessary to develop and strengthen the sincere believers in the truth.

"Our hopes now centered on the coming of the Lord in 1844. This was also the time for the message of the second angel, who, flying through the midst of heaven, cried, 'Babylon is fallen, is fallen, that great city!' Many left the churches in obedience to the message of the second angel. Near its close the Midnight Cry was given: 'Behold the bridegroom cometh, go ye out to meet him!' Light was being given concerning this message, in every part of the land, and the cry aroused thousands. It went from city to city, from village to village, and into the remote country regions. It reached the learned and talented, as well as the obscure and humble.

"This was the happiest year of my life. My heart was full of glad expectation; but I felt great pity and anxiety for those who were in discouragement and had no hope in Jesus. We united, as a people, in earnest prayer for true inward experience and the unmistakable evidence of our acceptance with God.

"We needed unbounded patience, for the scoffers were many. We were frequently greeted by scornful allusions to our former disappointment. 'You have not gone up yet; when do you expect to go up?' and similar sarcasms were often vented upon us by our worldly acquaintances, and even by some professed Christians, who accepted the Bible yet failed to learn its great and important truths. Their blinded eyes seemed to see but a vague and distant meaning in the solemn warning, 'God hath appointed a day in the which he will judge the world,' and in the assurance that the saints will be caught up together to meet the Lord in the air.

"The formal churches used every means to prevent the belief in Christ's soon coming from spreading. No liberty was granted in their meetings to those who dared mention a hope of the soon coming of Christ. Professed lovers of Jesus scornfully rejected the tidings that he whom they claimed as their best friend was soon to visit them. They were excited and angered against those who proclaimed the news of his coming and who rejoiced that they should speedily behold him in his glory.

"Every moment seemed precious and of the utmost importance to me. I felt that we were doing work for eternity, and that the careless and uninterested were in the geatest peril. My faith was unclouded, and I appropriated the precious promises of Jesus to myself. He had said to his disciples, 'Ask, and ye shall receive.' I firmly believed that whatever I asked in accordance with the will of God would certainly be granted to me. I sank in humility at the feet of Jesus with my heart in harmony with the divine will.

"I often visited families and engaged in earnest prayer with those who were oppressed by fears and despondency. My faith was so strong that I never doubted for a moment that God would answer my prayers, and without a single exception the blessing and peace of Jesus rested upon us in answer to our humble petitions, and the hearts of the despairing ones were made joyful by light and hope.

"With diligent searching of hearts and humble confessions we came prayerfully up to the time of expectation. Every morning we felt that it was our first business to secure the evidence that our lives were right before God. We realized that if we were not advancing in holiness we were sure to retrograde. Our interest for each other increased;

we prayed much with and for one another. We assembled in the orchards and groves to commune with God and to offer up our petitions to him, feeling more clearly in his presence when surrounded by his natural works. The joys of salvation were more necessary to us than our food and drink. If clouds obscured our minds we dared not rest or sleep till they were swept away by the consciousness of our acceptance with the Lord.

"My health was very poor, my lungs were seriously affected, and my voice failed. The Spirit of God often rested upon me with great power, and my frail body could scarcely endure the weight of glory that flooded my soul. The name of Jesus filled me with rapture, I seemed to breathe in the atmosphere of heaven, and rejoiced in the prospect of soon meeting my Redeemer and living in the light of his countenance forever.

"The waiting people of God approached the hour when they fondly hoped their joys would be complete in the coming of the Saviour. But the time again passed unmarked by the advent of Jesus. Mortality still clung to us, the effects of the curse were all around us. It was hard to take up the vexing cares of life that we thought had been laid down forever. It was a bitter disappointment that fell upon the little flock whose faith had been so strong and whose hope had been so high. But we were surprised that we felt so free in the Lord, and were so strongly sustained by his strength and grace.

"The experience of the former year was, however, repeated to a greater extent. A large class renounced their faith. Some, who had been very confident, were so deeply wounded in their pride that they felt like fleeing from the world. Like Jonah they complained of God and chose death rather than life. Those who had built their faith upon the evidence of others and not upon the Word of God were now as ready to again exchange their views. The hypocrites, who had hoped to deceive the Almighty as well as themselves, with their counterfeit penitence and devotion, now felt relieved from impending danger, and launched into open opposition to the cause they had lately professed to love.

" The weak and the wicked united in declaring that there could be no more fears or expectations now. The time had passed, the Lord had not come, and the world would remain the same for thousands of years. This second great test revealed a mass of worthless drift that had been drawn into the strong current of the Advent faith, and been borne along for a time with the true believers and earnest workers.

" We were disappointed but not disheartened. We resolved to submit patiently to the process of purifying that God deemed needful for us; to refrain from murmuring at the trying ordeal by which the Lord was purging us from the dross and refining us like gold in the furnace. We resolved to wait with patient hope for the Saviour to redeem his tried and faithful ones.

" We are firm in the belief that the preaching of definite time was of God. It was this that led men to search the Bible diligently, discovering truths they had not before perceived. Jonah was sent of God to proclaim in the streets of Nineveh that within forty days the city would be overthrown; but God accepted the humiliation of the Ninevites and extended their period of probation. Yet the message that Jonah brought was sent of God, and Nineveh was tested according to his will. The world looked upon our hope as a delusion and our disappointment as its consequent failure; but though we were mistaken in the event that was to

occur at that period, there was no failure in reality
of the vision that seemed to tarry.

"The words of the Saviour in the parable of the
wicked servant apply very forcibly to those who
ridicule the near coming of the Son of man. But
and if that servant say in his heart, My lord
delayeth his coming; and shall begin to beat their
fellowservants, and to eat and drink with the
drunken; the lord of that servant shall come in a
day when he looketh not for him, and in an hour
when he is not aware of, and shall cut him asunder,
and shall appoint him his portion with the hypocrites.

"We found everywhere the scoffers which Peter
says shall come in the last days, walking after their
own lusts, and saying, Where is the promise of his
coming? For since the fathers fell asleep, all things
continue as they were from the beginning of the cre-
ation. But those who had looked for the coming
of the Lord were not without comfort, they
had obtained valuable knowledge in the searching
of the word. The plan of salvation was plainer
to their understanding. Every day they discovered
new beauties in its sacred pages and a wonderful
harmony running through all, one scripture explaining another and no word used in vain.

"Our disappointment was not so great as that of
the disciples. When the Son of man rode trium-
phantly into Jerusalem they expected him to be
crowned king. The people flocked from all the
region about and cried, 'Hosanna to the Son of
David!' And Jesus, when the priests and elders
besought him to still the multitude, declared that if
they should hold their peace even the stones
would cry out, for prophecy must be fulfilled. Yet
in a few days these very disciples saw their beloved
Master, whom they believed would reign on David's
throne, stretched upon the cruel cross above the

mocking, taunting Pharisees. Their high hopes were drowned in bitter disappointment, and the darkness of death closed about them.

"Yet Christ was true to his promises. Sweet was the consolation he gave his people, rich the reward of the true and faithful.

"Mr. Miller and those who were in union with him supposed that the cleansing of the sanctuary, spoken of in Dan. 8:14, meant the purifying of the earth prior to its becoming the abode of the saints. This was to take place at the advent of Christ, therefore we looked for that event at the end of the 2300 days, or years. But after our disappointment the Scriptures were carefully searched with prayer and earnest thought, and after a period of suspense as to our true position, light poured in upon our darkness; doubt and uncertainty was swept away.

"Instead of the prophecy of Dan. 8:14 refering to the purifying of the earth, it was now plain that it pointed to the closing work of our High Priest in heaven, the finishing of the atonement, and the preparing of the people to abide the day of his coming.

"I might give a more detailed explanation of the passing of the time as considered in the light of prophecy, but it is not in the legitimate province of this work to do so. I merely designed to give as brief an account as possible of these important events with which my life was so closely interwoven that they cannot consistently be omitted from these pages. I would, however, refer those readers who desire further information, to works on this subject which give a full exposition of it. Address REVIEW AND HERALD Battle Creek, Mich., or SIGNS OF THE TIMES, Oakland, Cal.

"I now return to my personal history from which I have necessarily digressed. After the passing of the time in 1844, my health rapidly failed. I could only speak in a whisper or broken tone of voice. One physician stated that my disease was dropsical consumption, he pronounced my right lung decayed and the left one considerably diseased, while the heart was seriously affected. He thought that I could live but a short time, and might die suddenly at any time. It was very difficult for me to breathe when lying down, and at night I was bolstered in almost a sitting posture, and was frequently wakened by coughing and bleeding at the lungs.

"About this time, while visiting a dear sister in Christ, whose heart was knit with mine, the first vision was given to me. There were but five of us, all women, kneeling quietly in the morning at the family altar, when this event transpired. I related this vision to the believers in Portland, who had full confidence that these manifestations were of God. A power attended them that could only emanate from the divine. A solemn sense of eternal interests was constantly upon me. An unspeakable awe filled me, that I, so young and feeble, should be chosen as the instrument by which God would give light to his people. While under the power of the Lord I was so inexpressibly happy, seeming to be surrounded by radiant angels in the glorious courts of heaven, where all is peace and joy, that it was a sad and bitter change to wake up to the unsatisfying realities of mortal life.

"In a second vision, which soon followed the first, I was shown the trials through which I must pass, and that it was my duty to go and relate to others the things that God had revealed to me. It was shown me that my labors would meet with great opposition, and that my heart would be wrought with anguish, but that the grace of God would be sufficient to sustain me through all. The teaching of this vision troubled me exceedingly, for it pointed that my duty was to go out among the people and teach the truth.

"My health was so poor that I was in actual bodily suffering, and, to all appearance, had but a short time to live. I was but seventeen years of age, small and frail, unused to society, and naturally so timid and retiring that it was painful for me to meet strangers. I prayed earnestly for several days and far into the night, that this burden might be removed from me and laid upon some one else more capable of bearing it. But the light of duty never changed, and the words of the angel sounded continually in my ears, 'Make known to others what I have revealed to you.'

"I was unreconciled to going out into the world, its sneers and opposition rose before my mind in formidable array. I had little self-confidence. Hitherto when the Spirit of God had urged me to duty I had risen above myself, forgetting all fear and timidity in the great theme of Jesus' love and the wonderful work he had done for me. The constant assurance that I was fulfilling my duty and obeying the will of the Lord, gave me a confidence that surprised me and was foreign to my nature. At such times I felt willing to do or suffer anything in order to help others into the light and peace of Jesus.

"But it seemed impossible for me to accomplish this work that was presented before me: to attempt it seemed certain failure. The trials attending it appeared more than I could endure. How could I, a child in years, go forth from place to place unfolding to the people the holy truths of God! My heart shrank in terror from the thought. My brother Robert, but two years my senior, could not accompany me, for he was feeble in health and his timidity greater than mine; nothing could have induced him to take such a step. My father had a family to support and could not leave his business ; but he repeatedly assured me that if God had called me to labor in other places, he would not fail to open the way for me. But these words of encouragement were little comfort to my desponding heart; the path before me seemed hedged in with difficulties that I was unable to surmount.

"I really coveted death as a release from the responsibilities that were crowding upon me. At length the sweet peace I had so long enjoyed left me, and my soul was plunged in despair. My prayers all seemed vain, and my faith was gone. Words of comfort, reproof or encouragement were alike to me, for it seemed that no one could understand me but God, and he had forsaken me. The company of believers in Portland were ignorant concerning the exercises of my mind that had brought me into this state of despondency, but they knew that for some reason my mind had become depressed, and they felt that this was sinful on my part, considering the gracious manner in which the Lord had manifested himself to me.

"A great fear possessed me that God had taken his favor from me forever. As I contemplated the light that had formerly blessed my soul, it seemed doubly precious as contrasted with. the darkness that now enveloped me. Meetings were held at my father's house, but my distress of mind was so great that I did not attend them for some time. My burden grew heavier until the agony of my spirit seemed more than I could bear.

"At length I was induced to be present at one of the meetings in my own home. The church made my case a special subject of prayer. Father Pearson, who in my earlier experience had opposed the manifestations of the power of God upon me, now prayed earnestly for me and counseled me to surrender my will to the will of the Lord. Like a tender father he tried to encourage and comfort me, bidding me believe I was not forsaken by the Friend of sinners.

"I felt too weak and despondent to make any special effort for myself on this occasion, but my heart united with the petitions of my friends. I cared little now for the opposition of the world, and felt willing to make every sacrifice if only the favor of God might be restored to me. While prayer was being offered for me, the thick darkness that had encompassed me rolled back and a sudden light came upon me. My strength was taken away. I seemed to be carried to heaven and into the presence of the angels. One of these radiant beings again repeated the words, 'Make known to others what I have revealed to you.'

"One great fear that haunted me was that if I obeyed the call of duty and went out into the open field, declaring myself to be one favored of the Most High with visions and revelations for the people, I might fall a prey to sinful exaltation and be lifted above the station that was right for me to occupy, bring upon myself the displeasure of God, and lose my own soul. I had before me several cases such as I have here described, and my heart had shrunk from the trying ordeal.

"I now entreated that if I must go and relate what the Lord had shown me I should be preserved from undue exaltation. Said the angel, 'Your prayers are heard and shall be answered. If this evil that you dread threatens you, the hand of God will be stretched out to save you, by affliction he will draw you to himself and preserve your humility. Deliver the message faithfully. Endure unto the end and you shall eat the fruit of the tree of life and drink of the water of life.'

"After recovering consciousness of earthly things,

I committed myself to the Lord ready to do his bidding whatever that might be. Providentially the way opened for me to go with my brother-in-law to my sisters in Portland, thirty miles from my home. I there had an opportunity to bear my testimony.

"For three months my throat and lungs had been so diseased that I could talk but little and that in a low and husky tone. On this occasion I stood up in meeting and commenced speaking in a whisper. I continued thus for about five minutes, when the soreness and obstruction left my throat and lungs, my voice became clear and strong, and I spoke with perfect ease and freedom for nearly two hours. When my message was ended my voice was gone until I stood before the people again, when the same singular restoration was repeated. I felt a constant assurance that I was doing the will of God, and saw marked results attending my efforts.

"The way providentially opened for me to go to the eastern part of Maine. Brother Wm. Jordan was going on business to Orington, accompanied by his sister, and I was urged to go with them. I felt somewhat reluctant to do so, but as I had promised the Lord to walk in the path he opened before me, I dared not refuse. At Orington I met Elder James White. He was acquainted with my friends and was himself engaged in the work of salvation.

"The Spirit of God attended the message I bore, hearts were made glad in the truth, and the desponding ones were cheered and encouraged to renew their faith. At Garland a large number collected from different quarters to hear my message. But my heart was very heavy for I had just received a letter from my mother begging me to return home for false reports were being circulated concerning me. This was an unexpected blow. My name had always been free from the shadow of reproach, and my reputation was very dear to me. I also felt grieved that my mother should suffer on my account; her heart was bound up in her children and she was very sensitive in regard to them. If there had been an opportunity I should have set out for home immediately; but this was impossible.

"My sorrow was so great that I felt too depressed to speak that night. My friends urged me to trust in the Lord; and at length the brethren engaged in prayer for me. The blessing of the Lord soon rested upon me and I bore my testimony that evening with great freedom. There seemed to be an angel standing by my side to strengthen me. Shouts of glory and victory went up from that house, and the presence of Jesus was felt in our midst.

"Soon after I went to Exeter, a small village not far from Garland. Here a heavy burden rested upon me from which I could not be free until I related what had been shown me in regard to some fanatical persons who were present. This I did, mentioning that I was soon to return home and had seen that these persons were anxious to visit Portland; but they had no work to do there, and would only injure the cause by their fanaticism. I declared that they were deceived in thinking that they were actuated by the Spirit of God. My testimony was very displeasing to these persons and their sympathizers. It cut directly across their anticipated course and in consequence aroused in them feelings of bitterness and jealousy towards me.

"I now returned to Portland, having traveled and labored for three months bearing the testimony that God had given me, and experiencing his approbation at every step.

"Soon after quite a number of us were assembled at the house of Brother Howland in Topsham.

Sister Frances Howland, a very dear friend of mine, was sick with the rheumatic fever and under the doctor's care. Her hands were so badly swollen that we could not distinguish the joints. As we sat together speaking of her case, Brother Howland was asked if he had faith that his daughter could be healed in answer to prayer. He answered that he would try to believe that she might, and presently declared that he did believe it possible. We all then knelt in earnest prayer to God in her behalf. We claimed the promise, ' Ask and ye shall receive.'

" The blessing of God attended our prayers, and we had the assurance that God was willing to heal the afflicted one. Elder D. cried out, ' Is there a sister here who has the faith to go and take her by the hand and bid her arise in the name of the Lord ? '

" Sister Frances was lying in the chamber above, and before he ceased speaking Sister Curtis was on her way to the stairs. She entered the sick room with the Spirit of God upon her, and taking the invalid by the hand said, ' Sister Frances, in the name of the Lord arise and be whole.' New life shot through the veins of the sick girl, a holy faith took possession of her, and obeying its impulse, she rose from her bed, stood upon her feet, walked the room praising God for her recovery. She was soon dressed and came down into the room where we were assembled, her countenance lighted up with unspeakable joy and gratitude.

" The next morning she took breakfast with us. Soon after, as Elder White was reading from the fifth chapter of James, for family worship, the doctor came into the hall, and, as usual, went up stairs to visit his patient. Not finding her there, he hurried down and with a look of alarm opened the door of the large kitchen where we were all sitting, his patient in our midst. He gazed upon her with astonishment and at length ejaculated, 'So Frances is better.'

"Brother Howland answered, 'The Lord has healed her,' and the reader resumed his chapter where he had been interrupted, 'Is any sick among you? let him call for the elders of the church; and let them pray over him.' The doctor listened with a curious expression of mingled wonder and incredulity upon his face, nodded, and hastily left the room. The same day Sister Frances rode three miles and returned home in the evening; although it was rainy she sustained no injury, and continued to rapidly improve in health. In a few days, at her request she was led down into the water and baptized. And although the weather and the water were very cold, and her disease rheumatic fever, she received no injury, but from that time was free from the disease, and in the enjoyment of her usual health

"At this time Brother Wm. Hyde was very sick with bloody dysentery. His symptoms were alarming, and the physician pronounced his case almost hopeless. We visited him and prayed with him, but he had come under the influence of certain fanatical persons, who were bringing dishonor upon our cause. We wished to remove him from their midst, and petitioned the Lord to give him strength to leave that place. He was strengthened and blessed in answer to our prayers, and rode four miles to the house of Brother Patten. But after arriving there he seemed to be rapidly sinking.

"The fanaticism and errors into which he had fallen through evil influence seemed to hinder the exercise of his faith. He gratefully received the plain testimony borne him, and made humble confession of his fault. Only a few who were strong in faith were permitted to enter the sick room.

The fanatics whose influence over him had been so injurious, and who had persistently followed him to Brother Patten's, were positively forbidden to come into his presence, while we prayed fervently for his restoration to health. I have seldom known such a reaching out to claim the promises of God. The salvation of the Holy Spirit was revealed, and power from on high rested upon our sick brother and upon all present.

"Brother Hyde immediately dressed and walked out of the room praising God, with the light of heaven shining upon his countenance. A farmer's dinner was ready upon the table. Said he, 'If I were well I should partake of this food; and as I believe God has healed me, I shall carry out my faith.' He sat down to dinner with the rest and ate heartily without injury. His recovery was perfect and lasting.

"From Topsham we returned to Portland and found there quite a number of our faith from the East. Among them were the very fanatics to whom I had borne my testimony at Exeter, declaring that it was not their duty to visit Portland. These persons had laid aside reason and judgment; they trusted every impression of their excitable and over-wrought minds. Their demonstrative exercises, while claiming to be under the Spirit of God, were unworthy of their exalted profession. We trembled for the church that was to be subjected to this spirit of fanaticism. My heart ached for God's people. Must they be deceived and led away by this false enthusiasm? I faithfully pronounced the warnings given me of the Lord; but they seemed to have little effect except to make these persons of extreme views jealous of me.

"These false impressions of theirs might have turned me from my duty, had not the Lord previously showed me where to go and what to do.

Although so young and inexperienced, I was preserved from falling into the snare of the enemy, through the mercy of God, in giving me special instructions whom to fear and whom to trust. Had it not been for this protection I now see many times when I might have been led from the path of duty.

"About this time I was shown that it was my duty to visit our people in New Hampshire. My constant and faithful companion at this time was Sister Louisa Foss, the sister of my brother-in-law. She has been dead several years: but I can never forget her kind and sisterly attention to me in my journeyings. We were also accompanied by Elder Files and his wife, who were old and valued friends of my family, Brother Ralph Haskins and Elder White.

"We were cordially received; but there were wrongs existing in that field which burdened me much. We had to meet a spirit of self-righteousness that was very depressing. I had previously been shown the pride and exaltation of certain ones whom we visited, but had not the courage to meet them with my testimony. Had I done so, the Lord would have sustained me in doing my duty.

"While visiting at the house of Elder Morse, the burden did not leave me, but I did not yet feel sufficiently strong to relieve my mind and place the oppressive burden upon those to whom it belonged. During our stay at this house I was very ill. Prayer was offered in my behalf, the Spirit of God rested upon me, and I was taken off in vision. While in this state, some things were shown me concerning the disappointment of 1844, in connection with the case of Elder Morse. He had been a firm and consistent believer that the Lord would come at that time. He was bitterly disappointed when the period passed without bringing the event that was expected. He was perplexed and unable to explain the delay.

"He did not renounce his faith as some did, calling it a fanatical delusion; but he was bewildered, and could not understand the position of God's people on prophetic time. He had been so earnest in declaring that the coming of the Lord was nigh, that when the time passed, he was despondent and did nothing to encourage the disappointed people, who were like sheep without a shepherd, left to be devoured by wolves.

"The case of Jonah was presented before me. God commanded him to go into Nineveh and deliver the message that he gave him. Jonah obeyed, and for the space of three days and nights the solemn cry was heard throughout the streets of the wicked city, 'Yet forty days and Nineveh shall be overthrown!' The city was a marvel of wealth and magnificence; yet the king believed the warning and humbled himself and his people before the Lord in fasting and sackcloth.

"A merciful God accepted their repentance and lengthened the days of their probation. He turned away his fierce anger and awaited the fruits of Nineveh's humiliation. But Jonah dreaded being called a false prophet. He murmured at the compassion of God in sparing the people whom he had warned of destruction by the mouth of his prophet. He could not bear the thought of standing before the people as a deceiver. He overlooked the great mercy of God toward the repentant city, in the personal humiliation of seeing his prophecy unfulfilled.

"Elder Morse was in a similar condition to that of the disappointed prophet. He had proclaimed that the Lord would come in 1844. The time had passed. The check of fear that had partially held the people was removed, and they indulged in derision of those who had lookd in vain for Jesus. Elder Morse felt that he was a bye-word among his neighbors, an object of jest. He could not be reconciled to his position. He did not consider the mercy of God in granting the world a longer time to prepare for his coming; that the warning of his judgment might be heard more widely, and the people tested with greater light. He only thought of the humiliation of God's servants.

" I was shown that although the event so solemnly proclaimed did not occur, as in the case of Jonah, the message was none the less of God, and accomplished the purpose that he designed it should. Subsequent light upon the prophecies revealed the event which did take place, in the High Priest entering the most holy place of the sanctuary in heaven to finish the atonement for the sins of man. Nevertheless God willed for a wise purpose that his servants should proclaim the approaching end of time.

" Instead of being discouraged at his disappointment, as was Jonah, Elder Morse should gather up the rays of precious light that God had given his people and cast aside his selfish sorrow. He should rejoice that the world was granted a reprieve, and be ready to aid in carrying forward the great work yet to be done upon the earth, in bringing sinners to repentance and salvation.

" It has been reported that on the occasion of this vision I declared that in forty days the end of the world would come. No such words were uttered by me. I had no light concerning the end of time. The subject of Nineveh, her lengthened probation, and the consequent grief of Jonah, was presented to me as a parallel case with our own disappointment in 1844. The case of Elder Morse was presented to me as one that represented the condition of a large class of our people at that time.

Their duty was plainly marked; it was to trust in the wisdom and mercy of God and patiently labor as his providence opened the way before them.

"It was difficult to accomplish much good in New Hampshire. We found little spirituality there. Many pronounced their experience in the movement of 1844 a delusion; it was hard to reach this class, for we could not accept the position they ventured to take. A number who were active preachers and exhorters in 1844, now seemed to have lost their moorings, and did not know where we were in prophetic time; they were fast uniting with the spirit of the world.

"Upon one occasion when I was delivering the message that the Lord had given me for the encouragement of his people, I was interrupted several times by a certain minister. He had been very active in preaching definite time; but when the appointed period passed, his faith utterly failed, and he wandered in darkness, doubting and questioning everything. He was ever ready to array himself against any one who claimed more light than he possessed. The Spirit of the Lord rested upon me, as I related what he had shown me. This minister interrupted me several consecutive times; but I continued speaking, when he became very angry and excited, violently opposing what I said. He raised his voice to a high key, and abused me till he was forced to stop from sheer exhaustion. In a few moments he left the house, being seized with hemorrhage of the lungs. He rapidly failed from that time, and died not long after.

"Our testimony was welcomed by some; but many received us suspiciously. Fanaticism and spiritual magnetism seemed to have destroyed the spirit of true godliness. Many appeared unable to discern or appreciate the motives that led me in my feebleness, to travel and bear my testimony to the people. Those who had little interest for the salvation of souls, and whose hearts had turned from the work of preparation, could not comprehend the love of God in my soul that quickened my desire to help those in darkness to the same light that cheered my path. Could they also have seen what had been revealed to me of God's matchless love for men, manifested in giving his only Son to die for them, they would not have doubted my sincerity.

"I believed all that had been shown me in vision. Truth was to me a living reality, and my labor was for eternity. However others might view my work, the weight of its importance was heavy on my soul. In feeble health I was toiling to do good to others unto eternal life. Moments seemed precious to me, delays dangerous.

"In New Hampshire we had to contend with a species of spiritual magnetism, of a similar character with mesmerism. It was our first experience of this kind, and happened thus: Arriving at Claremont, we were told there were two parties of Adventists; one holding fast their former faith, the other denying it. At other places we had visited and labored with this latter class, and found that they were so buried in worldliness, and had so far adopted the popular view in regard to our disappointment that we could not reach nor help them.

"But we were now pleased to learn that there was a little company here who believed that in their past experience they had been led by the providence of God. We were directed to Elders Bennett and Bellings as persons holding similar views with ourselves. We discovered that there was much prejudice against these men, but concluded that they were persecuted for righteousness' sake. We called on them and were kindly received and courteously treated. We soon learned that they professed sanctification, claiming they were above the possibility of sin, being entirely consecrated to God. Their clothing was excellent, and they had an air of ease and comfort.

"Presently a little boy about eight years old entered, literally clad in dirty rags. We were surprised to find that this little specimen of neglect was the son of Elder Bennett. The mother looked exceedingly ashamed and annoyed; but the father, utterly unconcerned, continued talking of his high spiritual attainments without the slightest recognition of his little son. But his sanctification had suddenly lost its charm in my eyes. Wrapped in prayer and meditation, throwing off all the toil and responsibilities of life, this man seemed too spiritually minded to notice the actual wants of his family, or give his children the least fatherly attention. He seemed to forget that the greater our love to God, the stronger should be our love and care for those whom he has given us; that the Saviour never taught idleness and abstract devotion, to the neglect of the duties laying directly in our path.

"This husband and father declared that the heavenly attainment of true holiness carried the mind above all earthly thoughts. Still he sat at the table and ate temporal food; he was not fed by a miracle, and some one must provide that food, although he troubled himself little about that matter, his time was so devoted to spiritual things. Not so his wife, upon whom rested the burden of the family. She toiled unremittingly in every department of household labor to keep up the home. The husband declared that she was not sanctified, but allowed worldly things to draw her mind from religious subjects.

"I thought of our Saviour as a constant worker for the good of others. He said 'My Father work-

eth hitherto, and I work.' The sanctification that
he taught was shown in deeds of kindness and
mercy, and the love that counteth others better
than themselves.

"While at this house a sister of Elder Bennett
requested a private interview with me. She had
much to say concerning entire consecration to God,
and endeavored to draw out my views in regard to
that subject. I felt that I must be guarded in my
expressions. While talking, she held my hand in
hers, and with the other softly stroked my hair. I
felt that angels of God would protect me from the
unholy influence this attractive young lady was
seeking to exercise over me, with her fair speeches,
and gentle caresses. She had much to say in regard
to the spiritual attainments of Elder Bennett, and
his great faith. Her mind seemed very much occupied with him and his experience. I was glad to
be relieved at length from this trying interview.

"These persons, who made such lofty professions,
were calculated to deceive the unwary. They had
much to say of love and charity covering a multitude of sins. I could not unite with their views
and feelings; but felt that they were wielding a
terrible power for evil. I wished to escape from
their presence as soon as possible.

"Elder Bennett, in speaking of faith, said, 'All we
have to do is to believe, and whatever we ask of
God will be given us.'

"Elder White suggested that there were condi-
tions specified. 'If ye abide in me, and my words
abide in you, ye shall ask what ye will, and it shall
be done unto you.' Said he, 'Your theory of faith
must have a foundation; it is as empty as a flour-
barrel with both heads out. True charity never
covers up unrepented and unconfessed sins. She
only drops her mantle over the faults that are confessed and renounced. True charity is a very del-

icate personage, never setting her pure foot outside of Bible truth.' As soon as the views of these people were crossed, they manifested a stubborn, self-righteous spirit that rejected all instruction. Though professing great humiliation they were boastful in their sophistry of sanctification, and resisted all appeals to reason. We felt that all our efforts to convince them of their error were useless, as they took the position they were not learners but teachers."

## CHAPTER VI.

### TRIALS AND VICTORIES.

"WHILE in New Hampshire we visited at the house of Brother Collier, where we proposed to hold a meeting. We supposed this family were in union with those whom we had met at Elder Bennett's, mentioned in the preceding chapter. We asked some questions in reference to these men; but Brother Collier gave us no information. Said he, 'If the Lord sent you here, you will ascertain what spirit governs them, and will solve the mystery for us.'

"Both of these men attended the meeting at Brother C's. While I was earnestly praying for light and the presence of God, they began to groan and cry 'Amen!' apparently throwing their sympathy with my prayer. Immediately my heart was oppressed with a great weight, the words died upon my lips, darkness overshadowed the whole meeting.

"Elder White arose and said, 'I am distressed. The Spirit of the Lord is grieved. I resist this influence in the name of the Lord! O God, rebuke this foul spirit!'

"I was immediately relieved, and rose above the

shadows. But again, while speaking words of encouragement and faith to those present, their groanings and amens chilled me. Once more Elder White rebuked the spirit of darkness, and again the power of the Lord rested upon me, while I spoke to the people. These agents of the evil one were then so bound as to be unable to exert their baneful influence any more that night.

"After the meeting Elder White said to Brother Collier, 'Now I can tell you concerning those two men. They are acting under a Satanic influence, yet attributing all to the Spirit of the Lord.'

"'I believe God sent you to encourage us,' said Brother Collier. 'We call their influence mesmerism. They affect the minds of others in a remarkable way, and have controlled some to their great damage. We seldom hold meetings here, for they intrude their presence, and we can have no union with them. They manifest deep feeling, as you observed to-night, but they crush the very life from our prayers, and leave an influence blacker than Egyptian darkness. I have never seen them tied up before to-night.'

"During family prayer that night the Spirit of the Lord rested upon me, and I was shown many things in vision. These professed ministers were presented to me as doing great injury to the cause of God. While professing sanctification they were transgressing the sacred law. They were corrupt at heart and all those in unison with them were under a Satanic delusion and obeying their own carnal instincts instead of the word of God. These two men exerted a marked and peculiar power over the people, holding their attention and winning their confidence through a baneful mesmeric influence that many who were innocent and unsuspecting attributed to the Spirit of the Lord. Those who followed their teachings were terribly deceived and led into the grossest errors.

"I was shown that the daily lives of these men were in direct contrast with their profession. Under the garb of sanctification they were practicing the worst sins and deceiving God's people. Their deception was all laid open before me, and I saw the fearful account that stood against them in the great book of records, and their terrible guilt in professing entire holiness, while their daily acts were offensive in the sight of God. Some time after this, the characters of these persons were developed before the people and the vision given in reference to them was fully vindicated.

"These men claimed to be sanctified, and that they could not sin. 'Believe in Jesus Christ,' was their cry, 'only believe and this is all that is required of us; only have faith in Jesus.' The words of John came forcibly to my mind: ' If we say that we have no sin, we deceive ourselves, and the truth is not in us.' I was shown that those who triumph, and claim that they are sinless, show in this very boasting that they are far from being without the taint of sin. The more clearly fallen man comprehends the character of Christ, the more distrustful will he be of himself, and the more imperfect will his works appear to him in contrast with those which marked the life of the spotless Redeemer. But those who are at a great distance from Jesus, whose spiritual senses are so clouded by error that they cannot comprehend the divine character of the great Examplar, conceive of him as altogether such an one as themselves, and talk of their own perfection of holiness with a high degree of satisfaction. They really know little of themselves, and less of Christ. They are far from God.

"Those who have experienced the cleansing efficacy of the blood of Christ upon their hearts will be like their Master, pure, peaceable, and lowly of heart. No matter how bold and earnest one may be in his claims of spiritual soundness, and perfection of character, if he lacks Christian grace and humility, the dregs of the disease of sin is in his nature, and, unless it is purged from him, he cannot enter the kingdom of heaven. The truly holy, who walk with God like Enoch of old, will not be boastful of their purity, but be courteous, humble, unselfish, free from spiritual pride and exaltation. Those who know most of God, and keep their eye fixed on the Author and Finisher of their faith will see nothing good or great in themselves. They will feel, after doing all in their power to be faithful, that they are yet unprofitable servants.

"They who claim to be sinless are in the position of the Pharisee, who made boast before God of his alms-giving, thanking God that he was not like the publican. But the poor publican had no piety or goodness to boast of, but, bowed down with grief and shame, sent up from his stricken soul a longing cry for God's mercy. He dared not even cast his sinful eyes toward heaven, but beat his breast and prayed, 'Lord, be merciful to me a sinner.' The sin-pardoning Redeemer tells us that this man went to his house justified rather than the other. Those who are whole need not a physician, and those who consider themselves sinless do not experience that yearning for the wisdom, light and strength of Jesus. They are content with their attainments, and hear not the blessed words, 'Thy sins be forgiven thee.' They feel no necessity for growth in grace. They feel not as Paul did, that he must keep his body under, lest, after preaching to others, he should himself be a cast-away. The apostle declared that he died daily. He was every day battling with temptation, and hiding himself in Christ. Men who boast of their holiness are far from God; they have not Jesus in their hearts, and do not realize their own unworthiness.

" Next morning we started on our way to Springfield. The road was very bad. We had to travel over bare ground, and then through snow drifts that still remained. I fell from the wagon and so injured my side that I rode many miles in great pain, and was not able to walk into the house when we arrived at our destination. That night I could not rest nor sleep, my sufferings were so great. Sister Foss and myself united in pleading with God for his blessing and relief from pain. About midnight the blessing sought rested upon me. Those in the house were awakened by hearing my voice while in vision. This was the first time I had a view of the voice of God in connection with the time of trouble.

" That night it was shown me that reproach was being brought upon the cause of God in Maine, and his children were being disheartened and scattered by a fanatical spirit. Persons in whom we had placed confidence, J. T. and J. H., under a cloak of godliness were casting fear among the trembling, conscientious ones. I saw that it was duty to go and bear our testimony in Maine.

" We soon returned to Portland, and found the brethren in great discouragement and confusion. A meeting was appointed at the house of Sister Hanes that I might have an opportunity to relate what had been shown me. While praying for strength to discharge that painful duty, the Spirit of God rested upon me and I was taken off in vision, and in the presence of J. T., was again shown his ungodly course. Those present said I talked it out before him. After coming out of vision he said I was under a wrong influence. He acknowledged that the part of my testimony which had no reference to his course was right, but that which reproved his conduct was wrong. He said it would take a critical spiritual observer to detect the difference ; that this was the same spirit that had always

followed him to crush him. I was convinced
that J. T. would from that time resist and oppose
my testimony and would deceive souls to their
ruin; my heart was oppressed as I thought of the
cause of God which would be reproached through
the influence of this man. I left the meeting in
anguish of spirit, for I had a message for his wife, a
message of comfort to her sorrowing heart. I found
her weeping at home and grieving as though her
heart would break. I related the vision of reproof
given me for her husband which she confirmed.
We learned from united testimony, that honest,
precious souls had been told by these fanatics that
they were rejected of God. These cruel words
coming from men whom they believed to be men of
God, wholly overthrew some, while others were
much discouraged for a time; but comforting testimonies were given me of God for them which gave
them hope and courage. We also learned that
these officious ones had been making my father's
house their home. J. T. and J. H. who were leaders in this rank fanaticism, followed impressions
and professed to have burdens from God. These
impressions and burdens the Lord had nothing to
do with, for they led to corruption, instead of
purity and holiness.

"My parents were disgusted as they saw reason
and judgment laid aside by them, and protested
against their fanatical course. But finding that they
could not be freed from this company, they closed
their house, and left the city for Poland, where my
two married sisters were living. This did not suit
J. T., and when we arrived at Portland he told me
that my father was a doomed man; that my
mother and sisters might be saved, but my father
would be lost. The reason offered was because my
father would not give him possession of his house
when he left it. We then went to Poland, where

my parents rehearsed their trials, and mentioned incidents which occurred at Portland, all of which confirmed the vision given me in New Hampshire.

"As I returned to Portland, evidences increased of the desolating effects of fanaticism in Maine. The fanatical ones seemed to think that religion consisted in great excitement and noise. They would talk in a manner that would irritate unbelievers, and have an influence to cause them to hate them and the doctrines they taught. Then they would rejoice that they suffered persecution. Unbelievers could see no consistency in their course. The brethren in some places were prevented from assembling for meetings. The innocent suffered with the guilty. I carried a sad and heavy heart much of the time. It seemed so cruel that the cause of Christ should be injured by the course of these injudicious men. They were not only ruining their own souls, but placing a stigma upon the cause not easily removed. And Satan loved to have it so. It suited him well to see the truth handled by unsanctified men; to have it mixed with error, and then altogether trampled in the dust. He looked with triumph upon the confused, scattered state of God's children.

"J. T. labored with some success to turn my friends and even my relatives against me. Why did he do this? Because I had faithfully related that which was shown me respecting his unchristian course. He circulated falsehoods to destroy my influence and to justify himself. My lot seemed hard. Discouragements pressed heavily upon me; and the condition of God's people so filled me with anguish that for two weeks I was prostrated with sickness. My friends thought I could not live; but brethren and sisters who sympathized with me in this affliction met to pray for me. I soon realized that earnest, effectual prayer was being offered in my behalf.

Prayer prevailed. The power of the strong foe was broken, and I was released, and immediately taken off in vision. In this view I saw that human influence should never afflict me again in like manner. If I felt a human influence affecting my testimony, no matter where I might be, I had only to cry to God, and an angel would be sent to my rescue. I already had one guardian angel attending me continually, but when necessary, the Lord would send another to strengthen, and raise me above the power of every earthly influence. Then I saw for the first time the glory of the new earth.

"With Jesus at our head we all descended from the city down to this earth, on a great and mighty mountain, which could not bear Jesus up, and it parted asunder, and there was a vast plain. Then we looked up and saw the great city, with twelve foundations, twelve gates, three on each side, and an angel at each gate. We all cried out, 'The city, the great city, it's coming! it's coming down from God out of heaven!' And it came down and settled on the place where we stood. Then we began to look at the glorious things outside of the city. There I saw most beautiful houses, which were to be inhabited by the saints. These had the appearance of silver, supported by four pillars set with pearls, most glorious to behold, and in each was a golden shelf. I saw many of the saints go into the houses, take off their glittering crowns and lay them on the shelf, then go out into the field by the houses to do something with the beautiful flowers and trees growing spontaneously everywhere. A glorious light shone above their heads, and they were continually offering praises to God.

"I saw a field of tall grass most glorious to behold; it was living green, and had a reflection of silver and gold, as it proudly waved to the glory of King Jesus. We entered a field full of all manner of beasts. The lion, the lamb, the leopard and the wolf were all together in perfect union. We passed through the midst of them, and they followed on peaceably after. Then we entered a wood, not like the dark woods we have here ; but light and beautiful. The branches of the trees waved to and fro as though making obeisance to God. We passed through the woods, for we were on our way to Mount Zion. As we were traveling along, we met a company who were also gazing with delighted wonder at the glories of the place. I noticed red as a border on their garments ; their crowns were brilliant and their robes were pure white. As we greeted them I asked Jesus who they were. He said they were martyrs who had been slain for him. With them was a great number of little ones who also had a hem of red on their garments. These, said Christ are children who were murdered for my sake and for the faith of their parents.

" Mount Zion was just before us, and on the mount was a building which looked to me like a temple. About it were seven other mountains, on which grew roses and lilies. I saw the little ones climb, or if they chose, use their little wings and fly to the top of the mountains, and pluck the never-fading flowers. There were all kinds of trees to beautify the place ; the box, pine, fir, olive, myrtle and pomegranate, and the fig tree, bowed down with the weight of its timely figs, made the place all over glorious. As we were about to enter the temple, Jesus raised his lovely eyes and said, Only the one hundred and forty-four thousand enter this place, and we shouted Alleluia.

"The temple was supported by seven pillars, all of transparent gold, set with pearls most glorious. The things I saw there I can but faintly describe. Oh! that I could talk in the language of Canaan, then could I tell something of the glory of the better world. I saw there tables of stone in which the names of the one hundred and forty-four thousand were engraved in letters of gold. After we beheld the glory of the temple, we went out, and Jesus left us, and went to the city. Soon we heard his lovely voice again, saying, 'Come, my people, you have come out of great tribulation, and have done my will, and suffered for me; come to the marriage supper; for I will gird myself and serve you.' We shouted Alleluia, glory, and entered into the city. And I saw a table of pure silver, it was many miles in length, yet our eyes could extend over it. I saw the fruit of the tree of life, the manna, almonds, figs, pomegranates, grapes, and many other kinds of fruit. I asked Jesus to let me eat of the fruit. He said, Not now. Those who eat of the fruit of this land, go back to earth no more. But in a little while, if faithful, you shall both eat of the fruit of the tree of life, and drink of the water of the fountain. And he said, You must go back to earth again and relate to others what I have revealed to you. Then an angel bore me gently down to this dark world.

"Brother Hyde, who was present during this vision, composed the following verses, which have gone the rounds of the religious papers, and have found a place in several hymn books. Those who have published, read and sung them have little thought that they originated from a vision of a girl, persecuted for her humble testimony.

"We have heard from the bright, the holy land,
　　We have heard, and our hearts are glad;
　For we were a lonely pilgrim band,
　　And weary and worn and sad.
　They tell us the pilgrims have a dwelling there—
　　No longer are homeless ones;
　And we know that the goodly land is fair,
　　Where life's pure river runs.

"They say green fields are waving there,
　　That never a blight shall know;

And the deserts wild are blooming fair,
    And the roses of Sharon grow.
There are lovely birds in the bowers green—
    Their songs are blithe and sweet ;
And their warblings gushing ever new,
    The angel's harpings greet.

" We have heard of the palms, the robes, the crowns,
    And the silvery band in white ;
Of the city fair with pearly gates,
    All radiant with light.
We have heard of the angels there, and saints,
    With their harps of gold, how they sing ;
Of the mount, with the fruitful tree of life,
    Of the leaves that healing bring.

" The King of that country, he is fair,
    He's the joy and the light of the place ;
In his beauty we shall behold him there,
    And bask in his smiling face.
We'll be there, we'll be there in a little while ;
    We'll join the pure and the blest ;
We'll have the palm, the robe, the crown,
    And forever be at rest.

"About this time I was subjected to a severe trial. If the Spirit of God rested upon a brother or sister in meeting, and they glorified God by praising him, some raised the cry of mesmerism. And if it pleased the Lord to give me a vision in meeting, some would say that it was excitement and mesmerism. Grieved and desponding, I often went alone to some retired place to pour out my soul before Him who invites the weary and heavy laden to come and find rest. As my faith claimed the promises, Jesus seemed very near. The sweet light of heaven shone around me, I seemed to be encircled by the arms of Jesus, and there have I been taken off in vision. Then I would relate what God had revealed to me alone, where no earthly influence could affect me, but was grieved and astonished to hear some intimate that those who lived nearest to God were most liable to be deceived by Satan.

"According to this teaching, I could see no safety in the Christian religion, our only safety from delusion was to remain quite a distance from God, in a backslidden state. Oh, thought I, has it come to this, that those who honestly go to God alone to plead his promises, and to claim his salvation, are to be charged with being under the foul influence of mesmerism? Do we ask our kind Father in heaven for bread, only to receive a stone or scorpion? These things wounded my spirit, and wrung my soul with keen anguish, well nigh to despair. Many would have me believe that there was no Holy Spirit, and that all the exercises that holy men of God experienced, were only mesmerism or the deceptions of Satan.

"At this time visions were given me to correct the errors of those who had taken extreme views of some texts of scripture, and refrained wholly from labor, and rejected all those who would not receive their views on this point, and some other things which they held to be religious duties. God revealed these errors to me in vision, and sent me to his erring children to declare them; but many of them wholly rejected the message, and charged me with conforming to the world. On the other hand, the nominal Adventists charged me with fanaticism, and I was falsely, and by some, wickedly, represented as being the leader of the fanaticism I was laboring constantly to arrest by bearing my testimony given me of God. Different times were set for the Lord to come, and were urged upon the brethren. But the Lord showed me that they would pass by, for the time of trouble must come before the coming of Christ, and that every time that was set, and passed, would only weaken the faith of God's people. For this I was charged with being the evil servant that said, 'My Lord delayeth his coming.'

" The above, relative to time-setting, was printed nearly thirty years ago, and the books have been circulated everywhere. Yet some ministers claiming to be well acquainted with me, make the statements that I have set time after time for the Lord to come and those times have passed, therefore my visions are false. These false statements no doubt are received by many as truth. Those who know me and are acquainted with my labors will make no such report in candor. This is the testimony I have borne ever since the passing of the time in 1844: ' Time after time will be set by different ones which will pass by; and the influence of this time-setting will be to destroy the faith of God's people.' If I had seen in vision, and borne my testimony to definite time, I could not have written and published, in the face of this testimony, that all times that should be set would pass, for the time of trouble must come before the coming of Christ. Certainly for the last thirty years, that is, since the publication of this statement, I would not be inclined to set time for Christ to come, and thus place myself under the same condemnation with those whom I was reproving. I had no vision until 1845 which was after the passing of the time of general expectation in 1844. I was then shown that many would be deceived, and would set different times for the Lord to come, and urge them upon their brethren. But the Lord showed me that these times would pass; for the time of trouble must come before the coming of Christ; and that every time thus set and passed, would only weaken the faith of God's people. Has not this testimony which has been before the public nearly thirty years in published form been fulfilled in every particular? The First-day Adventists have set time after time, and notwithstanding the repeated failures, they have gathered courage to set new times.

God has not led them in this. Many of them have denounced the prophetic time, and the fulfillment of marked events in prophecy, because the time passed in 1844, and did not bring the expected event. They rejected the true prophetic time, and the enemy has had power to bring strong delusions upon them that they should believe a lie. I have borne the testimony since the passing of the time in 1844, that there should be no definite time set by which to test God's people. The great test on time was in 1843 and 1844; and all who have set time since these great periods marked in prophecy were deceiving and being deceived.

"Up to the time of my first vision I could not write. My trembling hand was unable to hold my pen steadily. While in vision I was commanded by an angel to write the vision. I obeyed, and wrote readily. My nerves were strengthened, and my hand became steady.

"It was a great cross for me to relate to individuals what had been shown me concerning their wrongs. It caused me great distress to see others troubled or grieved. And when obliged to declare the messages, I often softened them down, and related them as favorably for the individual as I could, and then would go by myself and weep in agony of spirit. I looked upon those who had only their own souls to care for, and thought if I were in their condition I would not murmur. It was hard to relate the plain, cutting testimonies given me of God. I anxiously watched the result, and if the individual reproved, rose up against the reproof, and afterwards opposed the truth, these queries would arise in my mind: Did I deliver the message just as I should? Oh, God! could there not have been some way to save them? And then such distress hung upon my soul, that I often felt death would be a welcome messenger, and the grave a sweet resting place.

" I did not realize that I was unfaithful in thus questioning and doubting, and did not see the danger and sin of such a course, until in vision I was taken into the presence of Jesus. He looked upon me with a frown, and turned his face from me. It is not possible to describe the terror and agony I then felt. I fell upon my face before him, but had no power to utter a word. Oh, how I longed to be covered and hid from that dreadful frown. Then could I realize, in some degree, what the feelings of the lost will be when they cry, ' Mountains and rocks fall on us, and hide us from the face of Him that sitteth on the throne, and from the wrath of the Lamb.'

" Presently an angel bade me rise, and the sight that met my eyes can hardly be described. A company was presented before me whose hair and garments were torn, and whose countenances were the very picture of despair and horror. They came close to me, and took their garments and rubbed them on mine. I looked at my garments, and saw that they were stained with blood. Again I fell like one dead, at the feet of my accompanying angel. I could not plead one excuse, and longed to be away from such a holy place. Again the angel raised me up on my feet, and said, ' This is not your case now, but this scene has passed before you to let you know what your situation must be, if you neglect to declare to others what the Lord has revealed to you. But if you are faithful to the end, you shall eat of the tree of life, and shall drink of the river of the water of life. You will have to suffer much, but the grace of God is sufficient.' I then felt willing to do all that the Lord might require me to do, that I might have his approbation, and not feel his dreadful frown.

" While visiting my sisters in Poland, I was afflicted with sickness. Those present united in

prayer in my behalf, and the disease was rebuked.
Angels seemed to be in the room, and all was light
and glory. I was again taken off in vision, and
shown that I must go about three miles to a meeting, and when there should learn what the Lord
would have me do. We went and found quite a large
gathering of the brethren and sisters. None had
known of any special meeting. J. T. was there.
He had boasted that he understood the art of
mesmerism, and that he could mesmerize me;
that he could prevent me from having a vision, or
relating a vision in his presence. There were many
present who had heard this boast. I arose in the congregation. My visions came up fresh before me, and
I commenced relating them, when I felt a human
influence being exerted against me. I looked at J.
T. He had his hand up to his face, and was looking through his fingers, his eyes intently fixed upon
me. His lips were compressed, and a low groan
now and then escaped him. In a moment I remembered the promise which the Lord had given me,
that if I was in danger of being affected by a
human influence, to ask for another angel, who
would be sent to protect me. I then turned to this
man, and related what the Lord had shown me in
Portland; and, raising my hands to heaven earnestly cried, 'Another angel, Father: another angel.' I knew that my request was granted. I felt
shielded by the strong Spirit of the Lord, and was
borne above every earthly influence, and with freedom finished my testimony. The friends were comforted, and rejoiced in the Lord. J. T. was asked
why he had not stopped my relating the vision.
He answered, 'Oh, some of you would have her
talk.' We returned to my sister's with strong confidence, rejoicing in God.

"Some in Paris, Maine, believed that it was sin
to work. Elder Stevens was cader in this error,

and exerted a strong influence over others. He had been a Methodist preacher and was considered an humble, faithful Christian. He had won the confidence of many by his zeal for the truth, and apparent holy living, which caused some to believe him especially directed of God. The Lord gave me a reproof for him, that he was going contrary to the word of God in abstaining from labor, and urging his errors upon others, denouncing all who did not receive them. He rejected every evidence which the Lord gave to convince him of his error, and was firm to take nothing back in his course. He followed impressions and went weary journeys, walking great distances, where he would only receive abuse, and considered that he was suffering for Christ's sake. His reason and judgment were laid aside.

"The Lord gave me a faithful message for this man, and I was sent long distances to warn the people of God against the errors he was urging upon them. At one time I was shown that I must go to Paris, Maine, for there was a meeting appointed which I must attend. I followed the direction given me, and there learned that Elder S. had notified the brethren that there was to be a great meeting the next day at the house of Brother C., where important matter was to be brought out, and he urged all to attend.

"The next morning we went to the place appointed for meeting. When Elder S. came in and saw us present he seemed troubled. The meeting commenced with prayer. Then as I tried to pray, the blessing of the Lord rested upon me, and I was taken off in vision. Elder Stevens had declared that he would listen to nothing but Bible. I was shown the teachings of the Bible in contrast with his errors. I then saw that the frown of God was upon Elder S.; that he was leading honest, conscien-

tious souls astray. They feared to differ with him. Yet they saw inconsistencies in his faith, and their judgment told them he was wrong. His object in appointing that meeting was to make an effort to strengthen the cords of error with which he had bound these souls.

"I saw that God would work for the salvation of his people; that Elder S. would soon manifest himself, and all the honest would see that it was not a right spirit that actuated him, and that his career would soon close.

"Soon after this the snare was broken, and he could have but little influence over souls. He denounced the visions as being of the devil, and continued to follow his impressions, until Satan seemed to take full control of his mind. His friends at length were obliged to confine him, where he made a rope of some of his bed clothing with which he hung himself. Thus ended his career.

" After returning home to Portland, I was shown that I must go to Portsmouth the next day and bear my testimony there. My sister Sarah traveled with me, and Elder White accompanied us. I had no means with which to pay my fare, but prepared to go, trusting in the Lord to open the way. The first car bell was ringing, as I put on my bonnet. I looked out of the window, and saw a good brother driving very fast up to the gate. His horse was reeking with sweat. He quickly entered the house, and asked, 'Is there any one here who needs means? I was impressed that some one here needed money.' We hastily related that we were going to Portsmouth at the Lord's bidding, and had nothing to go with, but resolved to start, trusting in the providence of God to open the way. The brother handed us money enough to carry us to Portsmouth and back. Said he, 'Take a seat in my wagon, and I will carry you to the depot.' On

the way to the cars he told us that while on the
road to my father's, his horse would come with
great speed the whole distance of twelve miles.
We had just taken our seats in the cars when the
train started. Here the Lord tested and proved us,
and strengthened our faith as we were brought
into a very straight place, and were carried through
by the manifestation of his providence. I had freedom in bearing my testimony in Portsmouth.

"I was then shown that I must visit Massachusetts, and there bear my testimony. When we
reached Boston, I learned that J. T. who opposed
me in Maine, had arrived a few hours before. We
considered that our being sent to Massachusetts just
at that time, was to save God's people from falling
under his influence. It was arranged that I should
go to Roxbury and there relate my message. I found
a large company collected in a private house. I felt
the opposition that existed in the hearts of my
brethren and sisters, yet in the strength of the Lord
delivered my unpopular message. As I was speaking,
a sister who had been opposed to me, arose and interrupted me. She grasped my hand, saying, I said
that the devil sent you, but I can doubt no longer,
and she declared to those present that I was a child
of God, and that he had sent me. All in the meeting were greatly blessed. The power of the Lord
attended the testimony, and every heart was comforted and refreshed. The leader of the meeting
arose, his countenance beaming with joy, and said,
'The same power attends this that attended the
truth in 1844. I do not expect to find another so
green a spot this side of our deliverance.' We next
visited the family of Brother Nichols in Dorchester,
and had a meeting there of the deepest interest.
Again the leader of the meeting at Roxbury testified
that the Lord had abundantly blessed him, and that
he could go forty days on the strength he there re-

ceived. But J. T. was exerting his influence to discourage and close up my way by spreading lying reports concerning me. The leader who had been made so happy as he received my testimony, fell under his influence, and as his mind turned, he became unsettled, then unstable, unhappy, and finally went into the spiritual view of the second advent, and received the grossest errors.

"I next visited Randolph, New Bedford and Carver. The Lord gave me liberty in all these places to bear my testimony, which was generally received, and the desponding and weak were strengthened. I made my home at the house of Brother O. Nichols. They were ever ready with words of encouragement to comfort me when in trial, and their prayers often ascended to heaven in my behalf, until the clouds were dispersed, and the light of heaven again cheered me. Nor did their kindness end here. They were attentive to my wants, and generously supplied me with means to travel. They were reproached because they believed me to be a child of God, chosen to bear a special testimony to his people, and on account of this they were obliged to be in almost constant conflict, for many left no means untried to turn them against me. A faithful record is kept of their acts of love and benevolence. They will not lose their reward. He that seeth in secret is acquainted with every kind and generous act, and will reward them openly.

"In a few weeks I visited Carver, and found that a few had been influenced by the false reports of J. T. But in many instances where the way had been previously closed up for me to bear my testimony, it was now opened, and I had more friends than I had before. There was a young sister in the house where we tarried who was subject to fits, and she was afflicted with this most distressing disease while we were there. All seemed to be alarmed.

Some said, 'Go for the doctor;' others, 'Put on the tea-kettle for hot water.' I felt the spirit of prayer. We prayed to the Lord to deliver the afflicted. In the name and strength of Jesus I put my arms around her, and lifted her up from the bed, and rebuked the power of Satan, and bade her, Go free. She instantly recovered from the fit and praised the Lord with us. We had a solemn, refreshing season in this place. We told them that we had not come to defend character, nor to expose the wickedness of men who were laboring to destroy our influence, but to do our Master's will, and God would take care of the result of the efforts made by designing men. Our hearts were strengthened, and the church encouraged.

"About this time Sister C. S. Minor came from Philadelphia, and we met in Boston. Different errors were affecting the Adventist people. The spiritual view of Christ's coming, that great deception of Satan, was ensnaring many, and we were often obliged, through a sense of duty, to bear a strong testimony against it. Sister M.'s influence was in favor of the idea of a spiritual second advent, which prevailed at that time, although she felt unwilling to acknowledge it. Those who stood clear from this influence were obliged to be decided, and have nothing to do with it, but in the fear of God bear their testimony against it.

"As we were about to journey to New Bedford, a special message came from Sister M. for me to come and relate what the Lord had shown me. Brother Nichols took my sister and myself to the house where quite a number were collected. There were individuals present whom I had been shown were strong fanatics. They dealt in a human or Satanic influence, and called it the Spirit of God. I had not seen them before with my natural eyes, yet their countenances were familiar; for their errors and corrupting influence had been shown me, and I felt forbidden to relate my vision in such a company. There were some present that we loved; but they had been led away in this deception. The leading ones considered this a favorable opportunity to exert their influence over me, and cause me to yield to their views.

"I knew their only object was to mangle the visions, spiritualize away their literal meaning, throw a Satanic influence upon me, and call it the power of God. Sister Minor addressed me, urging me to relate the visions. I respected her, but knew she was deceived in regard to that company. I refused to relate my vision to them. We told them we had no fellowship with their spirit, and in the name of the Lord would resist it. They flattered, but it had no effect. Then they tried to terrify me, commanding me. They said it was my duty to tell them the visions. I faithfully warned those whom I believed to be honest, and begged them to renounce their errors, and leave the company that was leading them astray. I left them, free from their influence and spirit. A portion of that company in a few weeks were left to run into the basest fanaticism.

"Those were troublesome times. If we had not stood firmly then, we should have made shipwreck of our faith. Some said we were stubborn; but we were obliged to set our faces as a flint, and turn not to the right hand nor to the left. Those who believed in the spiritual coming of Christ, were insinuating, like the serpent in the garden. When it suited their purpose they would profess such a mild, meek spirit, that we had to be on our guard, strengthened on every side with Scripture testimony concerning the literal, personal appearing of our Saviour.

"I had often been shown the lovely Jesus, that

he is a *person*. I had asked him if his Father was
a person, and had a form like himself. Said Jesus,
'I am in the express *image* of my Father's person.'
I had often seen that the spiritual view took away
the glory of heaven, and that in many minds the
throne of David, and the lovely person of Jesus
had been burned up by the fire of spiritual interpretation.

"By invitation of Brother and Sister Nichols, my
sister and myself again went to Massachusetts, and
made their house our home. There was in Boston
and vicinity a company of fanatical persons, who
held that it was a sin to labor. Their principal
message was, 'Sell that ye have, and give alms.'
They said they were in the jubilee, the land should
rest, and the poor must be supported without
labor. Sargent, Robbins, and some others, were
leaders. They denounced my visions as being of
the devil, because I had been shown their errors.
They were severe upon all who did not believe
with them. While we were visiting at the house of
Brother S. Nichols, Sargent and Robbins came from
Boston to obtain a favor of Brother Nichols, and
said they had come to have a visit, and tarry over
night with him. Brother Nichols replied that he
was glad they had come, for Sisters Sarah and
Ellen were in the house, and he wished them to
become acquainted with us. They changed their
minds at once, and could not be persuaded to come
into the house. Brother Nichols asked if I could
relate my message in Boston, and if they would
hear, and then judge. 'Yes,' said they, 'Come
into Boston next Sabbath, we would like the privilege of hearing her.'

"We accordingly designed to visit Boston, but in
the evening, at the commencement of the Sabbath,
while engaged in prayer, I was shown in vision
that we must not go into Boston, but in an oppo-

site direction to Randolph; that the Lord had a work for us to do there. We went to Randolph, and found a large room full collected, and among them those who said they would be pleased to hear my message in Boston. As we entered, Robbins and Sargent looked at each other in surprise and began to groan. They had promised to meet me in Boston, but thought they would disappoint us by going to Randolph, and while we w re in Boston, warn the brethren against us. They did not have much freedom. During intermission one of their number remarked that good matter would be brought out in the afternoon. Robbins told my sister that I could not have a vision where he was.

"In the afternoon while we were pleading with God in prayer, the blessing of the Lord rested upon me, and I was taken off in vision. I was again shown the errors of these wicked men and others united with them. I saw that they could not prosper, their errors would confuse and distract; some would be deceived by them; but that truth would triumph in the end, and error be brought down. I was shown that they were not honest, and then I was carried into the future and shown that they would continue to despise the teachings of the Lord, to despise reproof, and that they would be left in total darkness, to resist God's Spirit until their folly should be made manifest to all. A chain of truth was presented to me from the Scriptures, in contrast with their errors. When I came out of vision, candles were burning. I had been in vision nearly four hours.

"As I was unconscious to all that transpired around me while in vision, I will copy from Brother Nichols' description of that meeting.

"'Sister Ellen was taken off in vision with extraordinary manifestations, and continued talking in vision with a clear voice, which could be distinctly understood by all present, until about sundown. The opposition was much exasperated, as well as excited, to hear Sister E. talk in vision, which they declared was of the devil; they exhausted all their influence and bodily strength, to destroy the effect of the vision. They would unite in singing very loud, and then alternately would talk and read from the Bible in a loud voice, in order that she might not be heard, until their strength was exhausted, and their hands would shake so they could not read from the Bible. But amidst all this confusion and noise, Sister Ellen's clear and shrill voice, as she talked in vision, was distinctly heard by all present. The opposition of these men continued as long as they could talk and sing, notwithstanding some of their own friends rebuked them, and requested them to stop. But Robbins said, " You are bowed to an idol; you are worshiping a golden calf."

" ' Mr. Thayer, the owner of the house, was not fully satisfied that her vision was of the devil, as Robbins declared it to be. He wanted it tested in some way. He had heard that visions of Satanic power were arrested by opening the Bible and laying it on the person in vision, and asked Sargent if he would test it in this way, which he declined to do. Then Thayer took a heavy, large quarto family Bible which was lying on the table, and seldom used, opened it, and laid it upon Sister Ellen while in vision, as she was then inclined backward against the wall in the corner of the room. Immediately after the Bible was laid upon her, she arose upon her feet, and walked into the middle of the room, with the Bible open in one hand, and lifted as high as she could reach, and with her eyes steadily looking upward, declared in a solemn manner, " The inspired testimony from God," or words of the same import. While the Bible was thus extended in one hand, and her eyes looking upwards, and not on the Bible, she continued for a long time, to turn over the leaves with her other hand, and place her finger upon certain passages, and correctly repeat their words with a solemn voice. Many present looked at the passages where her finger was pointed, to see if she repeated them correctly, for her eyes at the same time were looking upwards. Some of the passages referred to were judgments against the wicked and blasphemers, and others were admonitions and instructions relative to our present condition.

"'In this state she continued all the afternoon until near sunset, when she came out of vision. When she arose in vision upon her feet, with the heavy open Bible in her hand, and walked the room, uttering the passages of scripture, these men were silenced. For the remainder of the time they were troubled, with many others; but they shut their eyes and braved it out without making any acknowledgment of their feelings.'

"Opposition to our faith increased in Portland. One evening as we were engaged in prayer, the window was broken in just above my head, and the glass came down upon me. I continued praying. One man in his blind rage was cursing and swearing while we continued to plead with God, that when his indignation should come upon the shelterless head of the poor sinner, we might be hid in the secret of his pavilion. The man's voice hushed, and he was seen hastening from the place. He could not endure the sound of prayer, nor the thought of the judgment.

"Some of our wicked, profane neighbors complained that they were disturbed by our frequent praying, and we were several times interrupted by them. One afternoon an officer was sent to visit us, while some of our neighbors raised their windows to hear the result. Father was away at his busi-

ness, and mother stepped to the door. He told her
that complaints had reached him that we disturbed
the peace of the neighborhood by noisy praying,
and sometimes praying in the night, and he was
requested to attend to the matter. Mother
answered that we prayed morning and night, and
sometimes at noon, and should continue to do so;
that Daniel prayed to his God three times a day,
notwithstanding the king's decree.

"He said he had no objection to prayer; if there
was more of it in the neighborhood, it would be
better. 'But,' said he, 'they complain of your
praying in the night.' He was told that if any
of the family were sick, or in distress of mind
in the night, it was our custom to call upon God for
help, and we found relief. He was referred to our
near neighbor who used strong drink. His voice was
often heard cursing and blaspheming God. Why
did not the neighbors send you to him, to still the
disturbance he causes in the neighborhood? He
serves his master, we serve the Lord our God. His
curses and blasphemy seem not to disturb the
neighbors, while the voice of prayer greatly troubles
them. 'Well,' said the officer, 'what shall I tell
them that you will do?' My mother replied,
'Serve God, let the consequences be what they
may.' The officer left, and we had no further
trouble from that quarter.

"A few days after, while our family were quietly
engaged in evening prayer, some young men, imi-
tating the example of their parents, commenced
making a noise around the house. At length they
ran for an officer. He came, and they told him
to listen. Said he, 'Is this what you have called
me out for? That family is doing what every family ought to do. They are making no disturbance;
and if you call me for this purpose again, I will put
you in the lock-up, for disturbing a peaceable fam-

ily while attending to their religious duties. After this we were not molested.

"That summer the neighbors were terrified by frequent thunder and lightning. A number were instantly killed; and if there was an appearance of a thunderstorm, some parents sent their children to our house to invite one of the family to visit them, and stay until the storm was over. The children innocently told the whole story, saying: 'Ma says the lightning will not strike a house where the Advent people are.' One night there was a fearful storm. The heavens presented a continual sheet of lightning. A few rushed from their beds into the street, calling upon God for mercy, saying, 'The judgment day has come.' My brother Robert, who was a devoted Christian, was very happy. He went out of the house and walked to the head of the street, praising the Lord. He said he never prized the hope of the Christian as he did that night, when he saw the terror and insecure position of those who had no hope in Christ.

"While on a visit to New Bedford, Massachusetts in 1846, I became acquainted with Elder Joseph Bates. He had early embraced the Advent faith, and was an active laborer in the cause. I found him to be a true Christian gentleman, courteous and kind. He treated me as tenderly as though I were his own child. The first time he heard me speak, he manifested deep interest. After I had ceased speaking he arose and said, 'I am a doubting Thomas. I do not believe in visions. But if I could believe that the testimony the sister has related to-night was indeed the voice of God to us, I should be the happiest man alive. My heart is deeply moved. I believe the speaker to be sincere, but cannot explain in regard to her being shown the wonderful things she has related to us.'

"Elder Bates was keeping the Sabbath, and urged

its importance. I did not feel its importance, and thought that Elder B. erred in dwelling upon the fourth commandment more than upon the other nine. But the Lord gave me a view of the heavenly sanctuary. The temple of God was opened in heaven, and I was shown the ark of God covered with the mercy-seat. Two angels stood one at either end of the ark, with their wings spread over the mercy-seat, and their faces turned toward it. This my accompanying angel informed me represented all the heavenly host looking with reverential awe toward the law of God which had been written by the finger of God. Jesus raised the cover of the ark, and I beheld the tables of stone on which the ten commandments were written. I was amazed as I saw the fourth commandment in the very center of the ten precepts, with a soft halo of light encircling it. Said the angel, 'It is the only one of the ten which defines the living God who created the heavens and the earth and all things that are therein. When the foundations of the earth were laid, then was also laid the foundation of the Sabbath. I was shown that if the true Sabbath had been kept there would never have been an infidel or an atheist. The observance of the Sabbath would have preserved the world from idolatry. The fourth commandment has been trampled upon, therefore we are called upon to repair the breach in the law and plead for the broken down Sabbath. The man of sin who exalted himself above God, and thought to change times and laws, brought about the change of the Sabbath from the seventh to the first day of the week. In doing this he made a breach in the law of God. Just prior to the great day of God, a message is sent forth to warn the people to come back to their allegiance to the law of God which antichrist has broken down. Attention must be called to the breach in the law by precept and example. I was shown that the third angel proclaiming the commandments of God and the faith of Jesus, represents the people who receive this message and raise the voice of warning to the world, to keep the commandments of God and his law as the apple of the eye, and that in response to this warning many would embrace the Sabbath of the Lord."

## CHAPTER VII.

### MARRIAGE AND UNITED LABORS.

THE subject of this narrative was very feeble. She seemed like one rapidly going to the grave with consumption. Her weight was only eighty pounds. As she traveled on the steamboats and in the cars, she would very frequently faint and remain breathless several minutes. In this condition it was necessary that she should have one or more attendants. Either her sister Sarah, or Sister Foss traveled with her. And as neither her aged father nor feeble brother were suitable persons to travel with one so feeble, and introduce her and her mission to the people, the writer, fully believing that her wonderful experience and work was of God, became satisfied that it was his duty to accompany them. And as our thus traveling subjected us to the reproaches of the enemies of the Lord and his truth, duty seemed very clear that the one who had so important a message to the world should have a legal protector, and that we should unite our labors. Mrs. W. says:

"August 30, 1846, I was married to Elder James White. In a few months we attended a conference in Topsham, Maine. Elder Joseph Bates was present. He did not then fully believe that my visions were of God. It was a meeting of much interest;

but I was suddenly taken ill and fainted. The brethren prayed for me, and I was restored to consciousness. The Spirit of God rested upon us in Brother C.'s humble dwelling, and I was wrapt in a vision of God's glory, and for the first time had a view of other planets. After I came out of vision I related what I had seen. Elder B. then asked if I had studied astronomy. I told him I had no recollection of ever looking into an astronomy. Said he, 'This is of the Lord.' I never saw him as free and happy before. His countenance shone with the light of heaven, and he exhorted the church with power.

"I was shown that I would be much afflicted, and that we would have a trial of our faith on our return to Gorham, where my parents had moved. On our return I was taken very sick, and suffered extremely. My parents, husband and sisters, united in prayer for me; but I suffered on for three weeks. Our neighbors thought I could not live. I often fainted like one dead, but in answer to prayer revived again. My agony was such that I plead with those around me not to pray for me, for I thought their prayers were protracting my sufferings. Brother and Sister Nichols, of Dorchester, Mass., heard of my afflictions, and their son Henry visited us, bringing things for my comfort. My sufferings increased until every breath came with a groan. The neighbors gave me up to die. Many prayers had been offered to God in my behalf, yet it pleased the Lord to try our faith. After others had prayed, Brother Henry commenced praying, and seemed much burdened, and with the power of God resting upon him, rose from his knees, came across the room, and laid his hands upon my head, saying, 'Sister Ellen, Jesus Christ maketh thee whole,' and fell back prostrated by the power of God. I believed that the work was of God, and the pain left me.

My soul was filled with gratitude and peace. The language of my heart was, There is no help for us but in God. We cannot be in peace only as we rest in him and wait for his salvation.

"The next day there was a severe storm, and none of the neighbors came to our house. I was able to be up in the sitting room. And as some saw the windows of my room raised they supposed I was not living. They knew not that the Great Physician had graciously entered the dwelling, rebuked the disease, and set me free. The next day we rode thirty-eight miles to Topsham. Inquiries were made of my father, at what time the funeral would be. Father asked, 'What funeral?' 'Why, the funeral of your daughter.' Father replied, 'She has been healed by the prayer of faith, and is on her way to Topsham.'

"Soon we took passage in the steamboat at Portland for Boston. The boat rolled fearfully, and the waves dashed into the cabin windows. The large chandelier fell to the floor with a crash. The tables were set for breakfast, but the dishes were thrown upon the floor. There was great fear in the ladies' cabin. Many were confessing their sins, and crying to God for mercy. Some were calling upon the Virgin Mary to keep them, while others were making solemn vows to God that if they reached land they would devote their lives to his service. It was a scene of terror and confusion. As the boat rocked, one lady above me fell out of her berth to the floor, crying out at the top of her voice. Another turned to me and asked, 'Are you not terrified? I suppose it is a fact that we may never reach land.' I told her I had made Christ my refuge, and if my work was done, I might as well lie in the bottom of the ocean as in any other place; but if my work was not done, all the waters of the ocean could not drown me. My trust was in God, that he would bring us safe to land if it was for his glory.

"At this time I prized the Christian's hope. This scene brought vividly to my mind the day of the Lord's fierce anger, when the storm of his wrath will come upon the poor sinner. Then there will be bitter cries, tears and confession of sin, and pleading for mercy when it will be too late. 'Because I have called and ye refused, I have stretched out my hand and no man regarded, but ye have set at naught all my counsel, and would none of my reproof, I also will laugh at your calamity, I will mock when your fear cometh.' Through the mercy of God we were all landed safe. But some of the passengers who manifested much fear in the storm made no reference to it only to make light of their fears. The one who had so solemnly promised that if she was preserved to see land she would be a Christian, as she left the boat mockingly cried out, 'Glory to God, I am glad to step on land again.' I asked her to go back a few hours, and remember her vows to God. She turned from me with a sneer.

"I was forcibly reminded of death-bed repentance. Some who serve themselves and Satan all their lives, as sickness subdues them, and a fearful uncertainty is before them, manifest some sorrow for sin, and perhaps say they are willing to die, and their friends make themselves believe that they have been truly converted and fitted for heaven. But if these should recover they would be as rebellious as ever. I am reminded of Prov. 1:27, 28: 'When your fear cometh as desolation, and your destruction cometh as a whirlwind; when distress and anguish cometh upon you, then shall they call upon me, but I will not answer; they shall seek me early, but they shall not find me.'

"August 26, 1847, our eldest son, Henry Nichols White, was born. In October Brother and Sister Howland kindly offered us a part of their dwelling

which we gladly accepted, and commenced housekeeping with borrowed furniture. We were poor
and saw close times. My husband worked at haul-
ing stone on the railroad, which wore the skin on
his fingers through, and the blood started in many
places. We had resolved not to be dependent, but
to support ourselves, and have wherewith to help
others. But we were not prospered. My husband
worked very hard, but could not get what was due
him for his labor. Brother and Sister H. freely
divided with us whenever they could; but they
were in close circumstances. They fully believed
the first and second messages, and had generously
imparted of their substance to forward the work,
until they were dependent on their daily labor.

"My husband left the railroad, and with his axe
went into the woods to chop cord-wood. With
a continual pain in his side he worked from early
morning till dark to earn about fifty cents a day.
He was prevented from sleeping nights by severe
pain. We endeavored to keep up good courage and
trust in the Lord. I did not murmur. In the
morning I felt grateful to God that he had preserved us through another night, and at night I
was thankful that he had kept us through another
day. One day when our provisions were gone,
husband went to his employer to get money or provisions. It was a stormy day, and he walked three
miles and back in the rain, passing through the village of Brunswick, where he had often lectured,
carrying a bag of provisions on his back, tied in different apartments. As he entered the house very
weary my heart sunk within me. My first feelings
were that God had forsaken us. I said to my husband, Have we come to this? Has the Lord left
us? I could not restrain my tears, and wept aloud
for hours until I fainted. Prayer was offered in
my behalf. When I breathed again, I felt the

cheering influence of the Spirit of God. I regretted that I had sunk under discouragement. We desire to follow Christ and be like him; but we sometimes faint beneath trials and remain at a distance from him. Sufferings and trials bring us nigh to Jesus. The furnace consumes the dross and brightens the gold.

"At this time I was shown that the Lord had been trying us for our good, and to prepare us to labor for others; that he had been stirring up our nest, lest we should settle down in ease, and that our work was to labor for souls; that if we had been prospered, home would be so pleasant that we would be unwilling to leave it to travel, and that we had been suffering trial to prepare us for still greater conflicts that we would suffer in our travels. We soon received letters from brethren in different States inviting us to come and visit them; but we had no means to take us out of the State. Our reply was that the way was not open before us. I thought that it would be impossible for me to travel with my child, and that we did not wish to be dependent, and were careful to live within our means. We were resolved to suffer rather than get in debt. I allowed myself and child one pint of milk each day. One morning before my husband went to his work he left me nine cents to buy milk for three mornings. It was quite a study with me whether to buy the milk for myself and child or get an apron for him. I gave up the milk, and purchased the cloth for an apron to cover the bare arms of my child.

"But little Henry was soon taken very sick, and grew worse so fast that we were much alarmed. He lay in a stupid state. His breathing was quick and heavy. We gave remedies with no success. We called in one of experience, who said he was a very sick child, and that his recovery was doubtful.

We had prayed for him, but there was no change. We had made the child an excuse for not traveling and laboring for the good of others, and we feared the Lord was about to remove him. Once more we went before the Lord, praying that he would have compassion upon us, and if the child was to be taken from us in wrath, because we had not been willing to travel, to spare the life of the child, and we would go forth trusting in him wherever he might send us.

"Our petitions were fervent and agonizing. By faith we claimed the promises of God. We believed the child would recover. From that hour he began to amend. Light from heaven was breaking through the clouds, and shining upon us again. Hope revived. Our prayers were graciously answered. Sister Frances Howland offered to take care of the child, while we should lie down for an hour's rest. It was daylight when we awoke. The child had slept sweetly through the night, and was fast recovering.

"While at Topsham we received a letter from Brother Chamberlain of Connecticut, urging us to attend a conference in that State. We decided to go if we could obtain means. Husband settled with his employer, and found that there was ten dollars due him. With five of this I purchased articles of clothing which we much needed, and then patched my husband's overcoat, even piecing the patches, making it difficult to tell the original cloth in the sleeves. We had five dollars left to take us to Dorchester. Our trunk contained nearly everything we possessed on earth. We enjoyed peace of mind and a clear conscience, and this we prized above earthly comforts. We called at the house of Brother Nichols, and as we left, Sister N. handed my husband five dollars, which paid our fare to Middletown, Conn. We were strangers in that city, and had never seen one of the brethren in the State. We had but fifty cents left. My husband did not dare to use that to hire a carriage, so he threw the trunk upon a pile of boards, and we walked on in search of some one of like faith. We soon found Brother C. who took us to his house.

"The conference was held at Rocky Hill, in the large, unfinished chamber of Brother Belden's house. I will here give an extract of a letter from my husband to Brother Howland respecting that meeting. 'April 20, Brother B. sent his wagon to Middletown for us and the scattered brethren in that city. We arrived at this place about four in the afternoon, and in a few minutes, in came Brethren Bates and Gurney. We had a meeting that evening of about fifteen. Friday morning the brethren came in until we numbered about fifty. These were not all fully in the truth. Our meeting that day was very interesting. Brother Bates presented the commandments in a clear light, and their importance was urged home by powerful testimonies. The word had effect to establish those already in the truth, and to awaken those who were not fully decided.'

"Soon after this we were invited to attend a conference at Volney, N. Y., August, 1848. Two years before this I had been shown that we should visit New York at some future time. Brother Edson wrote that the brethren were generally poor, and that he could not promise that they would do much toward defraying our expenses. We had no means to travel with. My husband was suffering with dyspepsia, and his diet was very spare. But the way opened for him to get work in the field to mow hay. It seemed then that we must live by faith. When we arose in the morning we bowed beside our bed, and asked God to give us strength to labor through the day. We would not be satisfied unless we had the assurance that the Lord heard us pray. My husband then went forth to swing the scythe, not in his own strength, but in the strength of the Lord. At night when he came home, we would again plead with God for strength to earn means to spread his truth. We were often greatly blessed. I will give an extract from a letter he wrote to Brother Howland, July 2, 1848.

"'It is rainy to-day so that I do not mow, or I should not write. I mow five days for unbelievers, and Sunday for believers, and rest on the seventh day, therefore I have but very little time to write. God gives me strength to labor hard all day. Praise the Lord! I hope to get few dollars to use in his cause.' Again he wrote to Brother H. July 23: 'We have suffered from labor, fatigue, pain, hunger, cold, and heat, while endeavoring to do our brethren and sisters good, and we hold ourselves ready to suffer more if God requires. I rejoice to-day that ease, pleasure and comfort in this life are a sacrifice on the altar of my faith and hope. If our happiness consists in making others happy we are happy indeed. The true disciple will not live to gratify beloved self, but for Christ, and for the good of his little ones. He is to sacrifice his ease, his pleasure, his comfort, his convenience, his will, and his own selfish wishes for Christ's cause, or never reign with him on his throne.'

"My husband earned forty dollars in the hay field. With a part of this we purchased some clothing, and had means left to take us to Western New York and to return. I had been troubled with a pain in my lungs and a severe cough, but I believed the Lord would give me strength to endure the long journey. We left our little Henry, then ten months old, in Sister Bonfoey's care at Middletown. This was a severe trial to me. I had not been separated from him before for one night. My health was poor, and it was impossible for me to travel and have the care of our child, and we dared not let our affection for the child keep us from the path of duty. Jesus laid down his life to save us. How small is any sacrifice we can make compared with his. We took the steamboat for New York City. On board the boat I coughed almost incessantly. Remarks were made as follows : 'That cough will carry her to the grave-yard. She cannot live long.' Some said that I would not live to see New York. But I knew in whom I believed. He that had bid me go would give me relief when it would best glorify him. One word from him would heal my irritated throat and lungs.

"The next morning we reached New York City, and called upon Brother Moody. We there met Brethren Bates and Gurney. My cough increased. I knew I must have relief soon. I had not had a good night's rest for weeks. I followed the directions given in the fifth chapter of James, and asked the brethren to pray for me. They prayed earnestly, but as often as I attempted to pray I was broken off by severe coughing. I relied upon the promise of God, 'Ask, and ye shall receive.' I tried to tell those present that I believed, but severe coughing prevented my speaking. I retired to rest trusting in the Lord. I commenced coughing as usual, but soon fell asleep, and did not awake till daylight. I then awoke with gratitude in my heart, and the praise of God on my lips. I felt the blessing of Heaven resting upon me. My cough was gone. In the morning my friends noticed a pimple on my face which increased and spread and did not leave me for several years. I was not troubled again with a cough on that journey.

"Our first conference in Western New York was at Volney in Brother Arnold's barn. There were

about thirty-five present, all that could be collected
in that part of the State, but there were hardly two
agreed. Each was strenuous for his views, declaring that they were according to the Bible. All
were anxious for an opportunity to advance their
sentiments and preach to us. They were told that
we had not come so great a distance to hear them,
but we had come to teach them the truth. Brother
Arnold held that the one thousand years of the
twentieth chapter of the Revelation were in the
past, and that the one hundred and forty-four thousand of the Revelation were those raised at Christ's
resurrection. And as we had the emblems of our
dying Lord before us, and were about to commemo-
rate his sufferings, Brother A. arose and said he had
no faith in what we were about to do, that the
Lord's supper was a continuation of the passover to
be observed but once a year.

"These strange differences of opinion rolled a
heavy weight upon me, especially as Brother A.
spoke of the one thousand years being in the past.
I knew that he was in error, and great grief pressed
my spirits, as it seemed to me that God was dishon-
ored, and I fainted under the burden. Brethren
Bates, Chamberlain, Gurney, Edson and my husband,
prayed for me. Some feared I was dying. But
the Lord heard the prayers of his servants, and I
revived. The light of Heaven rested upon me. I
was soon lost to earthly things. My accompanying
angel presented before me some of the errors of
those present, and also the truth in contrast with
their errors, that these discordant views which they
claimed to be according to the Bible were only according to their opinion of the Bible, and that they
must yield their errors and unite upon the third
angel's message. Our meeting ended victoriously.
Truth gained the victory. Those who held the
strange diversity of errors there confessed them

and united upon the third angel's message of present truth, and God greatly blessed them and added many to their numbers.

" From Volney we went to Port Gibson to attend a meeting in Brother Edson's barn. There were those present who loved the truth but were listening to, and cherishing error. But the Lord wrought for us in power before the close of that meeting. I was again shown in vision the importance of the brethren in Western New York laying their differences aside, and uniting upon Bible truth. When we left Brother Edson's we intended to spend the next Sabbath in New York City. But we were too late for the packet, so we took a line boat, designing to change when the next packet came along. And as we saw the packet approaching we commenced making preparations to step aboard ; but the packet did not stop, and we had to spring aboard while the boat was in motion. Brother Bates was holding the money for our fare in his hand, saying to the captain of the boat, ' Here, take your pay.' As he saw the boat moving off he sprang to get aboard, but his foot struck the edge of the boat, and he fell back into the water. He then commenced swimming to the boat, with his pocket-book in one hand and a dollar bill in the other. His hat came off, and in saving it he lost the bill, but held fast his pocket-book. The packet halted for him to get aboard. but his clothes were wet with the dirty water of the canal, and as we were near Centerport, we decided to call at the home of Brother Harris, and put them in order. Our visit proved a benefit to that family. Sister H. had been a sufferer for years with catarrh. She had used snuff for this affliction and said she could not live without it. She suffered much pain in her head. We recommended her to go to the Lord, the Great Physician, who would heal her affliction. She decided to do so, and we had a season of prayer for her. She left the use of snuff entirely. Her difficulties were greatly relieved, and her health from that time was better than it had been for years.

"While at Brother Harris' I had an interview with a sister who wore gold, and yet professed to be looking for Christ's coming. We spoke of the express declarations of Scripture against it. But she referred to where Solomon was commanded to beautify the temple, and to the statement that the streets of the city of God were pure gold. She said that if we could improve our appearance by wearing gold so as to have influence in the world it was right. I replied that we were poor fallen mortals, and instead of decorating these bodies because Solomon's temple was gloriously adorned, we should remember our fallen condition, and that it cost the sufferings and death of the Son of God to redeem us. This should cause in us self-abasement. Jesus is our pattern. If he would lay aside his humiliation and sufferings, and cry, If any man will come after me, let him please himself, and enjoy the world, and he shall be my disciple, the multitude would believe, and follow him. But Jesus will come to us in no other character than the meek, crucified One. If we would be with him in heaven, we must be like him on earth. The world will claim its own, and whoever will overcome, must leave what belongs to it.

"We took the packet on our way to Madison county, N. Y. It left us within twenty-five miles of Brother Abbey's. Here we hired a carriage to complete the journey. It was Friday when we arrived at the house, and it was proposed that one should go to the door and make inquiries, so that if we should be disappointed in receiving a welcome we could return with the driver, and keep the Sabbath at a public house. Sister Abbey came to the door, and my husband introduced himself as one who kept the Sabbath. Said she, 'I am glad to see you. Come in.' He replied, 'There are three more in the carriage with me. I thought if we all came in together, we might frighten you.' 'I am never frightened at Christians,' was the reply. Heartily were we welcomed by Sister A. and her family. She expressed much joy at seeing us, and when Brother Bates was introduced she said, 'Can this be Brother Bates who wrote that hewing book on the Sabbath? And come to see us? I am unworthy to have you come under my roof. But the Lord has sent you to us, for we are all starving for the truth.'

"A child was sent to the field to inform Brother Abbey that four Sabbath-keepers had come. He was in no hurry, however, to make our acquaintance, for he had previously been imposed upon by some who had often visited them, professing to be God's servants, but whose work was to scatter error among the little flock who were trying to hold fast the truth. Brother and Sister A. had warred against them so long that they dreaded to come in contact with them. Brother A. thought we were of the same class. When he came into the house he received us coldly, and then commenced asking a few plain, direct questions, whether we kept the Sabbath and believed the past messages to be of God. When he had become satisfied that we had come with truth, he joyfully welcomed us. This dear family were just coming out from the furnace of affliction. They had been visited with that dreadful scourge, small-pox, and were just recovering.

"While we were there, we had an exhibition of some of the trials they had passed through from those visiting them who made great pretensions, but were Satan's agents to worry and devour. A spiritualizer came in, and talked in such a fanatical and blasphemous manner that it was painful to hear

him.  He at last declared himself to be Jesus
Christ, and that there would be no literal, personal
appearing of Jesus.  My spirit was stirred within
me.  I could hold my peace no longer.  I told him
that my Saviour did not bear such a disgusting appearance as he manifested.  Then I described the
lovely person of Jesus, his glorious appearance in
the clouds of heaven, as he comes to earth the second time ; with what majesty and power he rides
forth upon the cloudy chariot, escorted by all the
angelic host, and with the glory of the Father.  He
grew angry, and raised his umbrella as if to strike
me.  He was vehement.  In great rage he left the
house, showering denunciations upon us as he went.
But a sweet spirit rested upon us.

"Our meetings in that place were cheering to the
few who loved the truth.  We felt to rejoice that
the Lord in his providence had directed us that
way.  We enjoyed the presence of God together,
and were comforted to find a few who had stood
firm all through the scattering time, and held fast the
messages through the mist and fog of spiritualizing
and fanaticism.  This dear family helped us on our
way after a godly sort.  We continued our journey to
Brooklyn, and held meetings in Brother Moody's
house.

"Thursday afternoon, we were to take the boat for
Middletown, Conn.  It was our last opportunity to
get to our appointment at Rocky Hill, unless we
should travel on the Sabbath.  We had a season of
prayer before leaving.  All present did not realize that the boat would not wait for us, and the
season of prayer was made too long for the occasion,
and we had but a few moments to get to the boat.
I took my husband's arm, and we ran about a mile
to reach the boat.  Brethren Gurney and Bates
were on the boat waiting for us.  The captain was
about to withdraw the plank, when Brother Bates

interceded, telling him that he had friends that were detained, and he must wait a few moments. He was prevailed upon to wait five minutes. He then declared he would not wait another moment. Just then we appeared in sight. Brother Bates cried out, 'They are coming! They must go on the boat to-night! You must wait!' We sprung upon the plank as it was being withdrawn, the boat started, and we were on our way.

"At Middletown we met Sister Bonfoey and our little Henry. My child grew feeble. We had used simple herbs, but they had no effect. The neighbors who came in said we could not keep him long, for he would die with consumption. One advised us to use one medicine, another something else. But it did not affect the child favorably. Finally he could take no nourishment. Townsend's Sarsaparilla was recommended as the last resort. We concluded to try it. We could send by a friend to Hartford that day, and must decide in a few moments. I went before the Lord in my room alone, and while praying obtained the evidence that our only source of help was in the Lord. If he did not bless and heal the child, medicine could not save him.

"I there decided to venture the life of the child upon the promises of God. I had a lively sense of his willingness and power to save, and there alone before God exclaimed, 'We will believe, and show to these unbelieving neighbors, who are expecting the death of the child, that there is a God in Israel, whose ear is open to the prayers of his children. We will trust alone in thee.' I felt the power of God to that degree that for a short time I was help-less. My husband opened the door to say to me that the friend was waiting for our decision, and asked, 'Shall we get the Sarsaparilla?' I answered, 'No, tell him we will try the strength of God's promises.'

"The neighbors looked upon me with astonishment. They were confident the child would die. That night we anointed him, and my husband prayed for him, laying his hands upon him in the name of the Lord. He looked up with a smile. A light seemed to rest upon his features, and we there had the evidence that the Lord had answered our prayers. We gave him no more medicine. He gained strength fast, and the next day could stand upon his feet.

"We were anxious to visit the brethren in Maine, but the sickness of our child had hindered us. We immediately made preparations for our journey. The first day we rode to Hartford. The child seemed very weary, and could not sleep. We again sought unto the Lord, who heard our prayer, and the nerves of the child were quieted; and while we were praying he fell into a sweet sleep and rested undisturbed through the night. The next day we traveled about one hundred and forty miles to the good home of Brother Nichols in Dorchester, Mass. The powers of darkness were again permitted to afflict the child. He would cling to my neck, and then with both hands seem to be fighting off something, crying, No, no, and then again cling with all his strength to me. We could not tell what these strange actions meant, but thought he must see something invisible to us. Satan was unwilling to lose his prey. Was he troubling the child? or were his evil angels by their presence exciting his fears, and causing him to act thus? In our season of prayer that morning we rebuked the power of the enemy, and our child was no more afflicted. We took the boat for Portland, but I was very sick, and could not take care of my child. I fainted a number of times. When I grew better my little Henry expressed great joy. He would climb upon the sofa, throw his little arms around my neck, and kiss me many times. He was then one year old.

"Again I was called to deny self for the good of souls. We must sacrifice the company of our little Henry, and go forth to give ourselves unreservedly to the work. My health was poor, and he would necessarily occupy a great share of my time. It was a severe trial, yet I dared not let my child stand in the way of our duty. I believed that the Lord had spared him to us when he was very sick, and that if I should let him hinder me from doing my duty, God would remove him from me. Alone before the Lord, with most painful feelings and many tears, I made the sacrifice, and gave up my only child for another to have a mother's care and feelings. We left him in Brother Howland's family in whom we had the utmost confidence. They were willing to bear burdens to leave us as free as possible to labor in the cause of God. We knew that they could take better care of Henry than we could while journeying with him, and it was for his good that he should have a steady home and good discipline, that his sweet temper be not injured. It was hard parting with my child. His little sad face, as I left him, was before me night and day; yet in the strength of the Lord I put him out of my mind, and sought to do others good. Brother Howland's family had the whole charge of Henry for five years, without any recompense, and provided him all his clothing, except a present I would bring him once a year, as Hannah did Samuel.

"One morning during family prayers at Brother Howland's, I was shown that it was our duty to go to Dartmouth, Mass. Soon after, my husband went to the postoffice and brought a letter from Brother Collins, urging us to come to Dartmouth, for their son was very sick. We immediately went and found that the young man, thirteen years old, had been sick nine weeks with the whooping cough, and was wasted almost to a skeleton. He had fits of coughing which would stop his breath, and his father was obliged to rush to the door with him in his arms that he might regain his breath. The parents thought him to be in consumption, and were greatly distressed that their only son must be taken from them. We felt a spirit of prayer for him, and earnestly besought the Lord to spare his life. We believed that he would get well, although to all appearances there was no possibility of his recovery. It was a powerful season. My husband raised him in his arms, and exclaimed, 'You will not die, but live!' We believed that God would be glorified in his recovery. We left Dartmouth, and were absent about eight days. When we returned, the sick boy came out to meet us. He had gained four pounds in flesh. We found the household rejoicing in God for his wonderful work.

"We then received a request to visit Sister Hastings of New Ipswich, N. H. She was greatly afflicted. We made it a subject of prayer, and obtained evidence that the Lord would go with us. We tarried on our way with Brother Nichols' family. They informed us of the affliction of Sister Temple of Boston. There was a sore upon her arm which caused her much suffering. It had extended over the bend of the elbow. She had suffered such agony that she had resorted to human means until she saw it was of no use. The last effort drove the disease to her lungs, and unless she should obtain immediate help, the disease would end in consumption. She left word for us to come and pray for her. We went with trembling, having tried in vain to get the assurance that God would work for us. We went into the sick room relying upon the naked promises of God which seemed so firm that we felt that we could venture out upon them. Her arm was in such a condition that we could not touch it, and were obliged to pour the oil upon it. Then we united in prayer, and claimed the promises of God. The pain and soreness left the arm while we were praying, and we left her recovering.

"We found Brother Hastings' family in deep affliction. Our dear Sister H. met us with tears, exclaiming, 'The Lord has sent you to us in time of great need.' She had an infant about eight weeks old which cried continually when awake. This, added to her wretched state of health, was fast wearing away her strength. We prayed earnestly to God for the mother, following the direction given in James, and we had the assurance that our prayers were heard. Jesus was in our midst to break the power of Satan, and release the captive. But we felt sure that the mother could not gain much strength until the cries of the child should cease. We anointed the child and prayed over it, believing that the Lord would give both mother and child peace and rest. It was done. The cries of the child ceased, and we left them doing well. The gratitude of the mother could not be expressed. Our interview with that dear family was precious. Our hearts were knit together; especially was the heart of Sister Hastings knit with mine as were those of David and Jonathan. Our union was not marred while she lived.

"In about one year from that time while in Oswego, N. Y., a sad letter reached us, giving information of Sister H.'s sudden death. This news fell upon me with crushing weight. It was difficult to be reconciled to it. She was capable of doing much good in the cause of God. She was a pillar in the cause of truth, and it seemed indeed to us like a mysterious providence that she should be laid away from our sight in the grave, and her talents be hid. But God works in a mysterious way his

wonders to perform. Her death was indeed to save
her children. Her earnest prayers had gone up to
God, to save them in any way that he should choose.
The mother was snatched away, and then her faithful admonitions, her earnest prayers and many
tears were regarded, and had an influence upon the
smitten flock. We visited the place after the
mother's death, in June, 1850, and found the father
bereaved and lonely, but living for God, and bearing well his double burden. He was comforted in
his great grief by seeing his children turning unto
the Lord, and earnestly seeking a preparation to
meet their dear mother when the Life-giver shall
break the fetters of the tomb, release the captive,
and bring her forth immortal. My husband baptized the four eldest children. Since that visit the
eldest daughter has died in hope, and rests in the
silent grave.

"On our return from New Ipswich to Boston,
about eight days after we had prayed for Sister
Temple, we found her at the wash-tub in the enjoyment of good health.

"Again we visited Connecticut, and in June, 1849,
Sister Clarissa M. Bonfoey proposed to live with us.
Her parents had recently died, and a division of
furniture at the homestead, had given her everything necessary for a small family to commence
housekeeping. She cheerfully gave us the use of
these things, and did our work. We occupied a part
of Brother B.'s house at Rocky Hill. Sister Bonfoey
was a precious child of God. She possessed a cheerful and happy disposition, never gloomy, yet not
light and trifling.

"My husband attended meetings in New
Hampshire and Maine, and during his absence I
was much troubled, fearing he might take the cholera which was then prevailing. But one night I
dreamed that many were dying with the cholera.

My husband proposed that we should walk out, and in our walk I noticed that his eyes looked bloodshot, his countenance flushed, and his lips pale. I told him I feared that he would be an easy subject for the cholera. Said he, 'Walk on a little further and I will show you a sure remedy for the cholera.' As we walked on we came to a bridge over a stream of water, when he abruptly left me and plunged out of sight into the water. I was frightened; but he soon arose, holding in his hand a glass of sparkling water. He drank it, saying, 'This water cures all manner of diseases.' He plunged in again out of sight, brought up another glass of clear water, and as he held it up, repeated the same words. I felt sad that he did not offer me some of the water. Said he, 'There is a secret spring in the bottom of this river which cures all manner of diseases, and all who obtain it must plunge at a venture. No one can obtain it for another. Each must plunge for it himself.' As he drank the glass of water, I looked at his countenance. His complexion was fair and natural. He seemed to possess health and vigor. When I awoke, all my fears were dispelled, and I trusted my husband to the care of a merciful God, fully believing that he would return him to me in safety.

"On his return, my husband was impressed that it was his duty to write and publish the present truth. He was greatly encouraged and blessed as he decided thus to do. But again he would be in doubt and perplexity as he was penniless. There were those who had means, but they chose to keep it. He at length gave up in discouragement, and decided to look for a field of grass to mow. As he left the house, a burden was rolled upon me, and I fainted. Prayer was offered for me, and I was blessed, and taken off in vision. I saw that the Lord had blessed and strengthened my husband to labor in the field one year before; that he had made a right

disposition of the means he there earned; and that
he would have a hundred fold in this life, and, if
faithful, a rich reward in the kingdom of God; but
that the Lord would not now give him strength to
labor in the field, for he had another work for him;
that if he ventured into the field he would be cut
down by sickness; but that he must write, write,
write, and walk out by faith. He immediately
commenced to write, and when he came to some
difficult passage we would call upon the Lord to
give us the true meaning of his word.

"My husband then began, to publish a small
sheet at Middletown, eight miles from Rocky Hill,
and often walked this distance and back again,
although he was then lame. When he brought the
first number from the printing-office, we all bowed
around it, asking the Lord, with humble hearts and
many tears, to let his blessing rest upon the feeble
efforts of his servant. He then directed the paper
to all he thought would read it, and carried it to
the postoffice in a carpet-bag. Every number was
taken from Middletown to Rocky Hill, and always
before preparing them for the postoffice, they were
spread before the Lord, and earnest prayers mingled with tears, were offered to God that his blessing would attend the silent messengers. Very soon
letters came bringing means to publish the paper,
and the good news of many souls embracing the
truth.

"July 28, 1849, my second child, James Edson
White, was born. When he was six weeks old we
went to Maine. September 14, a meeting was
appointed at Paris. Those who observed the Sabbath of the Lord had not had a meeting for one
year and a half. Brethren Bates, Chamberlain and
Ralph were present, also brethren and sisters from
Topsham. One F. T. Howland, a notable fanatic,
was present. He had long troubled God's children

with his errors and harsh spirit. Honest souls whom the Lord loved, but who had long been in error, were at the meeting. While engaged in prayer the Spirit of the Lord rested upon Brother S. Howland. His face was white, and a light seemed to rest upon it. He went towards F. T. Howland, and in the name of the Lord bid him leave the assembly of the saints. Said he, ' You have torn the hearts of God's children and made them bleed. Leave the house, or God will smite you.' That rebellious spirit, never before known to fear or to yield, sprang for his hat and in terror left the house. The power of God descended something as it did on the day of Pentecost, and five or six who had been deceived and led into error and fanaticism, fell prostrate to the floor. Parents confessed to their children, and children to their parents, and to one another. Brother J. N. Andrews with deep feeling exclaimed, ' I would exchange a thousand errors for one truth.' Such a scene of confessing and pleading with God for forgiveness we have seldom witnessed. That meeting was the beginning of better days to the children of God in Paris, to them a green spot in the desert. The Lord was bringing out Brother Andrews to fit him for future usefulness, and was giving him an experience that would be of great value to him in his future labors. He was teaching him that he should not be influenced by the experience of others, but decide for himself concerning the work of God.

"At that meeting I learned that my mother had stepped upon a rusty nail which had passed through her foot. She had tried every remedy, but nothing removed the inflammation, or relieved the pain. We went immediately to Gorham, and found her foot dreadfully swollen. The neighbors had proposed every remedy they could think of, but they accomplished nothing. Mother was threatened with lockjaw. The next morning we united in prayer for her. I believed that God would restore her to perfect soundness. She was unable to kneel. With a deep sense of my unworthiness, I knelt at my mother's feet and besought the Lord to touch her with his healing power. We all believed that the Lord heard prayer. With the Spirit of the Lord resting upon me, I bid her in the name of the Lord rise up and walk. His power was in the room, and shouts of praise went up to God. Mother arose and walked the room, declaring that the work was done, that the soreness was gone, and that she was entirely relieved from pain. That day she rode thirty-eight miles to Topsham to attend a conference there, and had no more trouble with her foot.

"Some present at the meeting were anxious to have us visit New York State again; but feeble health sunk my spirits, and it was a time of despondency with me. I told them that I dared not venture unless the Lord should strengthen me for the task. They prayed for me, and the clouds were scattered, yet I did not obtain that strength I so much desired. I resolved to walk out by faith and go, clinging to the promise, 'My grace is sufficient for you.' God had been my helper hitherto, and why should I now doubt? The language of my heart was, 'I will still trust in the strong arm of Jehovah. If like Paul I am to be troubled with a thorn in the flesh, I will not murmur. It will cause me to feel my dependence upon God, and to walk tremblingly before him.' On that journey our faith was tried, but we obtained the victory. My strength increased, and I could rejoice in God. All the strength the Lord had given me was needed to labor in New York. Many had united upon the truth since our first visit, but there was much to be done for them. I will here give an extract of a letter written by my husband, from Volney, N. Y., November 13, 1849:—

"'DEAR BROTHER HOWLAND: November 3, we attended a conference at Oswego. There was a large gathering. The increase of Sabbath-keepers since last spring in this region has been more than one-half. But there are trials here of a serious nature. We find work enough. Here are some fiery spirits who have much zeal and but little judgment, whose principal message is, 'Sell that ye have and give alms.' They press the truth in such a manner and spirit as to disgust, try, and harden those who have hundreds of dollars they might use in the cause of God. Thus a sore dividing spirit exists. The Lord has revealed these things to my wife, and she has borne her testimony that both parties were wrong. This testimony I think is received. Tobacco and snuff are being cleared from the camp with very few exceptions. Selling is a subject that should be treated in a cautious manner. A great responsibility rests upon God's stewards. With their money they may ruin some of us, and by withholding it from those whom God has called to feed the flock, souls may sink, and starve, and die. The Lord will straighten out all who will be straightened. His work will move on.'

"Our labors at this time were difficult. Some of the poor seemed to be envious of the rich, and it needed much wisdom to reprove the errors of the poor without strengthening the hands of the rich. If we reproved the selfishness of the rich, the poorer class would respond, 'Amen.' We presented before both classes the responsibility resting upon the wealthy to make a right use of that which God had lent them, and held up before them the suffering cause of God which was the true object of their liberalities. I was also shown that it was not the duty of the wealthy to help those who had health and could help themselves, that some were in very poor circumstances who need not be thus situated.

They were not diligent in business. They lacked economy and good management, and it was their duty to reform. Instead of receiving help from their brethren, they should carefully husband their time and provide for their own families and have something with which to help the cause of God. They were as accountable to God for the strength which he had given them as the rich man is for his property.

"Some of the poor were zealous to attend every conference, taking their whole families with them, consuming a number of days to get to the place of meeting, and then burdening those who provided for the meeting, with their unruly children. These persons were no help in the meetings and they manifested no fruits of receiving any benefit themselves. They seemed to possess a careless, loafing spirit which was an injury to the cause. In this way precious time for which they were accountable was wasted, and in cold weather they must suffer unless helped by their brethren. These things stood in the way of those who had means, as they were constantly vexed with the course of these individuals. And as we labored for the good of the wealthy, these stood directly in our way. It was difficult to impress both classes with a sense of their duty. Yet after much labor and many trials, there seemed to be a reform, and there was more order in the church. The Lord blessed our labors, and often revealed himself to us in remarkable power.

"We designed going to Lorraine to hold a meeting, but our little Edson was taken very sick. We carried this matter before the Lord, and felt it to be our duty to go, trusting in him. We prayed for our sick child, and then I took him in my arms in winter, and rode thirty miles, keeping my heart uplifted to God for his recovery. When we arrived the child was in a perspiration, and was better.

But again our faith was tried. In the course of the meeting the fever returned upon the child. He was suffering with inflammation upon the brain. All night we watched over him, earnestly praying that the disease might be effectually rebuked. We tried to exercise faith, regardless of appearance. Our petitions were heard, and the child recovered. It did seem to us that an angel of God touched him. Our meeting in Lorraine was greatly blessed of God. The hearts of the scattered ones were comforted, and some acknowledged with tears that they had been fed with truth. We returned to Volney free in the Lord.

"We then decided that it was our duty to labor in the State of New York. My husband felt a burden upon him to write and publish. We rented a house in Oswego, borrowed furniture from our brethren, and commenced housekeeping. There my husband wrote, published, and preached. It was necessary for him to keep the armor on every moment, for he often had to contend with professed Adventists who were advocating error, preaching definite time, and were seeking to prejudice all they could against our faith. We took the position that the time they set would pass by. I was shown that the honestly deceived would then see the deception of some whom they then had confidence in, who were zealously preaching time, and they would be led to search for truth.

"We visited Camden about forty miles from Oswego. Previous to going I was shown the little company who professed the truth there, and among them, saw a woman who professed much piety, but was a hypocrite, and was deceiving the people of God. Sabbath morning quite a number collected, but the deceitful woman was not present. I inquired of a sister if this was all their company. She said it was. This woman lived four miles from the place, and the sister did not think of her. Soon she entered, and I immediately recognized her as the woman whose real character the Lord had shown me. In the course of the meeting she talked quite lengthily, and said that she had perfect love, and enjoyed holiness of heart, that she did not have trials and temptations, but enjoyed perfect peace and submission to the will of God. The brethren and sisters were strangers to me, and they seemed to have confidence in her, and I feared that they would not receive my testimony if I should state what had been shown me in regard to her. I inquired concerning this person, and was informed that she appeared to be the most zealous one among them. I left the meeting with sad feelings, and returned to Brother Preston's. That night I dreamed that a secret closet was opened to me, filled with rubbish, and I was told that it was my work to clear it out. By the light of a lamp I removed the rubbish, and told those with me that the room could be supplied with more valuable things.

"Sunday morning we met with the brethren, and my husband arose to preach on the parable of the ten virgins. He had no freedom in speaking, and proposed that we have a season of prayer. We bowed before the Lord and engaged in earnest prayer. The dark cloud was lifted, and I was taken off in vision, and again shown the case of this woman. She was represented to me as being in perfect darkness. Jesus frowned upon her and her husband. That withering frown caused me to tremble. I saw that she had acted the hypocrite, professing holiness while her heart was full of corruption. After I came out of vision I related with trembling, yet with faithfulness, what I had seen. I was severely tried, and anxious for the people of God. Would those present believe the testimony? The woman put on a calm appearance

and said, 'I am glad the Lord knows my heart.
He knows that I love him.' Then her husband
rose in anger, and laying his hand on the Bible
said, 'The Bible is all we want, I shall not give up
the Bible for visions.' His wife affected to check
him, saying, 'Don't, husband, dear, don't talk ; the
Lord knows me, and will take care of it all.' Then
she vindicated herself, saying, 'If my heart could
only be opened that you might see it.' I knew the
minds of some were unsettled, whether to believe
what the Lord had shown me, or let her appearance
weigh against the testimony borne. Her appearance was perfectly calculated to gain their sympathy. But I had discharged a painful duty and God
would take care of the result. At the close of the
meeting she stated that she had no hard feelings
against me, and that she should pray for me, and
if I got to heaven I would see her there. We returned with Brother P.'s family, and that night the
Lord met with us. I believed that the Lord would
show his people the truth, and justify the vision.
The neighbors said that I had abused the poor
woman.

"Not long after this, terrible fear seized this
woman. A horror rested upon her, and she began
to confess. She even went from house to house
among her unbelieving neighbors, and confessed
that the man she had been living with for years
was not her husband, that she ran away from
England and left a kind husband and one child.
She also confessed that she had professed to understand medicine, and had taken oath that the bottles
of mixture she made cost her one dollar when they
cost her only twelve cents, that she had taken
thirty dollars from a poor man by taking a false
oath. Many such wicked acts she confessed, and
her repentance seemed to be genuine. In some
cases she restored where she had taken away

wrongfully. In one instance she started on foot forty miles to confess. We could see the hand of God in this matter. He gave her no rest day nor night, until she confessed her sins publicly. This fully justified in the minds of the brethren and those also of their neighbors who sympathized with her for a time what God had shown me of her vileness under the garb of sanctification.

"While in Oswego, N. Y., we decided to visit Vermont and Maine. I left my little Edson, then nine months old, in the care of Sister Bonfoey while we went on our way to do the will of God. We labored very hard, suffering many privations to accomplish but little. We found the brethren and sisters in a scattered and confused state. Almost every one was affected by some error, and all seemed zealous for their own opinions. We often suffered intense anguish of mind in meeting with so few who were ready to listen to Bible truth, while they eagerly cherished error and fanaticism. We were obliged to make a tedious route of forty miles by stage to get to Sutton, the place of our appointment. I was sick, and rode in much pain. My husband feared every moment that I would faint, and often whispered to me to have faith in God. Our silent yet earnest prayers were going up to heaven for strength to endure. Every ten miles the horses were changed. This was a great relief to me as I could step into a hotel a few minutes and rest by lying down. The Lord heard us pray, and strengthened me to finish the journey.

"The first night after reaching the place of meeting, despondency pressed upon me. I tried to overcome it, but it seemed impossible to control my thoughts. My little ones burdened my mind. We had left one in the State of Maine two years and eight months old, and another babe in New York, nine months old. We had just performed a tedious journey in great suffering, and I thought of those who were enjoying the society of their children in their own quiet homes. I reviewed our past life, calling to mind expressions which had been made by a sister only a few days before, who thought it must be very pleasant to be riding through the country without anything to trouble me. It was just such a life as she should delight in. At that very time my heart was yearning for my children, especially my babe, in New York, and I had just come from my sleeping room where I had been battling with my feelings, and with many tears had besought the Lord for strength to subdue all murmuring, and that I might cheerfully deny myself for Jesus' sake. I thought that perhaps all regarded my journeyings in this light, and had not the least idea of the self-denial and sacrifice required to travel from place to place, meeting cold hearts, distant looks and severe speeches, separated from those who are closely entwined around my heart.

"While riding in the cars to that meeting I was unable to sit up. My husband made a bed on the seat, and I laid down with aching head and heart. The burden borne for others I dreaded above everything else. These things came before me the following night, and I found myself saying, 'It won't pay! So much labor to accomplish so little.' In this state of mind I fell asleep and dreamed that a tall angel stood by my side, and asked me why I was sad. I related to him the thoughts that had troubled me, and said, 'I can do so little good, why may we not be with our children, and enjoy their society?' Said he, 'You have given to the Lord two beautiful flowers, the fragrance of which is as sweet incense before him, and is more precious in his sight than gold or silver, for it is a heart gift. It draws upon every fiber of the heart as no other sacrifice can. You should not look upon present appearances, but keep the eye single to your duty, single to God's glory, and follow in his opening providence, and the path shall brighten before you. Every self-denial, every sacrifice is faithfully recorded, and will bring its reward.'

"The blessing of the Lord attended our conference at Sutton, and after the meeting closed we went on our way to Canada East. My throat troubled me much, and I could not speak aloud, or even whisper, without suffering. We rode praying as we went for strength to endure the journey. About every ten miles we were obliged to stop that I might rest. My husband braided the tall grass and tied the horse to it, giving him a chance to feed, then spread my cloak upon the grass for a resting place for me. Thus we continued until we arrived at Melbourne. We expected to meet opposition there. Many who professed to believe in the near coming of our Saviour fought against the law of God. We felt the need of strength from God. I could not speak aloud, and often inquired, For what have I come this long distance? Again we tried to exercise faith, knowing that our only help was in God. We prayed that the Lord would manifest himself unto us. My earnest prayer was that the disease might leave my throat, and that my voice might be restored. I had the evidence that the hand of God there touched me. The difficulty was instantly removed, and my voice was clear. The candle of the Lord shone about us during that meeting, and we enjoyed great freedom. The children of God were greatly strengthened and encouraged.

"We then returned to Vermont, and again my voice failed me, yet we met our appointment at Johnson, and found quite a number of brethren and sisters collected. Some were in a perplexed and nine in condition. Certain fanatics had imposed upon them, and cast a fear over them which held them in bondage. The conscientious were so fearful of offending God, and had so little confidence in themselves, that they dared not rise and assert their liberty. The night after we arrived I fainted a number of times through weakness. But in answer to prayer I was revived, and strength was given me of the Lord to go through the meeting. We knew that on the next day we should have to battle with the powers of darkness, and that Satan would muster his forces. In the morning the two individuals, Libbey and Bailey, who had so long deceived and oppressed God's children came into the meeting with two women dressed in white linen to represent the righteousness of the saints, and with their long, black hair, hanging loose about their shoulders. I had a message for them, and while I was speaking L. kept his black eyes fastened upon me, but I had no fear of his influence. Strength was given me from Heaven to rise above their satanic power. The children of God who had been held in bondage began to breathe free, and rejoice in the Lord.

"As our meeting progressed, these fanatics sought to rise and speak, but they could not find opportunity. But as prayer was being offered at the close of the meeting, B. came to the door and commenced speaking. The door was closed upon him. He opened it and again began to speak. The power of God fell upon my husband, and the color left his face, as he arose from his knees, and laid his hand upon B., exclaiming, 'The Lord does not want your testimony here. The Lord does not want you here to distract and crush his people!' The power of God filled the room, and B. commenced to fall backward against the house. The power of God in the house was painful to that fanatical party. B. looked terrified. He staggered and came near falling to the floor. The place was awful on account of the presence of the Lord. All that company of darkness left the place, and the sweet Spirit of the Lord rested upon his dear, tried children. The cause of God in Vermont had been cursed by fanatical spirits, but at this meeting these wicked persons received a check from which they never recovered.

"From Vermont we returned to the State of New York, very anxious to see our child whom we had left. We had been from him five weeks, and as we met him and he clasped his little arms about my neck and laid his head upon my shoulder, I saw that a great change had taken place in him. He was very feeble. My feelings cannot be described. It was difficult to suppress murmuring feelings. These thoughts would arise, I left him in the hands of God to go and do his work, and now I find him in this condition. My agonized feelings found relief in tears. Then I became more calm and reconciled to the will of God. We tried to look at the child's case in as favorable a light as possible, and were comforted with these words, ' The Lord doth not afflict willingly, nor grieve the children of men.' We felt that our only hope was in God, and prayed for the child and obtained signal answers to our prayers. The Spirit of the Lord rested upon us, and his symptoms became more favorable, so that we journeyed with him to Oswego to attend a conference there.

"From Oswego we went to Centerport in company with Brother and Sister Edson, and made it our home at Brother Harris', where we published a monthly magazine, called the *Advent Review*. My child grew worse, and three times a day we had special seasons of prayer for him. Sometimes he would be blessed, and the progress of disease would be stayed, then our faith would be severely tried as

his symptoms became alarming. At one time we
left him to go about two miles to Port Byron.
Brother R. accompanied us intending to take the
packet to Port Gibson. When we returned Sister
H. met us at the door much agitated, saying, 'Your
babe is struck with death!' We hastened to the
child who lay unconscious. His little arms were
purple. The death dampness seemed to be on his
brow, and his eyes were dim. Oh, the anguish of
my heart then! I could give up my child. I did
not idolize him, but I knew that our enemies were
ready to triumph over us and say, 'Where is their
God!' I then said to my husband, There is but
one thing more that we can do, that is to follow
the Bible rule, and call the elders; but where should
we go? We thought of Brother R. who had just
left on the line-boat, intending to step aboard the
first packet. In a moment we were decided for my
husband to go for Brother R., drive on the tow-
path until he overtook the line-boat, and bring him
back. He drove five miles before overtaking the
boat. While my husband was gone we were praying for the Lord to spare the life of the child until
his father returned. Our petitions were answered.
When they arrived, Brother R. anointed the child
and prayed over him. We all united in the prayer
offered. The child opened his eyes and knew us.
A light shone upon his features, and the blessing of
God rested upon us all. We had the assurance
that the power of the enemy was broken.

"The next morning I was greatly depressed in
spirits. Such queries as this troubled me, Why
was not God willing to hear our prayers and raise
the child to health? Satan, ever ready with his
temptations, suggested that it was because we were
not right. I could think of no particular thing
wherein I had grieved the Lord, yet a crushing
weight seemed to be on my spirits, driving me to

despair. I doubted my acceptance with God, and could not pray. I had not courage so much as to lift my eyes to heaven. I suffered intense anguish of mind until my husband besought the Lord in my behalf. He would not yield the point until my voice was united with his for deliverance. It came, and I began to hope, and my trembling faith grasped the promises of God. Then Satan came in another form. My husband was taken very sick. His symptoms were alarming. He cramped at intervals, and suffered excruciating pain. His feet and limbs were cold. I rubbed them until I had no strength to do so longer. Brother Harris was away some miles at his work, and there were only Sisters Harris and Bonfoey and my sister Sarah present, and I was just gathering courage to dare believe in the promises of God. If ever I felt my weakness it was then. We knew that something must be done immediately. Every moment his case was growing more critical. It was clearly a case of cholera. He asked us to pray, and we dared not refuse, and in great weakness we bowed before the Lord. With a deep sense of my unworthiness, I laid my hands upon his head, and prayed the Lord to reveal his power. A change was effected immediately. The natural color of his face returned, and the light of Heaven beamed upon his countenance. We were all filled with gratitude unspeakable. We never had witnessed a more remarkable answer to prayer.

"That day was appointed for us to go to Port Byron to read the proof-sheets of the paper that was being printed at Auburn. It appeared to us that Satan was trying to hinder the publication of truth that we were laboring to get before the people. We felt that we must walk out upon faith. My husband said he would go to Port Byron for the proof-sheets, and we helped him harness the horse,

and then I accompanied him. The Lord strengthened him on the way. He received his proof and a
note stating that the paper would be off next day,
and we must be at Auburn to receive it. That
night we were awakened by the screams of our
little Edson who slept in the room above us. It
was about midnight. Our little boy would cling to
Sr. B., then with both hands fight the air, for we
could see nothing, and then in terror he would cry,
No, no, and cling closer to us. We knew this was
Satan's work to annoy us, and we knelt in prayer,
and husband rebuked the evil spirit in the name of
the Lord, and Edson quietly fell asleep in Sr. B.'s
arms, and rested well through the night.

"Then my husband was again attacked. He was
in much pain. I knelt at the bedside and prayed
the Lord to strengthen our faith. I knew the Lord
had wrought for him, and rebuked the disease, and
we could not ask him to do what had already been
done. But we prayed that the Lord would carry
on his work. We repeated these words, 'Thou
hast heard prayer! Thou hast wrought! We believe without a doubt! Carry on the work thou
hast begun!' Thus we plead two hours before the
Lord, and while we were praying, he fell asleep and
rested well till daylight. He then arose very weak,
but we would not look at appearance. We trusted
the promise of God. He said it should be done,
and we believed and determined to walk out by
faith. We were expected at Auburn that day to
receive the first number of the paper. We believed
that Satan was trying to hinder us, and my husband decided he should go, trusting in the Lord.
Brother H. made ready the carriage, and Sister B.
accompanied us. My husband had to be helped
into the wagon, yet every mile we rode he gained
strength. We kept our minds stayed upon God,
and our faith in constant exercise as we rode on

peaceful and happy. We hired a room in a hotel for the purpose of reading proof for the last time and in the afternoon as I looked out of the window I saw my husband carrying a heavy case of type from one office to another. This alarmed me, but the Lord gave him strength, and when we received the paper all finished, and rode back to Centerport, we felt sure that we were in the path of duty. The blessing of God rested upon us. We had been greatly buffeted by Satan, but through Christ strengthening us we had come off victorious. We had a large bundle of papers with us containing precious truth for the people of God.

"Our child was recovering, and Satan was not permitted to afflict him again. We worked early and late, sometimes not allowing ourselves time to sit at the table to eat our meals, but having a piece by our side we would eat and work at the same time. By overtaxing my strength in folding large sheets, I brought on a severe pain in my shoulder which did not leave me for years. We had been anticipating a journey East, and our child was again well enough to travel. We took the packet for Utica. There was on the boat a young woman from Centerport who was busy relating to others some things concerning us. And they would occasionally promenade back and forth the length of the boat to get a view of me. They had been informed that I had visions, and the young lady was heard to say, 'They are such a strange people! They can be heard praying at all times in the day, and often in the night. Most of their time is spent in prayer.' Many curious eyes were turned towards us, to examine us, especially the one who had visions. There was at one time some trouble on the boat. The chamber-maid had been abused by one of the passengers. She went with her complaint to the captain of the boat, and gained many sympathizers. While she was describing the one who had abused her, many eyes were turned towards me, as the dress described answered very nearly to my dress. It was whispered round, 'It is her! It is her! The one that has visions! What a shame!' And a zealous one spoke up and asked if it was me, pointing towards me. 'Oh no, no,' said she in her Irish tongue, 'Surely she is as nice a little woman as there is on the boat.' I could but notice how gladly they would have had me the guilty one, because I had visions.

"Next they inquired if I believed in the spirit rapping that had just commenced in Rochester. I told them that I believed there was a reality in it, but it was an evil spirit instead of a good one. They looked at each other and said, 'What blasphemy! I would not repeat those words for my life.' With religious horror they withdrew from our company, and manifested a fear to approach us afterwards. Some were very curious to know what physician had been attending my child. We told them we had not applied to any earthly physician. A minister and his wife and children were on board. Two of their children were very sick, and the mother inquired in regard to the remedies we had used. I told her the course we had pursued, that we had followed the prescription of the apostle James, chapter 5, and the Lord had wrought for us as no earthly physician could, and we were not afraid to trust our child in his hands, and he was fast improving. The only answer was, 'If that was my child, and I had no physician, I should know it would die.' At Utica we parted with Sister B., my sister S. and our child, and went on our way to the East, while Brother Abbey took them home with him. We had to make some sacrifice in our feelings to separate from those who were bound to us by tender ties; especially did our hearts cling to little Edson whose life had been so much in danger. We then journeyed to Vermont and held a conference at Sutton."

— • • •

## CHAPTER VIII.

### PUBLISHING AND TRAVELING.

" My husband soon commenced the publication of the *Advent Review and Sabbath Herald* at Paris Maine. The brethren there were all poor, and we suffered many privations. We boarded in Brother A.'s family. We were willing to live cheaply that the paper might be sustained. My husband was a dyspeptic. We could not eat meat or butter, and were obliged to abstain from all greasy food. Take these from a poor farmer's table and it leaves a very spare diet. Our labors were so great that we needed nourishing food. We had much care, and often sat up as late as midnight, and sometimes until two or three in the morning to read proof-sheets. We could have better borne these extra exertions could we have had the sympathy of our brethren in Paris, and had they appreciated our labors and the efforts we were making to advance the cause of truth. Mental labor and privation reduced the strength of my husband very fast.

" About this time we received a special invitation to attend a conference at Waterbury, Vt. We decided to go, but let Brethren R. and A. have our horse to visit the brethren in Canada and Northern Vermont, while we took the cars for Boston and New Ipswich, N. H. It took us two days to go forty miles to Washington, by private conveyance. The blessing of the Lord attended our meetings in that place. We then rode fifteen miles to visit Brother S. who was befogged with spiritualism.

We were anxious he should attend the conference at Waterbury. But he had no horse, and to help him, we told him if he would get a horse we would ride in the sleigh with him, and give him our fare which would be about five dollars on the cars. He purchased a horse for thirty dollars. It was in mid-winter, and we suffered with cold, but we were anxious to see Elder Joseph Baker who was shut up at home, and encourage him to attend the Waterbury meeting. Weary, cold and hungry, we arrived at Brother B.'s. Next morning we had a solemn season of prayer, and Brother B. was deeply affected. We urged him to attend the conference. He said he had not health and strength to drive his horse through the cold. My husband handed him five dollars to pay his fare on the cars. He was very reluctant to accept it, but said, 'If it is your duty to give me this, I will go.' We were the greater part of three days more in reaching Waterbury. There were three of us in an open sleigh, without a buffalo robe or even a horse-blanket to protect us from the cold, and we suffered very much.

"At this meeting we had to labor against a great amount of unbelief, and this was not all we had to meet. Satan had tempted some of the brethren to think that we had too good a horse, although we had given it up for others to use, and had come that journey in the tedious manner described. Jealousy was aroused by N. A. H. that Brother White was making money, and it awakened the same feelings in those who should have stood in our defense. As N. A. H. was very poor, my husband, only seven or eight months before, handed him twenty dollars which was put into his hands to help the cause, took his coat from his back and gave it to him, and interested the brethren in his behalf, so that a horse and carriage were given him at the conference at Johnson. But this was the reward he received.

We were forced to wade through a tide of oppression. It seemed that the deep waters would overflow us, and that we should sink.

"At the close of that meeting means was raised to defray the expenses of those who had come to the meeting. The question was asked, how it should be appropriated. A brother, who knew our poverty, and that we suffered for suitable food and clothing, hastily took the means and placed it in the hands of one whom my husband had helped to the meeting. And although we had been specially invited to attend the conference, we received nothing to defray our traveling expenses. But the Lord did not forsake us in our extremity. While engaged in prayer around the family altar, I was taken off in vision and shown some things concerning this cruel work. I saw that it had been carried on underhanded, and was as cruel as the grave. We found some relief, still our spirits were almost crushed to receive such treatment from our brethren. We then went to Waitsfield and Granville, and visited the family of our dear Sister Rice, who rests in the grave, and tried to aid them a little in their need. Brother K. took us to Bethel. We ascended a long mountain, and suffered with the cold extremely. We were five hours going fifteen miles. We held meetings among dark spirits, but Brother Philips there embraced the truth. We then returned to Massachusetts and Maine. But the influence that had worked against us in Vermont effected individuals in other States, and one good brother in Massachusetts wrote us many pages of reproof. He had received prejudice from others.

"My husband was borne down with care, and suffering from severe colds taken on the journey to the Waterbury meeting and in returning, which had settled on his lungs. He sunk beneath his trials. He was so weak he could not get to the printing

office without staggering. Our faith was tried to
the uttermost. We had willingly endured privation, toil and suffering, yet but few seemed to appreciate our efforts, when it was even for their good
we had suffered. We were too much troubled to
sleep or rest. The hours in which we should have
been refreshed with sleep, were often spent in
answering long communications occasioned by the
leaven of envy which commenced to work at the
Waterbury meeting; and many hours while others
were sleeping we spent in agonizing tears, and
mourning before the Lord. At length my husband
said, 'Wife, it is no use to try to struggle on any
longer. These things are crushing me, and will
soon carry me to the grave. I cannot go any farther.
I have written a note for the paper stating that I
shall publish no more.' As he stepped out of the
door to carry it to the printing office, I fainted.
He came back and prayed for me, and his prayer
was answered, and I was relieved.

"The next morning, while at family prayer, I
was taken off in vision and was shown concerning
these matters. I saw that my husband must not
give up the paper, for such a step was just what
Satan was trying to drive him to take, and he was
working through agents to do this. I was shown
that he must continue to publish, and that the Lord
would sustain him, and those who had been guilty
in casting upon him such burdens would have to
see the extent of their cruel course, and come back
confessing their injustice, or the frown of God would
rest upon them; that it was not against us merely
they had spoken and acted, but against Him who
had called us to fill the place he wished us to occupy,
and that all their suspicions, jealousy, and secret
influence which had been at work, was faithfully
chronicled in heaven, and would not be blotted out
until every one who had taken a part in it should

see the extent of their wrong course, and retrace every step. The exposures of that journey to Vermont my husband felt for years, and were not overcome until a few years since, when the Lord mercifully healed him in answer to prayer. The brother referred to in Massachusetts, was convinced that he was wrong, and wrote a humble acknowledgement which melted us to tears. But he was not satisfied to confess with pen and ink, but came all the way to Paris, Maine, to see us, and confess his error, and our hearts were more firmly united than ever. He had been influenced by one in whom he had the utmost confidence.

"We soon received urgent invitations to hold conferences in different States, and decided to attend general gatherings at Boston, Mass., Rocky Hill, Ct., Camden and West Milton, N. Y. These were all meetings of labor, but very profitable to our scattered brethren.

"The conference at West Milton was held in a barn which was well filled. This was an interesting and profitable meeting. We tarried at Ballston Spa a number of weeks, until we became settled in regard to publishing at Saratoga Springs, then rented a house, and with borrowed household stuff commenced housekeeping, and here my husband published the second volume of the *Advent Review and Sabbath Herald.*

"Sister Annie Smith, who now sleeps in Jesus, came to live with us and assist in the work. Her help was needed. My husband expresses his feelings at this time in a letter to Brother Howland, dated February 20, 1852, as follows: 'We are usually well, all but myself. I cannot long endure the labors of traveling, and the care of publishing. Wednesday night we worked until 2 o'clock in the morning, folding and wrapping No. 12 of the *Review and Herald;* then I retired and coughed till daylight.

Pray for me. The cause is prospering gloriously. Perhaps the Lord will not have need of me longer, and will let me rest in the grave. I hope to be free from the paper. I have stood by it in extreme adversity, and now when its friends are many, I feel free to leave it, if some one can be found who will take it. I hope my way will be made clear. May the Lord direct. We hope to hear from you and your dear family, and from our little Henry. I can hardly pen these lines from incessant coughing. Consumption is my portion unless God delivers immediately.'

"While at Saratoga we met with many discouragements. The brethren in that vicinity were not in a prosperous condition. There were errors and wrong influences to be corrected. H. C. had but little of this world's goods, and took an extreme position on the subject of selling and giving alms, and was dissatisfied with his wealthy brethren because they were not more liberal. They were accused by him of being worldly-minded, covetous and selfish. Neither party was right. Some of those possessing property were covetous, and on the other hand, H. C. did not employ his time and strength as he should, that he might provide for his own, and have something himself to aid the cause. His course cut off our testimony, while we tried to hold up the true object which called for means. Brother S. was willing to do anything for the cause of God when a suitable object was presented, but he did not feel called upon to sell his home farm, while he had available means which would meet the present wants of the cause. But H. C.'s family gave him no rest. 'Sell that ye have and give alms, and help the poorer brethren,' was their cry. Brother S. was desponding, and this reason was assigned, 'He is covetous, and God will not bless him until he disposes of his possessions.' But

it was H. C. who was covetous. He coveted the
good things of Brother S., and felt tried if he was
not willing to divide with him the fruits of his
hard labor in cultivating his land, while H. C. took
an easy course, trusting in the Lord as he said, and
did but very little.

"Often did this oppressed brother come from
Milton to Saratoga to ask our advice as to the
course he should pursue. Said he, 'They say this
heavy weight about my heart is the frown of God
upon me because I do not sell.' He said he had
ready means to use wherever the Lord called. We
told him not to sink in discouragement, that if it
was his duty to sell, the Lord was as willing to let
him know it and feel the burden, as to teach it to
his brethren. Once he came to see us, dizzy and
distressed, having become nearly blind on the way.
We felt sure his distress was in consequence of
disease of the heart and told him so, that it was
not because of neglected duty, for he was willing to
do anything. The next day Brother S. handed
us thirty dollars which was much needed by
one of the brethren to enable him to labor in
the gospel field. After we moved from Saratoga
Springs to Rochester, we received a letter informing us that Brother S. was dead. He died of apoplexy. Oh, thought I, some who have oppressed
that dear brother, and reproached him so unspar-
ingly, and had false dreams and burdens which
they spun out of their own bowels to extort from
him means which should have been applied to
God's cause, will have to give an account of these
things. He received no sympathy from them while
his heart was pressed as though a heavy weight
was upon it. When in distress he was told, 'When
you do your duty, sell and give alms, you will be
free and in the light.' That aching heart is now
still. He rests until the morning of the resurrec-

tion when we believe he will come forth immortal. Our testimony at Saratoga and vicinity was rejected by the covetous poor and also by the rich. We moved to Rochester and the cause went down.

" In a vision given me at Saratoga Springs I was shown a company in Vermont with a woman among them who was a deceiver, and the church must be enlightened as to her character lest poisonous error should become deeply rooted among them. I had not seen the brethren in that part of the State with my natural eyes. We visited them, and as we entered Brother B.'s dwelling a woman came forward to receive me whom I thought to be Sister B.'s mother. I was about to salute her when the light fell upon her face and lo! it was Mrs. C., the woman I had seen in vision. I dropped her hand instantly and drew back. She noticed this and remarked upon it afterwards. The church in Vergennes and vicinity collected together for meeting. There was confusion of sentiment among them. Brother E. E. held the age to come and some were in favor of S. Allen, a notable fanatic, who held views of a dangerous character which if carried out would lead to spiritual union and breaking up of families. I delivered the message in the Sabbath meeting which the Lord had given me. Sunday noon Mrs C. was talking quite eloquently in regard to backbiting. She was very severe, for she had heard that speeches had been made against her fanatical proceedings. Just then Sister B. entered saying, ' Will you please walk out to dinner?' Mrs. C. instantly replied, saying, ' This kind goeth not out save by fasting and prayer. I do not wish any dinner.' In a moment my husband was upon his feet. The power of God was upon him, and the color had left his face. Said he, ' I hope it will go out! In the name of the Lord, I hope it will go out!' and said he to Mrs. C., ' That evil spirit is in you, and I hope it will go out! I rebuke it in the name of the Lord!' She seemed to be struck dumb. Her glib, smart tongue was stilled for once.

"But she had sympathizers. This is generally the case. It commenced with the fall of Satan in heaven, and angels who sympathized with him fell also. Those who are wrong and co-workers with Satan will ever find those who will sympathize with them when they are reproved. These sympathizers have great fear that the feelings of those who receive just reproof will be hurt. Brother and Sister B. sympathized with this deceitful woman. They thought her to be about right. But we did not feel discouraged. The Lord had taken this matter in his own hands, and would deliver his church who had been burdened and oppressed.

"That afternoon as we united in prayer, the blessing of the Lord rested upon us, and I was again shown the case of this deceived woman, and the danger of the church in listening to such teaching as came from her lips. Her course was calculated to disgrace the cause of God. Mrs. C. had a lawful protector and with him should she abide or in his company travel, and that by her fanatical course she had forfeited all claims to Christian fellowship, and that the course of H. A. and Mrs. C. should be protested against, and if the church did not cut loose from those who pursued such a course, and lift their voices against it, they would incur God's frown and be partakers with them in their evil deeds, and that the Lord had sent us to the church with a message which if received would save them from greater danger than they yet realized.

"Many had known and deeply felt these wrongs, but others had viewed things differently. But the brethren began to breathe free again, and receive strength to bear their plain testimony against wrongs which they knew had existed. They knew that I had not received information from any earthly source, and that the Lord had revealed these things to me, and they testified that I had related the matter better than those could who were acquainted with all the circumstances. We had another interview with Brother and Sister B. The Lord was opening their eyes to see things in their true light. We returned from that journey with feelings of satisfaction, knowing that the Lord had wrought for his people.

"April, 1852, we moved to Rochester, N. Y., under most discouraging circumstances. We had not money enough to pay the freight on the few things we had to move by railroad, and were obliged to move out by faith. I will give a few extracts of a letter to Brother Howland's family, dated April 16, 1852: 'We are just getting settled here in Rochester. We have rented an old house for one hundred and seventy-five dollars a year. We have the press in the house. Were it not for this we should have to pay fifty dollars a year for Office room. You would smile could you look in upon us and see our furniture. We have bought two old bedsteads for twenty-five cents each. My husband brought me home six old chairs, no two of them alike, for which he paid one dollar, and soon he presented me with four more old chairs without any seating, for which he paid sixty-two cents for the lot. The frames were strong, and I have been seating them with drilling. Butter is so high we do not purchase it, neither can we afford potatoes. We use sauce in the place of butter, and turnips for potatoes. Our first meals were taken on a fire board placed upon two empty flour barrels. We are willing to endure privations if the work of God can be advanced. We believe the Lord's hand was in our coming to this place. There is a large field for labor and but few laborers. Last Sabbath our meeting was excellent. The Lord refreshed us with his presence.'

"Soon after our family became settled in Rochester, we received a letter from my mother informing us of the dangerous illness of my brother Robert, who lived with my parents in Gorham, Me. Wrong influences had affected him, and separated him in faith from us. He became bewildered as to our position and was unwilling to listen to any evidence in favor of the third message. He did not oppose, but entirely evaded the matter. This caused us many sad hours. When the news of his sickness reached us, my sister Sarah decided to go immediately to Gorham. To all appearance my brother could not live but a few days, yet contrary to the expectations of all he lingered six months, a great sufferer. My sister faithfully watched over him until the last. As soon as he was afflicted his voice was often heard pleading with God for the light of his countenance, and upon his sick bed he weighed the evidences of our position, and fully embraced the third message. He grieved that he had not looked into the subject before, and would frequently exclaim, 'How plain! How clear that there must be a third message as well as a first and second,' and he would say, 'The third angel followed them, the two former, it is all plain now. I have deprived myself of many blessings that I might have enjoyed. I thought that brother White and sister Ellen were in error. I have felt wrong towards them and want to see them once more.'

"My brother seemed to be ripening for heaven. He took no interest in worldly matters, and felt grieved when any conversation, except that of a religious character was introduced in his room. He seemed to be holding communion with God daily and to regard every moment as very precious, to be spent in preparing for his last change. We had the privilege of visiting him before his death, It was an affecting meeting. He was much changed yet his wasted features were lighted up with joy. Bright hope of the future constantly sustained him. He did not once murmur or express a wish to live. We had seasons of prayer in his room, and Jesus seemed very near. We were obliged to separate from our dear brother, expecting never to meet him again this side of the resurrection of the just. The bitterness of the parting scene was much taken away by the hope he expressed of meeting us where parting would be no more.

"My brother continued to fail rapidly. If he felt a cloud shutting Jesus from him, he would not rest until it was dispelled, and bright hope again cheered him. To all who visited him he conversed upon the goodness of God, and would often lift his emaciated finger, pointing upwards, while a heavenly light rested upon his countenance, and say, 'My treasure is laid up on high.' It was a wonder to all that his life of suffering was thus protracted. He had hemorrhage of the lungs, and was thought to be dying. Then an unfulfilled duty presented itself to him. He had again connected himself with the Methodist church, from which he was expelled in 1843 with the other members of the family on account of his faith. He said he could not die in peace until his name was taken from the church-book, and requested father to go immediately and have it taken off. In the morning father visited the minister, stating my brother's request. He said that he would visit him, and then if it was still his wish to be considered no longer a member of their church, his request should be granted. Just before the minister arrived my brother had a second hemorrhage and whispered his fears that he should not live to do this duty. The minister visited him, and he immediately expressed his desire, and told him he could not die in peace until his name was taken from the church-book, and that he should not have united with them again if he had been standing in the light. He then spoke of his faith, and hope, and the goodness of God to him. A heavenly smile was upon his countenance, and those lips, a few moments before stained with blood, were opened to praise God for his great salvation. As the minister left the room he said to my parents, 'That is a triumphant soul, I never saw so happy a soul before.' Soon after this my brother fell asleep in Jesus, in full hope of having a part in the first resurrection. The following lines were written upon his death by Sister Annie R. Smith :—

"He sleeps in Jesus—peaceful rest—
No mortal strife invades, his breast ;
No pain, or sin, or woe, or care,
Can reach the silent slumberer there.

"He lived, his Saviour to adore,
And meekly all his sufferings bore.
He loved, and all resigned to God ;
Nor murmured at his chastening rod.

" 'Does earth attract thee here ?' they cried,
The dying Christian thus replied :
While pointing upward to the sky,
' *My treasure is laid up on high.*'

" He sleeps in Jesus—soon to rise,
When the last trump shall rend the skies ;
Then burst the fetters of the tomb,
To wake in full, immortal bloom.

" He sleeps in Jesus—cease thy grief ;
Let this afford thee sweet relief—
That, freed from death's triumphant reign,
In heaven will he live again.

" We toiled on in Rochester through much perplexity and discouragement. The cholera visited

R., and while it raged, all night long the carriages bearing the dead were heard rumbling through the streets to Mount Hope cemetery. This disease did not cut down merely the low, but it took from every class in society. The most skillful physicians were laid low, and borne to Mount Hope. As we passed through the streets in Rochester, at almost every corner we would meet wagons with plain pine coffins in which to put the dead. Our little Edson was attacked and we carried him to the great Physician. The disease was stayed in its progress. I took him in my arms and in the name of Jesus rebuked the disease. He felt relief at once and as a sister commenced praying for the Lord to heal him the little fellow of three years looked up in astonishment and said, 'They need not pray any more, for the Lord has healed me.' He was very weak, but the disease made no further progress, and he gained no strength. Our faith was still to be tried. For three days he ate nothing, and we had appointments out for two months, reaching from Rochester, N. Y., to Bangor, Me., and this journey we were to perform with our good horse Charlie, given to us by brethren in Vermont, and covered carriage. We hardly dared to leave the child in so critical a state, but decided to go unless there was a change for the worse. In two days we must commence our journey in order to reach the first appointment. We presented the case before the Lord, taking it as an evidence that if the child had appetite to eat we would venture. The first day there was no change for the better. He could not bear the least food. The next day about noon he called for broth and it nourished him.

"We commenced our journey that night. About four o'clock I took my sick child upon a pillow and we rode twenty miles. He seemed very nervous that night. He could not sleep and I held him in

my arms nearly the whole night. My husband
would frequently awake, and as he heard the sound
of my rocking-chair would groan, for he thought of
the tedious journey before us. I obtained no sleep
through the night.

"The next morning we consulted together
whether to return to Rochester, or go on. The
family who had entertained us said we would bury
the child on the road. And to all appearance it
would be so. But I dared not go back to Rochester. We believed the affliction of the child was
the work of Satan to hinder us from traveling, and
we dared not yield to him. I said to my husband,
'If we go back I shall expect the child to die. He
can but die if we go forward. Let us proceed on
our journey trusting in the Lord.' We had a journey before us of about one hundred miles to perform
in two days, yet we believed that the Lord would
work for us in this time of extremity. I was much
exhausted and feared I should fall asleep and let
the child fall from my arms, so I laid him upon my
lap and tied him to my waist and we both slept that
day over much of the distance. The child revived
and continued to gain strength the whole journey
and we brought him home quite rugged.

"The Lord greatly blessed us on our journey to
Vermont. My husband had much care and labor.
At the different conferences he did most of the
preaching, sold books, and took pay for the papers.
And when one conference was over we would
hasten to the next. At noon we would feed the
horse by the roadside and eat our lunch. Then my
husband, with paper and pencil upon the cover of
our dinner-box, or the top of his hat would write
articles for the *Review* and *Instructor*. Our
meeting at Wolcott was of special interest. A can-
vas was attached to the house to accommodate the
people. The Lord blessed us with freedom and the

truth affected hearts. I had a vision in the congregation and had perfect liberty in relating it. I there became acquainted with our dear Sister Pierce, who was in despair. My heart was drawn out in sympathy and love for her as I had been in a similar state of mind. At this meeting our dear Brother Benson was convicted of the truth. He believed the vision he witnessed to be the power of God, and was affected by it. He fully embraced the truth. Others decided at that meeting to obey all of God's commandments and live. Since that meeting we have met Brother B.'s cheerful countenance in every conference we have attended in Vermont. But we shall meet him in this mortal state no more. He died in hope, and will rest in the silent grave until the resurrection of the just.

"Again at Panton, Vt., the Lord met with his people. Brother and Sister Pierce were present. The Spirit of the Lord affected hearts in that meeting. Brother E. Churchill was much broken in spirit, and decided fully to take his stand with the remnant people of God. At this meeting the Lord revealed himself to me and I was taken off in vision. A comforting message was given me for Sister Pierce. The following is their statement:—

"'My wife has for many years been subject to occasional, and sometimes protracted, seasons of the most hopeless despair. They began with her when quite young, and have from time to time afflicted her till since we embraced the present, the last message of truth. Some time after having embraced the Sabbath, and some other truths pertaining to the present message, the climax of darkness settled down upon her laboring mind, insomuch that the most encouraging conversation, elicited from the most cheering promises of the Bible, appeared to have no good effect upon her mind whatever. And although naturally possessed of a social disposition, and a cast of mind very favorable to friendly associations, yet so great was the weight of her mental oppression, and so vividly, in her estimation, was portrayed before the mind her forlorn, abject and wretched condition, that she was disinclined to participate in what by her had usually been deemed interesting social interviews, and rather inclined to absent herself from the presence of those who belonged to the circle of her acquaintance generally, and even some of her most endeared friends: Further, she had no disposition to attend any religious meetings, nor could she scarcely stimulate herself to go about the business of her usual avocation.

" 'This state of mind commenced, I believe, in the month of May, 1852, and continued with increased severity until the first of September following—the time of the Wolcott meeting, which myself and some other of her especial friends constrained her to attend. Nor was the weight of that mental anguish essentially abated then. Though she realized that it was an interesting meeting, that the Spirit of the Lord was there; and though the gift of prophecy was especially developed through Sister White, in a manner that satisfactorily convinced her that the visions were of God, yet at that time she had no hope that she had any part or lot in the matter of interest which then passed before her. Thus she remained till the time of the Panton meeting, four weeks afterwards. It was at this meeting the Lord gave Sister White a vision, a part of which so clearly showed up her case, and so perfectly instructed her what to do, that from that time forward the scene with her was in a great measure the most happily changed. Previously those seasons of despair had worn off more gradually; but in this case it seemed that the word was spoken, and the work was done. For even on our return from the meeting, instead of gloom and horror being depicted on her countenance it was. lighted up with cheering hope.

"'Those sleepless hours and restless nights which before had been the effect of a mind tortured with forebodings more dreadful than it seemed able to endure, have scarcely since recurred to disturb our accustomed repose. Instead of a manifest shrinking from the attendance of religious meetings, which only seemed to aggravate her woes, she then engaged zealously in the work necessary in order to establish meetings periodically at our own house.

"'I believe this favorable change in her condition at that time to be exclusively the effect of the visions then given. Untiring efforts had previously been put forth by those who had been in a similar condition, in conversation eliciting many of the great and precious promises, to try to buoy up the sinking mind, but it all produced no beneficial effect. Truly I have since believed there was occasion for gratitude that this gift is in the church.

"'Stephen Pierce.

"'According to my best recollection, the above account of my mental trials, and the effect of Sister White's visions, written by my husband, is essentially correct. 'Almira Pierce.'

"While we were absent from Rochester on this eastern tour the foreman of the Office was attacked with cholera. He was an unconverted young man. The lady of the house where he boarded died with the same disease, also her daughter. He was then brought down and no one ventured to take care of him, fearing the disease. The Office hands watched over him until the disease seemed checked, then took him to our house. He had a relapse and a physician attended him and exerted himself to the utmost to save him, but at length told him that his case was hopeless, that he could not survive through the night. Those interested for him could not bear to see the young man die without hope. They prayed around his bedside while he was suffering great agony. He also prayed that the Lord would have mercy upon him, and forgive his sins. Yet he obtained no relief. He continued to cramp and toss in restless agony. The brethren continued in prayer all night that he might be spared to repent of his sins and keep the commandments of God. He at length seemed to consecrate himself to God, and promised the Lord he would keep the Sabbath and serve him. He soon felt relief. The next morning the physician came, and as he entered, said, ' I told my wife about one o'clock this morning that in all probability the young man was out of his trouble.' He was told that he was alive. The physician was surprised and immediately ascended the stairs to his room, and as he examined his pulse, said, ' Young man, you are better, the crisis is past, but it is not my skill that saved you, but a higher power. With good nursing you may get about again.' He gained rapidly, and soon took his place in the Office, a converted man.

"After we returned from our eastern journey I was shown that we were in danger of taking burdens upon us that God did not require us to bear. We had a part to act in the cause of God, and should not add to our cares by increasing our family to gratify the wishes of any. I saw that to save souls we should be willing to bear burdens; and that we should open the way for my husband's brother Nathaniel and sister Anna to come and live with us. They were both invalids, yet we felt to extend to them a cordial invitation to come to our house. This they accepted. As soon as we saw Nathaniel we feared that consumption had marked him for the grave. The hectic flush was upon his cheek, yet we hoped and prayed that the Lord would spare him, that his talent might be employed in the cause of God. But the Lord saw fit to order otherwise. Nathaniel and Anna came into the truth cautiously yet understandingly. They weighed the evidences of our positions, and conscientiously decided for the truth.

"Nathaniel died May 6, 1853, in the 22d year of his age. The following particulars of his sickness and death, are from a letter I wrote to our bereaved parents :—

"'Dear Nathaniel, we miss him much. It seems hard for us to realize that we are no more to have his society here. He bore up through his sickness with remarkable cheerfulness and fortitude. I never heard him groan but once, and that was the Tuesday before he died. I loved him when he first came because he was brother to my husband, and I felt that I could do anything for his comfort, but soon he seemed as near to me as a natural brother. I read some in the Bible to him Wednesday, and told him about my poor brother Robert, who, after six months of great suffering, died of consumption. Said he, "I should not wish to have such lingering sickness as he had." He enjoyed his mind well, and told us not to look sad when we came into his room. Said he, "I am happy; the Lord blesses me abundantly. I have obtained the victory over impatience, and have the evidence that the Lord loves and owns me as his child." That night he suffered much with wakefulness. Thursday morning he expressed his joy that the long night had passed, and day had finally come. As he walked out to breakfast in the large parlor that morning, he looked around the room, and said, "Any one cannot help but get well in such a beautiful house as this, with such large, airy rooms."

"'Anna generally took his meals to him from

choice, and then sat by his side while he ate; as she did not wish to eat until after he had. Said he, "Ellen, I wish you would make Anna sit down and eat with the rest of the family, for there is no need of her sitting by me while I eat." He seemed to love Anna very much, and through his sickness often spoke of his coming to Rochester to accompany her, because she was so feeble, and now she was waiting upon him, and often said, "Anna, you did not know when you made up your mind to come to Rochester that you were coming to wait upon me." That night [Thursday] we went into his room and prayed with him, and he was abundantly blessed. He praised the Lord aloud, while his face lighted up with the glory of God. We especially prayed that he might have sleep and rest that night. He rested very well through the night. Friday morning, the last morning that he lived, he called us into his room. He said that he wished us to pray there, but first he had something to say. He then with remarkable clearness called up little things that had transpired while he had been with us, and every word that he thought he had spoken hastily or wrong he confessed heartily. He confessed wherein he had distrusted God in times past, and asked forgiveness of the family. "I regret," said he, "that I have been unreconciled to my sickness. I have felt that I could not have it so, and that the Lord dealt hard with me. But I am now satisfied it is just; for nothing but this sickness could bring me where I am. God has blessed me much of late, and has forgiven me all my sins. It often seems that if I should reach out my hand I could embrace Jesus, he is so near. I know that I love God and he loves me."

"'After he had said what he wished to, we united in prayer. It was a sweet season. He manifested great interest while we were praying, responding to

our prayers, saying, "Amen ! Praise the Lord ! Glory
to God ! I will praise him, for he is worthy to be
praised ! His name is Jesus, and he will save us from
our sins !" He prayed earnestly and in faith for a
full consecration to God's will, to be baptized with
his Spirit, and purified by his blood. Said he, "Thou
hast forgiven me all my sins. Thou hast sanctified
me to thyself, and I will honor thee as long as I
have breath." His face shone, and he looked very
happy. He said that the room seemed light, and
he loved us all. After we arose from prayers he
said, "Anna, I love you, come here." She went to
his bedside, and he embraced her, and said, "I am
very happy, the Lord has blessed me." Nathaniel
was triumphant in God through the day, although
he was very sick. I remained in his room and entertained him by reading the Bible and conversing
with him. As I read he would say, "How appropriate that is ! How beautiful ! I must remember
that !"

"'I then said, "Nathaniel you are very sick.
You may die in two hours, and unless God inter-
poses, you cannot live two days." He said, very
calmly, "Oh, not so soon as that, I think." He immediately arose from the bed, sat in the rocking-
chair, and commenced talking. He began back
to the time when he was converted, and told
how much he enjoyed, and how afraid he was of
sinning, and then when he began to forget God,
and lose the blessing, how high his hopes were
raised. He "meant to be a man in the world, to get an
education and fill some high station." And then he
told how his hopes had died, as afflictions had
pressed heavily upon him, and how hard it was for
him to give up his expectations. He said he felt he
could not have it so, he *would* be well, he *would*
not yield to it. Then he spoke of his coming to
Rochester. How trying it was to have us wait

upon him, and to be dependent. "It seemed to me," said he, "that the kindness of you all was more than I could bear, and I have desired to get well to pay you for all this." He then spoke of his embracing the Sabbath. Said he, "At first I was not willing to acknowledge the light I saw. I wished to conceal it, but the blessing of God was withheld from me until I acknowledged the Sabbath. Then I felt confidence towards God." Said he, "I love the Sabbath now. It is precious to me. I now feel reconciled to my sickness. I know that it is the only thing that will save me. I will praise the Lord, if he can save me through affliction."

" 'At our usual supper-time, we prepared poor Nathaniel's supper, but he soon said that he was faint, and did not know but he was going to die. He sent for me, and as soon as I entered the room, I knew that he was dying, and said to him, "Nathaniel dear, trust in God, he loves you, and you love him. Trust right in him as a child trusts in its parents." Don't be troubled. The Lord will not leave you. Said he, "Yes, yes." We prayed and he responded, "Amen, praise the Lord!" He did not seem to suffer pain. He did not groan once, nor struggle, nor move a muscle of his face, but breathed shorter and shorter until he fell asleep.' The following lines occasioned by his death, were written by Sister Annie R. Smith :—

" Gone to thy rest, brother ! peaceful thy sleep ;
　While o'er thy grave bending, in sorrow we weep,
　For the loved and the cherished, in life's early bloom,
　Borne from our number, to the cold, silent tomb.

" Sweet be thy slumber ! in quiet repose ;
　Beneath the green turf, and the blossoming rose ;
　Oh, soft is thy pillow, and lowly thy bed ;
　Mournful the cypress that waves o'er the dead.

" Dark though the pinion that shaded his brow,
　The truth which he followed illumined it now ;
　In the arms of his Saviour he fell to his rest,
　Where woes that await us pervade not his breast.

" Weep not for the Christian whose labor is done ;
Who, faithful to duty, the treasure has won,
The jewel was fitted forever to shine,
A gem in the casket, immortal, divine.

" Not long will earth's bosom his precious form hide,
And death's gloomy portals from kindred divide ;
For swiftly approaching, we see the bright day,
That brings the glad summons, Arise ! come away !

" After Nathaniel's death, my husband was much afflicted. Trouble and anxiety of mind had prostrated him. He had a high fever, and was confined to his bed. We united in prayer for him, and he was relieved, but still remained very weak. He had appointments out for Mill Grove, N. Y., and Michigan, and feared that he could not fill them. We decided, however, to venture as far as Mill Grove, and if he grew no better to return home. While at Elder R. F. Cottrell's, at Mill Grove, he suffered such extreme weakness that he thought he could go no farther. We were in great perplexity. Must we be driven from the work by bodily infirmities ? Would Satan be permitted to exercise his power upon us, and contend for our usefulness and lives as long as we remain in the world ? We knew that God could limit the power of Satan. He may suffer us to be tried in the furnace, but will bring us forth purified and better fitted for his work.

" I went into a log house near by, and there poured out my soul before God in prayer that he would rebuke the fever and strengthen my husband to endure the journey. The case was urgent, and my faith firmly grasped the promises of God. I there obtained the evidence that if we should proceed on our journey to Michigan the angel of God would go with us. When I related to my husband the exercise of my mind, he said that his mind had been exercised in a similar manner, and we decided to go trusting in the Lord. My husband was so

weak that he could not buckle the straps to his
valise and called Brother Cottrell to do it for him.
Every mile we traveled he felt strengthened. The
Lord sustained him. And while he was upon his
feet preaching the word I felt assured that angels
of God were standing by his side to sustain him in
his labors.

"At Jackson we found the church in great confusion. In their midst the Lord showed me their
condition, and I related that portion of it which
was clear before me which related to the wrong
course of one present. C. and R. were greatly prejudiced against this sister and cried out, 'Amen!
amen!' and manifested a spirit of triumph over
her, and would frequently say, 'I thought so! It
is just so!' I felt very much distressed, and sat
down before I had finished relating the vision.
Then C. and R. arose and exhorted others to receive
the vision, and manifested such a spirit that my
husband reproved them. The meeting closed in
confusion. While at family prayer that night at
Brother S.'s I was again taken off in vision, and
that portion of the vision that had passed from me
was repeated, and I was shown the overbearing
course of R. and C., that their influence in the
church was to cause division. They possessed an
exalted spirit, and not the meek spirit of Christ. I
saw why the Lord had hid from me the part of
the vision that related to them. It was that they
might have opportunity to manifest before all what
spirit they were of. The next day a meeting was
called, and I related the things which the Lord had
shown me the evening before. C. and R., who zealously advocated the visions the day before, were
dissatisfied when shown to be wrong, and did not
receive the message. They had stated before I
came to the place that if I saw things as they
looked upon them, they should know that the vis-

ions were of God, but if I saw that they had taken
a wrong course, and that the ones whom they regarded wrong were not faulty, they should know
the visions were incorrect. But both parties were
shown me to be wrong, especially C. and R. and
some others. They now began to fight against my
testimony, and here commenced what is called the
'*Messenger* party.' I will here give an extract
from a letter written to my parents in Gorham,
Me., June 23, 1853:—

"'While in Michigan we visited Tyrone, Jackson,
Sylvan, Bedford and Vergennes. My husband in
the strength of God endured the journey and his
labor well. His strength did not entirely fail him
but once. He was unable to preach at Bedford.
He went to the place of meeting, and stood up in
the desk to preach, but became faint and was obliged
to sit down. He asked brother Loughborough to
take the subject where he had left it, and finish his
discourse. He went out of the house into the open
air and lay upon the green grass until he had somewhat recovered, when brother Kelsey let him take
his horse, and he rode alone one mile and a half to
Brother Brooks'. Brother Loughborough went
through with the subject with much freedom. All
were interested in the meeting. The Spirit of the
Lord rested upon me and I had perfect freedom in
bearing my testimony. The power of God was in
the house, and nearly every one present was affected
to tears. Some took a decided stand for the truth.
After the meeting closed, we rode through the
woods to a beautiful lake, where six were buried
with Christ in Baptism. We then returned to
Brother B.'s and found my husband more comfortable. While alone that day his mind had been exercised upon the subject of Spiritualism, and he there
decided to write the book entitled, 'Signs of the
Times.' Next day we journeyed to Vergennes, trav-

cling over rough log-ways and sloughs. Much of the way I rode in nearly a fainting condition, but our hearts were lifted to God in prayer for strength, and we found him a present help, and were able to accomplish the journey, and bear our testimony there.'

"Soon after our return my husband engaged in writing the 'Signs of the Times.' His health was poor. He was troubled with aching head and cold feet. He could sleep but little, but the Lord was his support. When his mind was in a confused, suffering state, we would bow before the Lord, and in our distress cry unto him. He heard our earnest prayers and often blessed my husband so that with refreshed spirits he went on with the work. Many times in the day did we thus go before the Lord in earnest prayer. That book was not written in his own strength. In the fall of 1853 we attended conferences at Buck's Bridge, N. Y., Stowe, Vt., Boston, Dartmouth and Springfield, Mass., Washington, N. H., and New Haven, Vt. This was a laborious and rather dircouraging journey. Many had embraced the truth, who were unsanctified in heart and life, and the elements of strife and rebellion were at work, and it was necessary that a movement should take place to purify the church. The '*Messenger* party' soon drew off and the cause was relieved.

"In the winter and spring I suffered much with heart disease. It was difficult for me to breathe lying down, and I could not sleep unless raised in nearly a sitting posture. My breath often stopped, and fainting fits were frequent. But this was not all my trouble. I had upon my left eye-lid a swelling which appeared to be a cancer. It had been more than a year increasing gradually until it was quite painful and affected my sight. In reading or writing I was forced to bandage the afflicted eye. And I was constantly afflicted with the thought that my eye might be destroyed with a cancer. I looked back to the days and nights spent in reading proof-sheets, which had strained my eyes, and thought, If I lose my eye, and my life, I shall be a martyr to the cause.

"A celebrated physician visited Rochester, who gave counsel free. I decided to have him examine my eye. He thought the swelling would prove to be a cancer. He felt my pulse and said, 'You are much diseased, and will die of apoplexy before that swelling will break out. You are in a dangerous condition with disease of the heart.' This did not startle me, for I had been aware that unless I received speedy relief I must lie in the grave. Two other women had come for counsel who were suffering with the same disease. The physician said that I was in a more dangerous condition than either of them, and it could not be more than three weeks before I would be afflicted with paralysis. I inquired if he thought his medicine would cure me. He did not give me much encouragement. I purchased some of his medicine. The eye-wash was very painful, and I received no benefit from it. I was unable to use the remedies the physician prescribed.

"In about three weeks I fainted and fell to the floor, and remained nearly unconscious about thirty-six hours. It was feared that I could not live, but in answer to prayer again I revived. One week later, while conversing with sister Anna, I received a shock upon my left side. My head was numb, and I had a strange sensation of coldness and numbness in my head, with pressure, and severe pain through my temples. My tongue seemed heavy and numb; I could not speak plainly. My left arm and side were helpless. I thought I was dying, and my great anxiety was to have the evidence in my sufferings that the Lord loved me. For months I had suffered such constant pain in my heart that I did not have one joyful feeling. My spirits were constantly depressed. I had tried to serve God from principle without feeling, but I now thirsted for the salvation of God, that I might realize his blessing notwithstanding the pain in my heart.

"The brethren and sisters came together to make my case a special subject of prayer. My desire was granted. Prayer was heard, and I received the blessing of God, and had the assurance that he loved me. But the pain continued, and I grew more feeble every hour. The brethren and sisters again came together to present my case to the Lord. I was then so weak that I could not pray vocally. My appearance seemed to weaken the faith of those around me. Then the promises of God were arrayed before me as I had never viewed them before. It seemed to me that Satan was striving to tear me from my husband and children and lay me in the grave, and these questions were suggested to my mind, Can you believe the naked promise of God? Can you walk out by faith, let the appearance be what it may? Faith revived. I whispered to my husband, 'I believe that I shall recover.' He answered, 'I wish I could believe it.' I retired that night without relief, yet relying with firm confidence upon the promises of God. I could not sleep, but continued my silent prayer to God. Just before day I slept.

"As I awoke, the rising sun was seen from my window. I was perfectly free from pain. The pressure upon my heart was gone, and I was very happy. I was filled with gratitude. The praise of God was upon my lips. Oh, what a change! It seemed to me that an angel of God had touched me while I was sleeping. I awoke my husband and related to him the wonderful work that the Lord had wrought for me. He could scarcely comprehend it at first; but when I arose and dressed and walked around the house, and he witnessed the change in my countenance, he could praise God with me. My afflicted eye was free from pain. In a few days the cancer was gone, and my eyesight was fully restored. The work was complete.

"Again I visited the physician, and as soon as he felt my pulse he said, 'Madam, you are better. An entire change has taken place in your system; but the two women who visited me for counsel when you were last here are dead.' I stated to him that his medicine had not cured me, as I could take none of it. After I left, the doctor said to a friend of mine, 'Her case is a mystery. I do not understand it.'"

## CHAPTER IX.

### GOD'S PROVIDENCES.

"WE soon visited Michigan again, and I endured riding over log-ways, and through mud-sloughs, and my strength failed not. We felt that the Lord would have us visit Wisconsin, and were to take the cars at Jackson at ten in the evening. About five in the afternoon a young man of very pleasing appearance called at Brother Palmer's and inquired if they wished books bound, and stated that he was going out on the evening train, and would bind them at Marshall, and return them in a few weeks.

"As we were preparing to take the train we felt very solemn, and proposed a season of prayer. And as we there committed ourselves to God, we could not refrain from weeping. We went to the depot with feelings of deep solemnity. We looked for seats in a forward car, which had high backs, with the hope that we might sleep some that night, but were disappointed. We passed back into the next car, and there found seats. I did not, as usual when traveling in the night, lay off my bonnet, but held my carpet-bag in my hand, as if waiting for something. We both spoke of our singular feelings.

"The train had run about three miles from Jackson when its motion became very violent, jerking backward and forward, and finally stopping. I opened the window and saw one car raised nearly upon one end. I heard most agonizing groans. There was great confusion. The engine had been thrown from the track. But the car we were in was on the track, and was separated about one hundred feet from those before it. The baggage car was not much injured, and our large trunk of books was safe. The second-class car was crushed, and the pieces, with the passengers, were thrown on both sides of the track. The car in which we tried to get a seat was much broken, and one end was raised upon the heap of ruins. The coupling did not break, but the car we were in was unfastened from the one before it, as if an angel had separated them.

"We hastily left the car; and my husband took me in his arms, and, wading in the water, carried me across a swampy piece of land to the main road. Four were killed or mortally wounded. One of them was the young book-binder referred to. Many were much injured. We walked one-half mile to a dwelling, where I remained while my husband rode to Jackson with a messenger sent for physicians. I had opportunity to reflect upon the care which God has for those who serve him. What separated the train, leaving our car back upon the track? I have been shown that an angel was sent to preserve us. We reached the home of Brother

Smith in Jackson, about two o'clock, thankful to God for his preserving care.

"We took the afternoon train for Wisconsin. Our visit to that State was blessed of God. Souls were converted as the result of our efforts, yet it was a hard field of labor. The Lord strengthened me to endure the tedious journey. We returned from Wisconsin much worn, desiring rest; but were distressed to meet sister Anna afflicted. She had changed much in our absence. We also found brethren and sisters assembled at our house for Conference. Without rest we were obliged to engage in the meeting. After the labor of the Conference was over, Sister Bonfoey was taken down with fever and ague, and was a great sufferer for several weeks. It was a sickly summer. Deep affliction was in our family, and we felt the necessity of help from God. Many and fervent were our prayers that his blessing might be felt throughout our dwelling. Especially was sister Anna a subject of our earnest prayers; but she did not seem to feel her danger, and unite with us for the recovery of health, until disease had fastened upon her, and she was brought very low.

"Trials thickened around us. We had much care. The Office hands boarded with us, and our family numbered from fifteen to twenty. The large Conferences and the Sabbath meetings were held at our house. We had no quiet Sabbaths; for some of the sisters usually tarried all day with their children. Our brethren and sisters generally did not consider the inconvenience and additional care and expense brought upon us. As one after another of the Office hands would come home sick, needing extra attention, I was fearful that we should sink beneath the anxiety and care. I often thought that we could endure no more; yet trials increased, and with surprise I found that we were not overwhelmed. We learned the lesson that much more suffering and trial could be borne than we had once thought possible. The watchful eye of the Lord was upon us, to see that we were not destroyed.

"August 29, 1854, another responsibility was added to our family in the birth of Willie. He took my mind somewhat from the troubles around me. About this time the first number of the paper falsely called the *Messenger of Truth* was received. Those who slandered us through that paper had been reproved for their faults and wrongs. They would not bear reproof, and in a secret manner at first, afterward more openly, used their influence against us. This we could have borne, but some of those who should have stood by us were influenced by these wicked persons, some of whom were comparative strangers to them; yet they readily sympathized with them, and withdrew their sympathy from us, notwithstanding they had acknowledged that our labors among them had been signally blessed of God.

"The Lord had shown me the character and final come-out of that party; that his hand was against them, and his frown upon those connected with that paper. And although they might appear to prosper for a time, and some honest ones be deceived, yet truth would eventually triumph, and every honest soul would break away from the deception which had held them, and come out clear from the influence of those wicked men; as God's hand was against them, they must go down.

"Sister Anna continued to fail. Father and mother White, and her sister, E. Tenny, came from Maine to visit her in her affliction. Anna was calm and cheerful. This interview with her parents and sister she had much desired. She bade her parents and sister farewell, as they left to return to

Maine, to meet them no more until the trump of God shall call forth the precious dust to health and immortality. In the last days of her sickness, with her own trembling hands she arranged her things, leaving them in order, and disposed of them according to her mind. She expressed the greatest interest that her parents should embrace the Sabbath, and live near us. 'If I thought this would ever be,' said she, 'I could die perfectly satisfied.'

"The last office performed by her emaciated, trembling hand, was to trace a few lines to her parents. And has not God regarded her last wishes and prayers for her parents? In less than two years, father and mother White were keeping the Bible Sabbath, happily situated within less than one hundred feet from our door. We would have kept Anna with us; but we were obliged to close her eyes in death, and habit her for the tomb, and lay her away to rest. Long had she cherished a hope in Jesus, and she looked forward with pleasing anticipation to the morning of the resurrection. We laid her beside dear Nathaniel in Mount Hope Cemetery.

"After Anna's death, my husband's health became very poor. He was troubled with cough and soreness of lungs, and his nervous system was prostrated. His anxiety of mind, the burdens which he bore in Rochester, his labor in the Office, the sickness and repeated deaths in the family, the lack of sympathy from those who should have shared his labors, together with his traveling and preaching, were too much for his strength, and he seemed to be fast following Nathaniel and Anna to a consumptive's grave. That was a time of gloom and darkness. A few rays of light occasionally parted these heavy clouds, giving us a little hope, or we should have sunk in despair. It seemed at times that God had forsaken us.

"The '*Messenger* party,' the most of whom had been reproved for their wrongs, framed all manner of falsehoods concerning us. These words of the Psalmist were often brought forcibly to my mind: 'Fret not thyself because of evil doers, neither be thou envious against the workers of iniquity; for they shall soon be cut down like the grass, and wither as the green herb.' Some of the writers of that sheet even triumphed over the feebleness of my husband, saying that God would take care of him, and remove him out of the way. When he read this he felt some as Wickliffe did as he lay sick.* Faith revived, and my husband exclaimed, 'I shall not die, but live, and declare the works of the Lord, and may yet preach at their funeral.'

"The darkest clouds seemed to shut down over us. Wicked men, professing godliness, under the command of Satan were hurried on to forge falsehoods, and to bring the strength of their forces against us. If the cause of God had been ours alone, we might have trembled; but it was in the hands of Him who could say, No one is able to pluck it out of my hands. Jesus lives and reigns. We could say before the Lord, The cause is thine, and thou knowest that it has not been our own choice, but by thy command we have acted the part we have in it.

"My husband became so feeble that he resolved

---

* Monks and aldermen "hastened to the bedside of the dying man, hoping to frighten him with the vengeance of heaven." Said they, "You have death on your lips: be touched by your faults, and retract in our presence all you have said to our injury."

"He begged his servants to raise him on his couch. Then feeble and pale, and scarcely able to support himself, he turned toward the friars who were waiting his recantation, and opening his livid lips, and fixing on them a piercing look, he said with emphasis, 'I shall not die, but live, and again declare the evil deeds of the friars.'" They left the room in confusion, and the reformer recovered to perform his most important labors.—*D'Aubigne's History of the Reformation, Vol. V, p. 93.*

to free himself from the responsibilities of publishing, which had been urged upon him. He was editor and proprietor of the *Review and Herald*, until it reached Vol. vii., No. 9. No one ever asked him to give the *Review, Instructor*, and the publication of books, into other hands, or leave the position of editor. No one suggested anything of the kind to him. It was his choice that he might be relieved, and that the Office might be established beyond the influence of those men who had cried, Speculation! He never claimed the property at the Office which had been donated to be used for the benefit of the cause. He called upon the church to take the Office at Rochester, and establish it where they pleased, and suggested that it be managed by a publishing committee, and that no one connected with the Office should have a personal interest in it.

" As no others claimed the privilege, the brethren in Michigan opened the way for the Office to be removed to Battle Creek. At that time my husband was owing between two and three thousand dollars, and all he had besides the books on hand was accounts for books, and some of them doubtful. The cause had apparently come to a halt, and orders for publications were very few and small, and he feared that he would die in debt. Brethren in Michigan assisted us in obtaining a lot and building a house. The deed was made in my name, so that I could dispose of it at pleasure after the death of my husband.

" Those were days of sadness. I looked upon my three little boys, soon, as I feared, to be left fatherless, and thoughts like these forced themselves upon me: My husband dies a martyr to the cause of present truth; and who realizes what he has suffered, the burdens he has for years borne, the extreme care which has crushed his spirits, and ruined his health, bringing him to an untimely grave, leaving his family destitute and dependent? Some who should have stood by him in this trying time, and with words of encouragement and sympathy helped him to bear the burdens, were like Job's comforters, who were ready to accuse and press the weight upon him still heavier. I have often asked the question, Does God have no care for these things? Does he pass them by unnoticed? I was comforted to know that there is One who judgeth righteously, and that every sacrifice, every self-denial, and every pang of anguish endured for his sake, is faithfully chronicled in Heaven, and will bring its reward. The day of the Lord will declare and bring to light things that are not yet made manifest.

"About this time I was shown that my husband must not labor in preaching, or with his hands: that a little over-exercise then would place him in a hopeless condition. At this he wept and groaned. Said he, 'Must I then become a church pauper?' Again I was shown that God designed to raise him up gradually; that we must exercise strong faith, for in every effort we should be fiercely buffeted by Satan; that we must look away from outward appearance, and believe. Three times a day we went alone before God, and engaged in earnest prayer for the recovery of his health. This was the whole burden of our petitions, and frequently one of us would be prostrated by the power of God. The Lord graciously heard our earnest cries, and my husband began to recover. For many months our prayers ascended to heaven three times a day for health to do the will of God. These seasons of prayer were very precious. We were brought into a sacred nearness to God, and had sweet communion with him. I cannot better state my feelings at this time than they are expressed in the following extracts from a letter I wrote to Sister Howland:—

"'I feel thankful that I can now have my children with me, under my own watchcare, and can better train them in the right way. For weeks I have felt a hungering and thirsting for salvation, and we have enjoyed almost uninterrupted communion with God. Why do we stay away from the fountain, when we can come and drink? Why do we die for bread, when there is a storehouse full? It is rich and free. O my soul, feast upon it, and daily drink in heavenly joys. I will not hold my peace. The praise of God is in my heart, and upon my lips. We can rejoice in the fullness of our Saviour's love. We can feast upon his excellent glory. My soul testifies to this. My gloom has been dispersed by this precious light, and I can never forget it. Lord, help me to keep it in lively remembrance. Awake, all the energies of my soul! Awake, and adore thy Redeemer for his wondrous love.

"'Souls around us must be aroused and saved, or they perish. Not a moment have we to lose. We all have an influence that tells for the truth, or against it. I desire to carry with me unmistakable evidences that I am one of Christ's disciples. We want something besides Sabbath religion. We need the living principle, and to daily feel individual responsibility. This is shunned by many, and the fruit is carelessness, indifference, a lack of watchfulness and spirituality. Where is the spirituality of the church? Where are men and women full of faith and the Holy Spirit? My prayer is, Purify thy church, O God. For months I have enjoyed freedom, and I am determined to order my conversation, and all my ways, aright before the Lord.

"'Our enemies may triumph. They may speak

bitter words, and their tongue frame slander, deceit, and falsehood, yet will we not be moved. We know in whom we have believed. We have not run in vain, neither labored in vain. A reckoning day is coming, when all will be judged according to the deeds done in the body. It is true the world is dark. Opposition may wax strong. The trifler and scorner may grow bold in his iniquity. Yet for all this we will not be moved, but lean upon the arm of the Mighty One for strength.

"'God is sifting his people. He will have a clean and holy church. We cannot read the heart of man. But the Lord has provided means to keep the church pure. A corrupt people has arisen who could not live with the people of God. They despised reproof, and would not be corrected. They had an opportunity to know that their warfare was an unrighteous one. They had time to repent of their wrongs; but self was too dear to die. They nourished it, and it grew strong, and they separated from the trusting people of God, that he was purifying unto himself. We all have reason to thank God that a way has been opened to save the church; for the wrath of God must have come upon us, if these corrupt individuals had remained with us.

"'Every honest one that may be deceived by these disaffected ones, will have the true light in regard to them, if every angel from Heaven has to visit them, and enlighten their minds. We have nothing to fear in this matter. As we near the Judgment all will manifest their true character, and it will be made plain to what company they belong. The sieve is moving. Let us not say, Stay thy hand, O God. The church must be purged, and will be. God reigns; let the people praise him. I have not the most distant thought of sinking down. I mean to be right and do right. The

Judgment is to set and the books be opened, and we are to be judged according to our deeds. All the falsehoods that may be framed against me will not make me any worse, nor any better, unless they have a tendency to drive me nearer my Redeemer.'

"About this time I wrote as follows, which appeared in the *Review* for Jan. 10, 1856: 'We have felt the power and blessing of God for a few weeks past. He has been very merciful. He has wrought in a wonderful manner for my husband. We have brought him to our great Physician in the arms of our faith, and like blind Bartimeus have cried, 'Jesus, thou Son of David, have mercy on us;' and we have been comforted. The healing power of God has been felt. All medicine has been laid aside, and we rely alone upon the arm of our great Physician. We are not yet satisfied. Our faith says, Entire restoration. We have seen the salvation of God, yet we expect to see and feel more. I believe without a doubt that my husband will yet be able to sound the last notes of warning to the world. For weeks past our peace has been like a river. Our souls triumph in God. Gratitude, unspeakable gratitude, fills my soul for the tokens of God's love which we have of late felt and seen. We feel like dedicating ourselves anew to God.'

"From the time we moved to Battle Creek, the Lord began to turn our captivity. We found sympathizing friends in Michigan who were ready to share our burdens and supply our wants. Old, tried friends in Central New York and New England, especially in Vermont, sympathized with us in our afflictions, and liberally assisted us in time of distress. At the Conference at Battle Creek in November, 1856, God wrought for us. The minds of the servants of God were exercised as to the gifts of the church. If God's frown had been brought upon his people because the gifts had been slighted and neglected, there was a pleasing prospect that his smiles would again be upon us, and he would graciously revive the gifts, and they would live in the church to encourage the fainting soul, and to correct and reprove the erring. New life was given to the cause, and success attended the labors of our preachers.

"The publications were called for, and proved to be just what the cause demanded; so that by turning them out to the Committee at a discount, my husband was enabled to pay all his debts. His cough ceased, and the pain and soreness left his lungs and throat, and he was gradually restored to health, so as to preach three times on the Sabbath and three times on first-day with ease. This wonderful work in his restoration is of God, and he shall have all the glory.

"The paper called the *Messenger of Truth* soon went down, and the discordant spirits who spoke through it are now scattered to the four winds. We leave them, with the falsehoods they have framed. They will have to render an account to God. All their sins are faithfully registered in Heaven, and they will be judged according to their deeds.

"The publication of the *Review, Instructor,* and books, was commenced under most discouraging circumstances. The friends and supporters of the cause were then very few, and generally poor; and it was by extreme labor and economy that the truth was published. For several years we suffered more or less for want of suitable food and clothing, and deprived ourselves of needed sleep, laboring from fourteen to sixteen hours out of the twenty-four, for want of means and help to push forward the work.

"Again, the present truth was not then as clear as now. It has been opening gradually. It required much study and anxious care to bring it out, link after link. By care and incessant labor and anxiety has the work moved on, until the great truths of our message are clear. And now, as there are many writers, it is a light task to conduct the *Review* compared with what it was at first. In the struggle to bring up the *Review* and *Instructor* where the number of paying subscribers would be sufficient to meet the expenses, and in the publication of numerous tracts, pamphlets, and books, my husband nearly lost his life. He then gave all away into the hands of the Publishing Committee as the property of the church, like a man who commences in poverty to make a farm, and when he has spent the strength of manhood in improving it, gives it to others.

"I do not make these statements with one murmuring feeling. It is a pleasure to me in this work to state the facts in the case. We have acted from choice, for the good of the cause. Its prosperity and the confidence of its true friends are worth a thousand times more to us than the good things of this life. We are raised above want; and this is sufficient for all true believers in the third message. For this we feel grateful to God. I would here express our gratitude to our friends who lent my husband money without interest to publish with. This enabled him to purchase stock at the lowest rates, publish large editions of our books, and manage his business to advantage. Had it not been for this, the Office must have gone down, unless sustained in some other way.

"Our numerous personal friends have been liberal. Many to whom I sent the several numbers of the Testimonies, sent to me in return, some tenfold, and some more. Some who have never helped us have appeared to feel very much annoyed to see us raised above want and dependence. But if the Lord has put it into the hearts of our personal friends to raise us above want, that our testimony may not be crippled by the galling sense of dependence, I do not see how these persons can help it.

"In December, 1853, I fell and sprained my ankle, which confined me to crutches six weeks. The confinement was an injury to my lungs. I attended meeting in my afflicted state, and tried to labor for the good of some souls who seemed to manifest interest to become Christians. At the close of one of these meetings I felt very weary; but a request came for us to visit a family, and pray for some of their children who had been afflicted. My judgment told me that I had not strength to go farther. But I finally consented to go. While praying, something seemed to tear on my left lung. After I returned home, I could not breathe without pain. My lung seemed to be filling.

Our family bowed before the Lord, and earnestly prayed that I might be relieved. I found relief, but discharged blood from my lung. I have not been entirely free from pain in the left lung since that time. After this, I suffered with a dull, heavy pain in my head, which increased for three weeks, when it became intense. I tried every means in my power to remove it; but the pain overcame me. It was inflammation of the brain. I entreated those around me not to let me sleep, fearing I should never wake to consciousness. I did not expect to live, and wished to spend my moments, while reason lasted, in talking with my husband and children, and giving them up into the hands of God. At times my mind wandered, and then again I realized my critical situation. My husband called for a few who had faith to pray for me. The Spirit of the Lord rested upon me, and my grateful thanks ascended to our great Physician who had mercifully relieved me.

"A Conference was held at Battle Creek in May, 1856. While we were very busy preparing for the meeting, I was startled by a scream of distress. My little Willie, then about twenty months old, was brought to me by Sister Fraser apparently lifeless. While playing around a tub of dirty suds, he had fallen into it, and had not one of his little feet appeared above the dark surface, he would not have been discovered in season to save him. His arms and face were purple, and he was entirely breathless. We cut off his wet clothes, and rolled him on the grass, when he manifested a faint sign of life. We took him before a fire, and by heating flannels produced some heat in his body. He breathed with difficulty. I kissed him, and he opened his eyes languidly, and tried to return the token of affection with his pale, cold lips.

"The Lord spared our dear babe to us, when to all appearance he was already in death's embrace. Oh, how grateful we felt to God for his mercy to us! I felt very solemn as I heard in the still evening the cry, "Child lost!" and then the description of some mother's little one whose fate was in uncertainty. I clasped my little Willie to my heart, which throbbed with love and gratitude to the Lord who had spared our dear boy.

"But we were yet to pass through another severe trial. At the Conference a very solemn vision was given me. I saw that some of those present would be food for worms, some subjects for the seven last plagues, and some would be translated to Heaven at the second coming of Christ, without seeing death. Sister Bonfoey remarked to a sister as we left the meeting-house, 'I feel impressed that I am one who will soon be food for worms.' The Conference closed Monday. Thursday, Sister B. sat at the table with us apparently well. She then went to the Office as usual, to assist in mailing the *Review.* In about two hours she sent for me. She had been suddenly taken very ill. My health had been very poor, yet I hastened to suffering Clara. In a few hours she seemed some better.

"The next morning we had her brought home in a large chair, and she was laid upon her own bed, from which she was never to rise. Her symptoms became alarming, and we had fears that a tumor, which had troubled her for nearly ten years, had broken inwardly. It was so, and mortification was doing its work. Friday evening, about seven o'clock, she fell asleep. She had her senses until her eyes closed in death. She stated that her pilgrimage was ended, and that she had no fears of death. We united in prayer, and she responded. She kissed us, and bade us an affectionate farewell. She seemed very solicitous for my health, and was grieved if I manifested distress. We were unprepared for her death. To lose her was a living loss. Eight years she had shared our joys and trials, and she had never proved untrue. We have missed her cheerful society, and her sisterly affection, and her care in our family. We laid her in Oak Hill Cemetery to rest until the sleeping saints awake to immortality.

"Immediately after the funeral my health failed rapidly. I had a severe cough, and raised some blood. I thought that I, too, should soon rest in the grave. There was to be a tent-meeting at Monterey, and we were invited to attend. My children were my greatest anxiety. How could I leave them? They had been deprived of our care so much that they needed attention from one who could feel an interest for them. I left them, with a mother's keenest feelings, and thought, as I parted with them, that I might not be permitted to return to them alive. I was assured by one of the sisters that my children need not trouble my mind, that she would have especial care for them. I rode in much suffering to Monterey, Mich., coughing almost incessantly.

" Sabbath morning we retired to a grove to have a season of prayer. We were soon to go to the tent, and I was so weak that it was impossible for me to sit up long at a time. We felt like pleading with the Lord for his sustaining grace. We there committed my case to Him who while on earth was ever touched with human woe, and claimed the promises for strength and grace. The Spirit of the Lord rested upon me, and with a firm trust in the promises of God, we went to the meeting. I bore my testimony during that meeting five times, and continued to grow stronger. My cough did not leave me at once, yet I knew the Lord had given me strength as I needed it; for nothing but his power could have carried me through that meeting.

" When I returned home, I found that my children had been neglected by those who had assured me that they should have their care. I felt grieved. My greatest anxiety had been for my children, to bring them up free from evil habits. Our work had been to travel, and then write and publish. Henry had been from us five years, and Edson had received but little of our care. For years at Rochester, our family was very large, and our home like a hotel, and we from that home much of the time. I often felt grieved as I thought of others who would not take burdens and cares, who could ever be with their children, to counsel and instruct them, and to spend their time almost exclusively in their own families. And I have inquired, Does God require so much of us, and leave others without burdens?

Is this equality ? Are we to be thus hurried on from one care to another, one part of the work to another, and have but little time to bring up our children ? Many nights, while others have been sleeping, have been spent by me in bitter weeping.

"I would plan and frame some course more favorable for my children, then objections would arise which would sweep away these calculations. I was keenly sensitive to faults in my children, and every wrong they committed brought on me such heartache as to affect my health. I have wished that some mothers could be circumstanced for a short time as I have been for years; then they would prize the blessings they enjoy, and could better sympathize with me in my privations. We have prayed and labored for our children, and have restrained them. We have not neglected the rod, but before using it have first labored to have them see their faults, and then have prayed with them. We have our children understand that we should merit the displeasure of God, if we excused them in sin. And our efforts have been blessed to the good of our children. Their greatest pleasure is to please us. They are not free from faults, but we believe that they will yet be numbered with the lambs of Christ's fold."

The volume from which the foregoing is taken was written by Mrs. White in 1860. During the past twenty years many changes have taken place. Our godly parents, both by the name of White and Harmon, have passed away, and the old Bibles of both families, one printed in 1822, and the other in 1823, have fallen into our hands as an invaluable legacy. These dear old books, made still more precious by the marks of age, dimly bear the names of their first owners in gilt letters on their worn covers, John and Betsey White on the one, and Robert and Eunice Harmon on the other.

But it is not the aged alone that pass away to the silent grave. Death has twice stepped over our threshold, and has broken the eldest and youngest branches of our family tree. Little Herbert, born September 20, 1860, died December 14 of the same year. And when that tender branch was broken, how our hearts did bleed none may know but those who have followed their little ones of promise to the grave. A father may feel the blow keenly; but the tenderest earthly tie is between the mother and her child. She who bears the child, and from her body gives it the nourishment which nature provides, feels when the cord is severed, as the father cannot.

But oh, when our noble Henry died at the age of sixteen! when our sweet singer was borne to the grave, and we no more heard his early song, accompanied by the pure tones of the melodeon, ours was a lonely home. Both parents, and the two remaining sons, felt the blow most keenly. But God comforted us in our bereavements, and with faith and courage we pressed forward in the work he had given us, in bright hope of meeting our children, who had been torn from us by death, in that world where sickness and death will not come.

Since the death of our dear children, the Lord has opened before us a vast field of labor. Mrs. W. has taken the stand as a speaker, timidly at first, but as the providence of God has opened the way before her she has had confidence to stand before large audiences; and in power to move the people, has excelled all others of our speakers. Together we have attended our camp-meetings and other large gatherings, from Maine to Dakota—from Michigan to Texas and California.

Mrs. W. has spoken in twenty-four States and Territories, besides the Canadas. At our camp-meetings she has frequently held crowds of people ranging from five to twenty thousand. Her voice, which was imperfect in her earlier days of feebleness, has become clear and powerful, and her articulation is so distinct that acres of people can hear her out-of-doors addresses as easily as if seated in a church. The writer of a biographical sketch of Mr. and Mrs. White, published in a volume entitled, "The Eminent and Self-made Men of Michigan," speaks of Mrs. W. in these words: --

"As a speaker, Mrs. White is one of the most successful of the few ladies who have become noteworthy as lecturers in this country during the last twenty years. Constant use has so strengthened her vocal organs as to give her voice rare depth and power. Her clearness and strength of articulation are so great, that, when speaking in the open air, she has frequently been distinctly heard at the distance of a mile. Her language, though simple, is always forcible. When inspired with her subject, she is often marvelously eloquent, holding the largest audiences spell-bound for hours without a sign of impatience or weariness. The subject matter of her discourses is always of a practical character, bearing chiefly on fireside duties, the religious education of children, temperance, and kindred topics. On revival occasions she is always the most effective speaker. She has frequently spoken to immense audiences in the large cities on her favorite themes, and has always been received with great favor. On one occasion, in Massachusetts, twenty thousand persons listened to her with close attention for more than an hour."

The peculiar experience and extensive labors of Mrs. W. have called out expressions from the pious, from the curious, and from those who have cherished a spirit toward her and her work as bitter as gall. And the very nature of the case seems to demand that we should make the following points :—

1. Had Mrs. W. been spared the blow which made her an invalid in her childhood; had she grown to womanhood with health and strength to obtain a finished education; and had she come before the people, under these favorable circumstances, as a speaker and writer, the unbelief of our times, so ready to seize upon objections, would have given the credit of her work to the woman, and not to the Lord. For the special work connected with the last message, at this time of unparalleled skepticism, God chose a feeble means, that his power might be clearly manifested, and that the glory of his work might not be given to the instrument. The words of Paul are applicable: " Ye see your calling, brethren, how that not many wise men after the flesh, not many mighty, not many noble, are called : but God hath chosen the foolish things of the world to confound the wise; and God hath chosen the weak things of the world to confound the things which are mighty." 1 Cor. 1 : 26, 27.

2. At the age of nine years, Mrs. W. received a blow which broke her nose, and which made her an invalid during the period of her school-girl days, depriving her of the advantages of an education. At seventeen she received her first vision, as described on page 193. This occurred in the month of December, 1844. In a few weeks she left the home of her parents, in great feebleness, and went out in the cold of midwinter in Maine, to relate to others what God had revealed to her. Her work for the past thirty-five years, commenced under these discouraging circumstances, has continued with scarcely an interruption, up to the present time. During this time she has written thousands of personal testimonies, has raised her family, and, much of the time, been on the wing from State to State, to speak to the people. She has five thousand pages of her writings in the field.

3. Does unbelief suggest that what she writes in her personal testimonies has been learned from others? We inquire, What time has she had to learn all these facts? and who for a moment can regard her as a Christian woman, if she gives her ear to gossip, then writes it out as a vision from God? And where is the person of superior natural and acquired abilities who could listen to the description of one, two, or three thousand cases, all differing, and then write them out without getting them confused, laying the whole work liable to a thousand contradictions? If Mrs. W. has gathered the facts from a human mind in a single case, she has in thousands of cases, and God has not shown her these things which she has written in these personal testimonies.

4. In her published works there are many things set forth which cannot be found in other books, and yet they are so clear and beautiful that the unprejudiced mind grasps them at once as truth. A doctor of divinity once heard Mrs. W. speak upon her favorite theme, God in Nature. She dwelt largely upon the life and teachings of Christ. This Christian gentleman was instructed and highly edified; and at the close of the discourse, in private conversation, addressed her in these words: " Sister White, while you were speaking, I have been asking myself the question, Why is it that none of us have thought of these precious things which you have brought out this morning?"

If commentators and theological writers generally had seen these gems of thought which strike the mind so forcibly, and had they been brought out in print, all the ministers in the land could have read them. These men gather thoughts from books, and as Mrs. W. has written and spoken a hundred things, as truthful as they are beautiful and harmonious, which cannot be found in the writings of

others, they are new to the most intelligent readers
and hearers. And if they are not to be found in
print, and are not brought out in sermons from the
pulpit, where did Mrs. W. find them? From what
source has she received the new and rich thoughts
which are to be found in her writings and oral addresses? She could not have learned them from
books, from the fact that they do not contain such
thoughts. And, certainly, she did not learn them
from those ministers who had not thought of them.
The case is a clear one. It evidently requires a
hundred times the credulity to believe that Mrs. W.
has learned these things of others, and has palmed
them off as visions from God, that it does to believe
that the Spirit of God has revealed them to her.

5. The spirit of prophecy has been appealing to
the church through Mrs. W. during the past thirty-
five years in behalf of the Bible, the commandments
of God and the faith of Jesus, setting forth practical godliness as the test of Christian character.
The fruits of her teachings and labors have been
good, and only good. Here is the Lord's test:—

"Ye shall know them by their fruits. Do men
gather grapes of thorns, or figs of thistles? Even
so every good tree bringeth forth good fruit; but
a corrupt tree bringeth forth evil fruit." Matt. 7:
16, 17.

Gamaliel, a reputable doctor of the law, said,
"Refrain from these men, and let them alone; for
if this counsel or this work be of men, it will
come to naught; but if it be of God, ye cannot over-
throw it; lest haply ye be found even to fight
against God." Acts 5:38, 39.

The subject under consideration seems to demand
that the scriptural evidences of the perpetuity of
spiritual gifts, and their design, should constitute a
chapter of this work.

# CHAPTER X.

## THE SPIRIT OF PROPHECY—PERPETUITY AND DESIGN OF SPIRITUAL GIFTS.

ONCE, man walked with God in Eden. With open face he beheld the glory of the Lord, and talked with God, and Christ, and angels, in Paradise, without a dimming vail between. Man fell from his moral rectitude and innocency, and was driven from the garden, from the tree of life, and from the visible presence of the Lord and his holy angels. Moral darkness, like the pall of death, has since cast its shadows everywhere, and everywhere the blight and mildew of sin have been seen. And amid the general gloom and moral wretchedness, man has wandered from the gates of Paradise for nearly six thousand years, subject to sickness, pain, sorrow, tears, and death. He has also been subject to the temptations and wiles of the devil, so much so that it is the sad history of man, throughout the entire period of his fallen state, that Satan has reigned with almost universal sway.

When all was lost in Adam, and the shades of night darkened the moral heavens, there soon appeared the star of hope in Christ, and with it was established a means of communication between God and man through the gift of prophecy. In his fallen state, man could not converse face to face with God, and with Christ, and with angels, as when in his Eden purity. But through the ministration of holy angels could the great God speak to him in dreams and in visions. "If there be a prophet among you, I the Lord will make myself known unto him in a vision, and will speak unto him in a dream." Num. 12 : 6.

The manifestation of the spirit of prophecy was designed for all dispensations. The sacred Record nowhere restricts it to any particular period of time, from the fall to the final restitution. The Bible recognizes its existence alike in the patriarchal, Jewish, and Christian ages. Through this medium God communed with holy men of old. Enoch, the seventh from Adam, prophesied, and so extensive was the range of his prophetic vision, and so minute, that he could look down over long ages, and describe the coming of the Lord, and the execution of the last Judgment upon the ungodly. Jude, verses 14, 15.

God spoke to his prophets in the Jewish dispensation in visions and in dreams, and opened before them the great things of the future, especially those connected with the first advent of his Son to suffer for sinners, and his second appearing in glory to destroy his enemies, and complete the redemption of his people. If the spirit of prophecy nearly disappeared from the Jewish church for a few centuries toward the close of that dispensation, on account of the corruptions in that church, it re-appeared at its close to usher in the Messiah. Zacharias, the father of John the Baptist, "was filled with the Holy Spirit, and prophesied." Simeon, a just and devout man, who was "waiting for the consolation of Israel," came by the Spirit into the temple, and prophesied of Jesus as "a light to lighten the Gentiles, and the glory of Israel." And Anna, a prophetess, "spake of him to all them that look for redemption in Jerusalem." And there was no greater prophet than John, who was chosen of God to introduce to Israel "the Lamb of God, that taketh away the sin of the world."

The Christian age commenced with the outpouring of the Holy Spirit, and the manifestation of various spiritual gifts. Among these was the gift of prophecy. After commissioning his disciples to go into all the world and preach the gospel, Jesus says to them: "And these signs shall follow them that believe: In my name shall they cast out devils; they shall speak with new tongues; they shall take up serpents; and if they drink any deadly thing, it shall not hurt them; they shall lay hands on the sick, and they shall recover." Mark 16: 17, 18. On the day of Pentecost, when the Christian dispensation was fully opened, some of these gifts were manifested in a most wonderful manner. Acts 2: 1--11. Luke, in giving account of his travels with Paul and others, when a quarter of a century of the Christian age had already passed, after speaking of entering into the house of Philip the evangelist, says: "And the same man had four daughters, virgins, which did prophesy. And as we tarried there many days, there came down from Judea a certain prophet, named Agabus." Acts 21: 9, 10. Again, still later, we see the beloved John in the Isle of Patmos, imbued with the spirit of prophecy in all its fullness. The wonderful Revelation was given unto him when more than half a century of the Christian age had passed. And here the New Testament record leaves us, without a single intimation that the gifts of the Spirit should cease from the church till the day of glory should be ushered in by the second appearing of Jesus Christ.

Since the great apostasy, these gifts have rarely been manifested; and, for this reason, professed Christians generally suppose that they were designed to be limited to the period of the primitive church. But from the time of the primitive Christians to the present, there have been manifestations among the most devoted followers of

Jesus, which have been recognized by nearly all of the leading denominations as the gifts of the Holy Spirit. Then should not the errors and the unbelief of the church be assigned as reasons why these manifestations have been so seldom, rather than that God has taken these blessings from the church? When the people of God attain to primitive faith and practice, as they most certainly will under the last message, the latter rain will be poured out, and the gifts will be revived. The former rain was given at the commencement of the Christian age, in the time of sowing the gospel seed, to cause it to germinate and take good root. Then the church enjoyed the gifts. And when the latter rain shall be poured out at the close of this dispensation, to ripen the golden harvest for the garner of God, then will the gifts of the Holy Spirit be manifested in all their fullness.

To this agree the words of the prophet as quoted by Peter : " And it shall come to pass in the last days, saith God, I will pour out of my Spirit upon all flesh ; and your sons and your daughters shall prophesy, and your young men shall see visions, and your old men shall dream dreams ; and on my servants and on my handmaidens I will pour out in those days of my Spirit ; and they shall prophesy ; and I will show wonders in heaven above, and signs in the earth beneath ; blood, and fire, and vapor of smoke ; the sun shall be turned into darkness, and the moon into blood, before that great and notable day of the Lord come." Acts 2 : 17–20. Notice the following points:—

1. The spirit of prophecy is here mentioned as one of the especial signs of the last days. Its revival is to constitute one of the most noted signs of the approaching end.

2. The term last days embraces the very last day ; hence the manifestations of the spirit of

prophecy reach to the end. To say that these words of the Lord by the prophet were all fulfilled on the day of Pentecost, is virtually saying that the last days ended eighteen centuries ago.

3. There can be no mistake as to the time of the fulfillment of these signs. Christ, in his prophetic discourse to his disciples, in answer to the question, " What shall be the sign of thy coming, and of the end of the world," mentions the darkening of the sun and moon as signs of the end. He locates these signs in these words : " Immediately after the tribulation of those days shall the sun be darkened, and the moon shall not give her light." Matt. 24 : 29. The tribulation here mentioned is that which was upon the church of Christ for 1260 years, from 538 to 1798. It does not read, after those days ; but after the tribulation of those days. The days reached to 1798, eighteen years later than the dark day ; but the tribulation of the days ceased before the dark day of 1780. The days of tribulation were shortened for the elect's sake. Mark 13 : 24 makes the matter perfectly plain. " But in those days, after that tribulation, the sun shall be darkened." We are therefore shut up to the eighteenth century for the period of the fulfillment of the supernatural darkening of the sun and moon.

4. The same is a matter of prophecy in Rev. 6 : 12. The first event under the sixth seal is the great earthquake of 1755. Then follow the signs in the sun and moon, of 1780, in these words : " The sun became black as sackcloth of hair, and the moon became as blood." The full moon appeared, through the darkness of the night which followed the dark day of May 19, 1780, as a ball of blood.

5. The prophet Joel describes the same in these words : " The sun shall be turned into darkness,

and the moon into blood." This is in appearance only, as it would be absurd to suppose that the great center of light for our world would be actually turned into darkness, and the moon into literal blood. Classed with these signs of the approaching end is the manifestation of the spirit of prophecy.

Of all the blessings which God has bestowed upon his people, the gift of his Son excepted, none have been so sacred and so important to their welfare as the gifts of his holy law, and his Holy Spirit. And none have been so well calculated to thwart the plans of Satan, and consequently to stir his rage, as these. And when that people arise in the last generation of men, who shall observe all ten of the precepts of God's holy law, and recognize the revival of the spirit of prophecy, they may expect to feel that bitterness from their opponents which can arise only from the direct inspiration of Satan. "And the dragon was wroth with the woman, and went to make war with the remnant of her seed, which keep the commandments of God, and have the testimony of Jesus Christ." Rev. 12 : 17.

The dragon is a symbol of the first great rebel against God's government. The woman is a symbol of the true church. The common and well-understood figure of the remnant represents a small body of Christians in the last generation of men, just prior to the second coming of Christ. This body of Christians, waiting for the coming and kingdom of the Redeemer, are keeping the commandments of God, and have the testimony of Jesus Christ.

We now inquire, What is the testimony of Jesus Christ? The angel gives John the answer to this question in its broadest signification. "The testimony of Jesus is the spirit of prophecy." Rev. 19 : 10. The spirit, soul, and substance of prophecy, is the testimony of Jesus Christ. Or, the voice of the prophets relative to the plan and work of human redemption, is the voice of the Redeemer. Christ undertook the work of redemption, and who should inspire a book upon the subject but the Redeemer himself ?

The Jewish age, notwithstanding its apostasies, opened and closed with special manifestations of the Spirit of God. And it is not reasonable to suppose that the Christian age, the light of which, compared with the former dispensation, is as the light of the sun to the feeble rays of the moon, should commence in glory, and close in obscurity. And since a special work of the Spirit was necessary to prepare a people for the first advent of Christ, how much more important the work of the Spirit to prepare a people for his second advent.

God has never manifested his power to his people simply for their gratification : but according to their necessities has he wrought for them. Then we may safely conclude that, as his people are passing the perils of the last days in the final struggle with the aroused powers of darkness, when false prophets shall have power to show great signs and wonders, insomuch that, if it were possible, they would deceive the very elect, our gracious God will bless and strengthen his fainting people with the gifts, as well as the graces, of the Holy Spirit.

We have seen that the manifestation of the spirit of prophecy became necessary in consequence of man's being separated from the visible presence of God. But when the tabernacle of God shall be with men, and he shall dwell with them, and God himself shall be with them ; Rev. 21 : 3 ; when Christ shall come again with all the holy angels, and receive his people unto himself, that where he shall be, there they may be also ; John 14 : 3 ; and when man redeemed shall walk and talk with God, and Christ, and angels, in Eden restored ; *then* there will be no further need of the spirit of prophecy.

When man in Eden stood in all the perfection of his manhood, before the blight of sin had touched anything that God had made for him, and with open face beheld the glory of the Lord, he could have no need of the spirit of prophecy. But when Eden was lost in consequence of transgression, and man was doomed to grope his way from the gates of Paradise, enshrouded in the moral gloom that resulted from the curse and the reign of Satan, he needed this light. And his need in this respect will continue more or less urgent until the restitution, when the redeemed shall walk and talk with God, and with Christ, and with the holy angels, in Eden restored.

The apostle to the Corinthians clearly sustains this position. He introduces the subject by stating, "Now concerning spiritual gifts, brethren, I would not have you ignorant." 1 Cor. 12 : 1. He deemed the subject of too great importance to leave the church at Corinth in ignorance respecting it. He proposes to instruct them. We shall do well to avail ourselves of the benefit of his teachings.

In this chapter the apostle introduces the human body, with its several members acting in harmony, one dependent upon the other, as an illustration of the Christian church, with its members, and the several gifts God has set in the church. He then makes the application of the figure thus : "Now ye are the body of Christ, and members in particular. And God hath set some in the church, first apostles, secondarily prophets, thirdly teachers, after that miracles, then gifts of healings, helps, governments, diversities of tongues." Verses 27, 28.

Let it be borne in mind that *God has set* prophets, miracles, and gifts of healings, in the Christian church as verily as he has teachers, helps, and governments. And this expression, "God hath set" them in the church, means more than that he would communicate with his people by his Holy Spirit in the Christian age the same as he had in former dispensations. It conveys the idea that God had especially endowed the Christian church with them. He had established them in the church, to remain until the return of her absent Lord. This was done because the church needed them. Did the primitive church need them? So did the true church need them to light her pathway during the dark period of her persecutions and martyrdom. And much more does the church need the gifts in pressing her course through the perils of the last days, and in making ready to receive her soon-coming Lord.

• The design of the gifts, and also the time of their continuance in the church, are definitely expressed by the apostle to the Ephesians: "And he gave some, apostles; and some, prophets; and some, evangelists; and some pastors and teachers; for the perfecting of the saints, for the work of the ministry, for the edifying of the body of Christ; till we all come in the unity of the faith, and of the knowledge of the Son of God, unto a perfect man, unto the measure of the stature of the fullness of Christ." Chap. 4:11-13.

It cannot be shown that the church did, in the lifetime of Paul, reach the state of unity, knowledge, and perfection, here mentioned. And certainly the church did not enjoy these during her apostasy, 2 Thess. 2:3, and the period of her flight into the wilderness. Rev. 12:6. Nor has she reached this state of unity, knowledge, and perfection, since the labors of Martin Luther. The church to-day is almost infinitely below this state of unity, knowledge, and perfection. And not until the Christians of the last generation of men shall be brought to the enjoyment of it by the last warning message, and all the means God may employ to prepare them to be translated to Heaven without tasting death, will the ultimate design of the gifts be realized.

The gifts and callings of God, here mentioned by the apostle, were all given at the same time, for the same objects, and were all to reach to the same point of time. Were evangelists, pastors, and teachers to continue to the end? So was the gift of prophecy. Did the period for the manifestation of the spirit of prophecy close with Christ's first apostles? Then the commission of evangelists, pastors, and religious teachers, became obsolete eighteen hundred years since.

But Paul, in 1 Cor. 13, has distinctly shown when the gifts would cease. In the first part of this chapter the apostle discourses upon the pre-eminence of love (improperly translated *charity*) over the gift of tongues, gift of prophecy, faith, liberality to the poor, and courage to give one's body to be burned. These, in the absence of love, are valueless. He then describes the virtues and riches of love, closing with these words: "Charity [love] never faileth; but whether there be prophecies, they shall fail; whether there be tongues, they shall cease; whether there be knowledge, it shall vanish away." Verse 8. While love is the crowning Christian grace here, and will be the crowning glory of the redeemed to all eternity, the gifts will cease with faith and hope. At the glorious appearing of the Lord, faith will be lost in sight, hope in fruition, prophecies will fail to be any longer a light to the church, tongues will cease to be a sign, and the faint knowledge of the present dim night will vanish before the knowledge of the perfect day as the dim rays of the moon vanish before the light of the rising sun.

Next come the forcible words of verses 9 and 10: "For we know in part, and we prophesy in part; but when that which is perfect is come, then that which is in part shall be done away." We still wait for that which is perfect to come. And while we wait, may our dear, absent Lord manifest himself to his waiting people through the gifts. "For," says Paul, speaking of the present imperfect state, "we know in part, and we prophesy in part." How long shall the spirit of prophecy serve the church? When will it be done away? Answer: "But when that which is perfect is come, then that which is in part shall be done away." This should settle the question of the perpetuity of the gifts in the Christian church.

The popular view, however, is this: The gifts were given to the primitive church, to remain only during the lifetime of Christ's first apostles. At their death, the gifts were to be removed from the church. But let it be remembered that a great change takes place when the gifts are to cease, and that change is from an imperfect state to that which is perfect; from the dimness of night to the glory of perfect day. We need not inquire if such a change took place at the death of the first apostles; for all who have any knowledge of the history of the primitive church, know that whatever changes did take place in the church about the time of the death of the apostles, were not for the better, but decidedly for the worse. Even in Paul's day, the mystery of iniquity already worked in the church. 2 Thess. 2:7. And the apostle, addressing the elders of the church at Miletus, says: "For I know this, that after my departing shall grievous wolves enter in among you, not sparing the flock.

Also of your own selves shall men arise, speaking perverse things, to draw away disciples after them.' Acts 20:29, 30. But if we apply this great change to the close of the present dispensation, and the introduction of the eternal day of glory, all is plain. Here we have the clearest proof that the gifts were not to be done away until the second appearing of Christ.

Paul continues with an illustration of the present imperfect state, and the future life of perfection and glory: "When I was a child, I spake as a child, I understood as a child, I thought as a child; but when I became a man, I put away childish things." Verse 11. His childhood represents the present imperfect state; his manhood, the perfection of the immortal state. This is evident. Now suppose we are wrong, and that Paul's childhood represents the church in his day, endowed with the gifts; and that his manhood represents the church after his death, stripped of the gifts of the Holy Spirit, and fast sinking away toward the great apostasy! Absurdity!

And still the apostle continues with another beautiful illustration of the change from the present dispensation, during which the church was to enjoy the comparatively dim light of the gifts, as she walked by faith and hope, to the open glories of the world to come, when the redeemed shall walk with God in Eden restored, and talk face to face with Christ and angels. He says, "For now we see through a glass darkly; but then, face to face." Verse 21. To the view that the gifts were to cease at the death of the first apostles, and that with their death came the glorious change illustrated by these words of the apostle, we need only repeat, Absurdity!

The truth of God upon this subject is consistent and harmonious with itself, and with all divine

truth. The spirit of prophecy, in consequence of
the fall and man's separation from the visible presence of God, became a necessity. This necessity
has not been obviated by any past change of dispensation. No dispensation needs the gifts of
the Holy Spirit more than the Christian age; and
at no time in the long period of man's separation
from God's visible presence have they been so much
needed as amid the perils of the raging tempests of
the last days. But when the Redeemer shall
come, the controversy be ended, the saints' rest
given, and they, all immortal, meet around the
throne with angels, and face to face behold the
glory of God and the Lamb, the spirit of prophecy
will be numbered among Heaven's choicest blessings of the past.

But the skeptical objector inquires, "Where are
the gifts? If your position is correct, why have
they not been manifested in the church all along
down ever since God set them in the church? Why
are not the sick healed by faith now?" We are
aware that this is the principal objection brought
against the scriptural doctrine of the perpetuity of
the gifts, therefore it demands especial notice. We
reply as follows:—

1. The sick were not always healed by faith in
Paul's day. He says (2 Tim. 4 : 20), "Trophimus
have I left at Miletum sick." Again he says to
Timothy (1 Tim. 5 : 23), "Drink no longer water,
but use a little wine for thy stomach's sake and
thine often infirmities." God could have answered
the prayers of his servant Paul, and raised up
Trophimus, and healed Timothy's infirmities, if this
had been best. We conclude that God has not designed in any age of the church to manifest his
power so far that there should be no sick among
Christians. But in cases where it would be for the

good of the afflicted, and for his own glory, he has manifested his power, and will manifest it.

2. The unbelief of the professed followers of Christ in the manifestation of spiritual gifts is sufficient reason why they are not more fully manifested. It is said of Christ, "And he did not many mighty works there because of their unbelief." Matt. 13:58. There is an impious unbelief with many at this day, even of some who profess to take the Bible as their guide, which resembles that of those who, mockingly, said of Christ as he hung on the cross, "Let Christ, the King of Israel, descend now from the cross, that we may see and believe." It is sometimes said in reply to the Bible evidences of the perpetuity of spiritual gifts, "Just work a few miracles, and we will believe your doctrine." It is not God's plan to gratify such spirits; for should they see as powerful manifestations as were seen in the days of Christ, Paul, and Peter, they would scoffingly attribute it to the power of Satan, or some other cause besides the power of God.

It is humble, confiding faith that moves Omnipotence. Those only who have this faith may expect the manifestation of the gifts. Mark 2:5: "When Jesus saw *their faith*, he said unto the sick of the palsy, Son, thy sins be forgiven thee." Chap. 9:23: "Jesus said unto him, If thou canst believe, all things are possible to him that believeth." Matt. 9:21, 22: "For she said within herself, If I may but touch his garment, I shall be whole. But Jesus turned him about, and when he saw her, he said, Daughter, be of good comfort; *thy faith* hath made thee whole. And the woman was made whole from that hour." Chap. 15:28: "Then Jesus answered and said unto her, O woman, great is *thy faith*; be it unto thee even as thou wilt. And her daughter was made whole from that very hour."

3. The object of the gifts, as stated by Paul, was " for the perfecting of the saints, for the work of the ministry, for the edifying of the body of Christ, till we all come in the unity of the faith." But they have been superseded in the popular churches by human creeds, which have failed to secure scriptural unity. It has been truly said, " The American people are a nation of lords." In a land of boasted freedom of thought and of conscience, like ours, church force cannot produce unity ; but has caused divisions, and has given rise to religious sects and parties almost innumerable. Creed and church force have been called to the rescue in vain.

The remedy, however, for this deplorable evil is found in the proper use of the simple organization and church order set forth in the New-Testament Scriptures, and in the means Christ has ordained for the unity and perfection of the church. We affirm that there is not a single apology in all the book of God for disharmony of sentiment or spirit in the church. The means are ample to secure the high standard of unity expressed in the New Testament. Christ prayed that his people might be one, as he was one with his Father. John 17. And Paul appeals to the church at Corinth in these emphatic words: "Now I beseech you, brethren, by the name of our Lord Jesus Christ, that ye all speak the same thing, and that there be no divisions among you; but that ye be perfectly joined together in the same mind and in the same judgment." 1 Cor. 1:10. " Now the God of patience and consolation grant you to be like-minded one toward another according to Christ Jesus, that ye may with one mind and one mouth glorify God, even the Father of our Lord Jesus Christ." Rom. 15:5, 6. The gifts were given to secure this state of unity.

But the popular churches have introduced another means of preserving unity, namely, human creeds. These creeds secure a sort of unity to each denomination; but they have all proved inefficient, as appears from the New Schools and Reformed of almost every creed-bound denomination under heaven. Hence the many kinds of Baptists, of Presbyterians, of Methodists, and of others. There is not an excuse for this state of things anywhere to be found in the book of God. These sects are not on the foundation of unity laid by Jesus Christ, and taught by Paul, the wise master-builder. And the smaller sects who reject human creeds, professing to take the Bible as their rule of faith and practice, yet rejecting the gifts, are not a whit better off. In these perilous times they shake to fragments, yet cry, The Bible! the Bible! We, too, would exalt the Bible, and would say to those who would represent us as taking the gifts instead of the Bible, that we are not satisfied with a part of the sacred volume, but claim as ours the Bible, the whole Bible, the gifts and all.

All the denominations cannot be right, and it may not be wrong to suppose that no one of them is right on all points of faith. To show that they cannot have their creeds and the gifts too, that creeds shut out the gifts, we will suppose that God, through chosen instruments taken from each sect, begins to show up the errors in the creeds of these different denominations. If they received the testimony as from Heaven, it would spoil their creeds. But would they throw them away and come out on the platform of unity taught by Christ, Paul, and Peter? Never! They would a thousand times sooner reject the humble instruments of God's choice. It is evident that if the gifts were received, they would destroy human creeds; and that if creeds be received, they shut out the gifts.

4. When we consider the great apostasy of the church, the corruption of her pure doctrines, and her sojourn of 1260 years in the wilderness, we are not surprised that we do not find on the pages of her sad history any clearer records of the manifestations of spiritual gifts. We would here call attention to a work entitled "Miraculous Powers," published at the Office of the REVIEW AND HERALD, in which may be found testimonies from not only the eminently pious, but from many of the learned, and from some of the most reliable historians, fairly representing the faith of the church upon the subject of spiritual gifts. We do not rely upon the testimony of men as proof of our position; but after being established in the doctrine of the perpetuity of spiritual gifts from the plain testimony of God's word, it is a matter of unspeakable joy to find that on this vital doctrine our faith is in harmony with the good, the humble, and the prudent, ever since Christ said to his first ministers, "These signs shall follow them that believe."

Infinite wisdom has doubtless withheld the gifts to a great extent lest Satan take advantage of the ignorance and weakness of the people of God, and push them over into fanaticism. Many who have supposed that they were favored with manifestations of the Spirit of God, have regarded themselves as being quite out of danger. They soon became lifted up with pride in spiritual things, and were Satan's easy prey.

If it was necessary that Paul should have a thorn in the flesh, the messenger of Satan to buffet him, lest he become exalted through the abundance of revelations with which he was favored, it is a reasonable conclusion that all who seek to walk with God, and share all the spiritual

blessings of the Christian age, are also in danger
of exaltation and the wiles of the devil. If he can
push one such to extremes and fanaticism, he dis-
graces the vital part of Christianity, and gains a
greater victory than in holding a hundred souls in
cold formality. The history of Luther, the Wesleys, and others, who by the power of a living
faith led the church from the dark shades of error
and formality to a clearer light, proves the necessity of the mind's being well balanced with caution.
And he who sees no need of caution here is not far
from some delusive snare of Satan. But in walking softly and humbly before God, in strict watchfulness and fervent prayer to be kept by the power
of God from the wiles of Satan, there is safety.
God has great blessings in store for his people, and
will bestow them as fast as they can make a right
use of them to their good and his glory.

---

# CHAPTER XI.

## THE PUBLISHING DEPARTMENT.

THE publishing work of the S. D. Adventists
has grown to strength and great efficiency from
a small and humble commencement. The first
volume of the *Review* was printed upon an ordinary hand-press, at Paris, Maine, in the year
1850. Patrons were then so few that no subscrip-
tion price was given, the paper being supported
by donations from the friends of the cause, who
were generally poor. The most rigid economy
was necessary that it might maintain an existence.

The second volume was printed at Saratoga
Springs, N. Y. The growth of the cause was

slow. That which was gained in numbers was accomplished by great sacrifices and incessant toil. The accession of two or three preachers, and writers, and a corresponding increase of patrons, improved the condition of things; but up to this time the terms for the *Review* were gratis, the paper still being supported by donations.

May 6, 1852, the first number of volume three was printed at Rochester, N. Y., with material donated by our people. The cost of hand-press and types was seven hundred dollars. The present terms of the *Review*, two dollars per year in advance, were first made in June, 1855. By this time the paper was self-sustaining. The office remained at Rochester until October, 1855, when it was moved to its present location, Battle Creek, Michigan.

From this point the especial blessing of God attended the work, and as men were raised up in all parts of the field to proclaim the message of present truth, there was a more rapid increase of supporters; and it was soon seen that the hand-press was insufficient to supply the demand for our publications.

In 1857 a very encouraging change took place in the publishing department of our work. Twenty-five men were found in our feeble ranks, who cheerfully donated one hundred dollars each, for the purchase of a power-press and engine, which were put in successful operation in our wooden building, erected in 1855, the limited dimensions of which were 22 by 30 feet. This printing machine was then regarded the best for fine work. The excellent service it has done the past twenty-three years has contributed much to the reputation which the *Review* Office has earned of turning out the best printing done in the State.

Printing by steam was an important event in the history of our publishing work. The circulation of the *Review* and *Youth's Instructor* increased rapidly, new works were published, and new editions of those in print were issued. The building then occupied, which at first, before the introduction of the steam-press, seemed extravagantly large, soon proving to be too small for the work, an adjoining building was rented as a store-room of our publications and printers' stock. The pressing need of more room, and the inconveniences of the rooms then occupied, led to the conception of the plan, and the erection of the

first brick building, two stories high, in the form of a Greek cross, the main portion 26 x 66, the transverse section 26 x 44, as here represented. This building was located on the site of the first, at the south-east corner of Washington and West Main Streets. The plan of the building was not copied from any other. It was originated for the work to which it is so admirably adapted, the light pouring in through its ample windows on all sides of editors, compositors, pressmen, folders, and binders.

Up to this time we had been the legal proprietor of the publishing house, and sole manager of the work. We enjoyed the confidence of the active friends in the cause, who trusted to our care the means which they donated from time to time, as the growing cause demanded, to build up the publishing enterprise. And although the statement was frequently repeated through the *Review*, that the publishing house was virtually the property of the church, yet as we were the only legal manager, our enemies took advantage of the situation, and, under the cry of speculation, did all in their power to injure us, and to retard the progress of the cause. Under these circumstances we introduced the matter of organization, which resulted in the incorporation of the S. D. Adventist Publishing Association, according to the laws of Michigan, in the spring of 1861.

But there were those among us who did not take in the situation, and realize the embarrassing circumstances under which we were placed. Neither did they see the importance of order and organization in the church of God. And in their mistaken zeal, fearing that the S. D. Adventists were joining their hands with the world in forming a legally incorporated association, they gave their influence against the efforts which we were making to shift the financial responsibilities of the publishing house from our weary shoulders into the hands of an organized body. For a time this had its influence; but our good people soon saw the necessity and importance of an association to manage the rapidly increasing publishing work. And they came promptly and nobly to the rescue with their means, and immediately took stock to the amount of nearly $30,000.

While the discussion of the subject of organization was going on, the faithful friends of the cause, who gave us their confidence and sympathy, urged money into our hands in advance, to be invested in the stock of the Association, when it should be incorporated. This money we deposited with two brokers at Battle Creek, who were then paying ten per cent interest on deposits. In the advancement of the cause of the last message, God's providential care for the means consecrated to his cause by his trusting people has been manifested all the way. We give one marked case, with which we were connected.

While on a western tour in the autumn of 1860, we stopped at the house of Brother H. Patch, of Markesan, Wis., for the night. And while at family prayer we had a presentiment that our babe, then six weeks old, was sick. He appeared lying in his mother's lap, with head and face terribly swollen and inflamed. We immediately wrote to Mrs. W. that all was not well with the child. When she received the letter, three days later, and read it with the apparently healthy child on her lap, she stated to those around her, that if husband were there he would not have faith in his presentiment. But that night the bed was dressed with damp sheets, and the next morning the child was sick with erysipelas, affecting first the head and face.

Now we will go back in this narrative to the house of Brother Patch of Wisconsin. That night we dreamed that the brokers with whom we had deposited the money for the Office, were selling shop-worn shoes in an inferior store. And as we saw them we exclaimed, They have come down! These words awoke us, and for a moment we felt a little concerned for the Lord's money which was in their hands. But soon both the dream and the presentiment passed from our mind.

We had an appointment for a two-days' meeting at Monroe, Wis., and one the following week at Clyde, Ill. We filled the appointment at Monroe the next week, and then passed on to Clyde, and put up at the house of Brother Wicks. As we entered the house, Brother R. F. Andrews, who has since entered the ministry, handed us a telegram from Mrs. W. stating that the child was at the point of death, and requesting us to return home immediately. We then stated to those present that we were prepared to receive the news, that God had shown us the sickness of the child while at the house of Brother Patch. We were so confident in this matter that we told Sister Wicks that she would hear from us that the child's disease was in its head and face.

When we returned home we found the child lying in its mother's arms, in the same posture and condition in which it passed before our mind while bowed before the Lord at the house of Brother Patch at Markesan, Wis. The child lived four weeks. The funeral was in the forenoon. In the afternoon we went to the *Review* Office, and as we stepped over the threshold, the presentiment and the dream flashed before our mind. We immediately called those with whom we were associated in the publishing work, and related to them the dream and the presentiment, and stated that God had shown us in a figure that the money in the hands of the brokers was not safe, and that we should immediately draw it, which we did to purchase stone, brick, and lumber for the new building.

The first of July we made a tour east, stopping at Roosevelt and Buck's Bridge, N. Y. The day before we left we drew what remained of the principal and interest. When we reached the place of our second appointment we put up at the house of Elder Byington, where we received a note from his son, a printer in the *Review* Office, that the day after we left Battle Creek, these brokers both made an assignment. At that time not less than fifty thousand dollars from the citizens of Battle Creek and vicinity was in their hands on deposit, and no dividend whatever has been paid them.

Many at Battle Creek knew that we had deposited with these men, and they supposed that we had lost as others had done. And on our return from the east the question was frequently asked us, "How much did you lose by these men?" We had the pleasure of responding, "Not one dollar." "Well, you were lucky," was the frequent remark. The providence of God had cared for this investment that had been solemnly dedicated to the cause. And as we often related the foregoing facts, we felt justified in making the statement, that God sent his angel to warn us in season to secure the means which had been devoted to his work.

In 1871 a second building of the same size and form as illustrated on page 349, was erected to meet the wants of the increasing business.

And in 1873 a third building of the same kind was built for the same reason. These all stand, side by side, opposite the public square and the tabernacle, on the corners of Washington and West Main Streets.

In 1878 the first and third buildings were united by a four-story building, as shown on the following page. In the last-named building is located the bindery, furnished with modern machinery to do all branches of book-binding. In these buildings we have an aggregate

of twenty-seven thousand square feet of floor space, which is occupied in the various branches of editing, printing, folding, book-binding, electrotyping, stereotyping, mailing, and shipping. Including all departments, it is the best equipped printing office in the State of Michigan.

The different periodicals issued by the Association, the titles of which are given below, have an aggregate monthly circulation of 83,534 copies.

| | | | |
|---|---|---|---|
| REVIEW AND HERALD (weekly), | | | 6,104 |
| YOUTH'S INSTRUCTOR, | " | | 8,704 |
| " | " | (monthly) | 1,575 |
| GOOD HEALTH, | " | | 5,000 |
| COLLEGE RECORD, | " | | 3,929 |
| German paper, | " | | 2,000 |
| Swedish | " | " | 1,000 |
| Danish | " | (semi-monthly) | 1,265 |

The S. D. A. Publishing Association issues one hundred and fifty religious publications in English. These vary in size, from a four-page tract up to a volume of 528 pages. Of the smaller works, the Association publishes fourteen in French, twenty-one in German, thirty-nine in Danish, and twenty-three in Swedish. The Association also prints for GOOD HEALTH, twenty-nine health publications.

Most of these works have been written during the last twenty years by different authors. And it could hardly be expected that these writers, working to no general plan, would produce a line of publications which would cover the whole ground of our faith and duty, without some repetitions. It is now evident that we have too many books, some of which will go out of print, others will be revised and reduced in size, and some new ones will be written.

The great importance of our publications demands that we should give this branch of the work more attention for time to come than we have been able to do in the past. In consequence of arduous labor at camp-meetings and other general gatherings, we have lost time and strength to do this work, for which we have had an especial burden from the very commencement of our publishing work. This is a mistake on our part, which we number with the many of the past, and hope to have wisdom and grace for the future, to humbly and wisely pursue the work God has given us to do.

There has been a disposition on the part of some to bring all the pressure possible to bear on the prices of our publications. Yielding to this pressure, prices have been put so low as to seriously cripple our publishing houses. A favorable change, however, took place in December, 1879, since which time there have been greatly increased sales at better prices. The lower the prices, the less sales, has been the experience of the past. Against this ruinous policy of low prices we have pleaded, and have yielded the point for the last time. As a sample of our pleadings on this subject for the past ten years, we clip the following from the *Review:*—

"For several years past, our people have felt the importance of giving our publications a wide circulation. And the managers of our houses of publication have seconded the efforts of the people, in publishing largely, and in putting our publications down to very low prices. These efforts on the part of the publishers are praiseworthy, if not carried too far. But the present embarrassed condition of these houses shows that one of the mistakes which has resulted in this embarrassment is the ruinous prices at which our publications have been sold."

Sketches of the rise and progress of our publishing work contain liberal statements of our labor in connection with it, which give us more credit than we deserve. It is true that we have labored incessantly, ardently, and unselfishly. This being well understood by the writers of these sketches, has led them to attribute to us the great success of this important branch of the work, which should be shared by able and devoted co-laborers. With pleasure we here mention the names of Elders Andrews, Smith, and Waggoner, whose writings composed a large share of the matter of our earliest books and periodicals. And the glory of all the successes of our united labors should be given to the Guiding Hand which has been with us in all our consecrated efforts.

Has the writer had strength to labor and to endure? God has given it. Have we had wisdom to organize and to devise new and broader plans for the better prosecution of the work? It came from the Source of wisdom. Our course, especially when moving in our own wisdom and strength, has been marked all the way with imperfections and mistakes. It is the hand of God that has been with us in this great work. He has given it success, and this has given us the confidence of our people. In some degree, we realize our past mistakes, and God's merciful dealings with us; and that should we accept in our heart the statements now in print that give glory to us, which should be given to God alone, we would commit the greatest mistake of our life, and sin against God.

# CHAPTER XII.

THE press has been regarded by S. D. Adventists as the right arm of our strength. Our field of labor is the world. And as the number of our efficient preachers is small, a large portion of the work of giving the last message must of necessity be accomplished by our publications.

While on a tour through Northern Michigan by carriage, in the year 1868, our company, composed of several carriage-loads, was enjoying the second meal of the day in the shade of a pasture-oak, when kind friends from the nearest house gave us a call. Mrs. W. suggested giving them tracts. These they received with apparent gratitude. We were soon at the home of Sister Jeffrey, at Ithaca. To this faithful woman, who now sleeps, Mrs. W. related the circumstance of giving tracts to kind strangers, and remarked that the Lord had shown her that a great work is to be accomplished in the circulation of such reading matter, and that a book fund should be raised for this purpose. The statement touched the heart of this mother in Israel, and she left the room. Soon after, she returned with five dollars for the book fund, and as she handed it to Mrs. W., the donor wiped the tears that were rapidly falling.

At our first camp-meeting, held at Wright, Mich., Sept. 1-7, 1868, the sum of $1,400 was actually paid into the book fund, and pledges were taken on the ground sufficient to swell the sum to $2,400. The publication and circulation of tracts received especial attention, and during

the three years that followed not less than $35,-
000 was paid into this fund for the circulation
of our religious and health tracts. The work
rapidly increased, and became so extensive that
organization of the forces engaged in the tract
work seemed necessary in order to economize labor and means.

The first State tract society was organized in
the New England Conference, November, 1870.
In this country there are now twenty-two State
and Territorial organizations, embracing Maine,
New England, Vermont, New York, Pennsyl-
vania, Ohio, Michigan, Indiana, Illinois, Wisconsin, Minnesota, Iowa, Nebraska, Dakota, Mis-
souri, Kentucky, Tennessee, Kansas, Texas, California, Oregon, and Colorado. Local societies
were organized in Switzerland, Norway, and
Denmark in the years 1878 and 1879. The general tract society was organized August 15, 1874.

The tract societies, in carrying forward their
work during the past ten years, have employed
not less than $150,000. Thousands of volumes
of bound books have been placed in public libra-
ries and on vessels. The number of pages of
tracts and pamphlets which have been distributed
by the societies, as near as can be gathered from
printed reports, is 33,676,077. The number of
periodicals distributed is 1,016,346. And let it
be borne in mind that only thirty-seven per
cent of the members of the societies have reported, and this is only eighteen per cent of the
membership of the denomination. Had the full
amount of all the work of the societies been reported, the number of pages would probably
reach 50,000,000. Add to this the reading matter distributed before the organization of the societies, and by those outside of these societies,
and the entire amount would probably reach

100,000,000 pages, besides periodicals and health annuals. The entire sum of the pages of books, pamphlets, and tracts published by S. D. Adventists on all their presses is not less than 250,000,000.

Those only who have a lively interest in the tract work, and have taken part in it, have a just idea of its magnitude and extent.

Through the agency of the tract societies, periodicals and publications have been sent to all the States and Territories of our country, to the Canadas, Nova Scotia, England, Scotland, Ireland, Wales, Holland, France, Italy, Switzerland, Russia, Egypt, Denmark, Norway, Sweden, Portugal, East and West Indias, Australia, Japan, China, Central and South America, Vancouver's Island, Madeira Island, Cape of Good Hope, Finland, and to different points on the Mediterranean, Baltic, Red, and Black Seas.

The great and good work which the Lord has accomplished through Elder S. N. Haskell and his fellow-laborers in the tract cause will not be fully seen and appreciated in this life. Time can never reveal the importance of this work; eternity alone will unfold it. Those whom the Lord led out in the organization of our Conferences, the several associations and societies, and in the equitable plan adopted by our people to raise funds for the support of the cause, had but a faint idea of the great and important work they were then doing. Neither can the friends of the cause now comprehend a tithe of the results of the Tract Institutes being held in the several Conferences. These schools are educating the members of the tract societies to do their work wisely and well. And this will create a demand for our publications such as the most sanguine have had but a faint idea of, and will constitute our presses indeed a power in the land.

The men of this world understand the power of the printing-press. The politician seizes this lever to lift himself into office. Political campaigns are run principally through the press. Advertisements of this, that, and the other, posted and scattered everywhere, are evidences that the man of business understands the influence of the press.

This is a reading age. Active minds must be employed. The people will read. The masses prefer fiction to fact. The writers, publishers, and sellers of fictitious works fully comprehend the situation, and for gain flood the world with light literature. Thus the devil seizes the press to turn the minds of the people from the real facts and duties of this life, and a preparation for the life to come. The minds of the young are fevered with fiction to that degree that they lose relish for solid reading. They are so completely filled with trash that there is but little room in their minds and hearts for that which is real and substantial.

"Ye are the light of the world," said Christ in his memorable sermon on the mount. "A city that is set on a hill cannot be hid. Neither do men light a candle, and put it under a bushel, but on a candlestick ; and it giveth light unto all that are in the house. Let your light so shine before men, that they may see your good works, and glorify your Father which is in Heaven." Matt. 5 : 14–16.

Christians should be as wise in their generation as the men of this world. They should seize upon every means, and every opportunity, to let their light shine. They should let it shine from the hill-top. They should do all in their power to dissipate the darkness of error by the light of divine truth. The press, which in the

hands of the children of darkness is a power for
evil, may, in the hands of the children of light,
be a mighty power for good. Mrs. W., in an ar-
ticle headed "Our Publications," in Testimony to
the Church, No. 29, speaks of our publications,
their prices, their circulation, and the importance
of training men for the work of canvassing, in
these stirring words :—

"Many of our publications have been thrown
into the market at so low a figure that the profits
are not sufficient to sustain our Offices and keep
good a fund for continual use. And those of our
people who have no special burden of the various branches of the work at Battle Creek, and
at Oakland, do not become informed in regard to
the wants of the cause, and the capital required
to keep the business moving. They do not understand the liability to losses, and the expense
every day occurring to such institutions. They
seem to think that everything moves off without
much care or outlay of means, and therefore they
will urge the necessity of the lowest figures on
our publications, thus leaving scarcely any margin. And after the prices have been reduced to
almost ruinous figures, they manifest but a feeble interest in increasing the sales of the very
books on which they have asked such low prices.
This object gained, their burden ceases, when
they ought to have an earnest interest and a real
care to press the sale of the publications, thereby
sowing the seeds of truth, and bringing means
into the Offices to invest in other publications.

"There has been, on the part of ministers, a
very great neglect of duty in not interesting the
churches in the localities where they labor, in regard to this matter. When once the prices of
books are reduced, it is a very difficult matter
to get them again upon a paying basis, as men

of narrow minds will cry speculation, not discerning that no one man is benefited, and that God's instrumentalities must not be crippled for want of capital. Books that ought to be widely circulated are lying useless in our Offices of publication, because there is not interest enough manifested to get them circulated.

"The press is a power; but if its products fall dead for want of men who will execute plans to widely circulate them, its power is lost. While there has been a quick foresight to discern the necessity of laying out means in facilities to multiply books and tracts, plans to bring back the means invested, so as to reproduce our publications, have been neglected. The power of the press with all its advantages is in the hands of our people, and they can use it to the very best account, or they can be half asleep, and through inaction, lose the advantages which they might gain. They can extend the light, by judicious calculation, in the sale of books and pamphlets. They can send them into thousands of families who now sit in the darkness of error.

"With other publishers, there are regular systems of introducing into the market books of no vital interest. 'The children of this world are wiser in their generation than the children of light.' Golden opportunities occur almost daily where the silent messengers of truth might be introduced into families and to individuals; but no advantage is taken of these opportunities by the indolent, thoughtless ones. Living preachers are few. There is only one where there should be a hundred. Many are making a great mistake in not putting their talents to use in seeking to save the souls of their fellow-men. Hundreds of men should be engaged in carrying the light all through our cities, villages, and towns. The public mind must be agitated.

" Missionaries are wanted everywhere. In all parts of the field canvassers should be selected, not from the floating element in society, not from men and women who are good for nothing else, and have made a success of nothing; but they should be persons of good address, of tact, keen foresight and ability. Such are needed to make a success as colporteurs, canvassers, and agents. Men suited to this work undertake it; but some injudicious minister will flatter them that their gift should be employed in the desk instead of simply working as colporteurs. Thus the work of the colporteur is belittled. They are influenced to get a license to preach, and the very ones who might have been trained to make good missionaries to visit families at their homes, and talk and pray with them, are caught up to make poor ministers, and the field where so much labor is needed and where so much good might be accomplished for the cause, is neglected.

" If there is one work more important than another, it is that of getting before the public such publications as will lead men to search the Scriptures. Missionary work—introducing our papers and books into families, conversing, and praying with and for them—is a good work, and one which will educate men and women to do pastoral labor.

" Every one is not fitted for this work. Those of the best talent and ability, who will take hold of the work understandingly and systematically, and carry it forward with persevering energy, are the ones who should be selected. There should be a most thoroughly organized plan; and this should be faithfully carried out. Churches in every place should feel the deepest interest in the tract and missionary work.

"We now have great facilities for spreading the truth, but our people are not coming up to the privileges given them. They do not see and sense the necessity in every church of using their abilities in saving souls. They do not realize their duty to obtain subscribers for our periodicals, including our health journal, and to introduce our books and pamphlets. Men should be at work who are willing to be taught as to the best way of approaching individuals and families. Their dress should be neat, but not foppish, and their manners such as not to disgust the people. There is a great want of true politeness among us as a people. This should be cultivated by all those who take hold of the missionary work.

"Our publishing houses should show marked prosperity. Our people can sustain them if they will show a decided interest to work our publications into the market. But, should as little interest be manifested in the year to come as has been shown in the year past, there will be but small margin to work upon.

"The wider the circulation of our publications, the greater will be the demand for books that make plain the Scriptures of truth. Many are becoming disgusted with the inconsistencies, errors, and apostasy of the churches, and with the festivals, fairs, lotteries, and numerous inventions to extort money for church purposes. There are many who are seeking for light in the darkness. If our papers, tracts, and books, expressing the truth in plain Bible language, could be widely circulated, many would find that they are just what they want."

Since the foregoing extract appeared in print, favorable changes have taken place in book matters. More books have been shipped from this Office during the past six months than were shipped during the previous eighteen months. New works are in the press, and still others, of very great importance, are being prepared. Here is a good field of usefulness for young men who contemplate entering the ministry at some future time. The canvasser, in coming in contact with a great variety of minds, has a good opportunity to study human nature. He learns to come near the people, and adapt himself to changing circumstances, and hold on till he has accomplished his object. This is the self-training he needs to qualify him for the work of the last message, illustrated by the last urgent call in the parable of the great supper of Luke 14:16-24, "Go out into the highways and hedges, and compel them to come in."

## CHAPTER XIII.

### BATTLE CREEK COLLEGE.

THE subject of education, and the necessity of founding a denominational school, were brought before our people by Mrs. W. and the writer, in the early part of the year 1872, and several meetings were held at Battle Creek to consider these important matters. A committee was then chosen to take steps for the immediate establishment of a school, and to act in reference to the organization of an Educational Society at as early a date as it could be brought about. At a meeting held May 11, 1872, the matter was placed in the hands of the General Conference Committee.

April 16, 1873, a committee was appointed to solicit means, and by its vigorous action a sum of over $54,000 was pledged, and a sufficient amount was paid to render the organization of a legal society possible. March, 1874, the society was organized under the statutes of the State of Michigan, with full charter to grant such literary honors as are usually granted by colleges, and to give suitable diplomas in testimony thereof.

In 1874 grounds were purchased in the city of Battle Creek at a cost of $16,278. The grounds originally consisted of twelve acres. Since the purchase, tiers of building lots have been separated by West College Street and South College Street. It is the most beautiful site for a school-building in this vicinity. The grounds are tastefully adorned with a large number of evergreen and other ornamental trees.

The College building, represented on page 368, was erected in the autumn of 1874, at a cost of $27,858.20. It is situated on the west side of Washington Street, which runs nearly north and south. The building is 175 feet from this street on the east, and the same distance from West College Street on the west. It is 300 feet from Manchester Street on the north, and 200 feet from South College Street on the south.

The building is 72 feet from east to west, and the same distance from north to south. But there are at each of the four corners indentures of 17 feet. The building is of brick, and has three stories besides the basement. The ceiling of the basement is 9 feet from the floor. The ceilings of the first and second stories are 14 feet each. The third story is 17 feet from ceiling to floor. The College bell is the finest we have heard. It is of size and pitch to send forth a full and pleasant tone, delightful to the student's

ear. The building is heated by steam. A considerable portion of the basement is occupied by the philosophical and chemical laboratory and lecture-room. Here daily lectures are delivered on the subjects of philosophy, chemistry, and. geology, during the terms when these sciences are taught. The first and second stories are each divided into two spacious rooms, in which students are seated during school hours. The third story constitutes a fine, large lecture hall capable of seating 350 persons.

From the observatory there is a most delightful view of the surrounding country for several miles. Wooded hillsides, winding rivers, and fertile fields, together with the shaded streets and pleasant cottages of the city, in the suburbs of which the College is located, combine to make a varied and inviting prospect. Besides this central building, nine dwellings have been erected on the west and south.

Like most religious denominations, Seventh-day Adventists early felt the need of a school in which to educate young men and women to labor in the various departments of missionary work. They also felt a rapidly increasing demand for an institution where our youth might receive a thorough mental training, united with a high order of moral discipline, to secure the best preparation possible for the duties of manhood and womanhood.

This need was manifest in the demand for the special preparation of young men for ministerial and missionary work, and in the reluctance on the part of many parents to send their children to schools where a constant contact with corrupt youth cannot be avoided. In these schools there is a growing laxity of morals and a corresponding increase of crime. There was a deep conviction upon the minds of the friends of education among our people that at such a school much better mental and moral discipline could be attained in a given time than in most of the schools and colleges in the land, and that a wise and effective discipline could be better main-

tained and the interests of the youth be more
assiduously cared for than would be done elsewhere.

In the spring of 1874, when the College was
established, two departments of instruction were
opened; one in the Arts and Sciences, the other
in Theology. In the fall of 1876, a department
was opened for the preparation of teachers. In
the fall of 1877, a department of Hygiene was
established for those who desire to become familiar with the facts and principles upon which
health and temperance reforms are based. In
the fall of 1879, a Commercial department was
instituted, and a primary school opened.

The range of study in Battle Creek College
through its different departments, includes those
usually pursued in the very lowest grades and
upward through all the branches of a full colle-
giate course. There are two courses of study,
the Classical and the English, which, when completed, will entitle the graduate to a degree.
The former consists of four years, the latter of
three, each with a preparatory course of two
years. There is also a Teachers' course of four
years, including professional instruction in school
methods, designed to prepare teachers for their
work.

Besides these there is a course of three years
for students in Theology. This includes Biblical lectures, Ancient and Church History, Natural Sciences, English Language, and two years
in Greek. There are minor courses in the other
departments, for which diplomas are granted.
There are Commercial courses of various lengths,
a course of one year in the Hygienic department,
and a course of three years preparatory to the
Teachers' course.

The College receives its students from almost

every State and Territory in the Union. From the fall of 1873, to June 15, 1880, 1375, persons have been enrolled as students of this institution.

In the spring of 1875, one hundred students were in attendance. So rapid has been the increase of attendance up to date, that the present enrollment for the College year ending June 15 is four hundred and eighty-nine.

The important considerations which parents usually take into account in sending their children to school, are the character of the instruction, the influence under which their children will be placed, and the expense incurred while pursuing their studies.

It has become a kind of mania among young people in our public and preparatory schools throughout the country to attach very great importance to the higher branches, while the common branches are looked upon as something to be passed over in a superficial manner. The teachers of Battle Creek College are endeavoring to correct this false view among its students. Great importance is attached to the common branches, which are regarded as constituting a foundation for a liberal education. Indeed, the thoroughness with which the youth are taught to perform their tasks, will in a great measure determine their success in after-life. The habit of doing work well may become as firmly established in the character as the habit of doing it in a careless and superficial manner. This is eminently true of the student. With this fact before them, the teachers at our College make the principle of thoroughness a leading feature in their labors, and endeavor to inculcate like principles in the characters and minds of the students.

The good influences which surround the students at Battle Creek College, and the vigilance exercised by those in charge, warrant parents in intrusting their sons and daughters to the watch-care of the institution. Teachers and officers feel that the hearts and lives of those they seek to educate are in a peculiar sense consigned to their care. They recognize the responsibility thus devolving upon them. Students are not left to themselves without care or sympathy. A personal interest is taken in each one, and a strong moral and religious influence is thrown around each member of the school. The necessity of constant vigilance over the character and general deportment of the youth is fully realized, and a discipline is maintained which is firm, yet parental and effective. In our times, when serious and solid studies are becoming distasteful, when all kinds of inducements to waste and worse than idle away their time are forced upon our youth, and when morals are so lax, it is necessary that the character and general deportment of the student should be assiduously watched.

The necessary expenses of students attending Battle Creek College are probably less than at any similar institution in the land. The whole expense of board, room-rent, tuition, books, and incidentals, need not exceed one hundred and twenty dollars a year. The annual expense incurred by the majority is less than one hundred dollars for each. Club boarding is very popular among the students of this institution. This system enables them to economize, in this the greatest of college expenditures. As these students fully adopt the two-meal system, they assemble at the eating-house only twice each day, where order and sobriety are observed, becoming Christian gentlemen and ladies.

But the victories gained in adopting the restricted diet are of far more importance to young men and women who are preparing by study to bless others with their influence, than simply the sum of money saved. However important this may be to the poor student, dollars and cents can hardly compare with the moral value of practical lessons of self-control, and physical and mental culture. All scientific physicians in the land, who have not lost proper regard for truth and honesty, agree in testifying that a nutritious hygienic diet is the safest and best for the young student. Most of our students are conforming to hygienic rules of living, and, as a consequence, sickness is almost unknown among them, and they are able to make greater progress in their studies.

The true friends of the health reformation will be gratified to know that the experiment of the Hygienic Boarding Club system of our good school is proving a perfect success. Some may be ready to cry "starvation" when we state that restricted diet is adopted by these students. But the writer with pleasure looks back thirty-nine years, when, thirsting for education and grappling with poverty, he and his room-mate, now Judge Smith, lived three months on corn-meal pudding and raw apples. By way of variety we had flour-cakes for each Sunday morning. But these young gentlemen and ladies of the Hygienic Boarding Clubs of Battle Creek College feast twice each day on the best grains, fruits, and vegetables, at a cost of about one dollar a week. With them the keen relish of healthful appetite, secured by their restricted diet, far exceeds the gustatory enjoyment of the sweetened, spiced, salted, and buttered dishes of fashionable living. Thank God for health reform. It is a mighty lever to lift up the student to physical, mental, and moral improvement.

The nervous dyspeptic, who is forever anxious about what he shall eat, deserves but little credit for restricting his diet to simple and healthful food. With him it is a necessity. He must restrict his appetite in point of quantity as well as quality, or suffer next to death. But when our youth, who know nothing of enfeebled digestion and its consequences, adopt unfashionable and restricted diet from principle and choice, it is then that the friends of health reform may shout victory.

It is true that this school was brought into existence by S. D. Adventists, and that it is under the direction of the S. D. A. Educational Society; yet its doors are open to all worthy persons who choose to observe the rules deemed indispensable to good order and proper discipline. We welcome all such to the privileges which this institution offers. There is nothing in the regular course of study, or in the rules and practice of discipline, that is in the least sectarian. The Biblical lectures are before a class of only those who attend them from choice.

One of the principal objects of the College is the preparation of ministers and missionary workers. The results from the efforts already put forth are very encouraging. There are one hundred young men and almost as many young women laboring in the missionary field who received the impetus and preparation for their work at Battle Creek College. And of the many that have been students at our College, who made no profession of religion, not less than three-fourths have gone away hopefully converted. Hundreds of youth who have received their education at this institution, have been preserved from the ruin into which they would have been led, had they attended school under circumstances less favorable to morality. These results are noticed particularly because they are largely peculiar to our school. The mental training of students at Battle Creek College, and their preparation for active life, are not mentioned, notwithstanding they are of a superior character.

The rapid increase of students in attendance during the past five years will doubtless continue. This will create a demand for more buildings and enlarged plans.

The means necessary to remove the debt now on the College, and to meet the demand for more room, should be raised as cheerfully and promptly by the many of our people who have taken no stock, as the sum of $54,000 has been raised by the few who have already taken stock.

There should be equality in our sacrifices and efforts to build up the College. Appeals should be made at all our camp-meetings in behalf of our beloved school. Those who have not taken stock, should be urgently invited to bear their part of this happy burden. And those who are able and willing to increase their stock, should have the privilege of so doing.

And there are hundreds of aged and feeble brethren and sisters, in the possession of considerable wealth, who are liable to drop into the grave at any time. These should remember the wants of our College in a liberal manner in their wills. And while they live they should appropriate their means with their own hands, as they can do it better than others can when they are dead. We recommend the judicious maxim of Dr. Franklin, that " if you wish to have a thing half done, employ a hand; but if you would have it *done*, then do it yourself."

# CHAPTER XIV.

THE subject of Christian temperance was made very prominent in the lives and teachings of those who were first in the advocacy of the doctrines now held by S. D. Adventists. Elder Joseph Bates, of Fairhaven, Mass., was a thorough health and temperance reformer when we first met him in 1846.

That which makes his early history intensely interesting to his personal friends is the fact that he became a devoted follower of Christ, and a thorough practical reformer, and ripened into glorious manhood a true Christian gentleman, while exposed to the evils of sea-faring life, from the cabin-boy of 1807 to the wealthy retiring master of 1828, a period of twenty-one years.

Beauty and fragrance are expected of the rose, planted in the dry and well-cultivated soil, and tenderly reared under the watchful eye of the lover of the beautiful. But we pass over the expected glory of the rose to admire the living green, the pure white, and the delicate tint of the water-lily whose root reaches far down into the cold filth at the bottom of the obscure lake. And we revere that Power which causes this queen of flowers, uncultivated and obscure, to appropriate to itself all valuable qualities from its chilling surroundings, and to reject the evil.

So, to apply the figure, we reasonably expect excellence of character in those who are guarded against corrupting influences, and whose surroundings are the most favorable to healthy mental and moral development. In our hearts are blessings for all such. But he who, in the absence of all apparent good, and in the perpetual presence of all that is uncultivated and vile, with no visible hand to guard and to guide, becomes pure and wise, and devotes his life to the service of God and the good of humanity, a Christian philanthropist, is a miracle of God's love and power, the wonder of the age.

It was during his sea-faring life, while separated from the saving influences of the parental, Christian home, and exposed to the temptations of sailor life, that Elder Bates became thoroughly impressed with moral and religious principles, and gathered strength to trample intemperance and all other forms of vice beneath his feet, and to rise in the strength of God to the position of a thorough reformer, a devoted Christian, and an efficient minister of the gospel.

Among the most interesting, instructive, and valuable books for sale at our offices of publication, is the "Early Life, Later Experience and Labors of Elder Joseph Bates." In this remarkable narrative, the reader may learn how Elder Bates resisted the temptations which pressed him on every side, and gained the victory over tobacco, alcoholic drinks, tea and coffee, and triumphed as a victor over morbid appetite. This book should be in every family library for the especial benefit of the young. God evidently chose this holy man to be the first in the work of laying the foundation of a denomination of health and temperance reformers.

The experiences and labors of Elders Bates, Andrews, Loughborough. and others, have done much in building up the cause of Christian temperance among S. D. Adventists.

As early as 1847, Mrs. W. bore decided testimony of what the Lord revealed to her relative to the injurious effects of tobacco, tea, coffee, and highly seasoned food. Those who accepted her testimonies as the voice of the Lord through his humble instrument, laid those hurtful things aside, and soon reported favorably in point of physical and mental health. The work of reform in common habits of life has progressed until it can be truly said that we are a denomination of health and temperance reformers.

There are men in the ranks of S. D. Adventists who had used alcoholic drinks and tobacco to excess for fifty years, until the habit bound them as with fetters of steel. These are now rejoicing in the freedom they have gained over these injurious, debasing, and expensive indulgences. And there are women in the ranks who had for the same length of time used tea for the headache. These found it necessary to increase the amount of tea in proportion to the increasing headache and nervousness. But when they gave up their tea, the nervous headache went with it. These, also, now rejoice in the freedom they have gained, and are very happy in putting their tea money into the Lord's treasury, just where their converted brethren put their tobacco money.

This work has progressed among us until the disgusting sight and scent of tobacco cannot be recognized at the places of worship, in the clothing, or at the homes of S. D. Adventists. Tea, coffee, and alcoholic stimulants were nearly put out of the camp, before the recent health and temperance movement was introduced by J. H. Kellogg, M. D., of the Sanitarium. With this re-enforcement, which represents the highest type of Christian temperance, it is ardently hoped that all such idols and harmful indulgences will be purged from the denomination forever.

Here we introduce statements relative to Christian temperance, health reform, and the Sanitarium, prepared by the editor of *Good Health* :—

"The attention of S. D. Adventists was called to the subject of Christian temperance chiefly through the labors of Elder and Mrs. White. At the outset of their public labors they took a strong stand against the common use of tobacco and other narcotics, as well as against the use of alcoholic liquors. Elder Joseph Bates, who was one of the earliest temperance reformers in the country, having assisted in the organization of the first temperance society in America, was also associated with them in this work.

"In 1862, chiefly through the writings of Elder and Mrs. White, a more thorough-going reform was inaugurated. It was urged that a person's moral nature is largely affected by his physical condition. It was therefore seen that success in appealing to man's higher and spiritual nature is much more certain if he can be turned from wrong habits of life, which undermine the physical, and benumb the moral powers.

"At the present time the whole body of S. D. Adventists are abstainers from the use of alcoholic drinks of all kinds. Tobacco, in all its forms, is also discarded, none addicted to its use being received into church fellowship except upon the promise and expectation of its immediate abandonment. The result is, that, as a denomination, the sight and scent of tobacco are not found among this people. Pork, tea, and coffee are also little used. Rich and highly seasoned food is discarded. Grease and spices are seldom employed in cookery. Meat of any kind

is but rarely used. Two meals only a day are
considered preferable for most people, those to
be composed chiefly of grains, fruits, and vegetables, served up, however, in a great variety of
palatable and wholesome forms.

"These reformatory ideas, with the exception
of those respecting alcohol and tobacco, are not
made tests of fellowship, but a strong effort is
made to impress them upon the people in such
a manner as to secure attention to them. For
the purpose of keeping them constantly before
the members of the denomination, a society has
been recently organized known as the 'American
Health and Temperance Association,' which requires of its members to sign one of the following pledges :—

"TEETOTAL PLEDGE.—I do hereby solemnly
affirm that with the help of God I will wholly
abstain from the voluntary use, as a beverage, or
in any equivalent manner, of alcohol, tea and
coffee, and from the use of tobacco, opium, and
all other narcotics and stimulants.

"ANTI-RUM AND TOBACCO PLEDGE. — I do
hereby solemnly affirm that with the help of God
I will wholly abstain from the voluntary use of
alcohol in any form, as a beverage, or in any
equivalent manner, and from smoking, chewing,
or snuffing tobacco, or using it in any other form,
and from in any way encouraging the use of
these poisons.

"ANTI-WHISKY PLEDGE.— I do hereby solemnly affirm that with the help of God I will totally
abstain from the voluntary use, as a beverage, or in any equivalent manner, of all liquids
or substances containing alcohol.

"It is expected that every member of the denomination will sign the teetotal pledge. Those
who do not at first, are soon willing to do so.

The Association has subsidiary State societies and local clubs in nearly all parts of the United States.

" For the purpose of inculcating the principles of this reform and for the introduction of improved methods of medical treatment, especially for chronic invalids, the ' Health Reform Institute ' was founded Sept. 5, 1866. The institution was legally incorporated April 6, 1867.

Medical and Surgical Sanitarium.

Stock was sold to the amount of about $35,000, which by the earnings of the institution has been increased to more than double its original value.

" Increasing patronage demanding more facilities, a large building 120 x 130 feet, four stories in height above the basement, was erected, and opened for patients April 10, 1878. It is provided with an elevator, and all modern improvements for the convenience and comfort of patients. It is heated with steam, and lighted with gas. There is about eight thousand square feet of floor space devoted to treatment rooms; cost, about $80,000. Besides this, the old main building and seven cottages are occupied by the institution, which now goes by the name of the 'Medical and Surgical Sanitarium.'

"Since the introduction of improved facilities and methods of treatment, the patronage of the institution has increased very greatly, being at least three times as great at present as formerly. Seven to eight hundred patients are now annually treated, and with a wonderful degree of success.

"The Sanitarium is not a money-making enterprise, as its organization is such that no individual can derive pecuniary advantage from it, the stockholders having assigned their dividends for the benefit of the institution and to create in time a fund for the benefit of the sick poor. Even at the present time several thousand dollars are annually donated to the poor. The Sanitarium is managed by a Board of Directors who are annually elected at a meeting of the stockholders.

"This institution, though founded and managed by S. D. Adventists, is not conducted on a denominational basis. Only a small proportion of its patrons are members of the denomination. Members of all denominations, and all respectable people, are made equally welcome. A high moral tone is preserved in the management of the institution, but sectarianism is carefully avoided.

"A monthly magazine, formerly known as the *Health Reformer*, now called *Good Health*, was started in 1866. It is devoted to the consideration of all subjects pertaining to health, and to physical, mental, and moral culture. It is wholly undenominational in character, and has far the largest circulation of any health journal in the country."

The changes that have taken place in this institution during the past six years are highly gratifying. We have repeated it a hundred times, that it is a discredit to S. D. Adventists to do a second-class job at anything. Our publishing house, from a very small and humble beginning, has grown to great completeness and efficiency. Our College has arisen from a private school to an institution of learning of great importance to our people everywhere. The subject of Christian temperance at an early date worked its way into the minds and hearts of our people, until we became a denomination of health reformers. The need of an institution was felt, where the sick among us could be treated without being brought under the irreligious influences of existing health institutions, and where our feeble and worn ministers could find rest and relief from their arduous toils.

The greatest difficulty under which we have labored, has been to secure men and women of devotion to the work, and of sufficient breadth of character to act as physicians. Those who had charge of the work at the early and unfortunate period of our Health Institute, did better than could really be expected of them, judging by their failures since they have been superseded by those of efficiency and influence. Under their management, the institution suffered in its reputation, consequently it suffered financially.

We soon became satisfied that without thoroughly educated physicians, and men of superior financial ability, to stand at the head of our health institution, it could not arise to a position to meet the mind of God. But in our efforts to bring about these changes, we had to work against the narrow prejudices of those who held positions, and the discouragements of the stockholders and friends of the institution.

With but little sympathy and co-operation

from others, we have labored to bring about changes which are very gratifying. J. H. Kellogg, M. D., who now stands at the head of an able, refined and devoted faculty, has proved himself as true as steel, worthy of the confidence and respect of the medical and scientific men of our country, with whom he holds high rank. He has well earned the unwavering confidence and love of all our people.

The future of the Sanitarium is most hopeful. God has blessed the imperfect work of our health institution in the past to the physical and spiritual good of hundreds, and its mission and important work have only begun. If there were good reasons why brethren and sisters should take stock in it in the past, the reasons why all our people should now share in the work are doubly good. The debt should be lifted by our people. When this shall be accomplished, our feeble and weary ministers can share its benefits free of charge.

God has given us, as a people, the great subject of health reform, not that we should treat it in a manner to disgust the people, but that it may be a sort of John the Baptist to prepare the way for the greater light of the last message.

Among the inferior benefits of change from the common habits of life to those conducive to health and happiness, is money saved. The health journal makes its monthly visits to five thousand families. And we safely conclude that four thousand of these, at least, are true reformers. These four thousand families have left the use of tobacco, tea, and coffee, the annual expense of which, in cash paid out, would be from ten to fifty dollars a family. But we will put the average cost at twenty-five dollars to each family. The money saved, then, by four thousand families of reformers, in abstaining from tobacco, tea, and coffee, alone, would be the sum of $100,000 a year.

But this is not all the money saved by those who carry out the principles of health reform. The amount annually paid out to the doctors by those who adhere to old habits, is nearly as large as that paid out for tobacco, tea, and coffee. Then add to this the sum paid out for patent medicines, and the total would not be less than twenty-five dollars to a family. This, too, is saved by true health reformers, amounting, in four thousand families, to not less than a second $100,000 annually.

And, again, this is not all that is saved by the reform. The vegetarian diet, consisting of the grains, vegetables, and fruits, which are indeed the *fat of the land*, is far less expensive than the food usually eaten, of flesh, butter, sweet-cake, and pies, lard, saleratus, pepper, vinegar, pickles, allspice, cinnamon, ginger, and nutmeg. When we first discarded these, and purchased for our family only such articles as flour, meal, vegetables, and fruits, we were surprised to see how little it cost to live. The change was so great that we really felt embarrassed over the fact that our grocery bills were almost next to nothing. In our own family, ranging from ten to fifteen persons, we have saved annually, by adopting the reform diet, not less than one hundred dollars. But we will put the average saving in the four thousand families of health reformers, in consequence of changing to a more healthful diet, at twenty-five dollars to each family, making the third sum of $100,000. The total amount saved, in money alone, by those who have fully adopted the reform among our people, is the very handsome sum of $300,000 a year. But suppose the annual amount saved by discarding hurtful indulgences, and adopting healthful habits of living, is only one-half this sum. What a glorious offering to the Lord $150,000 would be to present before him each year for the benefit of the Battle Creek Sanitarium which has been established by his hand.

But the money saved by the health reform is hardly worthy to be compared with the physical, mental, moral, and spiritual benefits derived from correct habits of life. Health is man's capital, the value of which cannot be computed in dollars and cents. And self-denial of hurtful indulgences strengthens and elevates the moral powers, while the mental and spiritual become clearer, with an improved physical condition.

The real health reformer, who is true to the principles he adopts, enjoys a comparative freedom from pain, a clearness of thought, a calmness of nerve and temper, a release from dark forebodings and the horrors of a diseased conscience, which freedom constitutes, in a very great degree, the pleasure of existence. His senses are clear and keen, and he enjoys the glories of nature wherever his eye meets them, and the delights of a restored taste in the proper use of healthful food. Such an one finds himself, as it were, in a second Eden, almost in the enjoyment of the blessings of the first, when "out of the ground made the Lord God to grow every tree that is pleasant to the sight, and good for food."

True, we are not really in Paradise restored to its Eden glory; but having it in full prospect, soon to be given to the pure, we really do not see the need of passing an imaginary and self-made purgatory in reaching the heavenly plains. Thousands of health reformers know, by happy experience, the things of which we speak. To

those who do not, we would say, Change from
your gross habits of life, wash up, and cheer up.
God lives and reigns, and wills that you be
well and happy, and make the best of the ills of
this mortal life; and, if true to God and yourselves, he will, ere long, give you life eternal.

Health reform, with the money saved, and all
its inestimable blessings, is a Godsend. We appeal especially to our friends who rejoice in the
reform: What shall we render to the Lord for
these benefits? Shall we covetously invest the
money saved, in lands, houses, horses, carriages,
furniture, fine clothing, and the like? Or, shall
we consecrate it to the cause of health reform, as
a thank-offering to God for the good we have
received? Those who love self supremely will
do the former. Those who love God and humanity will sacredly consecrate to the Battle
Creek Sanitarium the money saved to them by
adopting the health reform.

## CHAPTER XV.

### BATTLE CREEK.

THE city of Battle Creek, Mich., having become the seat of the main branch of our publishing work, our College, and the Sanitarium, it is
thought proper to give a sketch of the work at
this important post from the commencement.

Elder Joseph Bates had visited Jackson in the
year 1848, when a number of persons of moral
value and devotion to the cause embraced the
doctrines connected with the last message. But
the first meeting of our people at Battle Creek
was held in a small private dwelling. Gathering

all the Sabbath-keepers in this vicinity, there were only as many persons as were in Noah's ark.

In company with Mrs. W. and Elder Lough-borough we held a meeting in the village of Battle Creek, June 6, 1853. Gathering in some from the adjoining towns, the congregation about half filled a private room. We there remarked that if the brethren and sisters were faithful, there might yet be quite a church raised up at Battle Creek. No one then present comprehended the significance of these words.

The growth of the cause and the work at Battle Creek is quite clearly indicated by the sizes of the several houses of worship occupied. The first house built by our people was 18x28 feet. The *Review* Office was moved from Rochester, N. Y., to its present location in the autumn of 1855. The increase of the work in two years from that time made a larger house of worship necessary, and a second one, 28x44 feet, was built. And for the same reason, a third house, 40x65, with gallery, was built in 1867. This third house would seat only about six hundred persons. The congregation of Sabbath-keepers rapidly increased, in consequence of the growth of the publishing work demanding more hands, and the increase in numbers of students at the College, and patients at the Sanitarium, to such a degree that in the winter of 1878-9 the Sabbath-school and Bible class were held in three rooms besides the house of worship, and a portion of the congregation had to retire to their homes during the regular service for want of room.

The necessity for a still larger house had been apparent for some years, and in August, 1878, the third house was moved from its site on Washington Street, fronting the public square, and the tabernacle was commenced on the same lo-

SEVENTH-DAY ADVENTIST TABERNACLE.

cation. The size of this building is 105x130.
The main auditorium will seat 900 persons.
This is surrounded by a north, an east, and a
south vestry, seating respectively 250, 350, and
250 persons. These rooms are separated from
the main auditorium by ground-glass sliding
partitions, which can all be raised when necessary, throwing the entire lower floor into one
room, capable of seating at least 1,750 persons.
A gallery running around three sides, seats 800;

wall-seats and chairs, 650 more; giving the entire building a seating capacity for 3,200 persons. The height of the central dome is 66 feet, clock tower, 108 feet. The arrangement of rooms described above adapts the house equally to large and small meetings, and makes it especially convenient for Sabbath-school work and inquiry meetings. The cost of the tabernacle was less than $27,000. It was dedicated April 20, 1879, and by actual count, 3,649 persons were present. For our own use, the Battle Creek church does not need so large a place of worship, but on special occasions, which will become more frequent in the future, there is need of just such a house as the Battle Creek Tabernacle.

In the organization and management of our institutions great care has been taken to secure the general good of the cause, and to prevent personal benefits. The highest officer of the Publishing Association and leading editors receive the same wages as printers. The result of this course has been the establishment of the confidence of all our people in the managers of the publishing department, resulting in union, strength, and unparalleled prosperity. The sacrifices and liberalities of those who have conducted this department have been great, which has inspired similar sacrifices and liberalities on the part of patrons.

The same policy has been pursued in the health department, with not quite so good results, for the reason that in its earlier history the influence of bigoted and selfish persons tended, in some degree, to cripple its influence. These influences being overcome in a good degree, and the Sanitarium now being established upon a broader and more liberal basis, we confidently expect that this work will be attended with prosperity similar to that seen in the publishing department.

Above all others, institutions of learning are objects of charity. We had supposed that it would be necessary to raise large sums of money annually to sustain our College ; but the friends of education among S. D. Adventists are happy to know that this institution, in its youth, is self-sustaining. Teachers, however, work on smaller salaries, by nearly one-half, than they could obtain elsewhere, and still continue their liberalities to help the cause in other branches. In these sacrifices, the entire church at Battle Creek, with few exceptions, sympathize and bear a part. These facts are not generally understood, hence the faithful workers at this important post do not share the confidence and sympathy of our people abroad, as they deserve.

In the prosecution of this work, the church at Battle Creek has borne very heavy burdens. And when the fact is taken into the account, that the entire membership of the Battle Creek church is composed of the poorer class, with very few exceptions, and that nearly all earn their bread as day-laborers, the amount that this church has given of their hard-earned means seems incredible. As early as 1879 the entire State of Michigan had taken stock in the Battle Creek College to the amount of $22,384.16. Of this sum the church at Battle Creek took $11,363.66, which is $343.16 more than has been taken by all others in the State.

The church at Battle Creek has taken stock in the Sanitarium and the Publishing Association in amounts nearly in the same proportion as the foregoing figures of College stock. Including what this church has given for the College, Sanitarium, Publishing House, book fund, missions, houses of worship, the support of the poor that have moved to Battle Creek from other churches, and tithes paid into the Michigan Conference Treasury, from 1860 to 1880, the entire sum would not be less than $60,000.

The church at Battle Creek has acted a part in building up our institutions worthy of the sympathy and confidence of our people everywhere. And we are happy to report that the working condition of the Publishing Association, the College, and Sanitarium, has never been as good as at the present time. It was necessary, in order to make ample provisions to prosecute the increasing work, to make debts. And that which increased the pressure of those debts was the hard times which immediately followed. But with the improved times, came lower rates of interest and greatly increased patronage.

The Sanitarium is actually worth, after the payment of all its debts, two dollars for every one taken in stock. The Publishing Association has two dollars and fifty cents for each dollar taken, and the College stock is worth one dollar and twenty-five cents on every dollar.

Those who have charge of these institutions are faithful men of God, close thinkers, judicious managers, and hard workers. They should have the confidence of our people everywhere.

It need not be denied that our people are beset with temptations and severe trials everywhere. This has ever been the portion of those who have devoted themselves to the work of God. And the more important their position in that work, and the more they are devoted to it, the sharper will be their conflicts with the powers of darkness. Those who hold no responsible position in the work and cause of God, and who are at ease in Zion, are not objects of solicitude with

Satan. He is indeed pleased that they are doing nothing to injure his cause, and he reposes quietly, as far as their cases are concerned.

His attacks are upon those who devote their lives to the service of God and the good of humanity, those whose efforts are constantly put forth to the injury of his cause. He will do all in his power to bring burdens upon the weary burden-bearers. If possible, he will divide, and grieve, and discourage the people of the Lord. And if there is one thing above another that fills Satan and his angels with hellish delight, and causes the holy angels to weep, it is the cool, selfish criticisms of those who will not bear burdens, upon those who are bearing heavy burdens.

During the late American war, Washington was fortified more thoroughly than any other Northern city, and was guarded by veteran troops; for the reason that the seat of government, being a very desirable point of attack, was in greater danger than any other city. Battle Creek has been the headquarters of this cause, a sort of Washington, during the last twenty-five years. Here Satan has rallied his forces. And it has not been as easy a task to manage the interests of the growing cause in all its branches, and maintain a life of Christian devotion under the constant fire of the enemy, as many have supposed. Our brethren generally, who had no practical knowledge of our toils and sacrifices and the difficulties under which we labored, were willing to let heavy burdens fall on us, which they themselves should have borne. And when we fell from paralysis, August 15, 1865, they were poorly prepared to bear the burdens that had crushed us. And in their ignorance of the work, they supposed that almost any one could fill the place we had occupied,

The paralytic stroke had so far touched the brain that for eighteen months we carried neither watch nor purse. And for the four years that immediately followed the war, we did not bear responsibilities at headquarters. During this time, sad changes took place at Battle Creek, in the spiritual and financial condition of things. Although it was the best time to do business in the history of the cause, not less than $20,000 was lost during that four years, at the Publishing House and Health Institute, when $30,000 should have been earned.

Here we wish to acknowledge the mercy and power of God in raising us to health, and giving us our position again in the work, and such a place in the confidence and love of the brethren as we had never before enjoyed. With the faithful co-operation of the brethren, and the especial blessing of God, the capital stock of the Publishing Association was raised, during the four years that followed, from $30,000 to $70,000, and corresponding success attended the work at the Health Institute.

The work rapidly increased everywhere. About this time, our camp-meetings were introduced into most of the State Conferences. And in company with Mrs. W., we went the rounds of the camp-meetings year after year. And as labors and cares increased, our work became fearfully hard, and soon we suffered a second paralytic stroke, which made it necessary that we should visit Colorado and California. Appeals were made for picked men at the head of the work. Having been connected with it from the very commencement, we understood the general management better than those of little experience. We needed helpers,—men willing to bear burdens, and to unite in patiently carrying out plans which those of experience might devise.

Those who moved to Battle Creek for this object, came with the best of intentions, and made sacrifices; but the difficulties attending the work, and the constant attacks of the powers of darkness, proved too much for them. It was a very trying position for these brethren, who were farmers at home. Like most of our brethren who are successful farmers, enjoying the quiet of their accustomed business, they did not comprehend the difficulties at this common point of attack, supposing that almost any one would be equal to the work here. Our own mistakes and errors in the experience of the past, while endeavoring to push the work in the face of a thousand difficulties, lead us to sympathize with those brethren who found the work at Battle Creek too much for them. They failed where others will probably fail, in taking the work in their own hands, without properly counseling with those who had long carried the burdens.

The prejudicial influence against the work at Battle Creek, which has been cast upon the minds of the brethren abroad in consequence of the failure of those who came to help in the work, is cruel and unjust. The Judgment will present this matter in its true character. God would have given these men grace, and wisdom to help bear the burdens at Battle Creek, had they stood in his counsel, and obeyed the testimonies of his Spirit.

And now, after an experience of a quarter of a century, we come to the deliberate conclusion that there is not a more sacrificing, burden-bearing, and devoted people in our ranks, than the church at Battle Creek. And taking as representatives those who came to help in the work at Battle Creek, it is hard to believe that those whom they represented would do as well at headquarters as the members of the Battle Creek church have done. In justice to the members of this church and to meet existing prejudices abroad, we make the foregoing statements, with a heart of love for the general cause, and of pity and forgiveness toward the erring.

In going the rounds of the camp-meetings we have robbed the church at Battle Creek, and our institutions located at this point, of that labor and counsel which was needed at the heart of the work. And when we have returned to this people, worn and weary, we have entered upon this work to great disadvantage. We now identify our interest with this people in hope of finding that repose with them, and in God, that will enable us to finish the work he has for us to do.

---

## CHAPTER XVI.

### LEADERSHIP.

In the providence of God, we have been permitted to bear a part in the work of the last message from its commencement. And it has fallen to our lot to lead out in the publishing work, church organization, systematic benevolence, and to take an active part in bringing our institutions into existence, and also in their management. The success which has attended the several branches of the great work, has come from the direct providence of God. This has given our people confidence in our plans and our general management. Some, taking extreme positions upon the subject of leadership, have been ready to acknowledge us as the leader of this people. This position, however, we have never for a moment accepted. Those who in all honesty took this position, did not clearly see the subject in all its bearings upon a people that might consent to be led, and upon the one who might accept the position of leader.

The leadership question, and the scriptural form of church organization and discipline, have been subjects of discussion in the Christian church for centuries. These are matters upon which men may have committed very grave errors in the past, and those who commit similar ones in our time should not be too severely censured.

Early in the history of our cause, at a time when distracting influences were at work among us, we took a decided position upon the subject of unity in the church of Christ. We have often repeated the statement that there is not a single apology in all the New Testament for the existing want of unity of sentiment and action in the professed churches of Christ. Our Lord prayed that his followers might be one, as he was one with the Father.

"I pray not that thou shouldest take them out of the world, but that thou shouldest keep them from the evil. They are not of the world, even as I am not of the world. Sanctify them through thy truth; thy word is truth. As thou hast sent me into the world, even so have I also sent them into the world. And for their sakes I sanctify myself, that they also might be sanctified through the truth. Neither pray I for these alone, but for them also which shall believe on me through their word; that they all may be one, as thou, Father, art in me, and I in thee, that they also may be one in us; that the world may believe that thou hast sent me." John 17:

15-21. And Paul, in his epistle to the church at Rome, praying that unity might exist with them according to Christ Jesus, doubtless refers to Christ's prayer that his people might be one.

"Now the God of patience and consolation grant you to be like-minded one toward another according to Christ Jesus; that ye may with one mind and one mouth glorify God, even the Father of our Lord Jesus Christ." Rom. 15:5, 6. He appeals to the church at Philippi in these stirring words:—

"If there be therefore any consolation in Christ, if any comfort of love, if any fellowship of the Spirit, if any bowels and mercies, fulfill ye my joy, that ye be like-minded, having the same love, being of one accord, of one mind. Let nothing be done through strife or vainglory; but in lowliness of mind let each esteem others better than themselves. Look not every man on his own things, but every man also on the things of others. Let this mind be in you, which was also in Christ Jesus." Phil. 2:1-5. He exhorts the church at Corinth:—

"Now I beseech you, brethren, by the name of our Lord Jesus Christ, that ye all speak the same thing, and that there be no divisions among you; but that ye be perfectly joined together in the same mind and in the same judgment." 1 Cor. 1:10.

"Finally, brethren, farewell. Be perfect, be of good comfort, be of one mind, live in peace; and the God of love and peace shall be with you." 2 Cor. 13:11. In connection with Paul's finally, we give Peter's, in these words:—

"Finally, be ye all of one mind, having compassion one of another; love as brethren, be pitiful, be courteous; not rendering evil for evil, or railing for railing, but contrariwise blessing,

knowing that ye are thereunto called, that
ye should inherit a blessing. For he that will
love life, and see good days, let him refrain his
tongue from evil, and his lips that they speak
no guile. Let him eschew evil, and do good; let
him seek peace, and ensue it. For the eyes of
the Lord are over the righteous, and his ears are
open unto their prayers."

The testimonies of Mrs. W., in harmony with
this position, were constantly appealing to our
people upon the subject of unity; and the position has been generally adopted, that no one of
our preachers should advance new views without counseling with his brethren in the ministry. God greatly blessed our united efforts, which
have done much to educate our people upon the
subject, and to secure the unparalleled unity of
sentiment and action that exists among us.

At the General Conference held at Battle
Creek, April, 1861, we spoke upon the resurrection, as set forth in the fifteenth chapter of Paul's
first epistle to the church at Corinth. The
strong tendency with many members of the
popular churches, to surrender the time-honored
doctrine of the literal resurrection of the dead,
led us to speak upon the subject before such representative men as Elders Andrews, Waggoner,
Loughborough, and Smith. We had adopted
the view that it was not necessary to a resurrection that the same particles of matter which
constitute the mortal man should enter into the
immortal being; and that the identity between
the present mortal and the immortal is not in
matter, but in organization.

We were happy to know that the position
taken relieved the subject of the resurrection
from the difficulties of the identical-particles-of-
matter theory, urged by skeptics, which difficul-

ties were leading thousands, like the Sadducees of old, to deny the resurrection of the dead. It seemed evident to us that Paul refers to these when he says, " But some man will say, How are the dead raised up ? and with what body do they come ?" 1 Cor. 15 : 35. He then shows by the figure of the grain, that the matter which constitutes the mortal body does not enter into the immortal being.

The ministers before mentioned did not accept our view of the subject, and conforming to the rule we had adopted, that new views should not be urged until there should be harmony among the leading men of the denomination, we let the matter rest during a period of sixteen years. But when writing upon the plan of redemption through Christ, given in the pamphlet entitled, "The Redeemer and Redeemed," the Spirit of God led us into the subject again. And while writing upon the identity question, Mrs. W. desired that we should listen to the reading of that which she was then preparing for the second volume of the "Spirit of Prophecy." The matter which she read, was what the Lord had shown her upon this subject in connection with the denial of the resurrection of the dead by the Sadducees. Both were writing upon the same subject, while neither knew of what the other was writing. With this evidence before us, that the Lord had taken the question in hand, we presented our views in the aforementioned pamphlet, and invited criticisms.

When we returned from California a few weeks later, we found Doctor Kellogg presenting to his physiology class the identity question from a scientific view. But the subject was still under the heavy pressure of the prejudice which would naturally exist in the minds of the brethren at Bat-

tle Creek, because of the position and influence of
leading ministers. Many of the students accepted
the Doctor's position, while but few of them dared
to express their real convictions, lest they should be
doomed to the regions of infidelity, where the Doctor had been consigned by those under the influence of narrow prejudice. We take pleasure, however, in here stating that the views of Mrs. W. on
this subject, in manuscript three years since, are
clear and definite. And when she can be spared
from arduous labors in the field, into which she
is urged, she will be able to give them in connection with other important matter in the fourth
volume of the "Spirit of Prophecy."

When the leadership question was especially
agitated among our people, the pressure of influences, at first opposite to each other, were
brought to bear upon us. On the one hand, we
were urged to acknowledge the position of
leader, and on the other hand, some were grieved
over the mistaken idea that we had accepted the
position, when, at this very time, our views on
the subject, given in the following pages, were in
manuscript, which was afterward given in the
*Signs of the Times.* We have been thus definite
in the foregoing, in order to bring out the following facts:—

1. That our position upon the subjects of
organization, and the means to secure unity
in the church of Christ, has been the same
during the past thirty years.

2. That, in the providence of God, we were
tested and proved on the very point where reproaches had fallen from those who were unfriendly. They had charged us with assuming
the very position which friends urged upon us
in vain.

3. In the matter of the identity question, we

were so far influenced by the opinions of others as to be silent upon an important point of truth for a period of sixteen years.

In the words of the Master we would here appeal to our brethren in the ministry. "One is your Master, even Christ, and all ye are brethren." Matt. 23 : 8. Jesus addressed these words to the twelve, in the hearing of the multitude. And while they were a rebuke to the scribes and Pharisees, who were striving for the mastery, they were also designed to impress the disciples with the great truth, which should be felt in all coming time, that Christ is the only head of the church.

The prophetic eye of the Son of God could look forward over the Christian age, and take in at a glance the errors and dangers of the church. And we may look back over her sad history and see that strict adherence to the principle set forth in the foregoing words of our Lord has been important to the purity of the church, while departure from it has marked the progress of different forms of corrupted Christianity. The most prominent among these is Catholicism, which has set over the church one man, whose claims to infallibility are sustained by the Roman Church.

Christ is the only authorized leader of his people. At the very commencement, in laying the foundation of the Christian church, as Jesus was walking by the Sea of Galilee he saw "two brethren, Simon called Peter, and Andrew his brother, casting a net into the sea; for they were fishers. And he saith unto them, Follow me, and I will make you fishers of men." Matt. 4 : 18, 19. "And as Jesus passed forth from thence, he saw a man named Matthew, sitting at the receipt of custom: and he saith unto him,

Follow me." "Then answered Peter and said unto him, I hold, we have forsaken all, and followed thee: what shall we have therefore? And Jesus said unto them, Verily I say unto you, That ye which have followed me, in the regeneration when the Son of man shall sit in the throne of his glory, ye also shall sit upon twelve thrones, judging the twelve tribes of Israel." Matt. 19 : 27, 28.

Was Moses the visible leader of the Jewish church? Christ was the invisible leader of that people, and is also the leader of the Christian church. Moses speaks of Christ in these words: "The Lord thy God will raise up unto thee a Prophet from the midst of thee, of thy brethren, like unto me; unto him ye shall hearken." Deut. 18 : 15. And Peter, in preaching Christ to the people on the occasion of healing the lame man at the gate of the temple, indorses the words of Moses thus: "For Moses truly said unto the fathers, A Prophet shall the Lord your God raise up unto you of your brethren, like unto me; him shall ye hear in all things whatsoever he shall say unto you." Acts 3 : 22.

The transfiguration was designed, not only to illustrate the future kingdom of glory after the resurrection and change to immortality, but to impress the church with the glory of Christ as her head and leader. No part of that grand scene could be more impressive than the bright cloud that overshadowed them, and the "voice out of the cloud, which said, This is my beloved Son, in whom I am well pleased. Hear ye him." Matt. 17 : 5.

And at no time during his public ministry does Christ intimate that any one of his disciples should be designated as their leader. He does say, however, that " he that is greatest among you shall be your servant." Matt. 23 : 11. And on the occasion of submitting the great commission to his first ministers, to be perpetuated in the Christian ministry to the close of the age, Christ gives the pledge that ever has been and ever will be the supporting staff of every true minister, "Lo, I am with you alway, even unto the end of the world." Matt. 28 : 20.

Christ's ministers have ever had a world-wide message: "Go ye therefore, and teach all nations." And wherever their footprints may be seen, upon the mountains or in the valleys, there Christ has been by the ministration of his holy angels, and the teachings of the Holy Ghost. "I am with you," is the soul-inspiring promise to every true minister. Christ proposes to lead his servants, and it is their privilege to approach the throne of grace, and receive from their sovereign Leader fresh rations, and orders direct from headquarters.

And there is no intimation that the apostles of Christ designated one of their number above another as their leader. Paul would have the Corinthians follow him only as he followed Christ. He says, "Be ye followers of me, even as I also am of Christ. Now I praise you, brethren, that ye remember me in all things, and keep the ordinances as I delivered them to you." 1 Cor. 11 : 1, 2. Paul, so far from claiming to be the head of the church at Corinth, and securing their obedience, sympathy, and benevolence on this ground, would shake them off from seeking to be directed by him. In the very first sentence of the very next verse he exalts Christ as their leader: "But I would have you know, that the head of every man is Christ.' Thank Heaven, the Christian church has no use for the pope.

In his epistle to the Hebrews, the apostle compares two faithful leaders. One was a servant in the Jewish church; the other is a Son over the Christian church. Who are these two leaders? Are they Moses and Peter? or Moses and Paul? or Moses and Luther? or Moses and Wesley? or Moses and Miller? We need not say that they are Moses and Christ. As a servant in the Jewish church, Moses was their visible leader. As a Son over his own church, both Jewish and Christian, Christ is the invisible leader. Moses led the Hebrews in the wilderness, not by his own wisdom, however superior, but by direct communications from Christ, who was the Angel that was with Moses in the church in the wilderness. Acts 7: 37, 38. And Christ leads the Christian church, through the ministration of angels attended by the Holy Spirit in harmony with the written word. Christ's ministers are shepherds of the flock, and leaders of the people in a subordinate sense. If faithful, they will receive a crown of unfading glory when the Chief Shepherd shall appear.

Paul enjoins obedience and submission on the part of the church; but he does not require this in particular for himself, or for any other one. He pleads in behalf of all faithful ministers in these words: "Remember them which have the rule over you, who have spoken unto you the word of God; whose faith follow, considering the end [object or subject] of their conversation, Jesus Christ, the same yesterday, and to-day, and forever." Chap. 13:7. Again he says, in verse 17 of the same chapter: "Obey them that have the rule over you, and submit yourselves; for they watch for your souls, as they that must give account, that they may do it with joy, and not with grief ; for that is unprofitable for you."

In Hebrews 12 : 1, 2, the apostle exalts Christ as the great head of the church, and the only one to whom she should look for leadership. He would have the church benefited by the experiences of the heroes of faith mentioned in the eleventh chapter, called in the first verse of the twelfth a cloud of witnesses. But he faithfully guards the church against looking back to them with a spirit of idolatry, or accepting any man as their leader, or pattern of the Christian life, in these three words : " Looking unto Jesus." Paul says : " Wherefore seeing we also are compassed about with so great a cloud of witnesses, let us lay aside every weight, and the sin which doth so easily beset us, and let us run with patience the race that is set before us, looking unto Jesus, the author and finisher of our faith : who for the joy that was set before him endured the cross, despising the shame, and is set down at the right hand of the throne of God."

All true ministers are Christ's ambassadors. " Now then we are ambassadors for Christ, as though God did beseech you by us ; we pray you in Christ's stead, be ye reconciled to God." 2 Cor. 5 : 20. In their ministry they are to represent the doctrine of Christ, and the interests of his cause in this world. They surrender their own judgment and will to Him who has sent them. No man can be Christ's ambassador until he has made a complete surrender of his right of private judgment to Christ. Neither can any man properly represent Christ who surrenders his judgment to his fellow-man.

But the subject must not be left here with the truth partly expressed. The words of Christ and his apostles relative to unity and the ordained means to secure it, and proper discipline, must have a qualifying bearing upon the subject, lest unsanctified men, who do not submit their will and judgment either to Christ or to church authority, assume the gospel ministry, and divide and scatter the flock of God.

But here we wish it distinctly understood that officers were not ordained in the Christian church to order or to command the church, or to "lord it over God's heritage." In the case of difference of opinion that arose in some of the primitive churches relative to circumcision and the keeping of the law of Moses, recorded in the fifteenth chapter of Acts, the apostles and elders at Jerusalem acted as counselors, in a manner to give room for the Holy Ghost to sit as judge. The report of that blessed meeting at Jerusalem to settle a festering difficulty, commences on this wise: "For it seemed good to the Holy Ghost and to us." And the brethren which were from among the Gentiles in Antioch, and Syria, and Cilicia, "rejoiced for the consolation." Differences settled in this way frequently seem more than settled, and generally remain settled: while those disposed of by the exercise of mere church authority are seldom really settled at all.

Between the two extremes, of church force, and unsanctified independence, we find the grand secret of unity and efficiency in the ministry and in the church of God. Our attention is called to this in a most solemn appeal from the venerable apostle Peter to the elders of his time: "The elders which are among you I exhort, who am also an elder and a witness of the sufferings of Christ, and also a partaker of the glory that shall be revealed: Feed the flock of God which is among you, taking the oversight thereof, not by constraint, but willingly: not for filthy lucre, but of a ready mind. Neither as being lords over God's heritage, but being ensamples to the flock. And when the Chief Shepherd shall appear, ye shall receive a crown of glory that fadeth not away. Likewise, ye younger, submit yourselves unto the elder. Yea, all of you be subject one to another, and be clothed with humility; for God resisteth the proud, and giveth grace to the humble. Humble yourselves, therefore, under the mighty hand of God, that he may exalt you in due time." 1 Pet. 5:1-6.

In painful contrast with the foregoing are those ecclesiastical conferences and assemblies of our time, where ministers distinguish themselves by a spirit of strife and debate, and in the use of language which would be regarded as ungentlemanly in all other respectable associations.

Organization was designed to secure unity of action, and as a protection from imposture. It was never intended as a scourge to compel obedience, but, rather, for the protection of the people of God. Christ does not drive his people. He calls them. "My sheep hear my voice, and I know them, and they follow me." Our living Head leads the way, and calls his people to follow.

We close this chapter with brief remarks upon the past, present, and future. We entered upon the work of the last message after the great disappointment in 1844, thirty-six years since, under the most discouraging circumstances. The money that paid the fare of Mrs. W. and the writer to the first Conference of our people, held in the State of Connecticut, we earned chopping cord-wood. The money that paid our fare to the second, held in Western New York, we earned in the hay-field.

Poverty, feebleness, and great discouragements

were our portion in the early history of the cause. The disappointment, and the scattering of the Advent people that followed, can hardly be described. After the disappointment, almost every conceivable fancy and fanaticism had divided the Advent people into contending factions. And it was from these, that the S. D. Adventists of those times were gathered. To organize and discipline a people composed of such elements, was a work that could be accomplished only by the especial help of God.

The Lord was speaking through Mrs. W. in messages of reproof and correction, which many were slow to receive; and some of those who rejected the reproofs seemed to be filled with a spirit of frenzy and bitterness against us and the work in which we were engaged. But God's grace is always proportionate to the work he requires of his trusting servants. It is frequently asked by the friends of the cause at the present time, "What sustained you in those days of poverty, feebleness, and reproach?" Our answer is, that the manifestation of the Spirit and power of God in answer to prayer, and comforting messages through the spirit of prophecy, so braced our faith that we threw ourselves into the work, and suffered sickness, want of suitable food and clothing, and bore the most bitter reproaches, with that composure and confidence which true faith gives. Saving faith, very scarce at this day, assumes the form of knowledge in the minds and hearts of the trusting, obedient children of God.

With such a faith, and Mrs. W. by our side, we have moved forward, venturing in this, in that, and in the other, as the cause has advanced. It was this that led us to venture our lives and to sacrifice our property in the work of building

up the cause on the Pacific coast. What we
have actually paid out in money, and what we
have lost in money, in consequence of our opera-
tions upon that coast, amounts to $8,000.

Under the faithful efforts of Elder Loughborough and his associate laborers, a great work has
been accomplished on the Pacific Coast. The
Pacific S. D. A. Publishing Association owns its
buildings and the land upon which they are
built, in the very center of the beautiful city of
Oakland, Cal., which has a population of 40,000.

**PACIFIC PRESS BUILDING.**

The main building, here represented on the left,
is in the form of a Greek cross, the main portion, 26x66, the transverse section, 26x44. It
faces the east on Castro Street. The portion on
the right is 30x84, facing the north on Central
Avenue.

The first object we had in view in establishing
this publishing house, was the dissemination in
print of the doctrines of S. D. Adventists upon
the Pacific coast. Had this object ever been
kept firmly in view by its managers, its denomi-

national patrons would now be more numerous,
and its finances would be in a better condition.
Both our Offices may be in danger of committing
the same error in a degree. God will bless his
own work. It is poor policy to do an outside
business, where there are risks, when in our own
work there are no risks, and the business is un
der our own control. Here has been the strength
of the *Review* Office in adhering more closely to
its legitimate work.

The present is a most interesting period in the
history of the publishing work, and in the cause
generally. We are under the conviction that it
would be a great error on our part to leave the
general oversight of this branch of the work to
others, to which God has especially called us.
The importance of the publishing work demands
our special attention in the preparation of books,
and the general oversight of this department in
all its branches.

Incessant toil away from Battle Creek has
worn us to such a degree that we needed rest on
returning. But instead of rest, we have usually
found work of the most perplexing character
waiting for us that had been piling up for weeks
or months. There was so much to be considered,
that decisions had to be made in thirty seconds
which should have had an hour of calm thought
of a rested mind. Under such a pressure we
have appeared to great disadvantage. The future is most hopeful. We are happy in the prospect of finding rest from the fatigue of camp-
meetings, and the work generally, and giving our
remaining energies to writing and the general
oversight of the publishing work.

# Catalogue of Publications

For sale at the Office of the Review and Herald, Battle Creek, Mich., and at the Pacific Press, Oakland, California.

## PERIODICALS.

THE ADVENT REVIEW AND SABBATH HERALD. A sixteen-page Religious Family Newspaper, devoted to a discussion of the Prophecies, Signs of the Times, Second Coming of Christ, Harmony of the Law and the Gospel, What We must Do to be Saved, and other Bible questions. $2.00 a year.

GOOD HEALTH. A monthly journal of hygiene, devoted to Physical, Mental, and Moral Culture. $1.00 a year.

THE YOUTH'S INSTRUCTOR. A four-page illustrated weekly for the Sabbath-school and the family. 75 cts. a year.

THE ADVENT TIDENDE. A Danish semi-monthly, sixteen pages, magazine form, devoted to expositions of prophecy, the signs of the times, and practical religion. $1.00 a year.

ADVENT HAROLDEN. A Swedish monthly, of the same size, and devoted to the same topics, as the *Advent Tidende*. 75 cts. a year.

STIMME DER WAHRHEIT. An eight-page German monthly. A religious family newspaper, frequently illustrated. 50 cts. a year.

THE COLLEGE RECORD. A four-page educational monthly. 10 cts. a year.

The above are published in Battle Creek, Mich. Terms always in advance.

THE SIGNS OF THE TIMES. A twelve-page weekly Religious Paper, devoted to the dissemination of light upon the same great themes treated in the *Review.* Published in Oakland, Cal. $2.00 a year.

LES SIGNES DES TEMPS. A religious monthly journal in French. Published in Bâle, Suisse. $1.00 a year.

(412)

# BOOKS, PAMPHLETS, AND TRACTS.

HISTORY OF THE SABBATH AND OF THE FIRST DAY OF THE WEEK, by Elder J. N. Andrews. This work contains an outline of the history of the Sabbath for the period of Six Thousand years. Part First is the Biblical history of the Sabbath and of the first day of the week. Part Second is the secular history of these two days since the time of the apostles. This volume has been prepared with most careful and patient study. In all cases of quotations from secular history, book, chapter, and page are given. And book, chapter and verse are given of all quotations from the word of God. 528 pp. $1.00

THE SANCTUARY AND THE 2300 DAYS OF DAN. 8:14, by Elder U. Smith. This question has developed the people known as Seventh-day Adventists, and is the pivotal doctrine upon which their applications of prophecy largely depend. It explains the past Advent movement, shows why those who looked for the Lord in 1844 were disappointed, reveals the fact so essential to be understood, that no prophetic period reaches to the second coming of Christ, and shows where we are, and what we are to expect in the future. A knowledge of this subject is indispensable to a correct application of the more important prophecies pertaining to the present time. 352 pp. $1.00
Condensed edition, paper, 224 " .30

THOUGHTS ON DANIEL, CRITICAL AND PRACTICAL, by Elder U. Smith. An exposition of the book of Daniel verse by verse. 400 pp. $1.00

THOUGHTS ON REVELATION, CRITICAL AND PRACTICAL, by Elder U. Smith. This work presents every verse in the book of Revelation with such remarks as serve to illustrate or explain the meaning of the text. 400 pp. $1.00

THE NATURE AND DESTINY OF MAN, by Elder U. Smith. This work, as its title implies, treats upon the constitution of man, his consequent condition in death, and destiny beyond the resurrection. All the passages in the Bible which have a bearing upon these questions are taken up and explained in full, thus giving the most comprehensive view of this whole question that has yet been presented. 356 pp. $1.00

LIFE SKETCHES. This work embraces sketches of the parentage, early life, Christian experience, and extensive labors of Elder James White, and also of his wife, Mrs. E. G. White. 416 pp. $1.00
With steel engraving of Elder W., 1.25

LIFE OF WILLIAM MILLER, with portrait. This work comprises sketches of the Christian Experience and Public Labors of this remarkable man, gathered from his Memoir by the late Sylvester Bliss, with Introduction and Notes by Elder James White. This book sets forth the true principles and real character of the man who was the leading spirit in the great American Second-Advent Movement.                    408 pp.   $1.00

LIFE OF ELDER JOSEPH BATES, with portrait. This is a reprint of his Autobiography, with introduction, and closing chapters relative to his public ministry, and last sickness, by Elder James White. The closing chapters relate to his labors in the ministry, and in moral reforms, and the triumphant close of his long and useful life. This book should be in every family library. Fine tinted paper,                    352 pp.   $1.00
Plain white paper,                    "          .85

THE SPIRIT OF PROPHECY; or, the Great Controversy between Christ and his Angels, and Satan and his Angels, in four volumes, by Mrs. Ellen G. White. These volumes cover the time from the fall of Satan to the destruction of sin at the close of the one thousand years of Rev. 20. The first three of these volumes are in print, and it is expected that the fourth, the most interesting and important of the series, will soon be ready.
Each,                    416 pp.   $1.00

THE BIBLE FROM HEAVEN, by Elder D. M. Canright. This work is what its name implies, an argument to show that the Bible is not the work of men, but is in deed and in truth the word of God. It is a candid, forcible, conclusive argument, sustained by a large array of facts and such deductions of science as rest upon any tolerable certainty. Just the work to put into the hands of honest skeptics, and those who are exposed to infidel influences. Adapted to the use of any and all persons who believe in the Bible.                    400 pp.   $1.00

THE BIBLICAL INSTITUTE. This is the title of a work containing a synopsis of the lectures given at the Institute held in Oakland, Cal., April 1-17, 1877. These cover all the main points of our faith, giving facts and dates, and the heads of the arguments.                    352 pp.   $1.00

HYMN BOOK. "Hymns and Tunes for those who keep the Commandments of God and the Faith of Jesus," is the title of this book. It has 537 hymns and 147 tunes.                    416 pp.   $1.00

CONSTITUTIONAL AMENDMENT; or, the Sunday, the Sabbath, the Change, and the Restitution. A discussion between W. H. Littlejohn and the editor of the *Christian Statesman.* This work discusses the proposed religious amendment to the Constitution, especially in its bearing upon the subject of the Sabbath and the first day of the week. This involves an examination of the alleged change of the Sabbath. 384 pp. $1.00

  In paper covers, 336 " .40

THE UNITED STATES IN THE LIGHT OF PROPHECY; or, an Exposition of Rev. 13:11-17, by Elder U. Smith. Dealing with our own land and applying to our time, this is a portion of prophecy which should possess surpassing interest for every American reader. This work shows by conclusive arguments the position which the United States government holds in prophecy, and the important part it is to act in the closing scenes of time. Issues are even now arising which it is of the greatest importance that all be prepared to meet. 160 pp. $ .40

  In paper covers, .20

THE SONG ANCHOR. A popular collection of songs for the Sabbath-school and praise service. 164 pp. 35 cts.

  Bound in muslin, 50 cts.

LIFE OF CHRIST, six pamphlets. By Mrs. E. G. White:

No. 1. His First Advent and Ministry. 104 pp. 10 cts.
" 2. His Temptation in the Wilderness. 96 pp. 10 cts.
" 3. His Teachings and Parables. 126 pp. 15 cts.
" 4. His Mighty Miracles. 128 pp. 15 cts.
" 5. His sufferings and Crucifixion. 96 pp. 10 cts.
" 6. His Resurrection and Ascension. 80 pp. 10 cts.

  LIFE OF THE APOSTLES, two pamphlets:--
No. 1. The Ministry of Peter. 80 pp. 10 cts.
" 2. The Teachings of Paul. 80 pp. 10 cts.

FACTS FOR THE TIMES: A collection of Valuable Extracts from Eminent Authors. 224 pp. 25 cts.

ELEVEN SERMONS ON THE SABBATH AND LAW, by Elder J. N. Andrews. 226 pp. 25 cts.

HISTORY OF THE IMMORTALITY OF THE SOUL, by Elder D. M. Canright. 209 pp. 25 cts.

MODERN SPIRITUALISM. Nature and Tendency of Modern Spiritualism, by Elder J. H. Waggoner. 184 pp. 20 cts.

REFUTATION OF THE AGE TO COME, by Elder J. H. Waggoner. 168 pp. 20 cts.

THE ATONEMENT, by Elder J. H. Waggoner. An examination of a remedial system in the light of Nature and Revelation. 168 pp. 20 cts.

THE MINISTRATION OF ANGELS, AND THE ORIGIN, HIS-

TORY, AND DESTINY OF SATAN, by Elder D. M. Canright. 144 pp., 20 cts.

OUR FAITH AND HOPE. Sermons on the Coming and Kingdom of Christ, by Elder James White. 182 pp. 20 cts.

MIRACULOUS POWERS. The Scripture Testimony on the Perpetuity of Spiritual Gifts, with Narratives of Incidents and Sentiments carefully compiled from the Eminently Pious and Learned of various denominations. 128 pp. 15 cts.

RESURRECTION OF THE UNJUST. A vindication of the doctrine, by Elder J. H. Waggoner. 100 pp. 15 cts.

THE SPIRIT OF GOD, its Gifts and Manifestations to the end of the Christian Age, by Elder J. H. Waggoner. 144 pp. 15 cts.

THE THREE MESSAGES OF REVELATION 14:6-12, particularly the Third Angel's Message and the Two-Horned Beast, by Elder J. N. Andrews. 144 pp. 15 cts.

THE TWO LAWS, as set forth in the Scriptures of the Old and New Testaments, by Elder D. M. Canright. 104 pp. 15 cts.

THE MORALITY OF THE SABBATH, by Elder D. M. Canright. 96 pp. 15 cts.

THE COMPLETE TESTIMONY OF THE FATHERS OF THE FIRST THREE CENTURIES CONCERNING THE SABBATH AND FIRST DAY OF THE WEEK, by Elder J. N. Andrews. 112 pp. 15 cts.

CHRIST IN THE OLD TESTAMENT AND THE SABBATH IN THE NEW, by Elder James White. 56 pp. 10 cts.

REDEEMER AND REDEEMED, by Elder James White. 48 pp. 10 cts.

THE SIGNS OF THE TIMES FROM THE FULFILLMENT OF PROPHECY, by Elder James White. 96 pp. 10 cts.

www.ingramcontent.com/pod-product-compliance
Lightning Source LLC
Chambersburg PA
CBHW021339110726
47900CB00005B/1532